Leslie Poles Hartley was born in Whittlesey, Cambridgeshire, in 1895 and was educated at Harrow and Balliol College, Oxford. During the First World War he was a junior officer in the British Army, though he was never on active service. For more than thirty years from 1923 he was indefatigable fiction reviewer for such periodicals as the *Spectator*, the *Saturday Review*, the *Sketch*, the *London Magazine* and *Time and Tide*. He published his first book, a collection of short stories entitled *Night Fears*, in 1924. *The Shrimp and the Anemone*, his first full-length novel, did not appear until 1944. The first volume of a trilogy, it was followed by *The Sixth Heaven* (1946) and *Eustace and Hilda* (1947), which won the James Tait Black Memorial Prize, and is also the title by which the whole work is generally known. It was recognized immediately as a major contribution to contemporary English fiction. His other novels include *The Boat* (1949) and *The Go-Between* (1953), which was awarded the Heinemann Foundation Prize of the Royal Society of Literature in 1954 and was later made into an internationally successful film, while the film version of *The Hireling* (1957) won the principal award at the 1973 Cannes festival. In 1967 he published *The Novelist's Responsibility*, a collection of critical essays. His later books include *My Sister's Keeper* (1970), *Mrs Carteret Receives* (1971) and *The Harness Room* (1971). He was awarded the CBE in the New Year's Honours List in 1956.

L. P. Hartley died in 1972. Lord David Cecil described him as 'One of the most distinguished of modern novelists; and one of the most original. For the world of his creation is composed of such diverse elements. On the one hand he is a keen and accurate observer of the processes of human thought and feeling; he is also a sharp-eyed chronicler of the social scene. But his picture of both is transformed by the light of a Gothic imagination that reveals itself now in a fanciful reverie, now in the mingled dark and gleam of a mysterious light and a mysterious darkness ... Such is the vision of life presented in [his] novels.'

Douglas Brooks-Davies was born in London in 1942 and educated at the Mercha

Oxford. He gained his Ph.D. from the University of Liverpool. Until 1993 he was Senior Lecturer in English Literature at the University of Manchester and is currently Honorary Research Fellow there, as well as being a stained-glass artist. His publications include *Number and Pattern in the Eighteenth-Century Novel* (1973); *Spenser's 'Faerie Queene': A Critical Commentary on Books 1 and 2* (1977); *The Mercurian Monarch* (1983); *Pope's 'Dunciad' and the Queen of Night* (1985); *Spenser: 'The Faerie Queene' Books 1–3* (1987); *Fielding, Dickens, Gosse, Iris Murdoch and Oedipal 'Hamlet'* (1989); *Silver Poets of the Sixteenth Century* (1992); and *Edmund Spenser: Selected Shorter Poems* (1995). He wrote the volume on Dickens's *Great Expectations* for Penguin Critical Studies (1989) and was Founder and General Editor of Manchester University Press's 'Literature in Context' series. Most recently he has prepared a modernized edition of Spenser's *Fairy Queen* (1996).

L. P. HARTLEY

The Go-Between

Edited by Douglas Brooks-Davies

PENGUIN BOOKS

Peng

Penguin Gro

Penguin

Penguin

Penguin Boo , India

Peng

Penguin Books (South Africa) (Pty) Ltd, 24 Sturdee Avenue,
Rosebank, Johannesburg 2196, South Africa

Penguin Books Ltd, Registered Offices: 80 Strand, London WC2R 0RL, England

www.penguin.com

First published by Hamish Hamilton 1953
Published in Penguin Books 1958
This edition published in Penguin Books 1997
Reprinted in Penguin Classics 2000

13

Typeset in 11/12 pt Monotype Perpetua
Typeset by Rowland Phototypesetting Ltd, Bury St Edmunds, Suffolk
Printed in England by Clays Ltd, St Ives plc

978-0-141-18778-5

www.greenpenguin.co.uk

MIX
Paper from responsible sources
FSC
www.fsc.org FSC™ C018179

Penguin Books is committed to a sustainable
future for our business, our readers and our
planet. This book is made from paper certified
by the Forest Stewardship Council.

For Timothy Webb

CONTENTS

ACKNOWLEDGEMENTS

The holograph of *The Go-Between*, and the letters of Hartley cited in this edition, are in the L. P. Hartley Archive, the John Rylands University Library, Manchester, and are quoted with the kind permission of the Librarian and Director.

It is, in addition, a great pleasure to record my thanks and gratitude to the following:

the late Miss Norah Hartley, for her encouragement and for kindly granting me permission to incorporate the textual changes recorded in the Note on the Text (pp. 263−5), to quote the textual variants and cancelled passages included in the Notes and Textual Appendix, and to quote, in the Introduction, from letters written by her brother. I am acutely aware of how generous she was with her time;

Mr William Riddington, without whose patient, prompt and courteous handling of my queries and requests I could not have completed this edition;

the staff of the John Rylands University Library, Deansgate, Manchester, who, despite the great difficulties imposed on them by extensive building renovation, aided my access to the L. P. Hartley Archive with a cheerful courtesy that made my work there a pleasure;

Tim Bates, to whose enthusiasm I owe the chance of undertaking this edition;

Mary Brooks-Davies, for the present of a first edition of *The Go-Between*, for helping me scrabble round floors at various fairs in search of copies of the songs mentioned in the novel, for enduring my singing of them, and for discussing my work with me;

the late Alan Marshall, for information about the early twentieth-century railway system, and for sharing with me his memories of East Anglia;

ACKNOWLEDGEMENTS

the Reverend Peter Nixson, for his enthusiasm and tenacity in helping me track down the precise English translation of Mendelssohn's *Lobgesang* alluded to in the novel;

Timothy Webb, without whose characteristic generosity in imparting his erudition (this time on Cato the Elder, cricket and fairy tales) this edition would have been much the poorer;

and Adrian Wright, who interrupted his work on the official biography of Hartley to share his knowledge with me with a warmth and cordiality for which I am most grateful. He even took time off to check the date of the statue of Sir Thomas Browne in Norwich.

My thanks again to all of you.

INTRODUCTION

The first sentence of *The Go-Between* – 'The past is a foreign country: they do things differently there' – has become almost proverbial, though it is probably true to say that in the minds of most of us it is indissociable from the voice of Michael Redgrave and the bleak opening images of the Losey/Pinter film of 1971. But the film is now a quarter of a century old, which – although we may forget it for the two hours or so it takes for its images to inhabit our television screens – adds curiously to the poignancy of the novel. For *The Go-Between* is not only nostalgic, it is *about* nostalgia: about the recovery of lost memories where those memories are not only personal (and, it turns out, deeply painful) but collective and cultural.

Leo remembers his stay with his schoolfriend Marcus Maudsley at Brandham Hall in the hot summer of 1900 and his involvement as messenger with Marcus's sister, Marian, and her lover, the farmer Ted Burgess; and in doing so he summons back to life, for a moment, the lost world of the late-Victorian upper classes. That world is Leo's Golden Age, his version of pastoral, glimpsed through the windows of memory. And his trauma leading to loss of memory, caused by Mrs Maudsley's hysterical reaction to seeing Marian and Ted making love, signals not just the erasure of personal memory but the loss of a cultural future in which the apparent stabilities of the Victorian gentry would continue. Leo stops remembering at the age of thirteen in 1900; we meet him carefully re-membering memory in 1952. When the memory is clarified he returns to Brandham, meets Marian again, and ends up endorsing her memory of the events at Brandham Hall in July 1900.

Summarized in this way the novel sounds rather precious, almost trivial. It is, in fact, an intelligent, complex and beautifully felt evocation of nascent boyhood sexuality that is also a searching exploration of the nature of memory and myth.

1 *Genesis and Autobiography*

The Go-Between was an immediate success when it appeared in the spring of 1953. It was a Book Society choice by early July, which meant the printing of some 17,000 extra copies; by September it was the *Daily Mail* Book of the Month; and by July 1954 Hamish Hamilton were reporting sales of somewhere near 50,000. Between mid 1954 and late 1955 there were plans for a film (with script by John Cresswell and starring Alec Guinness and Kenneth More) and, in 1959, an adaptation for the stage. By 1962, however, Cresswell was forgotten when Joseph Losey discussed the possibility of using a script by Peter Dehn for a film version starring Dirk Bogarde; and by 1967 Dehn had been superseded by Harold Pinter. Contracts were agreed by the end of July 1968, and Pinter had finished his first draft by December. After financial problems, the film was finally shot in the summer of 1970, the year that saw the fourth reprint of the Penguin edition (1958). Yet, superbly cast and shot though it is, the film is a partial reading of the novel, an interpretation that, suppressing some details, exaggerates others. But, then, the novel itself suppresses and exaggerates some of the elements which led to its composition, and it is with these that I shall begin.

In the Introduction he wrote for the 1963 Heinemann edition of *The Go-Between*, Hartley observed that his novel was to some extent autobiographical. Born in 1895, he had a vivid memory of the summer of 1900 because it was then that his family moved to Fletton Tower in Peterborough; and he mentions various incidents from a visit to a schoolfriend that found their way into the novel, including a letter asking to be called home. This emphasis on autobiography should not surprise us: all Hartley's novels, to a greater or lesser degree, are autobiographical, and in his critical writings he constantly returns to the relationship between fiction and the author's life: '[The novelist's world] must, in some degree, be an extension of his own life; its fundamental problems must be his problems, its preoccupations his preoccupations' (*The Novelist's Responsibility* (1967), p. 2); 'It is, of course, unsafe to assume that a novelist's work is autobiographical in any direct sense; but it is plausible to assume that his work is a transcription, an anagram of his own experience . . .' (*ibid.*, p. 62).

In fact, *The Go-Between* is the most searching novel Hartley wrote about his childhood, and more autobiographical than his conscious mind remembered – or pretended to remember – in the Introduction. We are indebted to his younger sister, Norah, for the perception that the formidably strong-willed Hilda in *Eustace and Hilda: a Trilogy* (1958) portrayed their mother (*Radio Times*, 19 March 1988, p. 15), which may suggest that the equally strong-willed Mrs Maudsley in *The Go-Between* has her origin there, too. But there is an abundance of less speculative clues in some of the letters that survive from Hartley's childhood. For example, a letter written to his mother in August 1909 records his arrival at Bradenham Hall (east of Swaffham, Norfolk) to stay with a schoolfriend, Moxey (with whom he is to sleep, together with the dog), and notes that there is to be a cricket match: Bradenham becomes the novel's Brandham; Moxey becomes Maudsley. Hartley's prep school, Northdown Hill, in Cliftonville, Thanet, becomes *The Go-Between*'s Southdown Hill, also in Thanet; Lambton House, against which is played the football match that releases the fatal word 'vanquished' into Leo's diary, thus setting the whole story in motion, is a second thought, for the holograph originally read 'Dumpton House', the actual name of a neighbouring prep school. Young Hartley reported the results of football matches against Dumpton House in letters of 21 November ('we beat them 3 – 2') and 5 December (another win, 5 – 0) 1909. Northdown possessed a master named 'Mr Lion ("Leo") . . . Mr Lion is very lionlike at times . . .', and the same early letter (9 October 1908) mentions that the nickname of another master, Mr Thomas, is 'old Tommy': it is at the very least interesting that *The Go-Between*'s Leo was originally called Tom (Prologue, n. 42).

The school's head, J. D. Holt – known as 'J. D.' compare Southdown's 'J. C., as we called him' (chapter 1) – had a toddler, the subject of a letter of 6 June 1909: 'A few days ago Mr Holt called me as I was going out from dinner, and said that the Baby (they call her the Babe) wanted to know if Norah was coming down here.' In *The Go-Between* this becomes the farewell at the premature close of Leo's summer term as the boys cheer, '"Mr Cross, Mrs Cross, and the baby!" How the baby came to be included I never knew . . . For that matter the baby was no longer a baby; she was nearly four, but for some reason it delighted us to cheer her' (chapter 1). The young Hartley's memory of being met off the school train in London by

Aunt Kathleen, who lived in Finchley (letter of 4 April 1909), becomes the meeting of Leo by 'Aunt Charlotte, a Londoner' off the Salisbury train as he breaks his journey to Norfolk (opening of chapter 1); and, like the Leo of the novel, as opposed to the film, he had a good voice – he refers to doing a solo in a letter of 17 October 1909, and his singing continued at Harrow.

Leo's excitement over swimming and, by today's standards, late development as a swimmer, are matched by the young Hartley who, in a letter of 14 May 1911, expresses the somewhat optimistic hope that he will be able to swim 75 yards 'soon', then, in a letter of a fortnight later (28 May), reports that he can now swim 30 yards across the school lake. (Note that in a cancelled passage from chapter 19, recorded in the Textual Appendix (p. 269), Ted gives Leo a long swimming lesson.) Most fascinating of all, though, is the letter to which Hartley refers in his 1963 Introduction about asking to be called home. He does not remember it himself, merely saying that his mother told him he wrote such a letter. In fact, a letter on this topic still exists. Addressed to his mother in mid-August 1910, from 72 St Helen's Road, Hastings, and headed 'Saturday', it reads:

Mrs Wallis wants me to stay till Wednesday, as she wants me to go to a party . . . You know I am not very fond of parties. And I *do* want to come home on Tuesday. However, they have asked me to write to you and ask if you would mind my staying. I am enjoying myself here, but I am sure we should both prefer me to be home.

Of course, if you think it would be better for me to stay, write to me and say so; it is only for a day. But still, I do want to be home again.

Leo is visiting a Norfolk stately home, and the young Leslie a south-coast villa; but here, in one letter, is the substance of Leo's two (see chapters 14, 16) as he reports being invited to stay on at Brandham and then asks to come home so that he can escape his birthday party. As he wrote the novel, Hartley thought himself back into his schoolboy self sufficiently deeply to recall an incident that was lost to his conscious recollection.

The letters from which I have quoted are now stored, in a symbolism Hartley would have appreciated, in a cardboard box alongside the two similar boxes housing the manuscript notebooks of *The Go-Between* itself: childhood record and fictional retrieval of that childhood thus mutely address each other. The letters were written from Thanet and Harrow; but the notebooks in which *The Go-Between* was written are Italian, which testifies to another element of autobiography in the novel.

In addition to the boyhood letters many survive from Hartley's adulthood – letters to and from Walter Allen, John Bayley, Phyllis Bentley, Edmund Blunden, Elizabeth Bowen, Maurice Bowra, Joyce Cary, Lord David Cecil, Nevill Coghill, Clifford Kitchin, C. Day Lewis, Daphne du Maurier, Aldous and Julian Huxley, Charles Morgan, and Dame Edith and Sir Osbert Sitwell, to name but a few. Among them are several to his elder sister, Enid, tracing the genesis of *The Go-Between*. They are mostly from Venice, where Hartley had lived intermittently from 1926 to the outbreak of the Second World War in 1939.

A letter of 24 May 1952 from Venice reports: 'I have begun another story, which means, or ought to mean, a return to slavery!', noting that Hartley's 'man' Sergio has been sent out to buy 'a very large exercise book'. ('Another' alludes to his already having begun *Facial Justice*, the 'new book' which, he complains in a letter of 9 February 1952, 'I haven't made much headway with' and on which he stopped working when the idea for *The Go-Between* struck him.) By 9 June, and still in Venice, inspiration is at a peak: 'I have been very busy with my book – and it *is* so time-taking. When it is going well I feel I must go on, so as not to lose the impulse – when it isn't, I feel I must go on trying till it comes back.' On 17 June he announces: 'My new novel has gone on quite fast, until now, when I am stopping to *think*, which perhaps I ought to have done before.' He wrote slightly more fully to Sir Roderick Meiklejohn on the same day: '. . . then I began to write a novel: this has occupied me rather obsessively – indeed, there *was* a moment when, if I had kept the pace up, I should almost have rivalled Stendhal, who . . . wrote the Chartreuse de Parme in about six months . . . Now I have slowed down, but still done quite a big chunk.' By 19 October, now at Bathford, he can tell Enid that the book is finished and he is 'trying to revise it'. Revision was still under way on 16 November.

Venice, the site of the novel's genesis, is a private backdrop, and a major clue, to *The Go-Between*'s meaning for Hartley. In *The Boat* (1949) he had made Timothy Carson, the protagonist, remember with anguish the way in which Venice had been lost to him through the Second World War, and the letters and the essay 'Remembering Venice' (reprinted in *The Novelist's Responsibility*) make the point yet again:

with increasing political tension, the fortified islands like Campalto grew so sensitive to my proximity that angry shouts greeted my appearance on the skyline.

Yes, the islands were forbidden country, emblems of what all Italy afterwards became. [p. 215]

We may suppose that freedom to return to Venice after the war did not remove the memories of hostility. In view of this, *The Go-Between*'s celebrated opening sentence sounds a particularly poignant note: *foreign* – repeated a few lines later, where the diary has 'a foreign look' – with its meanings *alien*, *other*, *strange*, registers the fundamental displacement that Hartley felt. Writing in Venice, which the war stole from him, he feels a foreigner, and the city that existed for him up to 1939 is itself now alien, foreign, belonging to a different world. The spatial distance between the Venice in which *The Go-Between* was written and the Norfolk in which it is set parallels the temporal distance between 1952 (the year in which Hartley writes is also the year in which Leo writes) and 1900, the year of Leo's visit to Brandham Hall. The title registers this, too; for although most obviously referring to Leo's role as messenger between Marian and Ted, it also suggests Hartley the authorial go-between, whose life was divided between England and Italy, denying foreignness until war brutally defined it for him; Leo, the man of sixty-four who, via the diary, goes-between his present and past selves much as Dickens – in an essay in *The Uncommercial Traveller* titled 'Travelling Abroad' – met and had a dialogue with his young self; and Mercury, the god with whom Trimingham identifies Leo (chapter 8) and who, mythologically, went-between heaven and earth as Jupiter's messenger.

II *Ghostly Memories*

Mercury was not, however, just Jupiter's messenger. One of his other roles was that of *psychopompos*, or guide of the souls of the dead into the lower world and leader of reincarnated souls back into the upper (see Virgil, *Aeneid*, 4. 242–4; Penguin Classics, tr. W. F. Jackson Knight, p. 104). Leo is thus particularly in a Mercurian role when, at the end of the Prologue, he recalls his memories to the light of day: 'I had kept them buried all these years . . . Was it true . . . that my best energies had been given to the undertaker's art? . . . The cerements, the coffins, the vaults, all that had confined them [the memories of the time at Brandham Hall] was bursting open.' Then, just as 'the clock struck twelve' – the hour when ghosts walk – his story of recalled memories begins, out of the diary and out of the opened combination lock.

It is no accident that this echoes the way Nelly Dean's tale, the central narrative of *Wuthering Heights*, emerges from Lockwood's (lockwould's) dream in the closet bed after he has been reading the diary scribblings of young Catherine Earnshaw written a generation before (*Wuthering Heights*, chapter 3), for Hartley admitted to an admiration for Emily Brontë's novel that stopped just short of idolatry (quoted in Peter Bien, *L. P. Hartley* (1963), p. 256). Leo, like Lockwood, summons memories that reappear as ghosts. And this reminds us in turn that Hartley made much of his reputation as a writer of ghost stories. Indeed, as a novel of boyhood *The Go-Between* has more in common with *Great Expectations* and Robert McCammon's *Boy's Life* (1991) than with *Huckleberry Finn*, Salinger's *The Catcher in the Rye* (1951) or Barry Hines's *A Kestrel for a Knave* (or *Kes*, 1968). As in Dickens's and McCammon's novels, the supernatural element is at once decoratively Gothic and a knowing exploitation of the uncanny to suggest the relationship between the rational self and those half-remembered somethings that we have to induce across the threshold of consciousness by enchantment, incantation and dream.

Emily Brontë stands at *The Go-Between*'s own threshold, for its epigraph is taken from one of her poems which tells of a child whose wish to see its future is granted by the sudden appearance of a spectre who, despite the child's attempts to thrust it away with its 'tiny hands', reveals that 'childhood's flower must waste its bloom/Beneath the shadow of the tomb'. While suggesting the premature blasting of Leo's childhood by Mrs Maudsley's reaction to Marian and Ted's love-making, the poem more significantly heralds the theme of the uncanny in the novel. The spectre brings from the tomb memories which become, in effect, the child's own and which the child then, like Leo, wishes to deny; with the difference that we see Leo now opening the tomb of his buried memories and willingly leading them forth, thereby allying himself, perhaps, more with Marcel Proust than with Brontë's 'child of dust'. For Proust's vast act of memorial recapture, *A la Recherche du Temps Perdu* (1913–27) – translated by C. K. Scott Moncrieff as *Remembrance of Things Past* – is a main inspiration of *The Go-Between*, as Hartley himself implied in his 1963 Introduction, maybe recalling as he did so what he had written in a review of his friend Osbert Sitwell's autobiography, *Left Hand, Right Hand!* (1944): '. . . *à la recherche du temps perdu* is a passion with him, and like Proust he can recapture the essential flavour of the act of living' (*The Novelist's Responsibility*, p. 161).

But surely Leo's power to make buried memories live is closer still to what Macaulay attributed to Milton: '[his words] are words of enchantment. No sooner are they pronounced, than the past is present and the distant near . . . and all the burial-places of memory give up their dead' (Thomas Macaulay, *Critical and Historical Essays*, ed. F. C. Montague, 3 vols (London, 1903), 1. 16). The sixty-four-year-old Leo has not lost his younger self's magicianship after all: he has learned, finally, to divert its purpose from cursing to healing. His last exercise of it – which is also his last assertion of his Mercurian self – is directed at the recall of the dead that signals his own rejoining of the human race through feeling: 'Under those cliffs, I thought, I have been buried. But they should witness my resurrection, the resurrection that had begun in the red collar-box . . .' (end of Prologue); 'Tell him there's no spell or curse except an unloving heart' (end of Epilogue).

In learning this Leo is, though, actually remembering something that his young self had discovered, despite his power to curse, on his first visit to Brandham church (chapter 6). There, musing on the mural tablets' roll-call of dead Triminghams, he had suddenly realized that the ninth Viscount might still be alive and that if he were 'not buried in a wall but walking about, then the whole family came to life; it did not belong to history but to today'. At that moment distant became present and the skeleton of mere facts – history for the young Leo possesses the place that bibliographical data assume in his older life – developed living, vulnerable human flesh and spirit much as, at the beginning of chapter 3 of *Wuthering Heights*, the names inscribed on

the window ledge flicker, under Lockwood's sleepy gaze, into swarming, living Catherines. Leo's intuition about the ninth Viscount is,
of course, recalled in the Epilogue when he meets young Edward
Trimingham, the eleventh Viscount. With Ted's hair and face he
makes the fact of Marian and Ted's liaison live again, not in the form
of ghostly memory but as genetic statement.

By a strange twist, though, the past has become so real by the end
of *The Go-Between* that the narrating Leo of the Epilogue has turned
into a ghostly outsider, who can assume – and resume – life only by
a physical revisiting of the place he has recalled, through memory.
So, like the adult Pip returning from abroad 'unseen' to the scenes
of his childhood in *Great Expectations* (chapter 59), he returns to Brandham for the first time since 1900: 'The place had changed with all
the changes of fifty years – the most changeful half a century in history.
I did not even feel a revenant; I felt a stranger.' It is a subtle distinction.
A revenant is, in the material as well as ghostly sense, one who returns
to somewhere known; but a stranger is an alien – a foreigner in a
place he once knew. And as the word *stranger* tends to be charged
with a sense of the uncanny and ghostly in Hartley's private vocabulary
(Epilogue, n. 8), Leo is saying here that he returns as a ghostlike
outcast. As a stranger, then, he passes from the church to the village,
where he encounters the current Viscount Trimingham who directs
him to Marian; for she, too, is a survivor from the summer of 1900
– the only one, apart from Leo.

He has to see her because, unlike Miss Havisham buried in her
house in *Great Expectations*, she remembers the past in terms of love
fulfilled. Despite the element of self-delusion in her lonely memory
of what happened between herself and Ted, and of the way they used
Leo, she contributes to his 'resurrection' by asking him to take the
message of love to her grandson. By revealing the 'truth' that their
love was beautiful and blameless, Leo can lift the curse that the young
Edward Trimingham feels Marian and Ted imposed on him. Mercury
takes messages; he also blesses new life by leading souls to the light
again.

Yet, in a sense, Leo's return as a stranger merely echoes his marginality to the social world of the Hall way back in 1900. Central to
the cricket match and the celebratory concert he may be, but here
even his Norfolk jacket is clownishly wrong, and he is more at home

with the outhouses, the rubbish-heap, and the farm than he is at the Hall, finding an easy affinity with the outlaw Robin Hood once his Maid Marian has bestowed upon him his suit of Lincoln green (chapter 4), and with a distinct 'sense of being abroad' (chapter 7) as he observes the difference between the Norfolk corn stooks and his native Wiltshire ones. On one level these details reflect Leo's sense of freedom from parental and school restraints; but on another they remind us, again, that Leo's story is in part Leslie Hartley's own story of distance and dissociation from his past. For north Norfolk, together with the adjoining Lincolnshire fens, was the scene of his own childhood. Moreover, Leo's home, Court Place near Salisbury (chapter 1), shares its name and location with a house inhabited by Hartley during the early years of the war. Leo lives in West Hatch (the name of the village, originally 'Winterborne' in the holograph to recall the various Winterbournes to the north of Salisbury, seems to have been borrowed from the village near Taunton, in Somerset); Hartley's Court House was in Lower Woodford, north of Salisbury near the Winterbournes. He moved there on his return from Venice in 1939, remaining until 1941, when he leased a house called West Hayes (the name may have contributed to Leo's West Hatch) in Rockbourne, south of Salisbury, then, in 1946, bought his house in Bathford, east of Bath. The Leo who travels from Wiltshire to Norfolk thus negotiates the gap separating Hartley's own fenland boyhood from his middle-aged self, at home variously in Wiltshire, Hampshire and Somerset.

III *The Golden Age and the Virgin*

Memory often idealizes the past, and so, within the frame occupied by the older Leo as he performs his resurrection of buried memory, a pastoral idyll gleams. Shot through with summer sun and shimmering in a heat-haze, it contains a stately home, a fenland harvest, lazy waterways, a picnic and a cricket match. Osbert Sitwell remembered a similar world in the Introduction to *Left Hand, Right Hand!*:

So placid was this brief golden halt that often as a small child . . . I used to wonder whether its stream had not altogether dried up. The Diamond Jubilee, the Boer War, the Edwardian Decade, none of these, viewed separately, was history. . . Nothing had happened for so long, and nothing would happen again: nothing.

But *The Go-Between*'s portrayal of this period is somewhat different. For the calm of Leo's idyll is, upon closer inspection, only apparent, disturbed as it is by the ripples and waves of class tension and war.

What to Sitwell is a 'golden halt' is, to the young Leo of the Prologue, a dawning Golden Age. And since *The Go-Between* uses the phrase in its precise classical sense, it is worth defining it. The Golden Age of the ancient Greek and Roman poets was a period of lost perfection but, it was said, there was always the possibility of its return. The seminal description occurs in Book 1 of Ovid's *Metamorphoses* where, among other details, we are told that it was a period of peace during which there was perfect equality between individuals. As the Silver, Bronze and finally Iron Ages succeeded it, the perfection was eroded and, when greed and warfare began to dominate, the last immortal on earth fled to the heavens. She was Astraea, the goddess of Justice, who became enshrined as the Virgo of the zodiac. As Virgo, who presides over late August and most of September, she was the goddess of corn, the fruition and colour of which are also reminders of the Golden Age.

Leo is obsessed with Virgo: 'I can scarcely say what she meant to me,' he says, in the Prologue, of her picture in the front of his diary. When he goes to Brandham Hall, he meets her in person, in the form of Marian: 'She was holding the long coil of her hair in front of her. It made two curves with which I was familiar; they belonged to the Virgin of the Zodiac' (chapter 4). This goddess literally walks the earth, then, confirming Leo in his conviction that the Golden Age has arrived with the new century.

Yet Brandham Hall is immediately disqualified as the site of a returned Golden Age because, despite Marian's Virgo presence, its existence is predicated on class difference, as the affair with Ted demonstrates only too well. Moreover, the Boer War (1899–1902) intrudes at various points, providing an important backdrop to the novel's action (chapters 4, 9, 18, 19 and 20) and reminding us that, far from being Sitwell's 'not history', it was significant in itself and, at the threshold of the new century, prophetic of the wars to follow.

Trimingham's damaged face, which turns him into Janus, the god of thresholds (chapter 5, n. 3), stands as a warning of the wars to come, in an all-too-iron century, that will claim, among their other victims, Marcus, Denys, and Marian's son, the tenth Viscount, and his wife.

The older Leo recalls the past as an idyll and, simultaneously, reinterprets it, thereby acknowledging that his early twentieth-century Golden Age was a consciously constructed myth. In doing so he implicitly recognizes that the late Victorian–Edwardian summer was a class myth built on a wilful blindness to social and other realities. It is the Leo of 1952, writing with the Second World War just over and the Korean War in progress, who understands the meaning of Trimingham's face; sees that the Brandham Golden Age was possible only because of Mr Maudsley's City money (Leo perceives him as 'gnome-like, leaving a trail of gold' in chapter 2); and makes the parallels between the villagers at the cricket match 'in their motley raiment' and the ill-dressed, but nevertheless supremely effective, Transvaal farmers in the Boer War (chapter 11). He can also assess the degree to which his younger go-between self, in its marginality to the Hall's world, identified with the villagers (so that in the cricket match he wants and does not want Ted to win; and he wishes Marian to marry Trimingham while himself still feeling drawn to Ted and understanding why she is), and can manipulate the narrative irony that what the cricket match re-enacted in little was not just the Boer War and its analogue the class struggle, but a clash of ideologies in the shape of republican (the Transvaal) versus monarchist imperialist. He can also make a neat connection between the colour of his green suit and the republican Robespierre (chapter 22, n. 3).

Finally, he can exploit the irony of his birth year when juxtaposed against the year of his – and Hartley's – writing. For if he is thirteen in July 1900, then he was born in 1887, the year of Queen Victoria's Golden Jubilee, one of the mementoes of which was a 'Golden Age' design embossed-leather wallpaper by Walter Crane. The older Leo would be only too aware that 1952, a year after the Festival of Britain, with its patriotic euphoria and Britannia symbolism, began with the death of King George VI on 6 February – the month in which Hartley began work on his dark dystopia, *Facial Justice*. The writing of Leo's remembered Golden Age into *The Go-Between* therefore coincided with the emergence of the 'New Elizabethan Age' myth that almost immediately sprang up around the young Elizabeth II and drew parallels not only between her and Queen Victoria, but, more importantly, between her and Elizabeth I, the monarch who had been mythologized, above all, as Virgo/Astraea, the goddess of the Golden Age. With the neo-Elizabethan fêting of the new queen, Hartley recalled the application of the Virgo symbol to the first Elizabeth. In terms of the young Leo's story he did so to explore the boy's fantasies about the nature of the virginal feminine as he stood on the threshold of puberty, at once intrigued and repelled by the notion of 'spooning' and what produces babies; in terms of the older Leo's story he did so to demonstrate how strong the need for myth was at periods of national spiritual debility. Post-war Britain, still rationed, still remembering the deprivations caused by the terrible winter of 1947, reeling in 1952 from the shock of the Lynton and Lynmouth floods, the king's death and the Harrow and Wealdstone train disaster, was once again creating a Golden Age myth. But Hartley knew that this myth was as false as Leo's Golden Age Brandham.

The young Leo, then, creates a pastoral landscape, and the older Leo interprets it, showing how it is contradicted by Trimingham's disfigured face and finally denied when its virgin Astraea loses her virginity. These broad details are supported by smaller ones: the information that Brandham Hall contains a notable picture collection of Dutch landscapes, for instance. To the young Leo they mean nothing. But the older Leo knows exactly how they reflect the Hall's view of itself as existing against a backdrop of idyllic, Golden Age calm (chapter 2, n. 5), just as he knows the significance of the Teniers in the smoking room – those erotic peasant paintings, 'not shown' to the public (chapter 2), which say everything about the way the Hall is titillated by the sexual life of the lower classes while simultaneously distancing it into pictorial collectables. From the perspective of 1952 he now sees that, on 27 July 1900, Marian made pictorial titillation become fact: destined for Trimingham, the ninth Viscount, by her rich but non-aristocratic parents, she found love and sexual gratification with Farmer Ted. Their liaison evoked the time-honoured struggle between the arranged marriage (duty to parents and the social system) and passion and, though duty and the class system appeared to prevail with Ted's suicide, the older Leo discovers in 1952 that love won. Trimingham may have married Marian to prove the truth of his particular myth that 'nothing is ever a lady's fault'; but what the marriage really effected was the legitimization of Ted's baby and thereby the continuation in the Trimingham 'line' of a healthy dose of Burgess blood. Trimingham's gesture is born out of love for Marian and out of duty to his line: his awareness of *noblesse oblige* combined with the pragmatic recognition, first, that his family needed the Maudsley money and, second, that genetically there is not much difference between a Maudsley and a Burgess. Marry the one, import the other, and the continuation of the family will be guaranteed.

A similar recognition of dynastic hard-headedness underlies the rather subtle presence of Carthage and Virgil's *Aeneid* in *The Go-Between*. Leo's cursing of the belladonna plant as he uproots it modifies Cato the Elder's insistent reminder of the danger of Carthage to Rome, *delenda est Carthago* (Carthage must be destroyed: see chapter 21, n. 8). In chapter 17, Leo's recognition of the 'Danaan implication' of Marian's gifts locates her as a treacherous Greek via *Aeneid*, Book 2 (the reference is to the Danaans [Greeks] who have left the wooden horse as an apparent gift which will enable them to destroy Troy: chapter 17, n. 20).

The belladonna is easily identified with Marian, at once mysterious, sexually attractive and dangerous (chapter 2, n. 14; Hartley made the identification himself in the 1963 Introduction). It represents Marian from Leo's viewpoint as she starts to contradict the Virgo identity he has imposed on her; and it represents her from her mother's viewpoint, too, as she increasingly detects the threat her daughter's sexuality poses to her plans for Marian's marriage. Leo's association of the plant with Carthage suggests the extent to which his reading of Marian begins to coincide with Mrs Maudsley's, for to chant *delenda est* is to identify Marian's alliance with Ted as a threat to the upper-class *status quo* and hence to the state. But the Carthage invoked by this quotation connects with the *Aeneid* reference, for it is taken from Aeneas's account of the fall of Troy to Dido, Queen of Carthage. As he talks, she falls in love with him, agonized because the vow of fidelity she has made to the memory of her dead husband makes any subsequent sexual liaison a betrayal. Then, in Book 4, when she and Aeneas are out hunting, there is a sudden thunderstorm. The couple seek refuge in a cave and make love: 'Henceforward Dido cared no more for appearances or her good name' (*Aeneid*, 4. 169–71; Penguin Classics,

p. 102). Her shame is broadcast throughout North Africa by Rumour; and Mercury is sent to earth by Jupiter to remind Aeneas that it is his duty to proceed on his mission to found imperial Rome. Despite Dido's pleas, which include the request that he should make her pregnant ('if I had a son of yours . . . [to] bring you back to me if only in his likeness, I might not then have felt so utterly entrapped and forsaken': ll. 327–30; Penguin Classics, p. 107), Aeneas insists that he cannot stay. Dido asks her sister, Anna, to build her a funeral pyre which, she says, she will reluctantly use as part of a magic spell to rid her of Aeneas's power over her. Then she stabs herself.

The love-making of Marian and Ted in the outhouse to the accompaniment of a thunderstorm clearly alludes to Dido and Aeneas in the cave – with the difference that Leo's Dido gets her baby. The destruction of the belladonna relives Dido's death while keeping Marian alive (symbolically killing her sexuality, as it were, while retaining her body for marriage purposes); yet Leo had already anticipated Dido's funeral on the pyre by imagining the belladonna 'crackling in a fire: all that beauty being destroyed' at the end of chapter 2. But whereas Aeneas escapes death, Ted assumes Dido's role and kills himself – an act which, in saving Marian from blame, subscribes to the code that relieves a lady of blame for anything, thereby making Ted as much a gentleman as Hugh.

Leo's unwillingness, in spite of everything, to betray Marian and Ted touchingly reminds us of the intensity of his need for a mythical space where irreconcilables can be united. For if the *Aeneid*'s story of Dido touches rather too closely on that of Marian and Ted, then the songs at the cricket supper weave a fantasy world in which opposites unite and love is vindicated. This is especially true of Ted's 'If Other Lips', from Balfe's *Bohemian Girl* (chapter 13, n. 4). Rejecting the ruthless *realpolitik* of upper-class and aristocratic intermarriage for a land of shamelessly pastoral romance, this song makes radical Farmer Ted into the opera's Thaddeus, an exiled Polish rebel who, taking refuge with a band of Gypsies, encounters a beautiful Gypsy girl with whom he falls in love. Eventually, with her identity established as Arline, the daughter of Count Arnheim, who had been abducted twelve years previously and brought up as a Gypsy, and his own revealed as a Polish aristocrat, they marry, despite the opposition of the Gypsy Queen and Floretein, the Count's foolish nephew. If Ted is Thaddeus and Marian Arline, then Mrs Maudsley is the witch-like Gypsy Queen and Floretein is Trimingham, turned into a buffoon by the Saturnalian forces of wish-fulfilment.

IV Leo's Magic

Wishing is one way in which you can try to guarantee the stability of your myth. Another is – like Prospero's in Shakespeare's *The Tempest* – through magic. Although Leo's interest in the zodiac is associated with his growing sense of power, the magic proper begins with the cursing of Jenkins and Strode and, by increasing his prestige at school, leads to his invitation to Brandham with results that affect him for the rest of his life. It is initially born of anger over the defacing of the diary. His schoolfriends turn his own word 'vanquished' against him; he retaliates by turning it against them. It is an important detail that the curses originated, in part, from 'a translation of the *Peau de Chagrin* [*The Wild Ass's Skin*] at home' (Prologue), for Balzac's novel is another clue to Leo's character.

It tells of a young man, Raphael de Valentin, who is given by an antiquary a fragment of dried wild ass's (onager's) skin which has the power to grant any wish expressed by its owner but on the understanding that at every wish the skin shrinks, signifying the shortening of the owner's life. The Sanskrit characters copied by Leo for his curse are inscribed on the skin, and the skin's symbolism exemplifies Balzac's theory of the will, as the antiquary explains:

Man exhausts himself by two acts, instinctively accomplished, which dry up the sources of his existence. Two words express all the forms that these two causes of death can assume: will and power . . . The exercise of the *will* consumes us; the exercise of *power* destroys us; but the pursuit of *knowledge* leaves our infirm constitution in a state of perpetual calm. So desire or volition is dead in me, killed by thought . . . I have invested my life, not in the heart, so easily broken, nor in the senses which are so readily blunted, but in the brain which does not wear out but which outlasts everything [tr. H. J. Hunt, Penguin Classics, p. 52].

Later he says: 'Here you have . . . *power* and *will* united. Here are . . . your inordinate desires . . .' (Penguin, p. 54). And here, surely, is the contrast between the young and the old Leos: the former, like Raphael, leaps at the chance to assert his will. Intolerant of childhood sickness he bursts into the new century, prompted by the violation of his diary, with an assertion of will which equals power. That Leo's magic is nothing more than this is conveyed by the pun contained in the French word *chagrin*, which means both shagreen and vexation (Prologue, n. 30): vexation with Jenkins and Strode leads to the assertion of will which, at Brandham, destroys his memory. Destruction of memory is not, however, destruction of body and mind. The older Leo, broken by his attempt to control Marian's destiny in altering the final message, has saved himself by pursuing the career of bibliographer. In this life of self-preserving 'interment' he has become Balzac's antiquary, surrounded by testaments to the dead, safe in his pursuit of knowledge.

It is arguable as well that Leo's devotion to the zodiac has its origins with Balzac. For just after he has stated his belief that the zodiacal figures, unbounded by cyclical patterns, 'soared in an ascending spiral towards infinity', he says that 'the expansion and ascension, as of some divine gas, which I believed to be the ruling principle of my own life, I attributed to the coming century. The year 1900 had an almost mystical appeal for me . . .' (Prologue). For this 'gas' – which identifies the celestial zodiac with Leo's sense of his infallible growth upward – appears to be identical with Balzac's *substance éthérée*, the 'etherial substance' of which the traditional opposites, spiritual and physical, are manifestations (see H. J. Hunt's Introduction to *The Wild Ass's Skin*, p. 9). In other words, it unites the two, bringing heaven to earth and earth to heaven, much as the Golden Age did when zodiacal Virgo, among others, walked among mortals.

The Go-Between, then, begins at the moment when Leo, discovering the diary, explores how he lost his youthful magical power and became his own, antiquary-like shadow. The diary holds the clue to the point at which young Leo, the asserter of will as power, the liver of life to excess among the figures of his earthly zodiac in the summer heat of July 1900, was vanquished by wills greater than his own: those of Marian and Ted (for love is the strongest form of magic, and Leo's spell in chapter 21 could not prevent Virgin and Water-carrier from showing the mortal, passionate clay of which they were made); and that of Mrs Maudsley, whose hysteria finally broke his will, turning him into the devotee of facts (and enemy of passion) that he describes in the Epilogue. In Marian and Ted's coupling on the floor she saw that her – and Leo's – myth was dead; that the old consolation of hierarchy prevailing and anarchic Eros quelled, offered by Shakespeare in *A Midsummer Night's Dream* (chapter 21, n. 4), was a hollow fiction, and her 'repeated screams' conveyed that knowledge to Leo.

Leo loses his memory in sympathy with Mrs Maudsley's ensuing madness: she 'goes away'; he loses himself in books. Both, in other words, escape what, in the Epilogue, Leo calls 'the most changeful half a century in history'. If I am right in suggesting that the origin of Leo's memory loss is not psychoanalytical theory but, rather, an anecdote recounted by Osbert Sitwell in the Introduction to *Left Hand, Right Hand!* (Epilogue, n. 1), then the possibility emerges that the abrupt curtailment of Leo's hopes and personality, whatever its other causes, is explained by another of Sitwell's books. This is his first novel, *Before the Bombardment* (1926), the material for which, he tells us, was collected between the ages of three and twelve. I think that Hartley recalled *Before the Bombardment* when he came to write *The Go-Between*.

The two novels have more than the Boer War and a cricket match – and the sense that the generals initially regarded the war that began in 1914 as a cross between the two – in common: they share a remembered world. In Sitwell's novel that world, located in 'Newborough', is erased by a German shell that comes screaming out of the air with no warning. The obliteration of Leo's memory of the golden summer of 1900 is caused by Mrs Maudsley's screams. Shell and scream testify to the same thing: that the world which would follow would never be the same as the one that had been lost.

Hartley leaves Mrs Maudsley in that lost world. In the Epilogue he makes Leo revisit the scene to discover that loss is not necessarily such a bad thing if one learns how to relinquish grief and to rebuild. Asserting his will again by visiting Marian, and in doing so rediscovering the relationship between will and inclination that he had lost in his adulthood (Prologue), he acquiesces in her view of the past, thus rescuing himself for the life of feeling from the fate of the antiquary. The anonymous narrator of Hartley's short story 'The White Wand' (1954) – significantly, a writer who has returned to post-war Venice only to find himself a ghostly alien – says: 'I believe people still say to themselves, "I will really start to *feel* . . . as soon as, as soon as – the hydrogen bomb is perfected, or this business in Korea is settled"' (*Complete Short Stories*, 1973, p. 284). In 1952, with the Korean War continuing and the first hydrogen bomb just exploded, Leo stops waiting and 'start[s] to feel'. It is, perhaps, a little matter, but that is why it is important. For Hartley identified one of the problems of twentieth-century living as a loss of feeling, and individual significance, in the face of over-exposure to such vast atrocities as 'the atom bomb and the concentration camp, and the appalling sufferings they involved' (*The Novelist's Responsibility*, p. 11). Leo's self-rescue in the year Britain exploded its first atom bomb is his, and the author's, attempt to demonstrate that our moral redemption resides in losing the numbness born of our saturation in suffering, and acting on, and valuing, the tiniest human detail.

DOUGLAS BROOKS-DAVIES

1895 30 December: Leslie Poles Hartley born at Whittlesey, Cambridgeshire, to the solicitor Harry Bark Hartley and Mary Elizabeth Hartley, eldest daughter of William Thompson. A sister, Enid Mary, had been born on Christmas Day 1892.

1898 March: father becomes a director of the Whittlesey Central Brick Company Limited.

1900 Father purchases Fletton Tower, Peterborough (about five miles from Whittlesey). His mother's parents farmed at Crowland, Lincolnshire (about eight miles from Fletton and Whittlesey).

1903 Younger sister, Annie Norah, born.

1908 5 October: starts at Northdown Hill School, Cliftonville, Thanet, Kent.

1909 17 December: leaves Northdown.

1910 April–July: attends Clifton College, Bristol; 28 September, enters Harrow School, Middlesex.

1915 Leaf Scholar, Harrow; October, matriculates at Balliol College, Oxford.

1916 April: enlists in Norfolk Regiment.

1918 August: invalided out of the Army, in which he had served as a second lieutenant, though never on active service. Spends a year convalescing.

1919–21 October: returns to Balliol to read Modern History. Co-edits *Oxford Outlook*.

1920 January: 'The Cat' (short story), *Oxford Outlook*. 'Candlemas' (poem), *Oxford Poetry*.

1921 March: 'The Duke's Tragedy' (short story), *Oxford Outlook*. Graduates BA.

1922 'Disparity in Despair' (poem), *Oxford Poetry*. First visit to Venice, where he will live for a considerable period each year from 1926 until 1939.

1923 Begins fiction reviewing for *Nation and Athenaeum* (until April 1924).

1924 First volume of short stories, *Night Fears, and Other Stories* (Putnam, London and New York).

1925 Short novel, *Simonetta Perkins* (Putnam, London and New York). Reviews for *Calendar of Modern Letters*; begins to review for *Saturday Review* (regular weekly reviews of three or more novels from 21 November 1925–1 March 1930).

1927 January: 'Saki' (short story), *Bookman*, vol. 71.

1931 January: 'Sacred River' (short story), *Sewanee Review*, vol. 39.

1932 Short stories, *The Killing Bottle* (Putnam, London).

1933 4 October: begins weekly fiction reviewing for *Sketch* (–29 December 1943).

1939 Living at Court House, Lower Woodford, Salisbury.

1941 Moves to West Hayes, Rockbourne, Fordingbridge, Hampshire.

1944 Novel, *The Shrimp and the Anemone* (Putnam, London). Reviews for *Life and Letters Today*.

1945 US edition of *The Shrimp and the Anemone* published by Doubleday as *The West Window*.

1946 Moves to Avondale, Bathford, Bath. Novel, *The Sixth Heaven* (Putnam, London). US edition 1947 (Doubleday). Reviews for *Life and Letters Today*.

1947 Novel, *Eustace and Hilda* (Putnam, London).

1948 Awarded the James Tait Black Memorial Prize for *Eustace and Hilda*. Short stories, *The Travelling Grave and Other Stories* (Arkham House, Wisconsin). First English edition, 1951 (J. Barrie, London). Mother dies.

1949 Novel, *The Boat* (Putnam, London). US edition, Doubleday 1950. Reviews for *Time and Tide*.

1951 Novel, *My Fellow Devils* (J. Barrie, London). US edition, 1959 (British Book Centre, New York).

1953 Novel, *The Go-Between* (Hamish Hamilton, London). US edition, 1954 (Knopf, New York).

1954 Heinemann Foundation Prize of the Royal Society of Literature for *The Go-Between*. Short stories, *The White Wand and Other Stories* (Hamish Hamilton, London). Father dies.

1955 Novel, *A Perfect Woman* (Hamish Hamilton, London). US edition, 1956 (Knopf, New York).

1956 January: awarded CBE.

1957 Novel, *The Hireling* (Hamish Hamilton, London). US edition, 1958 (Rinehart, New York).

1958 *Eustace and Hilda: A Trilogy*, introduced by Lord David Cecil (Putnam, London and New York). Comprises: I *The Shrimp and the Anemone*; II *The Sixth Heaven*; III *Eustace and Hilda*; also contains *Hilda's Letter*.

1960 Novel, *Facial Justice* (Hamish Hamilton, London; Collins, Toronto). US edition, 1961 (Doubleday, New York). Acquires a flat at Rutland Gate, London, SW7, and begins to divide his time between London and Bathford.

1961 Short stories, *Two for the River* (Hamish Hamilton, London; Collins, Toronto).

1962 'The Ghost-Writers' (short story) in *Winter's Tales 8*, ed. A. D. Maclean.

1964 Easter term, Clark Lecturer, Trinity College, Cambridge. Novel, *The Brickfield* (Hamish Hamilton, London; Collins, Toronto).

1966 Novel, *The Betrayal* (Hamish Hamilton, London; Collins, Toronto). Edits *Royal Society of Literature: Essays by Divers Hands* (Oxford University Press, London).

1967 *The Novelist's Responsibility: Lectures and Essays* (Hamish Hamilton, London; Collins, Toronto). US edition, 1968 (Hillary House, New York).

1968 Novel, *Poor Clare* (Hamish Hamilton, London). *The Collected Short Stories of L. P. Hartley*, introduced by Lord David Cecil (Hamish Hamilton, London). US edition, 1969 (Horizon Press, New York). Sister Enid dies.

1969 Novel, *The Love-Adept: A Variation on a Theme* (Hamish Hamilton, London).

1970 Novel, *My Sister's Keeper* (Hamish Hamilton, London).

1971 Novel, *The Harness Room* (Hamish Hamilton, London). Short stories, *Mrs Carteret Receives and Other Stories* (Hamish Hamilton, London). Film of *The Go-Between* (screenplay by Harold Pinter).

1972 February: made Companion of Literature by the Royal Society of Literature. Novel, *The Collections* (Hamish Hamilton, London). 13 December: dies. 'The Ugly Picture' (short story), *Spectator*, vol. 229 (23 December).

1973 Novel, *The Will and the Way* (Hamish Hamilton, London). *The Complete Short Stories of L. P. Hartley*, introduced by Lord David Cecil (Hamish Hamilton, London). Film of *The Hireling* (script by Wolf Mankowitz).

FURTHER READING

1 *Works by Hartley*

NB: full publication details will be found in the Chronology.

Night Fears, and Other Stories (London and New York, 1924) short
  stories
Simonetta Perkins (London and New York, 1925) short novel
The Killing Bottle (London, 1932) short stories
The Shrimp and the Anemone (London, 1944) novel
The Sixth Heaven (London, 1946) novel
Eustace and Hilda (London, 1947) novel
The Travelling Grave and Other Stories (Wisconsin, 1948) short stories
The Boat (London, 1949) novel
My Fellow Devils (London, 1951) novel
The Go-Between (London, 1953) novel
The White Wand and Other Stories (London, 1954) short stories
A Perfect Woman (London, 1955) novel
The Hireling (London, 1957) novel
Facial Justice (London and Toronto, 1960) novel
Two for the River (London and Toronto, 1961) short stories
The Brickfield (London and Toronto, 1964) novel
The Betrayal (London and Toronto, 1966) novel
The Novelist's Responsibility (London and Toronto, 1967) criticism
Poor Clare (London, 1968) novel
The Collected Short Stories of L. P. Hartley (London, 1968)
The Love-Adept: A Variation on a Theme (London, 1969) novel
My Sister's Keeper (London, 1970) novel
The Harness Room (London, 1971) novel

Mrs Carteret Receives and Other Stories (London, 1971) short stories
The Collections (London, 1972) novel
The Will and the Way (London, 1973) novel
The Complete Short Stories of L. P. Hartley (London, 1973) short stories

2 Editions of 'The Go-Between'

In addition to those listed in the Note on the Text, see the list of translations and abridgements in Stanton, 1978 (see Bibliographies).

3 Bibliographies

BIEN, Peter, 'An L. P. Hartley Bibliography', *Adam International Review*, nos 294–6 (1961), 63–70.

STANTON, R. J., *A Bibliography of Modern British Novelists*, 2 vols, Troy, New York: The Whitston Publishing Company, 1978, 1. 281–405.

4 Selected Bibliography of Biography and Criticism Relevant to 'The Go-Between'

ALLEN, Trevor, 'L. P. Hartley in Focus', *Books and Bookmen* 18 (1972), 25–7.

ALLEN, Walter, *The Modern Novel in Britain and the United States*, New York: E. P. Dutton, 1964, pp. 253–7.

ANON., 'A Man in His Senses', *Times Literary Supplement* (4 November 1960), p. 708.

ANON., 'Hartley, Leslie Poles', in *Encyclopedia of World Literature in the Twentieth Century*, ed. W. B. Fleischman, New York: Frederick Ungar, 1969, p. 86.

ATHOS, John, 'L. P. Hartley and the Gothic Infatuation', *Twentieth Century Literature* 7 (1962), 172–9.

ATKINS, John, *Six Novelists Look at Society*, London: John Calder, 1977, pp. 77–111.

BIEN, Peter, *L. P. Hartley*, London: Chatto and Windus; University

Park, Pennsylvania: Pennsylvania State University Press, 1963.

BLOOMFIELD, Paul, 'L. P. Hartley: Short Note on a Great Subject', *Adam International Review*, nos 294–6 (1961), 5–7.

—, *L. P. Hartley*, Harlow, Essex: Longman for the British Council, 1962; revised edn, 1970. Writers and their Work, 217.

CURCURU, Monique, *Childhood and Adolescence in the Novels of L. P. Hartley*, Publications de l'Université des Langues et Lettres de Grenoble, 1978.

DAVIDSON, R. A., 'Graham Greene and L. P. Hartley: "The Basement Room" and "The Go-Between"', *Notes and Queries* 221 (1966), 101–2.

FOREY, Margaret, '*The Go-Between*', in *Reference Guide to English Literature*, ed. D. L. Kirkpatrick, 3 vols, Chicago and London: St James's Press, 1991, 3. 1602–3.

GILL, Richard, *Happy Rural Seat: The English Country House in the Literary Imagination*, New Haven, Connecticut: Yale University Press, 1972.

GORDON, Lois, '*The Go-Between* – Hartley by Pinter', *Kansas Quarterly* 4 (1972), 81–92.

GRINDEA, Miron, 'Un Maître du Roman Anglais', *Adam International Review*, nos 294–6 (1961), 2–4.

GROSSVOGEL, D. I., 'Under the Sign of Symbols: Losey and Hartley', *Diacritics* 4 (1974), 51–6.

HALL, James, *The Tragic Comedians: Seven Modern British Novelists*, Bloomington, Indiana: Indiana University Press, 1963, pp. 111–28.

HARTLEY, L. P., 'Introduction' to *The Go-Between*, London: Heinemann Educational Books, 1963, pp. 1–8.

HIGDON, D. L., *Time and English Fiction*, London and Basingstoke: Macmillan, 1977, pp. 45–50.

—, *Shadows of the Past in Contemporary British Fiction*, London and Basingstoke: Macmillan, 1984, pp. 23–38.

JONES, E. T., 'Summer of 1900: A la Recherche of *The Go-Between*', *Literature/Film Quarterly* 1 (1973), 154–60.

—, *L. P. Hartley*, Boston: Twayne, 1978. Twayne's English Authors Series, 232.

JONES, Ernest, 'Schoolboy's World', *New Republic* 131 (1954), 19–20.

KITCHEN, C. H. B., 'Leslie Hartley – A Personal Angle', *Adam International Review*, nos 294–6 (1961), 7–12.

LEARMONT-BATLEY, K. E., '"The Past is a Foreign Country: They Do Things Differently There": Some Views on Teaching L. P. Hartley's *The Go-Between*', *Crux: A Journal on the Teaching of English* 19 (1985), 3—17.

MCEWAN, Neil, *York Notes on L. P. Hartley: 'The Go-Between'*, Harlow, Essex: Longman, 1980. Longman Literature Guides.

MELCHIORI, Giorgio, 'The English Novelist and the American Tradition', *Sewanee Review* 68 (1960), 502—15.

MOAN, M. A., 'Setting and Structure: An Approach to Hartley's *The Go-Between*', *Critique: Studies in Modern Fiction* 15 (1973), 27—36.

MUDRICK, Marvin, 'Humanity is the Principle', *Hudson Review* 7 (1955), 614—15.

MULKEEN, Anne, *Wild Thyme, Winter Lightning: The Symbolic Novels of L. P. Hartley*, London: Hamish Hamilton; Detroit, Michigan: Wayne State University Press, 1974.

PARKER, Derek, 'The Novelist L. P. Hartley Talks About His Childhood', *Listener* 88 (31 August 1972), 274—5.

PINTER, Harold, *Five Screenplays*, London: Methuen, 1971. (Screenplay of *The Go-Between*.)

PRITCHARD, R. E., 'L. P. Hartley's *The Go-Between*', *Critical Quarterly* 22 (1980), 45—55.

RADLEY, Alan, 'Psychological Realism in L. P. Hartley's *The Go-Between*', *Literature and Psychology* 33 (1987), 1—10.

RICHARDSON, Sallyann, 'L. P. Hartley', *Twentieth Century Writing: A Reader's Guide to Contemporary Literature*, ed. Kenneth Richardson, London: Newnes Books, 1969, pp. 278—81.

RILEY, Michael, and James Palmer, 'Time and the Structure of Memory in *The Go-Between*', *College Literature* 5 (1978), 219—27.

SEYMOUR-SMITH, Martin, 'L. P. Hartley', in *Who's Who in Twentieth Century Literature*, New York: Holt, Rinehart and Winston, 1976, pp. 151—2.

SINYARD, Neil, 'Pinter's *Go-Between*', *Critical Quarterly* 22 (1980), 21—33.

WATTS, H. H., 'L. P. Hartley', in *Reference Guide to English Literature*, ed. D. L. Kirkpatrick, 3 vols, Chicago and London: St James's Press, 1991, 2. 699—700.

WEBSTER, H. C., 'The Novels of L. P. Hartley', *Critique: Studies in Modern Fiction* 4 (1961), 39—51.

—, *After the Trauma: Representative British Novelists Since 1920*, Lexington, Kentucky: University Press of Kentucky, 1970, pp. 152–67.

WILLMOTT, M. B., '"What Leo Knew": The Childhood World of L. P. Hartley', *English* 24 (1975), 3–10.

WOOD, Michael, 'Losey's Hartley: *The Go-Between*', *New Society* (23 September 1971), 574–5.

WRIGHT, Adrian, *Foreign Country: The Life of L. P. Hartley*, London: André Deutsch, 1996.

The Go-Between

To Miss Dora Cowell

But, child of dust, the fragrant flowers,
The bright blue sky and velvet sod
Were strange conductors to the bowers
Thy daring footsteps must have trod.
                                    EMILY BRONTË

PROLOGUE

The past is a foreign country:[1] they do things differently there.

When I came upon the diary it was lying at the bottom of a rather battered red cardboard collar-box,[2] in which as a small boy I kept my Eton collars.[3] Someone, probably my mother, had filled it with treasures dating from those days. There were two dry, empty sea-urchins;[4] two rusty magnets,[5] a large one and a small one, which had almost lost their magnetism; some negatives[6] rolled up in a tight coil; some stumps of sealing-wax; a small combination lock with three rows of letters; a twist of very fine whipcord, and one or two ambiguous objects, pieces of things, of which the use was not at once apparent: I could not even tell what they had belonged to. The relics were not exactly dirty nor were they quite clean, they had the patina of age; and as I handled them,[7] for the first time for over fifty years, a recollection of what each had meant to me came back, faint as the magnets' power to draw, but as perceptible. Something came and went between us: the intimate pleasure of recognition, the almost mystical thrill of early ownership – feelings of which, at sixty-odd, I felt ashamed.

It was a roll-call in reverse; the children of the past announced their names, and I said 'Here'. Only the diary refused to disclose its identity.

My first impression was that it was a present someone had brought me from abroad. The shape, the lettering, the purple limp leather curling upwards at the corners, gave it a foreign look; and it had, I could see, gold edges. Of all the exhibits it was the only one that might have been expensive. I must have treasured it, why then could I not give it a context?

I did not want to touch it and told myself that this was because it challenged my memory: I was proud of my memory and disliked having it prompted. So I sat staring at the diary, as at a blank space in a crossword puzzle. Still no light came, and suddenly I took the combination lock and began to finger it, for I remembered how, at school, I could always open it by the sense of touch when someone else had set the combination. It was one of my show-pieces, and when I first mastered it drew some applause, for I declared that to do it I had to put myself into a trance: and this was not quite a lie, for I did deliberately empty my mind and let my fingers work without direction. To heighten the effect, however, I would close my eyes and sway gently to and fro, until the effort of keeping my consciousness at a low ebb almost exhausted me; and this I found myself instinctively doing now, as to an audience. After a timeless interval I heard the tiny click and felt the sides of the lock relax and draw apart; and at the same moment, as if by some sympathetic loosening in my mind, the secret of the diary flashed upon me.[8]

Yet even then I did not want to touch it; indeed my unwillingness increased, for now I knew why I distrusted it. I looked away and it seemed to me that every object in the room exhaled the diary's enervating power, and spoke its message of disappointment and defeat. And as if that was not enough, the voices reproached me with not having had the grit to overcome them. Under this twofold assault I sat, staring at the bulging envelopes around me, the stacks of papers tied up with red tape – the task of sorting which I had set myself for winter evenings, and of which the red collar-box had been almost the first item; and I felt, with a bitter blend of self-pity and self-reproach, that had it not been for the diary, or what the diary stood for, everything would be different. I should not be sitting in this drab, flowerless room, where the curtains were not even drawn to hide the cold rain beating on the windows, or contemplating the accumulation of the past and the duty it imposed on me to sort it out. I should be sitting in another room, rainbow-hued,[9] looking not into the past but into the future:[10] and I should not be sitting alone.

So I told myself, and with a gesture born of will, as most of my acts were, not inclination, I took the diary out of the box and opened it.

Diary
for the year
1900

it said in a copper-plate script unlike the lettering of today; and round the year thus confidently heralded, the first year of the century,[11] winged with hope, clustered the signs of the Zodiac, each somehow contriving to suggest a plenitude of life and power, each glorious, though differing from the others in glory.[12] How well I remembered them, their shapes and attitudes; and I remembered too, though it was no longer potent for me, the magic with which they were then invested, and the tingling sense of coming fruition they conveyed — the lowly creatures no less than the exalted ones.

The Fishes sported deliciously, as though there were no such things as nets and hooks; the Crab had a twinkle in its eye, as though it was well aware of its odd appearance and thoroughly enjoyed the joke; and even the Scorpion carried its terrible pincers with a gay, heraldic air, as though its deadly intentions existed only in legend.[13] The Ram, the Bull, and the Lion epitomized imperious manhood; they were what we all thought we had it in us to be; careless, noble, self-sufficient, they ruled their months with sovereign sway. As for the Virgin,[14] the one distinctively female figure in the galaxy, I can scarcely say what she meant to me. She was dressed adequately, but only in the coils and sweeps of her long hair; and I doubt whether the school authorities, had they known about her, would have approved the hours of dalliance my thoughts spent with her, though these, I think, were innocent enough. She was, to me, the key to the whole pattern, the climax, the coping-stone, the goddess — for my imagination was then, though it is no longer, passionately hierarchical; it envisaged things in an ascending scale, circle on circle, tier on tier, and the annual, mechanical revolution of the months did not disturb this notion. I knew that the year must return to winter and begin again; but to my apprehensions the zodiacal company were subject to no such limitations: they soared in an ascending spiral towards infinity.

And the expansion and ascension, as of some divine gas, which I believed to be the ruling principle of my own life, I attributed to the coming century. The year 1900 had an almost mystical appeal for me; I could hardly wait for it: 'Nineteen hundred, nineteen hundred,' I would chant to myself in rapture; and as the old century drew to its close, I began to wonder whether I should live to see its successor. I had an excuse for this: I had been ill and was acquainted with the idea of death;[15] but much more it was the fear of missing something infinitely precious – the dawn of a Golden Age.[16] For that was what I believed the coming century would be: a realization, on the part of the whole world, of the hopes that I was entertaining for myself.

The diary was a Christmas present from my mother, to whom I had confided some, though by no means all, of my aspirations for the future, and she wanted its dates to be worthily enshrined.

In my zodiacal fantasies there was one jarring note, to which, when I indulged them, I tried not to listen, for it flawed the experience. This was my own role in it.

My birthday fell in late July[17] and I had an additional reason, an excellent one, though I should have been loath to mention it at school, for claiming the Lion as my symbol. But much as I admired him and what he stood for, I could not identify myself with him, because of late I had lost the faculty which, like other children, I had once revelled in, of pretending that I was an animal. A term and a half at school had helped to bring about this disability in my imagination; but it was also a natural change. I was between twelve and thirteen, and I wanted to think of myself as a man.

There were only two candidates, the Archer and the Water-carrier,[18] and, to make the choice more difficult, the artist, who probably had few facial types at his command, had drawn them very much alike. They were in fact the same man following different callings. He was strong and sturdy and this appealed to me, for one of my ambitions was to become a kind of Hercules.[19] I leaned to the Archer as the more romantic, and because the idea of shooting appealed to me. But my father had been against war,[20] which I supposed was the Archer's profession; and as to the Water-carrier, though I knew him to be a useful member of society I could not help conceiving of him as a farm-labourer or at best a gardener, neither of which I wanted to be. The two men attracted and repelled me at the same time: perhaps I was jealous of them. When I studied the title-page of the diary I tried not to look at the Sagittarius–Aquarius combination, and when the whole conception took wing and mounted to the zenith, drawing the twentieth century with it for a final heavenly romp, I sometimes contrived to leave it behind. A zodiacal sign without port-folio,[21] I then had the Virgin to myself.

One result of the diary was that I went to the top of the class for knowing the signs of the Zodiac. In another way its influence was less fortunate. I wanted to be worthy of the diary, of its purple leather, its gold edges, its general sumptuousness; and I felt that my entries must live up to all these. They must record something worthwhile, and they must reach a high standard of literary attainment. My ideas of what was worthwhile were already rather advanced and it seemed to me that my school life did not provide events fit for such a magnificent setting as my diary was, or for the year 1900.

What had I written? I remembered the catastrophe well enough, but not the stages that led up to it. I turned the pages. The entries were few. 'Tea with C's pater and mater – very jolly.' Then, more sophisticated, 'Jolly decent tea with L's people. Muffins, scones, cakes and strawberry jam.' 'Drove to Canterbury in 3 breaks. Visited Cathedral, very interresting. Thomas A'Beckett's blood.[22] Très riping.' 'Walk to Kingsgate Castle.[23] M. showed me his new knife.' This was the first reference to Maudsley; I turned the pages more quickly. Ah, here it was – the Lambton House saga.[24] Lambton House was a nearby preparatory school with which we felt ourselves on terms of special rivalry; they were to us what Eton is to Harrow.[25] 'Played Lambton House At Home. Match drawn 1 – 1.' 'Played Lambton House Away. Match drawn 3 – 3.' Then, 'Last and Ultimate and Final Replay. Lambton House VANQUISHED 2 – 1!!!! McClintock scored both goals!!!!'

After that, no more entries for a time. Vanquished! That was the word for which I was made to suffer.[26] My attitude to the diary was twofold and contradictory: I was intensely proud of it and wanted everybody to see it and what I had written in it, and at the same time I had an instinct for secrecy and wanted nobody to see it. I spent hours balancing the pros and cons of either course. I thought of the applause that would greet the diary as it was wonderingly passed from hand to hand. I thought of the enhancement to my prestige, the opportunities to swank of which I should avail myself discreetly but effectively. And on the other hand there was the intimate pleasure of brooding over the diary in secret, like a bird sitting on its eggs, hatching, creating; losing myself in zodiacal reveries, speculating upon the glorious destiny of the twentieth century, intoxicated by my almost sensuous premonitions of what was coming to me. These were joys that depended upon secrecy; they would vanish if I told them or even betrayed their source.

So I tried to get the best of both worlds: I hinted at the possession of hidden treasure, but I did not say what it was. And for a time this policy was successful, curiosity was aroused, questions were asked: 'Well, what is it? Tell us.' I enjoyed parrying these: 'Wouldn't you like to know?' I enjoyed going about with an 'I could if I would' air,[27] and a secret smile. I even encouraged questionnaires of the 'animal, vegetable, or mineral'[28] type, breaking them off when the scent became too hot.

Perhaps I gave too much away; at any rate the one thing I hadn't guarded against happened. I had no warning of it, none: it happened at break, in the middle of the morning, and I suppose I hadn't looked in my desk that day. Suddenly I was surrounded by a mob[29] of grinning urchins chanting: 'Who said "vanquished"? Who said "vanquished"?' And in a moment they were all upon me: I was borne to the ground: various forms of physical torture were applied, and my nearest tormentor – he was almost as breathless as I, so many were pressing on him, cried: 'Are you vanquished, Colston, are you vanquished?'

For a moment I certainly was, and for the whole of the next week, which seemed an eternity, I was subjected to the same treatment at least once a day – not always at the same hour, for the ringleaders chose their opportunity with care. Sometimes, as the day wore on, I thought I had escaped; then I would see the nefarious band in conclave; cries of 'vanquished' would break out and the pack would be upon me. As quickly as I could I admitted myself vanquished, but I was usually sore all over before quarter was given.

Strangely enough, though so idealistic about the future I was quite realistic about the present: it never occurred to me to connect my school life with the Golden Age or think that the twentieth century was letting me down. Nor did I have to restrain an impulse to write home or sneak to one of the masters. I had brought it on myself, I knew, by using that pretentious word, and did not dispute the right of public opinion to punish me. But I was desperately anxious to prove I was not vanquished; and as I clearly could not do that by physical force, I must resort to guile. Rather to my surprise the diary had been returned to me. Apart from having the word 'vanquished' scrawled all over it, it was uninjured. I attributed its restitution to magnanimity; I think now that it was probably due to prudential considerations, to a fear that I should report its disappearance as a theft. To report a theft was not against our code, it was not sneaking, as telling about my physical sufferings would have been. I gave them credit for this, but I was most anxious to put an end to the persecution and also to get even with them. Even, but no more: I was not vindictive. Luckily the jeering words were written in pencil. Retiring with the defaced diary to the lavatory I set about erasing them and it was there, in the relaxed state of mind that mechanical rubbing induces, that I had my idea.

They would believe, so I reasoned, that the diary had been discredited for ever as a talisman for self-esteem — and indeed, they were nearly right, for at first I felt that it had lost its magic by being violated: I could hardly bear to look at it. But as one by one the taunting words 'vanquished' disappeared, it began to recover its value for me, I felt its power returning. How wonderful if I could make it the instrument of my vengeance! There would be poetic justice in that. Moreover my enemies would be off their guard, they would never suspect danger from a gun they had so thoroughly spiked. And at the same time their consciences would not be quite easy about it, it would be a symbol of the injury they had done me, and they would be all the more sensitive to an attack from it.

In the privacy of my retreat I practised assiduously; and then I cut my finger, dipped my pen in blood, and transcribed the two curses into the diary.

I looked at them now, brown and faded, but still legible though not comprehensible, except for the two names printed in block letters, JENKINS AND STRODE, which stood out in sinister intelligibility. Comprehensible they never were, for they made no sense: I concocted them out of figures and algebraical symbols and what I remembered of some Sanskrit characters I had seen, and pored over, in a translation of the *Peau de Chagrin*[30] at home. CURSE ONE was followed by CURSE TWO. Each took a page of the diary. On the next page, which was otherwise blank, I had written:

CURSE THREE

AFTER CURSE THREE THE VICTIM DIES

Given under my hand and

written in my BLOOD

BY ORDER

THE AVENGER.

Faded though the characters were, they still breathed malevolence, they could still pluck a superstitious nerve, and I ought to have been ashamed of them. But I was not. On the contrary I felt a certain envy of the self of those days, who would not take things lying down, who had no notion of appeasement, and who was prepared to put all he had into making himself respected in society.

What I expected to be the outcome of my plan I hardly knew, but I put the diary in my locker, which I purposely left unlocked, even ajar, with the cover of the diary showing, and awaited results.

I did not have long to wait – the results came very soon and were very disagreeable. Within a few hours I was set upon, and the drubbing I got then was the worst of the whole series. 'Are you vanquished, Colston, are you vanquished?' cried Strode, bestriding me in the mêlée. 'Who's the avenger now?' And he pressed his fingers under my eyes, a trick which, it was commonly believed, would cause them to pop out.

That night, in bed, my smarting eyes shed tears for the first time. It was my second term at school; I had never been unpopular before, still less had I been systematically bullied, and I didn't know what to make of it. I felt I had shot my bolt.[31] All my persecutors were older than I was and I couldn't possibly gather together a gang to fight them. And failing that, I couldn't ask for sympathy. It was perfectly correct to enlist supporters if action was to be the outcome; but to confide in someone for the sake of confiding, that simply was not done. All the other four boys in my dormitory (Maudsley was one) knew of my trouble, of course; but not one would have dreamed of mentioning it, not even when they saw my scars and bruises – perhaps least of all then. Even to say 'Bad luck' would have been in bad taste, as suggesting that I was not able to look after myself. It would have been like pointing out some physical defect. The law that one must consume one's own smoke[32] was absolute, and no one subscribed to it more whole-heartedly than I. A late-comer to school, I had uncritically accepted all its standards. I was a conformist: it never occurred to me that because I suffered there was something wrong with the system, or with the human heart.

One act of consideration, however, my room-mates showed me and I still remember it with gratitude. It was our custom to talk for some few minutes after lights out, simply because to do so was against the rules; and if any of the five failed to join in he was pointedly reminded of it and told he was a funk, and letting down the good name of the dorm. Whether my sobs were audible I don't know, but I dare not trust my voice to speak and nobody censured my silence.

The next day at break I wandered about by myself, keeping close to the wall, for there, at any rate, I could not be surrounded. I was keeping a weather eye open for the gang (where there had been nobody suddenly there were six) when a boy I hardly knew came up with an odd look on his face and said,

'Have you heard the news?'

'What news?' I had hardly spoken to anybody.

'About Jenkins and Strode.' He looked at me narrowly.

'What is it?'

'They were out on the roofs last night and Jenkins slipped and Strode tried to hold him but he couldn't and was pulled off too. They're both in the San with concussion of the brain and their people have been sent for. Jenkins's mater and pater have just arrived. They came in a cab with the blinds drawn down and Jenkins's mater is in black already. I thought you might be interested.'

I said nothing and the boy, with a backward glance at me, went off whistling. I felt faint and didn't recognize myself: it was so extraordinary not to be afraid of the gang any more. But I was afraid — afraid of what they might do to me in case I was a murderer. The bell went and I began to walk towards the door in the corner, and two of the boys in my dorm came up and shook hands with me and said 'Congrats' with respect in their faces. So then I knew it was all right.

Afterwards I was quite a hero, for nobody, it turned out, had much liking for Jenkins and Strode, though nobody had raised a finger to stop them ragging me. Even their four chums who used to help them to knock me about said they only did it because Jenkins and Strode made them. Jenkins and Strode had told everyone about the curses, meaning to make a fool of me, and what the whole school wanted to know was: Did I mean to use the third curse? Even the boys in the top classroom spoke to me about this. It was generally agreed that it would be more sporting not to, but that I should be quite within my rights if I did: 'Those chaps want a lesson,' the Head of the School told me. However, I didn't use it. I was secretly terrified at what I had done, and if it hadn't been for the current of public opinion running my way I might easily have got into a morbid state about it. As it was, I devised a number of spells intended to make the victims recover, but these I did not enter into my diary, partly because they would have detracted from the sense of utter triumph I was being encouraged to feel, and partly because, if they failed, my public reputation as a magician would have suffered. Nor would it have been a popular move; for during the few days that the boys' lives hung in the balance we all went about in a subdued manner with long faces, but secretly hoping for the worst. Ghoulish reports – faces under sheets, parents in tears – were circulated, and the mood of tension and crisis demanded an outlet in catastrophe. Of this it was cheated, but very gradually; and during the drawn-out anticlimax I received many rather rueful congratulations on my forbearance in not having launched the third curse, which most of the boys, including in certain moods myself, believed would have been fatal.

'Are you vanquished, Colston, are you vanquished?' No, I was not; I had come through with flying colours. I was the hero of the hour, and though my vogue did not last long at that high level, I never quite lost it. I became a recognized authority on two subjects dear to the hearts of most boys at that time: black magic and code-making, and I was frequently consulted on both these subjects. I even made a little out of it, charging threepence a time for my advice, which I gave only after certain necromantic formalities had been gone through, passwords exchanged, and so on. I also invented a language and had the delirious pleasure, for a few days, of hearing it used round me. It consisted, if I remember, in making the syllable 'ski' alternately the prefix and suffix of each word in a sentence, thus: 'Skihave youski skidone yourski skiprep?' It was considered very funny so I got a reputation as a wag as well. And also as a master of language.[33] I was no longer made fun of if I used long words, on the contrary they were expected of me; the diary became a quarry for synonyms of the most ambitious kind. It was then that I began to cherish a dream of becoming a writer – perhaps the greatest writer of the greatest century, the twentieth. I had no idea what I wanted to write about: but

I composed sentences that I thought would look well and sound well in print: that my writing should achieve the status of print was my ambition, and I thought of a writer as someone whose work fulfilled print's requirements.

One question was often put to me, but I never answered it: What exactly was the meaning of the curses that had literally brought about the downfall of Jenkins and Strode? How did I translate them? I didn't, of course, myself know what they meant. I could easily have produced a translation but I felt for several reasons it would be wiser not to. Kept secret, they would still minister to my prestige; revealed, and used by irresponsible people, who knew what harm they might do? They might even be turned against me. Meanwhile a good deal of private curse-making went on: strips of paper covered with cabalistic signs were passed from hand to hand. But though their authors sometimes claimed to have obtained results, nothing happened to challenge the supremacy of mine.

'Are you vanquished, Colston, are you vanquished?' No, I was not; I had won, and my victory, though its methods were unorthodox, had fulfilled the chief requirement of our code: I had won it by myself, or at any rate without calling in the help of any human agency. There had been no sneaking. Also, I had kept within the traditional terms of schoolboy experience; so fantastic in some ways, so matter of fact in others. The curses were not really a shot in the dark, though their outcome had been so sensational. They were aimed at the superstitiousness that I instinctively knew my schoolfellows possessed. I had been a realist, I had somehow sized up the situation and solved it with the means at my command, and I enjoyed a realist's reward. If I looked on Southdown Hill School[34] as being in some way an adjunct of the twentieth century, or as being intimately related to the Zodiac – a hierarchy of glorious, perfected beings slowly ascending into the ether – what a cropper I should have come.

With an effort I took up the diary again and turned the closely written pages, so buoyant with success. February, March, April – with April the entries fell off for it was the holidays – May full up again and the first half of June. Again the dearth of entries and I was in July. Under Monday 9th I had written 'Brandham Hall'.[35] A list of names followed, the names of my fellow guests, and then: 'Tuesday 10th. 84.7 degrees.'

Each day after that I had recorded the maximum temperature and much else, until: 'Thursday 26th. 80.7 degrees.'

This was the last entry in July, and the last entry in the diary. I did not have to turn the pages to know they would be blank.

It was 11.5, five minutes later than my habitual bedtime. I felt guilty at being still up, but the past kept pricking at me and I knew that all the events of those nineteen days in July were astir within me, like the loosening phlegm in an attack of bronchitis, waiting to come up. I had kept them buried all these years, but they were there, I knew, the more complete, the more unforgotten, for being carefully embalmed. Never, never had they seen the light of day; the slightest stirring had been stifled with a scattering of earth.[36]

My secret – the explanation of me – lay there. I take myself much too seriously, of course. What does it matter to anyone what I was like, then or now? But every man is important to himself at one time or another; my problem had been to reduce the importance, and spread it out as thinly as I could over half a century. Thanks to my interment policy I had come to terms with life, I had made a working – working was the word – arrangement with it, on the one condition that there should be no exhumation. Was it true, what I sometimes told myself, that my best energies had been given to the undertaker's art? If it was, what did it matter? Should I have acquitted myself better, with the knowledge I had now? I doubted it; knowledge may be power, but it is not resilience, or resourcefulness, or adaptability to life,[37] still less is it instinctive sympathy with human nature; and those were qualities I possessed in 1900 in far greater measure than I possess them in 1952.[38]

If Brandham Hall had been Southdown Hill School I should have known how to deal with it. I understood my schoolfellows, they were no larger than life to me. I did not understand the world of Brandham Hall; the people there were much larger than life; their meaning was as obscure to me as the meaning of the curses I had called down on Jenkins and Strode; they had zodiacal properties and proportions. They were, in fact, the substance of my dreams, the realization of my hopes; they were the incarnated glory of the twentieth century; I could no more have been indifferent to them than after fifty years the steel could be indifferent to the magnets in my collar-box.

If my twelve-year-old self, of whom I had grown rather fond, thinking about him, were to reproach me: 'Why have you grown up such a dull dog, when I gave you such a good start? Why have you spent your time in dusty libraries, cataloguing other people's books instead of writing your own? What has become of the Ram, the Bull, and the Lion, the example I gave you to emulate? Where above all is the Virgin, with her shining face and long curling tresses, whom I entrusted to you' – what should I say?

I should have an answer ready. 'Well, it was you who let me down, and I will tell you how. You flew too near to the sun, and you were scorched.[39] This cindery creature is what you made me.'

To which he might reply: 'But you have had half a century to get over it! Half a century, half the twentieth century, that glorious epoch, that golden age that I bequeathed to you!'

'Has the twentieth century,' I should ask, 'done so much better than I have? When you leave this room, which I admit is dull and cheerless, and take the last bus to your home in the past, if you haven't missed it – ask yourself whether you found everything so radiant as you imagined it. Ask yourself whether it has fulfilled your hopes. You were vanquished, Colston, you were vanquished, and so was your century, your precious century that you hoped so much of.'

'But you might have tried. You needn't have run away. I didn't run away from Jenkins and Strode, I overcame them. Not at once, of course. I went to a private place and I thought about them a great deal, they were very real to me, I can tell you. I can still remember what they looked like. Then I took action. They were my enemies. I called down curses on them, and they fell off the roof and had concussion. Then I wasn't bothered with them any more. I didn't mind thinking about them a bit, I don't now. Did you take any action? Did you call down curses?'

'That,' said I, 'was for you to do, and you didn't do it.'

'But I did – I cast a spell.'

'What good was a spell, when it was curses that were needed? You didn't want to injure them, Mrs Maudsley or her daughter or Ted Burgess or Trimingham. You wouldn't admit that they had injured you, you wouldn't think of them as enemies. You insisted on thinking of them as angels,[40] even if they were fallen angels. They belonged to your Zodiac. "If you can't think of them kindly, don't think of them at all. For your own sake, don't think of them." That was your parting charge to me, and I have kept it. Perhaps they have gone bad on me. I didn't think of them because I couldn't think of them kindly, or kindly of myself in relation to them. There was very little kindness in the whole business, I assure you, and if you had realized that, and called down curses, instead of entreating me, with your dying breath, to think about them kindly – '

'Try now, try now, it isn't too late.'

The voice died away. But it had done its work. I *was* thinking of them. The cerements, the coffins, the vaults, all that had confined them was bursting open, and I should have to face it, I *was* facing it, the scene, the people, and the experience. Excitement, like hysteria, bubbled up in me from a hundred unsealed springs. If it isn't too late, I thought confusedly, neither is it too early: I haven't much life left to spoil. It was a last flicker of the instinct of self-preservation which had failed me so signally at Brandham Hall.

The clock struck twelve. Round me were ranged the piles of papers, dingy white and with indented outlines like the cliffs of Thanet.[41] Under those cliffs, I thought, I have been buried. But they should witness my resurrection, the resurrection that had begun in the red collar-box, whose contents were still strewn about it. I picked up the lock and looked at it again. What was the combination of letters that had opened it? I might have guessed without troubling to put myself into a trance: egotism might have prompted me. I said it aloud to myself wonderingly; for many years it had been only a written word. It was my own name, LEO.[42]

CHAPTER I

The eighth of July was a Sunday and on the following Monday I left West Hatch, the village where we lived near Salisbury, for Brandham Hall. My mother arranged that my Aunt Charlotte, a Londoner, should take me across London. Between bouts of stomach-turning trepidation I looked forward wildly to the visit.

The invitation came about in this way. Maudsley had never been a special friend of mine, as witness the fact that I have forgotten his Christian name. Perhaps it will come to me later: it may be one of the things that my memory fights shy of. But in those days schoolboys seldom called each other by their first names. These were regarded simply as a liability, though not such a heavy liability as one's middle name, which it was just foolhardy to reveal. Maudsley was a dark-haired, sallow, round-faced boy, with a protruding upper lip that showed his teeth; he was a year younger than I was, and distinguished neither in work nor games, but he managed to get by, as we should say. I knew him pretty well because he was a member of my dormitory, and just before the affair of the diary we discovered a mild liking for each other, chose each other as companions for walks (we walked out in a crocodile), compared some of our personal treasures and imparted to each other scraps of information more intimate, and therefore more fraught with peril, than schoolboys usually exchange. One of these confidences was our respective addresses; he told me his home was called Brandham Hall and I told him mine was called Court Place, and of the two he was the more impressed, for he was, as I afterwards discovered, a snob, which I had not begun to be, except in the world of the Heavenly Bodies — there, I was a super-snob.

The name Court Place predisposed him in my favour, as I suspect it also did his mother. But they were mistaken, for Court Place was quite an ordinary house, set a little back in the village street, behind looped chains, of which I was rather proud. Well, not quite ordinary, for part of the house was reputed to be very old; the bishops of Salisbury, it was said, once held their court there; hence the name. Behind the house we had an acre of garden, intersected by a stream, which a jobbing gardener attended to three days a week. It was not a Court in the grandiloquent sense of the word, such as Maudsley, I fancy, believed it to be.

All the same, my mother did not find it easy to keep up. My father was, I suppose, a crank. He had a fine, precise mind which ignored what it was not interested in. Without being a misanthrope he was unsociable and non-conforming. He had his own unorthodox theories of education, one of which was that I should not be sent to school.[1] As far as he could he educated me himself with the help of a tutor who came out from Salisbury. I should never have gone to school if he had had his way, but my mother always wanted me to and so did I, and as soon as was possible after his death I went. I admired him and revered his opinions, but my temperament had more in common with my mother's.

His talents went into his hobbies, which were book-collecting and gardening; for his career he had accepted a routine occupation and was quite content to be a bank manager in Salisbury. My mother fretted at his lack of enterprise, and was a little jealous and impatient of his hobbies, which enclosed him in himself, as hobbies do, and, so she thought, got him nowhere. In this she turned out to be wrong, for he was a collector of taste and foresight, and his books made a sum that astonished us when they were sold; indeed, I owe to them my immunity from the more pressing cares of life. But this was long after; at the time my mother fortunately never thought of selling his books: she cherished the things he had been fond of, partly from a feeling that she had been unfair to him; and we lived on her money, and the pension from the bank, and the little he had been able to put by.

My mother, though unworldly, was always attracted by the things of the world; she felt that if circumstances had been different, she could have taken her place in it; but thanks to my father's preferring objects to people she had very little chance. She liked gossip, she liked social occasions and to be dressed right for them; she was sensitive to public opinion in the village, and an invitation to some function in Salisbury would always set her a-flutter. To mix with well-dressed people on some smooth lawn, with the spire of the Cathedral soaring above, to greet and be greeted by them, to exchange items of family news and make timid contributions to political discussions – all this gave her a tremulous pleasure; she felt supported by the presence of acquaintances, she needed a social frame. When the landau² arrived (there was a livery stable in the village) she stepped into it with a little air of pride and self-fulfilment very different from her usual diffident and anxious manner. And if she had persuaded my father to go with her, she looked almost triumphant.

After he died what little social consequence we had diminished; but at no time was it such as anyone with a delicate sense of social nuances would have associated with the name Court Place.

I did not tell Maudsley this, of course – not from any wish for concealment, but because our code discouraged personal disclosures. Bragging about the wealth and grandeur of one's parents was not unknown, but Maudsley was not one of those who did it. In some ways he was precociously sophisticated; his corners must have been rubbed off before he came to school. I never understood him very deeply; perhaps there was little to understand, except an instinctive responsiveness to public opinion, a *savoir-faire* that enabled him to be, without appearing to seek it, on the winning side.

During the diary episode, he had remained neutral, which was all that one could hope for from one's friends. (This is not cynicism; belonging to a lower age group they could have done nothing for me effectively.) But when I was the winning side he made no secret of his pleasure at my success and, I afterwards learned, he told his family about it. He took lessons from me in magic and I remember drawing up for him, free, certain curses that he could use if he was in a tight place – though I never thought he would be in one. He looked up to me and I felt that his esteem was decidedly worth having. Once in an expansive moment he confided to me that he was going to Eton, and he was like a premature Etonian, easy, well-mannered, sure of himself.

The last weeks of the Easter term were the happiest of my schooldays so far, and the holidays were irradiated by them. For the first time I felt that I was someone. But when I tried to explain my improved status to my mother she was puzzled. Success in work she would have understood (and happily I was able to report this also) or success in games (of this I could not boast, but I had hopes of the cricket season). But to be revered as a magician! She gave me a soft, indulgent smile and almost shook her head. In a way she was religious: she had brought me up to think about being good, and to say my prayers, which I always did, for our code permitted it as long as it was done in a perfunctory manner: soliciting divine aid did not count as sneaking. Perhaps she would have understood what it meant to me to be singled out among my fellows if I could have told her the whole story: but I had to edit and bowdlerize it to such a degree that very little of the original was left; and least of all the intoxicating transition from a trough of persecution to a pedestal of power. A few of the boys had been a little unkind, now they were all very kind. Because of something I had written in my diary which was rather like a prayer, the unkind boys had hurt themselves and of course I couldn't help being glad about it. 'But ought you to have been glad?' she asked anxiously. 'I think you ought to have been sorry, even if they were a little unkind. Did they hurt themselves badly?' 'Rather badly,' I said, 'but you see they were my enemies.' But she refused to share my triumph and said uneasily, 'But you oughtn't to have enemies at your age.' In those days a widow was still a figure of desolation; my mother felt the responsibility of bringing me up, and thought that firmness should come into it, but she never quite knew when or how to apply it. 'Well, you must be nice to them when they come back,' she sighed; 'I expect they didn't mean to be unkind.'

Jenkins and Strode, who had had some bones broken, did not in fact return until the autumn. They were very much subdued, and so was I, and we had no difficulty in being nice to each other.

My mother was mistaken if she thought that I gloated over their downfall; it was the rise in my own stock that enlarged my spirit. But I was sensitive to atmosphere, and under my mother's half-hearted sympathy my dreams of greatness did not thrive. I began to wonder if they were something to be ashamed of, and when I went back to school it was in a private capacity, not as a magician. But my friends and clients had not forgotten; to my surprise they were as eager as ever to profit by my proficiency in the Black Arts. I was still the vogue and any scruples of conscience I retained soon fled. I was urged to put out more spells, one of which was that we should be given a whole holiday. Into this last I put all the psychic force I had, and I was rewarded. Soon after the beginning of June we had an outbreak of measles. By half-term more than half the school was down with it, and soon after came the dramatic announcement that we were to break up.

The delight of the survivors, of whom I was one and Maudsley another, can be imagined. The spiritual and emotional intoxication, which normally took thirteen weeks to brew, was suddenly engendered after seven; and added to it was the thrilling sense of having been favoured by fortune, for only once before in the history of the school had such a crowning mercy been vouchsafed.

The appearance at my bedside of my shiny black trunk with its imposing, rounded roof, flanked by my father's brown wooden tuck-box which still showed, by a patch of darker paint, where my initials had been painted over his – this ocular proof that we were really going back had an effect on my spirits more overwhelming than the Headmaster's brief announcement after prayers the previous evening. And not only the sight, the smell: the smell of home exhaled by the trunk and tuck-box, drowning the smell of school. For the whole of one day the vessels of salvation stood empty, and as long as they were empty there was always the fear that J. C., as we called him, might change his mind. The matron and her assistant were engaged in other dormitories. But our turn came, and, at last, stealing upstairs to look, I saw the trunk with its lid pushed back and its tray foaming with the tissue-paper in which were wrapped my lighter and more breakable possessions. This was a supreme moment: nothing that came afterwards surpassed it in pure bliss, although excitement steadily mounted.

Two brakes, instead of three, were drawn up before the school front-door. The apathy on the drivers' faces contrasted strongly but rather agreeably with the joy on ours. They knew the procedure, however; they did not start off as soon as the last small boy (even to me he looked extremely small) had climbed into his place. There was a last rite to perform – the only flourish we allowed ourselves, for we were not an emotional school. The head boy stood up and looking round him cried 'Three cheers for Mr Cross, Mrs Cross, and the baby!' How the baby came to be included I never knew: perhaps it was the spontaneous, facetious afterthought of a former head boy. Late in life (or so it seemed to us) Mr and Mrs Cross had been blessed with a third daughter. The other two were already, to our eyes, grown up, and them we did not cheer. For that matter the baby was no longer a baby; she was nearly four, but for some reason it delighted us to cheer her, as it plainly delighted her to be lifted up between her parents and to wave her hand. We waited for this to happen and when it did we laughed and nudged each other, relieved, as Englishmen, at not having to take our cheering too seriously.

The volume of sound was thin compared with normal times, but it lacked nothing in fervour nor did we stop to think how it would sound to the suffering prisoners in the San.[3] The 'baby's' acknowledgement left nothing to be desired: it was comically regal. The drivers raised their whips without raising their faces, and we were off.

How long did the ecstasy of escape continue? It was at its height in the train. Both coming and going, the school was allotted a special coach. It was a saloon of a kind not found now, upholstered in deep red plush, the seats facing each other the whole length of the compartment. They were impregnated with a most searching smell[4] of train smoke and tobacco, which, on the outward journey, at once turned my stomach. But going home it was the very breath of freedom and acted like an apéritif. Joy shone on every face; playful punches were exchanged; new variations were found of the theme of the South-Eastern and Smashem Railway.[5] Nonchalantly I took out my diary and began to decorate the date – it was Friday the 15th of June – with a red pencil. Covertly my neighbours watched me. Was a new spell being cast? Presently I tired of arabesques and whirligigs and decided to paint the whole day red.

Did I really believe that I had been responsible for the epidemic? Modestly, I took some credit for it, and in certain quarters credit was given me. My pretensions were not exploded, far from it; but the awe with which I had been regarded was now tempered with a certain good-natured banter that might easily have turned to ridicule had the term gone on. I expect I had got a little above myself, not, I prefer to think, in manner, but in my outlook on life. Once I had been too self-distrustful; now I was over-confident. I expected things to go my way, and without much conscious effort on my part. I had only to wish them to serve me, and they would. I had forgotten the era of persecution; I had relaxed and withdrawn the sentries. I felt myself to be invulnerable. I did not believe that my happiness was contingent on anything: I felt that the laws of reality had been suspended on my behalf. My dreams for the year 1900, and for the twentieth century, and for myself, were coming true.

It never occurred to me, for instance, that I might get measles, and it astonished me that my mother regarded this as not only possible but probable. 'You will tell me, won't you,' she said anxiously, 'the first moment that you don't feel well?' I smiled. 'Of course I shall be all right,' I assured her. 'I hope so too,' she said. 'But don't forget last year, and how ill you were.'

Last year, the year 1899, had been a disastrous year. In January my father died after a brief illness and in the summer I had diphtheria, with complications; almost all July and August I had spent in bed. They were phenomenally hot months; but what I recollected of the heat was my own fever, of which the heat in my room seemed only another aggravating aspect; heat was my enemy, the sun something to be kept out. I dreaded it; and whenever I heard people saying what a wonderful summer it had been, almost the hottest within living memory, I could not understand what they meant – I only thought of my aching throat and the desperate search of my fretful limbs for a cool place in the bedclothes. I had good reason to wish the century over.

The summer of 1900 would be a cool one, I decided; I should arrange for that. And the Clerk of the Weather hearkened to me. On July 1st the temperature was in the sixties and we had only had three hot days – the 10th, the 11th and the 12th of June. I had marked them in my diary with a cross.

The first of July also brought Mrs Maudsley's invitation, for in those days we still had a post on Sundays. My mother showed me the letter: it was written in a large, bold, sloping hand. I had just reached the age when I could read handwriting that was unfamiliar to me, and this accomplishment gave me some pride. Mrs Maudsley did not ignore the possibility of measles though she took it more light-heartedly than my mother did. 'If neither of our boys has come out in spots by July 10th,' she wrote, 'I should be so very pleased if you would allow Leo to spend the rest of the month with us. Marcus'[6] – ah, *that* was his name – 'has told me quite a lot about him, and I am most anxious to make his acquaintance, if you can spare him. It will be very nice for Marcus to have a boy of his own age to play with as he is the baby of the family, and a little apt to feel left out.

I understand that Leo is an only child and I promise you we will take great care of him. The Norfolk air . . .' etc. She ended up: 'You may be surprised that we should be spending the Season in the country but neither my husband nor I have been very well, and Town is no place for a small boy in the summer.'

I pored over the letter and soon committed it to memory. I imagined that its conventional phrases implied a deep and sympathetic interest in my personality; it was almost the first time I had felt myself real to somebody who didn't know me.

At first I was all agog to go and couldn't understand my mother's hesitation in accepting for me. 'Norfolk is such a long way off,' she would say, 'and you've never been away from home before, to stay with strangers, I mean.' 'But I've been to school,' I argued. She had to admit that. 'But I wish you weren't going for so long,' she said. 'You may not like it, and then what will you do?' 'I'm sure I shall enjoy myself,' I told her. 'And you will be there for your birthday,' she said. 'We've always been together for your birthday.' I said nothing to that, I had forgotten about my birthday and was visited by a pang of premature nostalgia. 'Promise me you'll let me know if you're not happy,' she said. I didn't like to say again I knew I should be happy, so I promised. But still she wasn't satisfied. 'Perhaps you'll get measles after all,' she told me hopefully, 'or Marcus will.'

A dozen times a day I asked her if she had written saying I might go until in the end she quite lost patience with me. 'Don't worry me – I have written,' she said at last.

Preparations followed – what should I take with me? One thing I shouldn't need, I said, was summer clothes. 'I know it won't be hot.' And the weather bore me out – cool day followed cool day. My mother saw eye to eye with me in this: she believed that thick clothes were somehow safer than thin ones. And she had another motive: economy. The hot months of last year I had spent in bed, so I had no hot-weather outfit suitable to my size. I was growing fast: the outlay would be considerable and perhaps money thrown away: my mother yielded to me. 'But try not to get hot,' she said. 'Getting hot is always a risk. You needn't do anything *violent*, need you?' We looked at each other in perplexity, and dismissed the idea that I should have to do anything violent.

In imagination, often in apprehension, she tried to foresee the kind of life I should lead. One day she said, apropos of nothing, 'Try to go to church if you can. I don't know what sort of people they are – perhaps they don't go to church. If they do, I expect they drive.' Her face grew wistful, and I knew she wished she was going with me.

I shouldn't have wanted that. I was haunted by the schoolboy's fear that my mother wouldn't look right, do right, be right in the eyes of the other boys and their parents. She would be socially unacceptable; she would make a bloomer. I could bear humiliation for myself, I thought, more easily than I could for her.

But as the day of departure drew nearer my feelings underwent a change. Now it was I who wanted to get out of going, and my mother who held me to it. 'You could so easily say I had got measles,' I pleaded. She was horrified. 'I couldn't say such a thing,' she cried indignantly. 'And besides they would know. You were out of quarantine yesterday.' My heart sank: I tried a spell for making spots come out on my chest, but it didn't work. On the last evening my mother and I sat together in the drawing-room on the two-humped settee which reminded me of a dromedary in profile. The room faced the street and was a little stuffy, for we used it seldom and when it was not in use the windows were fastened to keep out the dust which, in the dry weather, rose in clouds whenever a vehicle went by. It was our one formal room and I think my mother may have chosen it for its moral effect; its comparative strangeness would be a step towards the strangeness I should feel in another house. Also I suspect she had something special to say, which the room would lend weight to, but she never said it, for I was too near to tears to be open to practical or moral counsels.

CHAPTER 2

To my mind's eye, my buried memories of Brandham Hall are like effects of chiaroscuro, patches of light and dark: it is only with an effort that I can see them in terms of colour. There are things I know, though I don't know how I know them, and things that I remember. Certain things are established in my mind as facts, but no picture attaches to them; on the other hand there are pictures unverified by any fact which recur obsessively, like the landscape of a dream.

The facts I owe to my diary which I kept religiously, beginning on the 9th, the day I arrived, and going on until the 26th, the eve of the fateful Friday.[1] The last few entries are in code – how proud I was of having invented that! Not a pretence code such as I had used to call down curses on Jenkins and Strode, but a real one like Pepys's[2] – perhaps I had heard of his. I found it difficult to 'break', partly because, from motives of prudence and also, possibly, to display my virtuosity, I modified and embellished it each day. There are still two or three sentences which don't give up their secret, though the whole affair is clearer to me now than it was then.

Facts there are in plenty, beginning with 'M. met me on Norwich platform with the pony carriage and the Under-Coachman. We drove 13¾ miles to Brandham Hall, which came in site after about 12½ miles and then disapeared again.'

No doubt this was so but I have no recollection of the drive, no visual image to make it real for me; the first part of my visit remains in my memory as a series of unrelated impressions, without time sequence, but each with a distinct *feeling* attaching to it. Some of the entries might just as well refer to places I have never seen, and incidents I have never experienced. Even the look of the house is vague to me. I laboriously transcribed into my diary a description of it that I found in a directory of Norfolk.[3]

'Brandham Hall, the seat of the Winlove family,[4] is an imposing early Georgian mansion pleasantly situated on a plot of rising ground and standing in a park of some five hundred acres. Of an architectural style too bare and unadorned for present tastes, it makes an impressive if over-plain effect when seen from the S.W. The interior contains interesting family portraits by Gainsborough and Reynolds, also land- scapes by Cuyp, Ruysdael, Hobbema, etc. and in the smoking-room a series of tavern scenes by Teniers the Younger[5] (these are not shown). The first-floor apartments are approached by a double staircase[6] which has been much admired. The Winlove family has the gift of the livings of Brandham, Brandham-under-Brandham, and Brandham All Saints. At present the mansion, park and pleasure grounds are let to Mr W. H. Maudsley, of Princes Gate and Threadneedle Street,[7] who allows the public the same facilities to see the house that it enjoyed formerly. Permission to view should be obtained from the agent, Brandham Estate Offices, Brandham.'

Now of this all that remains clear in my mind's eye is the double staircase, which certainly was admired by me. I likened it to many things: a tilted horseshoe, a magnet,[8] a cataract; and both coming down and going up I made it a rule to use alternate routes; I persuaded myself that something awful might happen if I went the same way twice. But surprisingly enough (considering how ready I was to be impressed), the imposing façade, which I am sure I studied from the S.W., has faded from my mind. I can see the front of the house now, but through the eyes of the directory, not through my own.

Perhaps we came and went through a side-door – I think we did, and that there was a backstairs near it convenient for our bedroom – for I shared a bedroom, and indeed a bed, a four-poster, with Marcus. And not only with him, but with his Aberdeen terrier, an elderly, cross creature, whose presence soon became almost intolerable. My memories are of the hinder parts of the house, invisible from the S.W., which were higgledy-piggledy and rambling, and of passages with sudden bends and confusing identical doors, where you could easily lose your way and be late for meals. They were not well lighted, if I remember, which the Georgian addition must have been. Perhaps our bedroom was an old night-nursery. It had a broad, squat window, set high in the wall, Elizabethan possibly: sitting up in bed I could only see the sky. In those days even rich people did not always give their children the kind of sleeping-quarters we should think essential for them now.

No doubt there was a shortage of bedrooms, for a great many guests came and went and once we were eighteen to dinner. Marcus and I sat next to each other and when the ladies retired we retired too, to bed. I can remember the pink glow of the candles and the shine of the silver, the stately ample figure of Mrs Maudsley at one end of the table and the thin figure of her husband with his stiff upright carriage at the other. Sitting down he looked taller than when standing up. She always seemed to take up more space than was necessary to her, and he less.

I don't know what he did with himself all day but my impression is of meeting him unexpectedly in some passage or doorway and of his stopping to say 'Enjoying yourself?' and when I had said 'Yes, sir' he would say, 'That's good', and hurry on. He was a wispy little man with a long drooping moustache, eyelids that drooped over his blue-grey eyes, and a long thin neck round which he wore the highest of high collars. It would have been as difficult to think of him being master of the house as it would have been to think of his wife not being mistress of it.

Her face is a blur to me now, so many impressions have overlaid the original; but when I see her in dreams (for I have not been able to keep her out of them) it is not with that terrible aspect she wore the last time I saw her, when her face could hardly be called a face at all, but with the look of a portrait by Ingres or Goya,[9] a full, pale face, with dark, lustrous eyes, a fixed, unchanging regard, and two or three black curls, or crescents of curls, stealing down over her forehead. In dreams, oddly enough, her attitude towards me is as cordial as it was at the beginning of my stay when I only half-sensed the danger behind her fascination. Can it be that her spirit would like to make it right with me? – for she must long ago be dead – she was then, I suppose, in her middle or late forties, and seemed old to me. Marcus had her colouring, but not her beauty.

I suppose it was my first evening when, the honoured guest, I sat next to her at dinner.

'And so you are a magician?' she said smiling.

'Oh,' I replied modestly, 'not really. Only, you know, at school.'

'You're not going to bewitch us here?' she said.

'Oh no,' I answered, wriggling, a habit I had when I was nervous, and I made a mental note to reproach Marcus for this breach of trust.

She never looked at anyone, it seemed to me, except with intention and as if she didn't mean to waste the look. Her glance most often rested on her daughter who usually sat between two young men. What do they find to talk *about*? I remember thinking. They seem so interested – more interested than she is.

I didn't possess the ordinary schoolboy's royal gift for fitting names to faces – perhaps because I had been at school such a short time. I was introduced to everyone, of course, and Marcus told me who was coming and who was leaving and something about them; and I dutifully put their names down in my diary, Mr This and Miss That – they were generally single. But the few years that separated us were wider than an ocean; I think I should have had more in common with a Hottentot child than with these grown-ups in their late 'teens and early twenties. What they thought, what they did, how they occupied themselves, was a mystery to me. The young men down from the University (as Marcus assured me they were), the young women with even less to identify them, would greet me on their way to or from the tennis court or the croquet lawn; the men in white flannels, white boots, and wearing straw boaters, the women, also in white with hourglass figures and hats like windmills; all white, or nearly white, save for the men's black socks that sometimes showed above their buckskin boots. Some found more to say to me than others; but they were only part of the scene and I never had, or felt I ought to have, the smallest personal relationship with them. They were they, and Marcus and I were we – different age groups, as we should say now.

And that was why, for the first day or two, I never properly took in the fact that one of 'them' was my host's son, and another his daughter. Blond (as they mostly were), dressed in white, swinging their tennis-rackets, they looked so much alike!

Denys, the son and heir, was a tall, fair young man with unfinished features and a conceited expression (schoolboys are quick to diagnose conceit).[10] He was full of plans and opinions which he would press for more than they were worth – which even I could tell was not very much. He would grow warm enlarging upon the advantage of such and such a project until his mother, with a few cool words, would puncture it. I think he felt that she despised him, and he was

the more anxious to assert himself against her, and exercise the overt
authority which his father never exerted. Between Mr and Mrs
Maudsley I never saw a sign of disagreement; she went her way and
he went his, gnome-like, leaving a trail of gold.[11] I should hardly
have known they were married, accustomed as I was to the more
demonstrative manner of my parents. He alone, it seemed to me,
was not included in the plans that Mrs Maudsley made for everybody,
for she had us all, I gradually realized, on a string, which I came to
think of as the beam of her dark eye.[12] We seemed to come and go
unnoticed but really we did not.

'My sister is very beautiful,' Marcus said to me one day. He
announced it quite impersonally, as who should say 'Two and two
make four', and I received it in the same spirit. It was a fact, like
other facts, something to be learned. I had not thought of Miss Marian[13]
(I think I called her this to myself) as beautiful, but when I saw her
next I studied her in the light of Marcus's announcement. It must
have been in the front part of the house for I have an impression of
light, which was absent in our part, Marcus's and mine; I believe I
had some schoolboy notion that the front of the house, where the
grown-up people lived, was the 'private side' and that I was trespassing
when I went there. She must have been sitting still for my scrutiny,
for I have the impression that I was looking down on her, and she
was tall, even by grown-up standards. I must have taken her unawares,
for she was wearing what I afterwards came to think of as her 'hooded'
look. Her father's long eyelids drooped over her eyes, leaving under
them a glint of blue so deep and liquid that it might have been shining
through an unshed tear. Her hair was bright with sunshine, but her
face, which was full like her mother's, only pale rose-pink instead of
cream, wore a stern brooding look that her small curved nose made
almost hawklike. She looked formidable then, almost as formidable
as her mother. A moment later she opened her eyes – I remember
the sudden burst of blue – and her face lit up.

So that is what it is to be beautiful, I thought, and for a time my
idea of her as a person was confused and even eclipsed by the abstract
idea of beauty that she represented. It did not bring her nearer to
me, rather the opposite; but I no longer confused her with the other
young ladies who circled, planet-like, around the perimeter of my
vision.

Those early days were a time of floating impressions, unrelated to each other, making little sense, let alone a story. Scenes linger with me – generally in tones of light and dark, but sometimes tinged with colour. Thus I remember the cedar on the lawn, its dark foliage and the brightness of the turf around its shadow; and I also remember the hammock of crimson canvas slung on two poles beneath it. The hammock was a novelty that had just succeeded the corded, knotted kind that caught your buttons and dragged them off. It was much frequented by the young people and I can still hear them laugh as it tipped them out and spilt them on the grass.

Of this there is no mention in my diary. Of the stables there is more than one, but I have no recollection of them, though I carefully entered the names of five of the horses, Lady Jane, Princess, Uncas, Dry Toast, and Nogo – Nogo I thought deliciously funny, but I can't remember what he or any of them looked like. I can, however, remember the coach-house, though the diary is silent about it. The lamps, the springs, the shafts, the dashboards, with their shining paint and super-polish, fascinated me. And the smell of harness leather – to me more captivating than the stronger horse smells. The coach-house was a treasure-house to me.

Enough of the vagaries and inconsistencies of my memory. But one thing which I had forgotten the diary did bring back – and not only the fact but the scene with the utmost vividness. 'Wednesday 11th of July. Saw the Deadly Nightshade – Atropa Belladonna.'[14]

Marcus wasn't with me, I was alone, exploring some derelict outhouses which for me had obviously more attraction than the view of Brandham Hall from the S.W. In one, which was roofless as well as derelict, I suddenly came upon the plant. But it wasn't a plant, in my sense of the word, it was a shrub, almost a tree, and as tall as I was. It looked the picture of evil and also the picture of health, it was so glossy and strong and juicy-looking: I could almost see the sap rising to nourish it. It seemed to have found the place in all the world that suited it best.

I knew that every part of it was poisonous, I knew too that it was beautiful, for did not my mother's botany book say so? I stood on the threshold, not daring to go in, staring at the button-bright berries and the dull, purplish, hairy, bell-shaped flowers reaching out towards me. I felt that the plant could poison me, even if I didn't touch it, and that if I didn't eat it, it would eat me, it looked so hungry, in spite of all the nourishment it was getting.

As if I had been caught out looking at something I wasn't meant to see I tiptoed away, wondering whether Mrs Maudsley would think me interfering if I told her about it. But I didn't tell her. I couldn't bear to think of those lusty limbs withering on a rubbish-heap or crackling in a fire: all that beauty being destroyed. Besides I wanted to look at it again.

Atropa belladonna.

CHAPTER 3

It all began with the weather defying me.

The Monday I travelled on had been a cool temperate day, but the next day the sky was cloudless and the sun beat down. After we had fled from luncheon (I seem to remember we left all meals incontinently, like escaping prisoners, only staying to ask if we could get down) Marcus said, 'Let's go and look at the thermometer – it's one of those that mark the highest and lowest temperature of the day.'

Maddeningly, and unreasonably – considering how often I was to have recourse to it – I cannot remember where the thermometer was; but yes, I can; it hung on the wall of an octagonal structure with a pointed roof, situated under a yew tree. The building fascinated me – it had something withdrawn and magical about it. It was thought to be a disused game-larder, put under the yew tree for coolness' sake, but this was only an hypothesis: no one really knew what it was for.

Marcus told me how the instrument worked, and showed me the small, stumpy magnet which drew the markers up and down. 'Only we mustn't touch it,' he said, reading my thoughts, 'or my father would be angry. He likes to do the thermometer himself.'

'Is he often angry?' I asked. I could not imagine Mr Maudsley being angry, or indeed anything else, but this was almost the first thing one wanted to know about grown-up people.

'No, but my mother would be,' Marcus replied obliquely.

The thermometer stood at nearly eighty-three.[1]

We had run all the way from the luncheon-table, partly to make good our escape, partly because we often ran when walking would have done as well. I was perspiring a little, and remembered my mother's oft-repeated injunction, 'Try not to get hot'. How could I not get hot? I looked at Marcus. He was wearing a light flannel suit. His shirt was not open but it was loose at the neck; his knickers could not be called shorts, for they came well below his knees but they also were loose, they flapped, they let the air in. Below them, not quite meeting them, he wore a pair of thin grey stockings neatly turned over their supporting garters; and on his feet – wonder of wonders – not boots but what then were called low shoes.[2] To a lightly clad child of today this would seem thick winter wear; to me it might have been a bathing-suit, it looked so inadequate to the proper, serious function of clothes.

The record of these sartorial details is before me, for Marcus and I were photographed together;[3] and though the light has got in at one corner, and the background and ourselves are tilted alarmingly, the faded reddish-brown print does display the uncanny perception possessed by the camera in those days when it could not so easily lie. I am wearing an Eton collar and a bow tie; a Norfolk jacket[4] cut very high across the chest, incised leather buttons, round as bullets, conscientiously done up, and a belt which I have drawn more tightly than I need have. My breeches were secured below the knee with a cloth strap and buckle, but these were hidden by thick black stockings, the garters of which, coming just below the straps, put a double strain on the circulation of my legs. To complete the picture, a pair of obviously new boots, looking larger for being new, and with the tabs, which I must have forgotten to tuck in, standing up boldly.

I have my hand on Marcus's shoulder (I was an inch or two taller as well as a year older than he) in the attitude of affection which, in those days, was permitted to the male sex when they were photographed together (undergraduates and even soldiers draped themselves about each other), and though the unfortunate slant of the photograph makes me look as if I was trying to push him over, I also look fond of him – which I was, though the coolness and deep-seated conventionality of his nature made it difficult to be intimate with him. We were not much alike, and had been brought together by factors extraneous to our real personalities. His round face looks out on the world without much interest, and with a complacent acceptance of the situation; my rather long one is self-conscious and seems aware of the strain of adaptability.[5] Both of us were wearing straw boaters, his with a plain band, mine with the school colours; and their tilted crowns and brims make two hard diagonal lines, inclined planes along which we seem to be rushing violently down a steep place.

*

I was not unduly dismayed by the heat, my dread of which was at least as much moral and hypochondriacal as physical, for I still half-believed in my ability to influence the weather, and that night I prepared a good strong spell to bring the temperature down. But like an invalid whose fever defies the doctor, the weather did not respond, and next day, when our post-luncheon scamper had taken us to the game larder, the thermometer had climbed to nearly eighty-five, and was still pushing up the marker.

My heart sank and making a great effort I said to Marcus:

'I wonder if I should sport my cricket togs?'

He replied at once:

'I wouldn't if I were you. Only cads[6] wear their school clothes in the holidays. It isn't done. You oughtn't really to be wearing the school band round your hat, but I didn't say anything. And, Leo, you mustn't come down to breakfast in your slippers. It's the sort of thing that bank clerks do. You can put them on after tea if you like.'

Marcus was old for his age in most ways, just as in most ways I was young for mine. I winced at the reference to bank clerks, and remembered that on Sundays my father had always come down to breakfast in his slippers. But it had been a shot in the dark; I had never told Marcus of my father's lowly social status.

'And, Leo, there's another thing you mustn't do. When you undress you wrap your clothes up and put them on a chair. Well, you mustn't. You must leave them lying wherever they happen to fall – the servants will pick them up – that's what they're for.'

He spoke without emphasis but with so much authority that I never for a moment doubted he was right. He was the arbiter of elegance and fashion to me just as surely as – more surely than – I was to him an expert in the Black Arts.

At tea-time someone said to me, 'You *are* looking hot. Haven't you something cooler to wear?' The voice didn't betoken much solicitude for my state, it had an undertone of teasing; and defending myself against that I said at once, mopping my face with a handkerchief, for I did not yet know that one should dab it, 'Oh, I'm not really hot. It's just that Marcus and I have been running.' 'Running, this weather?' said another voice, with an affected sigh in which I detected sarcasm, the schoolboy's bugbear; and hot as I was a chill went through me and I seemed to hear the taunt 'vanquished' and see the grinning faces.

It was indeed the beginning of a mild persecution – very very mild and concealed in smiles and kindly faces; the grown-ups could not have known it was one. But it became the thing to say to me, when they came across me, 'Hullo, Leo, still feeling hot?' And 'Why don't you take your jacket off – you'd be more comfortable without it' – with a light laugh for this impossible request, for in those days dress was much more ceremonious and jackets were not lightly discarded. I came to dread these pleasantries, they seemed to spring up all round me like rows of gas-jets scorching me, and I turned redder than I was already. The frightful feeling of being marked out for ridicule came back in all its strength. I don't think I was unduly sensitive; in my experience most people mind being laughed at more than anything else. What causes wars, what makes them drag on so interminably, but the fear of losing face?[7] I avoided even Marcus, for I didn't dare to tell him what was troubling me.

That night I worked out a new spell. I could not sleep, partly from misery and excitement, partly because the Aberdeen, which was also feeling the heat, kept moving about in search of fresh places until he was lying half-way across my pillow. Under the pillow lay my diary. I got it from under the dog without disturbing him, and in the dark I managed to put down the spell on paper, without which formality I felt it would be useless. It was a good spell, hatched in the small hours with which I had then so little acquaintance, and it worked; next day the thermometer did not reach seventy-seven, and I felt calmer in my mind and much less hot.

I did not look so, for at tea-time the gentle raillery began again. I took it in better part this time, for I was fortified by the knowledge, which my well-meaning tormentors apparently did not possess, that the temperature had really dropped. But it went on and soon I became as wretched as before. I did not realize that *au fond*[8] they were trying to take an interest in me and were using my unseasonable clothes and perspiring face to draw me out. It seemed doubly hard that a Norfolk jacket should be out of place in Norfolk; I had imagined that everybody would be wearing one. Suddenly I caught sight of myself in a glass and saw what a figure of fun I looked. Hitherto I had always taken my appearance for granted; now I saw how inelegant it was compared with theirs; and at the same time, and for the first time, I was acutely aware of social inferiority.[9] I felt utterly out of place among these smart rich people, and a misfit everywhere. Nothing is more heating than embarrassment; my face flamed while it dripped. If only I could think of some verbal quip to turn the tables on them, the sort of thing a grown-up might say! 'I may look hot,' I said defiantly, 'but I'm quite cool underneath, I'm a chilly mortal, really.' At this they burst out laughing and tears started to my eyes. I hastily gulped down some tea and began to perspire anew. Suddenly from behind the silver tea-kettle I heard Mrs Maudsley's voice. It was like a current of cold air blowing towards me.

'Did you leave your summer clothes at home?'

'No . . . yes . . . I expect Mother forgot to put them in,' I blurted out.

The full enormity of this remark then dawned on me; it was at once a lie and a cruel aspersion on my mother, who would certainly have got some lighter clothes had I not discouraged her. I felt I had lowered her in their regard and burst into tears.

There was a moment's embarrassed silence; tea-cups were stirred, then Mrs Maudsley's cool-edged voice said:

'Well, won't you write and ask her to send them?'

For an answer I only gulped, and then Marian, who, I think, had never commented on my heated condition, said:

'Oh, that would take too long, Mama. You know what the posts are. Today is Thursday, he mightn't get them till well into next week. Let me take him into Norwich tomorrow and get him a new outfit. You'd like that, wouldn't you?' she said, turning to me.

I mumbled that I should. But among the clouds that were lifting a new black one appeared.

'I haven't any money. At least only fifteen shillings and eightpence halfpenny.'[10]

'That doesn't matter,' Marian said gaily. 'We've got some.'

'Oh, but I couldn't take yours,' I protested. 'Mother wouldn't like me to.'

'Don't forget, Marian, that he has the things at home,' her mother said.

I writhed, but Marian said quickly, 'Oh, but we'll give them to him as a birthday present; she wouldn't mind that, would she? And then he'll have two sets. When is your birthday, by the way?' she asked me.

'Well, actually – as a matter of fact . . . it's on the twenty-seventh.'

'What, of this month?'

Her interest drew me out.

'Yes. You see, I was born under the sign of Leo, though it's not my real name.'

'What is your real name?'

I saw Marcus looking at me, but I couldn't refuse to tell her.

'It's Lionel. But don't tell anyone.'

'Why not?'

'Because it's rather a *fancy* name.'

I saw her trying to probe this mystery of the schoolboy mind; by-passing it, she said:

'But how splendid that it's so soon, your birthday. Now we can all give you something to wear. That's the nicest kind of present. Shall I give you a mane?'

I thought that very funny, though a trifle silly.

'Or a lion-skin?'

I tried to enter into the joke.

'That might be rather hot.'

'It might, indeed.' Suddenly Marian looked bored, and almost yawned. 'Well, we'll go tomorrow,' she said.

'Or would you,' said her mother, 'rather wait till Monday, when Hugh[11] will be here, and make a party to go to Norwich?'

'Who will be here?' asked Marian.

'Hugh. He comes on Saturday. I thought you knew.'

'Hugh coming?' Mr Maudsley asked, making one of his rare contributions to a conversation.

'Yes, he's staying till the end of the month, perhaps longer.'

'Are you sure he is, Mama?' Denys put in. 'When I saw him he told me he was going to Goodwood.'[12]

'I had a letter from him yesterday.'

'You know he never misses Goodwood?'

'I think this year he means to.'

'I don't want to disagree with you, Mama, but I think it most unlikely that Trimingham will miss Goodwood. You see, he . . .'

'Well, I think you'll find that he means to give Goodwood up for us . . . Marian, are you sure you wouldn't like to wait till Monday?'

In an agony of impatience I listened for her answer. Who was this Hugh, or Trimingham, who was stealing my thunder? I felt resentful, even jealous of him. With him there, the expedition would be spoilt. And to wait till Monday! Yet Mrs Maudsley had made her wishes plain, and how dare anyone, even Marian, cross them?

'Wouldn't you rather wait till Monday?' Mrs Maudsley repeated.

Marian answered at once, and it was like two steel threads crossing each other.[13]

'Norwich wouldn't be any treat to Hugh, Mama. He knows it better than we do. He wouldn't want to go trailing around the shops with Leo and me – and in this heat too.' She looked up mischievously at her mother's expressionless face. 'Besides, by Monday Leo will have melted into butter, and all he'll need will be a muslin bag![14] But of course if anyone would like to go with us!'

Her glance strayed from face to face, a challenge, not an invitation, and my eyes followed hers, desperately anxious that there should be no acceptances. And there were not. They all excused themselves. I suppose my jubilation was plain to see.

'Then we may go, Mama?' asked Marian.

'Of course, unless your father wants the horses.'

Mr Maudsley shook his head.

'But don't go to Stirling and Porter,' Mrs Maudsley said, 'as you sometimes do. I never like their things.'

'I should go to Challow and Crawshay,' said Denys with sudden energy. 'They're much the best.'

'No, Denys, they're not,' his mother said.

'I know Trimingham sometimes goes there for his ties,' Denys persisted.

'Will Leo be needing ties?'

'I'll stand him a tie if you promise to get it at Challow's.'

I began to feel hot again.

'I tell you what,' said Marian, 'let each of the family give him something, and then we can share the blame if they're not right.'

'Bags I the bags,'[15] said Marcus suddenly.

'Oh, Marcus!'

A chorus of disapproval greeted Marcus's joke, and he looked quite sheepish until his mother said:

'Well, they can be *my* present, Marcus dear.'

I was surprised to see the fondness in her face.

Marian said she would find out what I needed. For this she would have to examine my exiguous wardrobe, an inquisition which I dreaded; but when it came, when all soft and flouncy she appeared in our room, heralded by Marcus, what a delight it was! – a transformation scene. She studied each garment almost reverently. 'How beautifully they are mended!' she said. 'I wish we had someone who could mend like that!' I didn't tell her that my mother had done it, but perhaps she guessed. She was quick at finding out things. 'Those clothes you had at home were a myth, weren't they?' she said. 'A myth?' I echoed. 'I mean you didn't really have them?' I nodded, happy to have been found out, delighting in the shared secret. But how could she have known?

CHAPTER 4

The expedition to Norwich was a turning-point: it changed everything. Of the expedition itself I remember little except a general sense of well-being which seemed to mount and mount in me, ever seeking higher levels, like wine filling a glass. Ordinarily, the process of buying clothes irked me, for I was not vain of my appearance and had no reason to be. I never felt that it had much to do with me until the amusement caused by my looking so hot convinced me that it had. The idea that I was somehow bound up with what I looked like was a revelation to me and at first a very disturbing one. When Marian told me that one thing suited me and another didn't (she was never for a moment in doubt), when I realized that her main concern was for clothes that would look well rather than wear well, a new feeling was born in me whose sweetness I remember, though it died so quickly. I came back not only feeling it was glorious to be me, but intimately satisfying to look like me.

We lunched at the Maid's Head in Wensum Street,[1] and this was a great occasion for me, for even when my father was alive it was held to be a great extravagance to go to a hotel: if we went out for a meal it was always to a restaurant.

We had started away from Brandham early and by lunch-time we had nearly finished our shopping. One by one the parcels were put into the carriage until the seat in front of us was covered with them. I could hardly believe that most of them were for me. 'Would you like to array yourself now,' Marian asked me, 'or would you rather wait till we get home?' I still remember the indecision that this question brought me; in the end, for the sake of prolonging anticipation, I said that I would wait. Hot as it must have been in Norwich – for the thermometer, when we visited it later in the day, still stood at eighty-three, and had been higher – I don't remember feeling the heat, for all my winter wear.

What did we talk about that has left me with an impression of wings and flashes, as of air displaced by the flight of a bird? Of swooping and soaring, of a faint iridescence[2] subdued to the enfolding brightness of the day?

It all seemed to depend on her presence, yet when after luncheon she dismissed me, asking me to amuse myself for an hour in the Cathedral, my ecstasy continued.[3] No doubt it was partly that I knew that I should soon see her again; but never had I felt in such harmony with my surroundings. It was as though the whole building, striving upwards to its famous vaulted roof, expressed what I was feeling, and later when I left the cool gloom of the interior for the heat and sunshine outside, the domain of Tombland[4] whose name fascinated me, I kept craning my neck to try to fix the point, the exact point, at which the summit of the spire pierced the sky.

O altitudo![5] She had asked me to meet her by the statue of Sir Thomas Browne; and in order not to be late I was early; the carriage was there with its two horses, the coachman raised his whip in salute. I hung around the statue, wondering who Sir Thomas Browne was, shy of getting into the carriage and sitting there as if I owned it; and then I caught sight of her on the far side of the square. She seemed to be saying good-bye to someone, at least I had the impression of a raised hat. She came slowly towards me, threading her way through the drowsy traffic, and did not see me till much later. Then she waved her parasol with its frilly, foamy edges, and quickened her step.

My spiritual transformation took place in Norwich: it was there that, like an emerging butterfly, I was first conscious of my wings. I had to wait until tea for the public acknowledgement of my apotheosis. My appearance was greeted with cries of acclaim, as if the whole party had been living for this moment. Instead of gas-jets, fountains of water seemed to spring up around me. I was made to stand on a chair and revolve like a planet, while everything of my new outfit that was visible was subjected to admiring or facetious comment. 'Did you get the tie from Challow's?' cried Denys. 'I won't pay for it unless you did!' Marian said yes. Actually, as I discovered afterwards, the tie had another name on it: we had gone to so many shops! 'What a cool customer he looks!' said someone, wittily. 'Yes,' said another, 'just like a cucumber, and the same shade of green!' They discussed what kind of green it was. 'Lincoln green!'[6] said another voice. 'He might be Robin Hood!' I was delighted by that, and saw myself roaming the greenwood with Maid Marian. 'Don't you *feel* different?' somebody asked me, almost as indignantly as if I had denied it. 'Yes,' I exclaimed, 'I feel quite another person!' – which was less than the truth. They all laughed at this. The talk drifted away from me, as it does from children, and I got down awkwardly from my pedestal, realizing that my moment was over; but what a moment it had been. 'Come here, my dear,' said Mrs Maudsley, 'and let me look at you near to.' I went towards her nervously, caught like a moth in the beam from her eye, that black searchlight, whose pressure and intensity never varied. She rubbed the soft, thin material between her fingertips. 'These smoked pearl buttons are nice, I think, don't you? Yes, I think it does very well, and I hope your mother will think so, too. By the way, Marian,' she added, turning to her daughter as if I and my concerns no longer existed for her, 'did you find time for those little commissions I gave you – the things we shall be wanting next week?' 'I did, Mama,' said Marian.

'And did you do any shopping for yourself?'

Marian shrugged her shoulders.

'Oh no, Mama; that can wait.'

'You mustn't wait too long,' said Mrs Maudsley evenly. 'You didn't see anyone in Norwich, I suppose?'

'Not a cat,' said Marian. 'We were hard at it all the time, weren't we, Leo?'

'Yes, we were,' I answered, so eager to agree with her that I forgot the hour I had spent in the Cathedral.

From being my enemy the summer had become my friend: this was another consequence of our Norwich shopping. I felt I had been given the freedom of the heat, and I roamed about in it as if I was exploring a new element. I liked to watch it rise shimmering from the ground and hang heavy on the tops of the darkening July trees. I liked the sense of suspended movement that it gave or seemed to give, reducing everything in Nature to the stillness of contemplation. I liked to touch it with my hand, and feel it on my throat and round my knees, which now were bare to its embrace. I yearned to travel far, ever farther into it, and achieve a close approximation with it;

for I felt that my experience of it would somehow be cumulative, and that if it would only get hotter and hotter there was a heart of heat I should attain to.[7]

The green suit, with its smoked pearl buttons and open collar that sat so lightly on me, the thin underclothes whose touch caressed me, the stockings hardly thick enough to protect my legs from scratches, the 'low' shoes that were my special pride – these, I felt, were only first steps towards my complete, corporeal union with the summer. One by one they would be discarded – in what order I couldn't decide, though it was a question which exercised me. Which garment would be the last I should retain, before the final release into nakedness? My notions of decency were vague and ill-defined, as were all my ideas relating to sex; yet they were definite enough for me to long for the release of casting them off with my clothes, and being like a tree or a flower, with nothing between me and Nature.

These yearnings for nudist[8] fulfilment hovered on the confines of my mind; perhaps I never thought them capable of realization. In the meantime my pride in my new rig-out had, at another level of consciousness, altered my outlook on the world, and my relation to it. New clothes are always a tonic, and the circumstances in which I had come by mine made them a super-tonic. I strutted, I preened myself. But I was not incapable of gratitude or awe, and both these feelings had been awakened in me. Gratitude for the gifts – how was it possible that my benefactors did not value me, how was it possible that I should not value them, when such pledges of amity had been bestowed? and awe for the way they had been given: the casual accumulation of colossal bills, mounting from shop to shop, as if money were nothing! The expenditure had been godlike; it belonged to another, ampler phase of being than the one I was accustomed to. My mind could not grasp it but my imagination could make play with it, for unlike my mind, which could dismiss what it did not understand, my imagination loved to contemplate the incomprehensible and try to express my sense of it by an analogy. And I had one ready-made. From those resplendent beings, golden[9] with sovereigns (and, I suspected, guineas), arriving, staying, leaving, apparently unaffected by any restrictions of work or family ties, citizens of the world who made the world their playground, who had it in their power (for I did not forget that) to make me miserable with a laugh and happy with a smile — from them it was but a short step to the hardly more august and legendary figures of the Zodiac.

One of the items in my trousseau[10] was a bathing-suit, and partly from the promptings of nudism, partly because I fancied the idea of myself in it (the day with Marian had made me conscious of myself in many ways) I badly wanted to put it on. I confessed that I couldn't swim unless somebody held me but Marian said she would arrange for that. Here, however, my hostess put her foot down. My mother had written to her that I was delicate and liable to colds; she would not take the responsibility of letting me bathe without first having my mother's permission. But of course I could watch the others bathe if I liked.

There was a bathing party afoot and I had just time to write the letter and go down and join them. It was Saturday the 14th — metcorologically a disappointing day, for the thermometer (which I now wished to soar to unprecedented heights) had not reached seventy-six. But this was a secret that I shared with Marcus and his father; the others, ignorant of the true state of affairs, complained loudly of the heat. I took my bathing-dress with me, to be in keeping with the spirit of the party. Marcus also had his, for use, though like me he could not swim. Neither of them, I ruefully realized, made many concessions to nakedness; I had tried mine on, it was disappointingly ample, and so was Marcus's.

I had never been to a grown-up bathing party before. There was nothing surprising in that, for in those days bathing was a pastime of the few and the word denoted an intenser experience than it does now. I was curious about it and almost frightened — this idea of surrendering oneself to an alien and potentially hostile element. Though my knowledge of it was to be only vicarious I felt a tingling on my skin and a faint loosening of my bowels.

We trooped down the path, six of us — Marian and Denys, a young man and a young woman whose names are in my diary but whose faces I cannot remember — and Marcus and I bringing up the rear. It was about six o'clock but the heat still lingered, not burning but diffused and benign. We went through a wicket gate into a belt of trees. I was often to go that way on hotter days; but never again did I get quite the same impression of cold succeeding heat. The trees were very thick, they wrapped us round; the stillness was infectious, no one spoke. We came to a road between the trees and followed it, and then scrambled down a steep tree-lined bank and over a stile into a meadow. Another stage nearer the experience! Under the renewed assault of the heat we started talking again, and Marcus said:

'Trimingham is coming this evening.'

'Oh, is he?' I answered, not much interested, but noting the name for my diary.

'Yes, but late, we shall be in bed.'

'Is he nice?' I asked.

'Yes, but dreadfully ugly. You mustn't start or anything when you see him, or it will put him off. He doesn't like you to feel sorry for him. You see he was wounded in the war and his face hasn't got right.[11] They say it never will.'

'Hard cheese,' I said.

'Yes, but you mustn't say so to him, or to Marian either.'

'Why not?'

'Mama wouldn't like it.'

'Why not?' I said again.

'Promise you won't tell anybody — not even under torture.'

I promised.

'Mama wants Marian to marry him.'

I digested this news in silence. It was extremely disagreeable to me. I already felt violently jealous of Trimingham, and the fact that he was a war-hero did not recommend him to me. My father had disapproved of the war, to the point of being a pro-Boer.[12] I was quite capable of lending my voice to 'The Soldiers of the Queen' and 'Good-bye, Dolly, I must Leave You,' and had gone almost mad with excitement at the relief of Ladysmith;[13] but I believed that my father was right. Perhaps Trimingham deserved to be disfigured. And why should Mrs Maudsley want Marian to marry a man who was horribly ugly and not even a Mr?

We were crossing the meadow on a raised causeway towards a curved line of rushes; the curve was concave, and we were aiming for the farthest part. It was one of those sedgy, marshy places in Norfolk where bog-cotton grows; despite the heat, which was drying up everything, one had to pick one's way, to avoid the pools of reddish water that were half concealed by grass. Squelch, squelch, and a brown trickle came over my low shoes.

There was a black thing ahead of us, all bars and spars and uprights, like a gallows.[14] It gave out a sense of fear – also of intense solitude. It was like something that must not be approached, that might catch you and hurt you; I wondered why we were walking towards it so unconcernedly. We had nearly reached it, and I saw how the pitch was peeling off its surfaces, and realized that no one could have attended to it for years, when suddenly the head and shoulders of a man rose from among the rushes. He had his back to us and did not hear us. He walked slowly up the steps on to the platform between the wheels and pulleys. He walked very slowly, in the exultation of being alone; he moved his arms about and hunched his shoulders, as if to give himself more freedom, though he was wearing nothing that could have cramped him: for a moment I thought that he was naked.

He stood almost motionless for a second or two, just raising his heels experimentally; and then he threw his hands up, stretched himself into an arc and disappeared. Until I heard the splash I hadn't realized how near the river was.

The grown-ups stared at each other in dismay, and we at them. Dismay turned to indignation. 'What cheek!' said Denys. 'I thought we had the whole place to ourselves. He must know he's trespassing. What shall we do? Shall we order him off?'

'He can't go quite as he is,' the other man said.

'Well, shall we give him five minutes to clear out?'

'Whatever you do, I'm going to change,' said Marian. 'It takes me a long time. Come along, Eulalie' (this was her friend's strange name) 'there's our bathing machine – it's better than it looks,' and she pointed to a hut among the rushes, which, like so many huts, had the appearance of a disused hen-coop. They went off, leaving us to face the situation.

We looked at each other irresolutely and then by common consent pushed through the rushes to the river bank. The river had been hidden until now.

At once the landscape changed. The river dominated it – the two rivers, I might say, for they seemed like different streams.

Above the sluice, by which we stood, the river came out of the shadow of the belt of trees. Green, bronze, and golden, it flowed through weeds and rushes; the gravel glinted, I could see the fishes darting in the shallows. Below the sluice it broadened out into a pool that was as blue as the sky. Not a weed marred the surface, only one thing broke it: the intruder's bobbing head.

He saw us and began to swim towards us; white above, brown below, his arms parted the water. Soon we could see his face and his eyes fixed on us with the strained expression of the swimmer. 'Why, it's Ted Burgess,'[15] said Denys in a low voice, 'the tenant of Black Farm. We can't be rude to him – it's his land on the other side for one thing, and Trimingham wouldn't like it, for another. You'll see, I shall be particularly nice to him. He doesn't swim badly, does he, for a farmer?' Denys seemed relieved at not having to make a scene; and I, who had been rather looking forward to it, and didn't think the farmer would be an easy man to order off, felt disappointed.

'I'll just say how do you do to him,' said Denys. 'We don't know him socially, of course, but he mustn't think us stuck-up.'

Burgess by now was almost under us. Clamped to the brickwork of the sluice a thick old post stuck out of the water. Exposure to the elements had grooved its sides and sharpened it almost to a point. To this post he clung and began to haul himself up. Crouching over the spike to change his foothold he looked as though he would be impaled; then his hand grasped a ring embedded in the coping and he was on the bank, the water running off him.

'What a way to land!' said Denys, giving his dry hand to the farmer's wet one; 'why didn't you get out comfortably, on the other side of the sluice? We've had some steps made there.'

'I know,' the farmer said, 'but this is the way I've always done it.' He spoke with a local accent; it lent a kind of warmth and substance to his words. He looked down at the water collecting in a puddle on the bluish brickwork at his feet, and suddenly seemed embarrassed at being so nearly naked in the presence of the clothed. 'I didn't know anyone was going to be here,' he said, apologetically. 'Harvest's just started, and I got that hot working I thought I'd run down and have a dip, being Saturday and all. I shan't be long, just one more header – '

'Oh please don't hurry on our account,' Denys broke in. 'It's quite all right for us. We were hot too, up at the Hall. By the way,' he added, 'Trimingham's coming tonight: he'll probably want to see you.'

'I shouldn't be surprised,' the farmer said, and giving Denys a half salute he ran up the staircase to the platform, leaving a dark footprint on each step. We watched him dive – it must have been a ten-foot drop – and then Denys said, 'I think I put him at his ease, don't you?' His friend agreed. They went off one way, we another, to find a lair in the rushes. Their feathery tops nodded invitingly. Within the rushes, we could see, but not, I thought, be seen: it was tinglingly secret and withdrawn. Marcus began to take his clothes off. I wanted to do the same but Marcus said, 'I shouldn't put on a bathing dress if you're not going to bathe. It would look funny.' So I stayed as I was.

The rushes rustled as the men walked out, and almost at the same moment we heard the hut door creak and the sound of women's voices. They all went together to the steps above the sluice and I followed, feeling I was no longer of their company. Somehow it was disappointing to see them so fully clad, almost as if they were bathing in their clothes; Marian's suit, I remember, seemed to cover her far more completely than her evening dresses. They lingered on the steps, playfully daring each other to go in first.[16] Denys and his friend pulled each other in and were carried by the current through the sluice, while Marian and Eulalie and Marcus stayed in the shallow water above, where it was only waist-deep; their feet showed softly white on the shining golden gravel, as they waded about with long, uneven steps, plunging into unsuspected holes, splashing each other, shrieking and giggling and laughing. Their thick clumsy dresses began to cling to them and take on the soft outlines of their bodies. Bolder now, they struck out purposefully. Resolution narrowed their eyes; their chins were tilted upwards; with long slow sweeps their outstretched hands pushed back the water, gathering it in again in armfuls. The motion began to come more easily to them; smiling beatifically they drew deep blissful breaths.

It was like looking on at a dance, unable to join in. I could not bear to watch them, and went round to the far side of the sluice, where Denys and the other man were floating on their backs in the deep water, sometimes kicking it into a foam, sometimes staring at the sky, only their faces showing. While I stood there admiring them, but not wishing to join them, I heard a sound beneath me; it was Ted Burgess clinging to the post, hauling himself out. His muscles bunched, his face tense with effort, he did not see me; and I retreated almost in fear before that powerful body, which spoke to me of something I did not know. I drew back into the rushes and sat down; while he stretched himself on the warm brickwork in the sun.

His clothes were lying at his side; he hadn't bothered to seek the shelter of the rushes. Nor did he now. Believing himself to be unseen by the other bathers, he gave himself up to being alone with his body. He wriggled his toes, breathed hard through his nose, twisted his brown moustache where some drops of water still clung, and looked himself critically all over. The scrutiny seemed to satisfy him, as well it might. I, whose only acquaintance was with bodies and minds developing, was suddenly confronted by maturity in its most undeniable form; and I wondered, what must it feel like to be him, master of those limbs which have passed beyond the need of gym and playing field, and exist for their own strength and beauty? What can they do, I thought, to be conscious of themselves?

Now he had a plantain stalk in his left hand and was rubbing it gently along the hairs of his right forearm; they glinted in the sun and were paler than his arms, which were mahogany-coloured to above the elbow. Then he stretched both arms high above his chest, which was so white it might have belonged to another person, except below his neck where the sun had burnt a copper breastplate; and he smiled to himself, an intimate, pleased smile, that would have looked childish or imbecile on most people, but on him had the effect of a feather on a tiger[17] – it pointed a contrast, and all to his advantage.

I wondered whether I ought to be spying on him but I could not move without betraying myself and I had a feeling that it would be dangerous to disturb him.

The bathers had been quiet all this time, but suddenly a cry came from the river – 'Oh my hair! my hair! It's come down, it's all wet! It'll never get dry! What shall I do? What shall I do? I'm coming out!'

The farmer sprang up. He didn't wait to dry himself. He pulled his shirt over his head, and his corduroy trousers[18] over his wet bathing-slip; stuffed his feet into thick grey socks and pulled his boots on. Coming after his previous quiescence, the furious energy he put into these movements almost frightened me. His leather belt gave him the most trouble; he swore as he was fastening the buckle. Then he strode off across the sluice.

A moment later Marian came by. She was holding the long coil of her hair in front of her. It made two curves with which I was familiar; they belonged to the Virgin of the Zodiac.[19] She saw me at once; she was half laughing and half angry. 'Oh Leo,' she said, 'you do look so smug sitting there, I should like to throw you in the river.' I suppose I looked alarmed, for then she said, 'No, not really. Only you do look so dreadfully *dry*, and it will be ages before I am.' She looked round and said 'Has that man gone?'

'Yes,' I said, always glad to be able to answer any question she asked me. 'He went off in a hurry. His name is Ted Burgess and he's a farmer,' I volunteered. 'Do you know him?'

'I may have met him,' Marian said, 'I don't remember. But you're still here, that's something.'

I didn't know what she meant, but it sounded like a compliment. She went on into the hut. Soon the others came up out of the river: Marcus joined me and began to tell me how ripping it had been. I envied him his wet bathing-suit, that seemed shrunk to half its size: my dry one was like a badge of failure. We had to wait a long time for the ladies. At last Marian came out, holding the coil of hair away from her. 'Oh, I shall never get it dry,' she wailed, 'and it's dripping on my dress!' It was funny to see her helpless and despairing, she who always took things so lightly, and all about a trifle like wet hair! Women were very odd. All at once I had an idea. It pierced me with joy: 'Here is my bathing-suit,' I said, 'It's *quite* dry. If you fasten it round your neck, so that it hangs down your back, then you can spread your hair on it, and your hair will get dry and your dress won't get wet.' I stopped, breathless; it seemed to me the longest speech I had ever made, and I was in terror that she wouldn't listen to it: children's suggestions were so often brushed aside. Imploringly I held the garment up, so that she could see for herself its fitness for the purpose. 'It might do,' she said doubtfully, 'has anyone a pin?' A pin was produced; the garment was draped round her neck; I was congratulated on my ingenuity. 'And now you must spread my hair on it,' she said to me. 'And take care not to pull it. Ooh!' I drew back in alarm; how could I have hurt her? I had hardly touched her hair, much as I wanted to. Then I saw that she was smiling and returned to my task. A labour of love it truly was, the first I had ever done.

I walked back with her through the lengthening shadows, anxious still to be 'something' to her, though I didn't know what. Every now and then she asked me how her hair was, and whenever I touched it to see, she pretended I had pulled it. She was in a strange, exalted mood, and so was I; and I thought that somehow our elations came from the same source. My thoughts enveloped her, they entered into her: I was the bathing-suit on which her hair was spread; I was her drying hair, I was the wind that dried it. I had a tremendous sense of achievement for which I couldn't account. But when she gave me back my property, damp with the dampness I had saved her from, and let me touch her hair once more, dry with the dryness I had won for it, I felt my cup was full.

CHAPTER 5

Breakfast at Brandham Hall started with family prayers at nine o'clock. These were read by Mr Maudsley sitting at the head of the table (all the dishes were on the sideboard). The chairs were drawn back and ranged round the walls; they were all alike, I think, but I had my favourite chair which I could distinguish by certain signs and I always tried to get it. After the gong had gone the servants filed in headed by the butler wearing his most solemn air. I always counted them but could never make them more than ten, though there were said to be twelve in the house. The family were less regular in attendance. Mrs Maudsley was always there; Marcus and I made it a point of honour; Denys came from time to time and Marian, who was seldom there at the opening, sometimes came in half-way through. On the whole, rather more than half the guests used to attend. It was in no way compulsory, Marcus told me; but most households that were not 'fast'[1] had family prayers (I dared not tell him that ours hadn't). His father rather liked one to go, but would not be angry if one didn't.

First we sat, then we turned round and knelt down. While we were sitting Mr Maudsley read a Lesson; while we were kneeling he read prayers; he read in a secular voice without inflections but not without reverence; his personality was so subdued that it seemed to fit in with anything he did.

While we were sitting was the best time to make observations, to study the guests, or, which was easier, the servants, for they sat opposite to us. Marcus was to some extent in their confidence; he knew, for instance, which of them had been getting into trouble, and why. If one of them could be thought of as looking red-eyed, it lent a touch of drama to the morning ceremony. Afterwards, kneeling, one could press one's knuckles into one's eyes to make the colours come, and one could observe intensely over a very restricted field of vision. Covertly to extend this, without incurring the charge of irreverence, was one of the tasks one set oneself.

This morning, my first Sunday morning at Brandham Hall, Marcus did not come down with me. He said he didn't feel well. He did not, as I should have, debate with himself whether he should get up or not or ask anyone's leave to stay in bed; he just stayed there. His pale cheeks were a little flushed and his eyes bright. 'Don't worry about me,' he said. 'Someone will come. Give Trimingham my kind regards.'

Secretly resolving to tell Mrs Maudsley as soon as prayers were over (for apart from real concern for his state I fancied myself as a breaker of bad news) I waited for the last stroke of the gong and presently found myself at the head of the double staircase. I had no difficulty in remembering which track to take.

Trimingham, I thought, as I went bumping down the cataract. (I was a Red Indian this morning; shooting the rapids I had to be some kind of explorer.) Trimingham: the mister-less Trimingham whom her mother wanted Marian to marry. But supposing she didn't want to marry him? I hated to think of her wishes being crossed or forced in any way. Trimingham was a weight on my thoughts. Perhaps I could cast a spell on him. Thinking how to word it I reached my favourite chair and composed my features. The other guests were coming in, and one of them sat down beside me. I didn't have to be told who it was, and in spite of having been warned I started.

On the side of his face turned to me was a sickle-shaped scar that ran from his eye to the corner of his mouth; it pulled the eye down, exposing a tract of glistening red under-lid, and the mouth up, so that you could see the gums above his teeth. I didn't think his eye could close, even in sleep, or his mouth either. He had grown a moustache, so I afterwards learned, to cover this, but it was a straggly affair and didn't do its job. His damaged eye watered a little: even as I was looking at him he dabbed it with a handkerchief. His whole face was lop-sided, the cheek with the scar on it being much shorter than the other.

I decided it would be impossible to like him, and immediately liked him better. He was nothing to be afraid of, even without the handicap of his ambiguous social position, which I judged to be below that of a gentleman but above that of, well, such a person as Ted Burgess. But why make all this fuss of him? It must be because of his disfigurement. The Maudsleys were, I thought, a religious family: perhaps he was some sort of dependant whom they didn't want to lose sight of, and they were being kind to him on Christian principles. So would I be, too, I thought, as I listened with more attention than usual to the Collect.[2]

I didn't get the opportunity to give him Marcus's message, he sat on the other side of the breakfast table, which was full to capacity; several guests had arrived on Saturday while we were bathing. Marian sat on one side of him, his good side: I soon came to think of him as two-sided, like Janus.[3] Together, they looked like Beauty and the Beast.[4] How nice of her, I thought, to take such trouble with him! She opened her blue eyes for him as she rarely did for anyone except, at times, for me.

The men walked about to eat their porridge. This, Marcus told me, was *de rigueur*;[5] only cads ate their porridge sitting down. I roamed about with mine, fearful of spilling it. The ladies, however, remained seated. Mrs Maudsley seemed preoccupied. Her inscrutable, beeline glance rested several times on Trimingham – it didn't have to travel, it was *there*. But it never turned my way, and when at last I did get her attention the meal was over, we were leaving the table, and she said: 'Oh, isn't Marcus here?' She hadn't even noticed that he wasn't, although he was such a favourite with her. But she went straight up to his room, where, after making sure the coast was clear, I followed her. To my astonishment I found an envelope with 'No Admittance' on it fixed with two drawing pins to our door. This was a challenge I at once took up: besides, it was my room as well as Marcus's, and no one had the right to keep me out. I opened the door and put my head in.

'What's up?' I said.

'It was decent of you to trickle along,' said Marcus languidly from the bed, 'but don't come in. I have a headache and some spots and Mama thinks it may be measles. She didn't say so, but I know.'

'Hard cheese, old man,' I said. 'But what about the jolly old quarantine?'

'Well, cases do develop when it's over. But the doctor's coming, and he'll know. What fun for you if you get it. Perhaps we shall all get it, like at school. Then we shan't be able to have the cricket match or the ball or anything. Lord, I shall laugh!'

'Is there to be a cricket match?'

'Yes, we have it every year. It helps to keep them quiet.'[6]

'And a ball?' I asked, apprehensively. I didn't feel equal to a ball.

'Yes, that's for Marian, and Trimingham, and all the neighbours. It's to be on Saturday the 28th. Mama's sent out the invitations. Cripes! The place will be a hospital by then!'

We both laughed like hyenas at the prospect, and Marcus said, 'You'd better not stay here breathing in my ruddy germs.'

'Oh God, perhaps you're right. That reminds me, I want my prayer-book.'

'What, are you going to the jolly old kirk?'

'Well, I thought I might.'

'Pretty decent of you, but you needn't, you know.'

'No, but I don't want to let the side down. We do it at home sometimes,' I told him, tolerantly. 'Shall I slink across the room and get my prayer-buggins?'

Last term it had been the fashion to call a book a 'buggins'.

'Yes, but hold your breath.'

I filled my lungs, dashed to the chest of drawers, snatched the prayer-book, and scarlet in the face regained the door.

'Good egg, I didn't think you could,' said Marcus, while I gasped. 'And have you got any old button or such-like for the collection?'

Again the under-water dash to the chest of drawers but this time I had to come up for air. As I gulped it down I had a distinct feeling of several germs, the size of gnats, going down my windpipe. To distract myself I opened my purse and sniffed it. The new leather had a pungent, aromatic smell almost as reviving as a smelling-bottle; and the central partition, which opened with a thief-proof catch, sheltered a half-sovereign. Other partitions had other coins, arranged in order of value; the outermost held pennies.

'Mama would give you something if you asked her,' Marcus said. 'She probably will anyhow. She's decent about that.'

An access of masculine secrecy about money suddenly stopped my tongue.

'I'll think it over,' I said, pinching the purse which crackled deliciously.

'Well, don't break the bank. So long, old chap. Don't pray too hard.'

'Ta-ta, you old shammer,' I replied.

At home we had one way of talking and at school another: they were as distinct as two different languages. But when we were alone together, and especially when any excitement – like Marcus's suspected measles – was afoot, we often lapsed into schoolboy talk, even away from school. Only when Marcus was instructing me in *les convenances*,[7] as he called them, for he liked to air his French, did he stick closely to an unadorned vocabulary. They were a serious matter.

Somewhere on the sunny side of the house, the private side, at the foot of the staircase, I expect, the party for church was assembling: a new atmosphere prevailed: voices and movements were restrained, everyone was wearing a decorous air. I admired the richness of the women's prayer-books: the men seemed to have concealed theirs, if they had them. I was wearing my Eton suit, Marcus said that would be right; and I could change into my green suit after luncheon. Composing my features into pious lines I strayed about among the gathering guests, but no one paid me much attention, until Mrs Maudsley drew me aside and said, 'Would you like to give that to the collection?' and she slipped a shilling into my hand. I suddenly felt enormously enriched and the thought flashed through me: should I substitute a smaller coin? That would be something to tell Marcus: but no, I thought, I won't. We were still hanging about; a feeling of tension communicated itself to me: churches don't wait. Mr Maudsley took out his watch: 'Do we wait for Trimingham?' he said.

'Well, perhaps another minute or two,' his wife replied.

My mother was wrong: we didn't drive: the church was only half a mile away. You could see it most of the time, you couldn't miss it, besides, it overlooked the cricket field. We straggled along, in twos and threes, not in a crocodile, as we did at school. At school we arranged beforehand whom we should walk with. Feeling strange without Marcus, I attached myself experimentally to one or two couples, and when they seemed to be occupied with each other I walked alone. Presently Marian, who was also alone, came up to me and I told her about Marcus. 'I expect he'll be all right,' she said. 'It's probably just a touch of the sun.' The sun was blazing down, and the dust blowing up at us.

'Is your hair dry now?' I asked solicitously.

She laughed and said, 'Thanks to your bathing-suit!'

I felt proud of having been of use to her, but I couldn't think of anything to say to her except, 'Does it only come down by accident?'

She laughed again and said, 'Haven't you any sisters?' which surprised and even wounded me; I had told her all about my family circumstances, for me an oyster-like disclosure, the day we went to Norwich. I reminded her of this.

'Of course you did,' she said. 'And I remember it all perfectly. But I have so many things to think about, it slipped out of my mind. I am so sorry.'

I had never heard her apologize to anyone before, and it gave me a strange feeling of sweetness and power; but I didn't know what to say next, and fell to looking at her, at her straw hat with a bow in it like the sails of a windmill, at the patterns her flowery light blue skirt made as it trailed the dust. Suddenly out of the corner of my eye I saw that Trimingham was following us, he wasn't dawdling as we were and would soon catch us up. I didn't want this to happen and calculated how long it would take him to overtake us, but in the end I felt compelled to say: 'Trimingham's coming after us,' as if he were a disease, or a misfortune, or the police.

'Oh is he?' she said, and turned her head, but she didn't call to him, or make a sign, and his pace slackened off, and when he did come abreast of us he passed us, to my great relief, with a smile, and joined the people who were walking in front.

CHAPTER 6

I forget how we got into the church or who told me where to sit. That was a thing that had been bothering me, for I knew it was important to sit in the right place. But I remember we sat in a transept,[1] at right angles to the rest of the congregation, and raised a step or two above them. A verger offered me a prayer-book and a hymn-book, and I was pleased to be able to show him that I was already provided.

I was relieved at being in church at last, it was like having caught a train. The first thing I did was to examine the Psalms for the Day, and add up the number of verses, for I knew that if there were over fifty I might feel faint and have to sit down, a thing I dreaded, for it made people turn and look at me: and once or twice I had been taken out and made to rest in the church porch till I felt better. I enjoyed the importance that this gave me, but I dreaded the preliminaries, the cold sweat, the wobbling knees and the wondering how long I could hold out. Perhaps they were a sign that religion didn't agree with me. In those days congregations were hardier than they are now, and the Psalms went their appointed length.

But there were only forty-four verses all told,[2] so my mind was set at rest, and I looked about for something to occupy it with. The transept wall was covered with mural tablets and on every one the same name occurred. 'To the memory of Hugh Winlove, Sixth Viscount Trimingham' I read. 'Born 1783, Died 1856.' I studied them carefully. All the Viscounts seemed to be called Hugh. Seven Viscounts were accounted for, but there should have been eight – no, nine. The fifth was missing; there was no record of him. And the ninth was missing, too. 'To the memory of Hugh, Eighth Viscount Trimingham, born 1843, died 1894.' It offended my sense of completeness. What was still more annoying, two of the Viscounts had perversely been called Edward.[3] What had happened to the fifth Viscount, that there was no memorial to him? He lived so long ago that he might have got into one of those fortunate periods when history seemed to get along without dates. But the eighth Viscount had died in 1894, so there must be a ninth. Why was he not there?

Suddenly it dawned on me that he might be still alive.

This discovery, or hypothesis, for I could not quite convince myself of its truth, caused a revolution in my attitude towards the assembled Viscounts. At first I had thought of them as so much church furniture, utterly dead and gone, more dead, more gone, than if they had been given proper graves instead of mere wall space. They were something out of a history book; the deeds recorded of them were just like those recorded in a history book: the battles they had fought in, the honours they had won, the positions in the Government they had held – what could be deader than all that? Their exploits were things to be learnt, to be forgotten, to be examined about, perhaps to be punished for forgetting. 'Write out the Sixth Viscount Trimingham ten times.'

But if there really was a ninth Viscount, not buried in a wall but walking about, then the whole family came to life;[4] it did not belong to history but to today; and the church was the citadel of its glory; the church, and Brandham Hall.

I brooded over this, and it seemed to me that the Maudsleys were the inheritors of the Trimingham renown. It was, I felt, local, and they enjoyed it by right of rent. And if they, so did their guests, including myself.

A glory brighter than the sunshine filled the transept. It filled my mind too, and reaching upwards and outwards began to identify itself with the Zodiac, my favourite religion.

Think about being good, my mother had told me, and I had no difficulty in doing this for I had a sense of worship. At school I took singing lessons, and among the pieces I learnt was one – 'My song shall be alway thy mercy praising'[5] – from which I got great pleasure: I felt I could really contemplate the mercy of God, and hymn its praises, if I didn't have to stand, for ever; but I thought of it simply as an attribute of God; I didn't connect it with the sins of men. And in the same way I did not associate goodness much with moral behaviour; it was not a standard to live up to, it was an abstraction to think about; it was included in the perfection of the heavenly bodies, though it was not their goodness that specially attracted me, it was their immunity from the disabilities I suffered from. I never thought of comparing my lot with theirs, except as a contrast.

Rapt in contemplation of the absolute, I missed some of the service and my nervous apprehension about the Psalms returned, but it was short-lived. At verse forty I examined my symptoms and found them normal: I knew by experience that in the space of four verses nothing untoward could develop.

But now came an ominous sound; the clergyman's voice changed gear and took on a deeper note: 'O God, the Father of Heaven.'[6] My spirits sank. We were in for the Litany. I at once took out my watch, for having a bet with myself as to how long it would last was the best way I knew of getting through the ordeal.

Usually I closed my mind completely to what was being intoned, only waiting for the drone to change its rhythm – the sign that the end was getting nearer. But this time some of the words came through, and 'miserable sinners',[7] instead of being a sound, reached me as a meaning with a challenge.

I rebelled strongly against it. Why should we call ourselves sinners? Life was life and people acted in a certain way, which sometimes caused one pain. I thought of Jenkins and Strode. Were they sinners? Even at the height of the persecution, I had never thought of them as such: they were boys like myself, and they had got me into a situation which I had to use my wits to get out of: and I had got out of it, I had turned the tables on them. If I had thought of them as sinners, requiring mercy from God, not resistance from me, the story of my deliverance would have lost its zest. I should deserve no credit for my victory: the solution to the problem would have been in God's hands, not mine, and I might even have to confess myself a sinner, for drawing down the curses.

No, I thought, growing more rebellious, life has its own laws[8] and it is for me to defend myself against whatever comes along, without going snivelling to God about sin, my own or other people's. How would it profit a man[9] if he got into a tight place, to call the people who put him there miserable sinners? Or himself a miserable sinner? I disliked the levelling aspect of this sinnerdom, it was like a cricket match played in a drizzle, where everyone had an excuse – and what a dull excuse! – for playing badly. Life was meant to test a man, bring out his courage, initiative, resource; and I longed, I thought, to be tested: I did not want to fall on my knees and call myself a miserable sinner.

But the idea of goodness did attract me, for I did not regard it as the opposite of sin. I saw it as something bright and positive and sustaining, like the sunshine, something to be adored, but from afar.

The idea of the assembled Viscounts contained it for me, and the Maudsleys, as their viceroys, enjoyed it too, not so incontestably, but enough to separate them from other human beings. They were a race apart, super-adults, not bound by the same laws of life as little boys.

I had just reached this conclusion when the last hymn was announced. What a long service, almost a record; it was 12.52. The sidesmen were doing their rounds; and the expression of the one who mounted the transept steps and came towards us justified me in thinking that we were something special, so respectful was it.

Walking back from church I again found myself the odd man out, and this time Marian didn't join me; she went at once to the head of the little procession, as if she had made up her mind beforehand. I lagged behind, trying to conceal the fact of my isolation by staring round me like a tourist. But again I was not the last: Trimingham had stayed at the church door chatting to the verger, who looked nothing if not obsequious. I was puzzled by all this deference shown to Trimingham and was still resenting it when he caught me up and said, very pleasantly, I had to admit:

'I don't think we've been introduced. My name is Trimingham.'

Being without experience of social usage I didn't know that I ought to tell him my name in return; I didn't give him credit for modesty and thought it rather silly of him to imagine I didn't know his name, when it had been on everybody's lips.

'How do you do, Trimingham?' I replied repressively, as who should say: 'Trimingham you are, and don't forget it.'

'You can call me Hugh, if you like,' he volunteered, 'I don't charge extra.'

'But your name is Trimingham, isn't it?' I couldn't help asking. 'You told me it was yourself.' To be on the safe side, and also with a certain guile, I added hastily, 'Mr Trimingham, I mean.'

'You were right the first time,' said he.

Overcome by curiosity I stared at his odd face, at the scar, the down-weeping, blank eye, the upturned mouth, as if they could tell me something. Then I suspected him of teasing me and said:

'But aren't all grown-up men called Mister?'

'Not all,' he said. 'Doctors aren't, for instance, or professors.'

I saw the flaw in this.

'But they're called Doctor or Professor,' I said. 'It's a . . . a title they have.'

'Well,' he said, 'I have a title, too.'

Then it dawned on me, and it was like the dawn of the unimaginable. Slowly, painfully I said:

'Are you *Viscount* Trimingham?'

He nodded.

I had to get it absolutely right.

'Are you the *ninth* Viscount Trimingham?'

'I am,' he said.

When I had got over the shock of this disclosure, which quite took away my powers of speech, my first impulse was to feel aggrieved. Why hadn't they told me? I might have made an even worse fool of myself. Then, with still greater force, it struck me that I ought to have known. It had been obvious from the start, too obvious. But I was like that. Two and two never made four for me, if I could make them five.

'Oughtn't I to call you my lord?' I asked at length.

'Oh no,' he said, 'not in ordinary conversation. Perhaps if you were writing me a begging letter . . . But Trimingham is quite in order, if you prefer it to Hugh.'

I was amazed at his condescension. The equivocal unmistered Trimingham I had pictured to myself vanished utterly, to be replaced by the ninth Viscount, whom I somehow felt to be nine times as glorious as the first. I had never met a lord before, nor had I ever expected to meet one. It didn't matter what he looked like: he was a lord first, and a human being, with a face and limbs and body, long, long after.

'But you haven't told me your name?' he said.

'It's Colston,' I brought out with difficulty.

'Mr Colston?'

I blushed at the hit, though it was a very gentle one.

'Well, Leo is my Christian name.'

'Then I shall call you Leo if I may.'

I mumbled something. I'm afraid he must have noticed the alteration in my manner: the sidesman and the verger had shown much more pride of bearing than I did.

'Does Marian call you Leo?' he asked suddenly. 'I noticed you were talking to her this morning.'

'Oh yes, she does,' I said, enthusiastically. 'And I call her Marian, she asked me to. Don't you think she is a ripping girl?'

'Why yes, I do,' he said.

'I call her spifflicating . . . A.1 . . . . I don't know what to call her,' I wound up lamely. 'I'd do anything for her.'

'What would you do?'

I scented a trap in this; I felt I had been caught out boasting. There was so little I could do for her that would sound important. Thinking of what it was within the compass of small boys to do, I said:

'If a big dog attacked her, I could go for it, or of course I could run errands for her – you know, carry things and take messages.'

'That would be most useful,' said Lord Trimingham, 'and kind as well. Would you like to take her a message now?'

'Crikey, yes. What shall I say?'

'Tell her I've got her prayer-book. She left it behind in church.'

Always glad to run, I trotted off. Marian was walking with a man, one of last night's new-comers. I circled round them.

'Please, Marian,' I said, trying not to seem to interrupt, 'Hugh asked me to tell you –'

She looked down at me, puzzled.

'Who asked you to tell me?'

'Yes, Hugh asked me to tell you –'

'But,' she said quite kindly but with a touch of impatience, 'how can I tell who asked you to tell me?'

The words 'Hugh', 'you', and 'who' danced before my mind and I was terribly embarrassed. 'Not who,' I stammered, 'Hugh.'

She still looked blank, and I said:

'Hugh, you know, Hugh the Viscount.'

They both laughed.

I was terribly ashamed. I thought she would think I was making free with his Christian name. 'Did I say it wrong?' I asked. 'He asked me to call him Hugh,' I added. I had only seen the word written and had forgotten how he pronounced it.

'Yes, but not who,' she said. 'Hugh, like well . . . stew, or phew, or whew. What words! Still I ought to have known, I wasn't thinking . . . What did Hugh say?'

'He said he'd got your prayer-book. You left it behind in church.'

'How careless of me. I seem to forget everything. Please thank him.'

I trotted back to Lord Trimingham and gave him Marian's message.

'Is that all she said?' he asked. He seemed disappointed. Perhaps he expected, as I had, that she would come and claim the prayer-book at once.

Outside the front door a high dog-cart[10] was drawn up. Its wheels were painted black and yellow; they had very thin spokes and were shod with indiarubber. A groom was standing by the horse's head.

'Do you know whose turn-out that is?' asked Lord Trimingham. He seemed to have recovered from his disappointment over the prayer-book.

I said I didn't.

'It's Franklin, Dr Franklin. You mustn't call him Mister. He's not a surgeon.'

I didn't quite see the point of this, but I laughed dutifully. I had taken a great liking to Lord Trimingham though I couldn't have told whether I liked the Viscount or the man.

'Doctors always come at lunch-time, it's one of their rules,' he said.

I was emboldened to ask:

'But how did you know it was Dr Franklin?'

Lord Trimingham gave a little shrug. 'Oh, I know everyone round here,' he said.

'Of course it all belongs to you really, doesn't it?' I asked. Then I brought out a phrase I had been pondering over. 'You are a guest in your own house!'

He smiled. 'And very pleased to be,' he said, a little crisply.

After luncheon, just as I was about to scamper off, Mrs Maudsley called me to her. It was always difficult for me to approach her, along the beam of that black ray that started from her eye, and I must have given the impression that I went unwillingly.

'Marcus isn't very well,' she told me, 'and the doctor says we must keep him in bed a day or two. He doesn't think it's anything infectious but to be on the safe side we're going to change your room. They're moving your things now, I think. It's across the passage from your old one – a room with a green baize door. Would you like me to show it to you?'

'Oh no, thank you,' I said, alarmed at the idea. 'I know the green baize door.'

'And don't go in to Marcus,' she called after me as I scurried off.

But presently my steps came slower. Should I have the room to myself, or should I be sharing it? When I opened the door should I find someone in the room, occupying it and resenting an intruder? Perhaps one of the grown-up guests, who would take up more than his share of the bed, who would have strange ways of dressing and undressing, and might not want me to look at him?

I paused at the door and knocked on the soft baize, a muffled knock. There was no answer, so I went in. I saw at a glance my fears were groundless.

It was a very small room, almost a cell: and the bed so narrow it could only be meant for one person. My things were all there, my hair brushes, my red collar-box;[11] but all in different places and looking different: and I felt different, too. I tiptoed about, as though exploring a new personality. Whether I was more or less than I had been, I couldn't decide: but I felt I was cast for a new rôle.

Then I remembered what Marcus had told me, about changing, and joyfully and furtively – all my movements in the new room were furtive – I began to take off my Eton suit. Then, a Robin Hood in Lincoln green, with a tingling sense of imminent adventure, I started off. I took all the precautions a bandit should take not to be observed, and I am certain no one saw me leave the house.

CHAPTER 7

The thermometer stood at eighty-four: that was satisfactory but I was confident it could do better.

Not a drop of rain had fallen since I came to Brandham Hall. I was in love with the heat, I felt for it what the convert feels for his new religion. I was in league with it, and half believed that for my sake it might perform a miracle.

Only a year ago I had devoutly echoed my mother's plaintive cry: 'I don't think this heat can last *much* longer, do you?' Now the sick self that had set so much store by the temperate was inconceivable to me.

And without my being aware of it, the climate of my emotions had undergone a change. I was no longer satisfied with the small change of experience which had hitherto contented me. I wanted to deal in larger sums. I wanted to enjoy continuously the afflatus of spirit that I had when I was talking to Lord Trimingham and he admitted to being a Viscount. To be in tune with all that Brandham Hall meant, I must increase my stature, I must act on a grander scale.

Perhaps all these desires had been dormant in me for years, and the Zodiac had been their latest manifestation. But the difference was this. In those days, I had known where I stood: I had never confused the reality of my private school life with the dreams with which I beguiled my imagination. That they were unattainable was almost their point. I was a schoolboy, assiduously but unambitiously subscribing to the realities of a schoolboy's life. The schoolboy's standards were my standards: in my daily life I did not look beyond them. Then came the diary and the persecution; and the success of my appeal for supernatural aid slightly shook my very earthbound[1] sense of reality. Like other dabblers in the Black Arts, I was willing to believe I had been taken in. But I was not *sure*; and now, superimposed on the grandeur of the Maudsleys, was the glory of the Triminghams militant here in earth: and the two together had upset the balance of my realistic–idealistic system. Without knowing it, I was crossing the rainbow bridge from reality to dream.[2]

I now felt that I belonged to the Zodiac, not to Southdown Hill School; and that my emotions and my behaviour must illustrate this change. My dream had become my reality: my old life was a discarded husk.

And the heat was a medium which made this change of outlook possible. As a liberating power with its own laws it was outside my experience. In the heat, the commonest objects changed their nature. Walls, trees, the very ground one trod on, instead of being cool were warm to the touch: and the sense of touch is the most transfiguring of all the senses. Many things to eat and drink, which one had enjoyed because they were hot, one now shunned for the same reason. Unless restrained by ice, the butter melted. Besides altering or intensifying all smells the heat had a smell of its own – a garden smell, I called it to myself, compounded of the scents of many flowers, and odours loosed from the earth, but with something peculiar to itself which defied analysis. Sounds were fewer and seemed to come from far away, as if Nature grudged the effort. In the heat the senses, the mind, the heart, the body, all told a different tale. One felt another person, one was another person.

Instinctively I looked round for Marcus. But Marcus wasn't there. I should have to spend the afternoon by myself; the others, the companions of the Zodiac, were all engaged on their own high concerns. I would not seek them out. I had lost my fear of them; they would be kind to me if I approached them; but I should be in their way. Also I wanted, I urgently wanted, to be by myself.

How best to explore the heat, that was the question; how best to feel its power and be at one with it. Marcus and I, in our afternoon playtime, had generally hung about the house, whose less exposed ramifications had a fascination for us. I would go further afield. The only road I knew that was not a carriage-road was the path to the bathing-place, and that I took.

Even since yesterday the water-meadow seemed to have dried up. The rusty pools beside the causeway had receded; the willows shimmered in a greyish haze. I wondered if I should find the farmer bathing but I didn't; the place was deserted, and without the shouts and the laughter and the splashing, it frightened me as it had the first time — with some suggestion of drowning, I suppose.[3] I mounted the black scaffold, which was almost too hot to touch, and looked down into the mirror which had been shattered by the farmer's dive.[4] How flawless it was now; a darker picture of the sky.

I crossed the sluice and followed a path between rushes as tall as I was. Soon came a second, smaller sluice, but with two drop-doors, instead of one. I crossed that too, and found myself in a cornfield. It had been lately reaped; some of the swathes were lying on the ground, others had been gathered into stooks. These had a slightly different outline from our Wiltshire ones, and confirmed me in my sense of being abroad.[5]

Here for the first time I regretted my low shoes, for the stubble came over them and pricked my ankles. Still it was not unpleasant to feel the hard sharp thrust against my skin. I saw a gate at the far corner and treading carefully made my way towards it.

It opened on a deep-rutted farm road. In some places the ruts were so deep and narrow, and baked so hard, that when I put my boot into them (from a feeling that I ought to) I could hardly get it out. Supposing I was left there, held by the foot, flinging myself this way and that, like a stoat in a trap, until help came!

Beyond the fields the road seemed to vanish into the hillside, there was no sign of it on the grey-green rise ahead. But when I got there I found it turned to the left, and switchbacked its way between spare hedgerows to a farmyard and a cottage. There it ended.

To a boy of my generation a farmyard was a challenge. It was an accepted symbol of romance, like a Red Indian's wigwam. All sorts of adventures might await one: a fierce sheep-dog, which ought to be braved; a straw-stack, which one must slide down, or admit oneself a funk.

There was no one about.

I opened the gate and went in. There, facing me, was a straw-stack with a convenient ladder running up it. Soft-footed, bending down and peering round, I made a reconnaissance. The stack was an old one, half of it had been cut away; but plenty was left to slide down. I didn't really want to, but there was no excuse whatever not to, if I was to retain my self-respect. I could not help acting as if the eyes of the whole school were on me. Suddenly a slight panic seized me;

I longed to get the sliding over; and I omitted a necessary and practical precaution always taken, and without loss of face, by experienced straw-stack sliders: to make a bed of straw to break my fall. I could have done it – there was plenty lying about – but I yielded to my sense of urgency.

The wild rush through the air, so near to flying, enraptured me: it was deliciously cool, for one thing, and devotee of heat though I now was, I saw nothing illogical in also relishing every experience that relieved me of it. I had already made up my mind to repeat the performance several times when crash! my knee hit something hard. It was a chopping-block, I afterwards discovered, submerged by the straw below the stack; but at the moment I could do nothing but moan and watch the blood flow from a long gash under my knee-cap. The fate of Jenkins and Strode flashed through my mind and I wondered if I had broken my bones or given myself concussion.

What I should have done next I don't know, but the decision was taken out of my hands. Striding across the farmyard came the farmer, a pail of water in each hand. I remembered him – it was Ted Burgess of the swimming pool, but he clearly didn't remember me.

'What the devil – !' he began, and his red-brown eyes sparkled with angry lights. 'What the hell do you think you're doing here? I've a good mind to give you the biggest thrashing you've ever had in your life.'

Oddly enough this didn't put me against him: I thought it was exactly what an angry farmer ought to say: in a way I should have been disappointed if he had spoken less harshly. But I was terribly frightened, for with his sleeves rolled up on the arms I remembered so well he looked quite capable of carrying out his threat.

'But I know you!' I gasped, as if that was sure to turn away his wrath. 'We . . . we've met!'

'Met?' said he disbelievingly. 'Where?'

'At the bathing-place,' I said. 'You were bathing by yourself . . . and I came with the others.'

'Ah!' he said, and his voice and manner changed completely. 'Then you are from the Hall.'

I nodded with such dignity as I could muster in my semi-recumbent position, hunched up, the straws sticking into the back of my neck, feeling, and no doubt looking, very small. Now that a greater physical danger was removed, I was becoming acutely conscious of the pain in my knee. Experimentally I touched the place, and winced.

'I suppose we'd better do that up for you,' he said. 'Come along. Can you walk?'

He gave me his hand and pulled me up. The knee was stiff and painful, and I could only hobble.

'Lucky it was Sunday,' he said, 'or I shouldn't have been here. I was taking the horses a drink when I heard you holler.'

'Did I holler?' I asked, crestfallen.

'You did,' he said, 'but some lads would have cried.'

I appreciated the compliment and felt I must make him some return. 'I saw you dive,' I said. 'You did it jolly well.'

He seemed pleased and then said: 'You mustn't mind if I spoke to you a bit hasty. That's the way I am, and these old boys[6] round here they drive me half demented.'

I did not despise him for changing his tune when he knew where I came from: it seemed to me right, natural, and proper that he should, just as it had seemed right and proper to me to change my tune with Trimingham when I realized that he was a Viscount. I carried my hierarchical principles into my notions of morality, such as they were, and was conscientiously a respecter of persons.

We entered the house, which struck me as a mean abode, through a door that led straight into the kitchen. 'This is where I mostly live,' he told me, defensively: 'I'm not what you call a gentleman farmer, I'm a working one. Sit down, will you, and I'll get something to put on that knee.'

It was not until I sat down that I realized how much the knock on my knee had shaken me up.

He came back with a tall bottle labelled 'carbolic' and several pieces of rag. Then from the sink he brought a white enamelled bowl and washed the gash, which had ceased to bleed.

'You were lucky,' he said, 'that it missed your knickers and your stockings. You might have spoilt that nice green suit.'

Relief surged up in me; I did feel lucky. 'Miss Marian gave it to me,' I said. 'Miss Marian Maudsley, at the Hall.'

'Oh, did she?' he said, swabbing the knee. 'I don't have much to do with those grand folks. Now this'll sting a bit.' He soaked a rag in carbolic and dabbed it on the place. My eyes watered but I managed not to flinch. 'You're a Spartan,' he said, and I felt exquisitely rewarded. 'Now we'll tie it up with this.' This was an old handkerchief.

'But won't you want it?' I asked.

'Oh, I've got plenty more.' He seemed a little put out by the question. He pulled the bandage rather hard: 'Too tight?' he asked.

I liked his half-unwilling gentleness.

'Now try walking with it,' he said.

I stumped about on the stone flags of the kitchen floor: the bandage held; I was beginning to feel better. To know that something that had begun badly was ending well acted like a tonic. What a story I should make of this! Then suddenly I realized that I owed him something; used as I was to having things done for me, as all children are, I was old enough to recognize a debt. But I dared not have offered him money, even if I had had any. What could I do? Could I give him a present? Presents were very much in my mind. I looked round the kitchen, which had no ornaments except a large stock-breeder's calendar and was so different from my recent surroundings, and said, rather grandly:

'Thank you very much indeed, Mr Burgess.' (I was glad to have got in the 'mister'.) 'Is there anything I can do for you?'

I fully expected him to say no, but instead he looked at me rather hard and said:

'Well, perhaps, there is.'

My curiosity was at once aroused.

'Could you take a message for me?'

'Of course,' I said, disappointed at being given such a trifling commission. I remembered Lord Trimingham's message, and how flat it had fallen. 'What is it, and who shall I give it to?'

He didn't answer at once, but took up the bowl of discoloured water and swilled it round in the sink. He came back and stood over me.

'Are you in a desperate hurry?' he said. 'Could you wait a minute or two?' He always seemed to speak with his whole body and it gave a curious intensity to his words.

I looked at my watch and calculated. 'We don't have tea till five o'clock,' I said. 'That's rather late, isn't it? At home we have it earlier. I could wait . . . well, ten or fifteen minutes.'

He smiled and said: 'You mustn't miss your tea.' He seemed to be debating with himself: his manner altered and he said: 'Would you like a look at the horses?'

'Oh yes.' I tried to sound enthusiastic.

We had reached a long brick-built shed, in which were four doors each flanked by a window, and from each window a horse's head looked out. 'This white one's Briton,' he said. 'He's the best puller I have, but he won't work with another horse, has to do it all himself. Funny, isn't it? This is the bay mare, her name's Smiler, she's a good, willing worker, but as soon as the harvest's over she'll be in foal, and this grey one's Boxer, but he's getting a bit long in the tooth. And this is the one I drive and use for hunting, sometimes. He has a nice head, hasn't he?' He stooped and kissed the velvet nose, and the horse showed its appreciation by dilating its nostrils and breathing hard through them.

'And what's he called?' I asked.

'Wild Oats,' he answered with a grin, and I grinned back, without knowing why.

All the heat of the afternoon seemed to be concentrated where we stood, intensifying the smell of horses, the smell of manure, and all the farmyard smells. It made me uncomfortable, almost giddy and yet it stimulated me;[7] and I was half sorry and half glad when, the inspection over, we turned to go back to the house.

As we were entering the kitchen the farmer said abruptly:

'How old are you?'

'I shall be thirteen on the twenty-seventh of this month,' I said impressively, hoping he would say, 'Why, fancy that!' for most grown-ups could be relied on to show an interest in one's birthday.

Instead he said, 'I should have given you a bit more. You're a big boy for your age.'

I was flattered at this tribute, especially coming from a man of his size.

'I wonder if I could trust you,' was the next thing he said.

I was very much taken aback, and half offended; but only half, because I thought it must be the prelude to a confidence.

However, I said rather indignantly: 'Of course you can. My report said I was trustworthy; "a trustworthy boy", the Headmaster said.'

'Yes, but can I?' he said, eyeing me. 'Can I trust you to keep your mouth shut?'

What an idiotic question, I thought, to ask a schoolboy. We were all sworn to secrecy. I looked at him almost pityingly. 'Do you want me to cross my heart?' I said.

'You can do what you like with yourself,' he answered. 'But if you let on –' he stopped, and the physical threat that his presence always implied seemed to vibrate through the room.

'Is it anything to do with this afternoon?' I asked. 'You can bet I shan't want to tell them, but they'll see my knee.'

He ignored that. 'There's a boy, isn't there,' he said, 'a lad of your age?'

'Yes, my friend Marcus,' I said, 'but he's in bed.'

'Oh, he's in bed,' repeated the farmer thoughtfully. 'So you are on your own, like.'

I explained that we usually played together in the afternoon, but that this afternoon I had taken a walk instead.

He listened with half an ear, and then he said; 'It's a big house, isn't it, a great big house, lots of rooms in it?'

'Counting the bedrooms,' I said, 'I don't know how many.'

'And always people about, I suppose, chatting to each other and so on? You're never alone with anybody?'

I couldn't imagine what this catechism was leading to.

'Well, they don't talk to me very much,' I said. 'You see, they're all grown up, and they have grown-up games like whist and lawn tennis, and talking, you know, just for the sake of talking' (this seemed a strange pursuit to me). 'But sometimes I talk to them a little, like I did to Viscount Trimingham this morning after church, and once I spent a whole day with Marian – she's Marcus's sister, you know, a topping girl – only that was in Norwich.'

'Oh, you spent a day with her?' the farmer said. 'That means you're pretty pally with her, I expect?'

I considered. I did not want to claim for myself, in respect of Marian, more than was my due. 'She talked to me again this morning,' I told him, 'on the way to church, although she could have talked to Viscount Trimingham if she'd wanted to.' I tried to think of other occasions when she had talked to me. 'She talks to me quite often when grown-ups are about – she's the only one that does. Of course

I don't expect them to. Her brother Denys said I was her sweetheart. He said so several times.'

'Oh, did he?' said the farmer. 'Does that mean that you are alone with her sometimes? I mean, just the two of you in a room, with no one else?'

He spoke with great intensity, as if he was envisaging the scene.

'Well, sometimes,' I said. 'Sometimes we sit together on a sofa.'

'You sit together on the sofa?' he repeated.

I had to enlighten him. At home there were two sofas; here there appeared to be none; at Brandham Hall –

'You see,' I said, 'there are so many sofas.'

He took the point. 'But when you are together, chatting – ?'

I nodded. We were together, chatting.

'You are near enough to her – ?'

'Near enough?' I repeated. 'Well of course, her dress – '

'Yes, yes,' said he, taking that point too. 'These dresses spread out quite a long way. But near enough to – to give her something?'

'Give her something?' I said. 'Oh yes, I could give her something.' It sounded like a disease; my mind was still slightly preoccupied by measles. He said impatiently:

'Give her a letter. I mean without anybody seeing.'

I almost laughed – it seemed such a small thing for him to have got so worked up about. 'Oh yes,' I said. 'Quite near enough for that.'

'Then I'll write it,' he said, 'if you can wait.'

As he was moving away a thought struck me. 'But how can you write to her when you don't know her?' I asked.

'Who said I didn't know her?' he countered almost truculently

'Well, you did. You said you didn't know them at the Hall. And she told me she didn't know you, because I asked her.'

He thought for a moment, with the strained look in his eyes that he had when he was swimming.

'Did she say she didn't know me?' he asked.

'Well, she said she might have met you, but she didn't remember.'

He drew a long breath.

'She does know me, in a way,' he said. 'I'm a kind of friend of hers, but not the sort she goes about with. That's what she meant, I expect . . .' He paused. 'We do some business together.'

'Is it a secret?' I asked eagerly.

'It's more than that,' he said.

All at once I felt rather faint, as if the Psalms had exceeded fifty verses: to my surprise (for grown-ups could be very dense about this) he noticed it, and said: 'You look all in. Sit down and put your feet up. Here's a stool. I haven't any sofas, I'm afraid.' He established me in the one easy chair. 'I won't be long,' he said.

But he was. He got out a bottle of Stephens' blue-black ink (I was rather shocked that it was not a proper inkstand),[8] and a sheet of blue-lined writing paper, and wrote laboriously. His fingers seemed too large to hold the pen.

'Should I just give her a message?' I said.

He looked up with narrowed eyes.

'You wouldn't understand it,' he said.

At last the letter was done. He put it in an envelope, licked the flap, and laid his fist on it like a hammer. I stretched out my hand: but he didn't give it to me.

'If you can't get her alone,' he said, 'don't give it to her.'

'What shall I do with it?'

'Put it in the place where you pull the chain.'

One part of me wished he hadn't said this, for I was beginning to see my mission in romantic colours; but the other appreciated the practical side of the precaution; I was a born intriguer.

'You can be sure I will,' I said.

Now, I thought, he will really let me have the letter, but still he kept it under his clenched fist, like a lion guarding something with its paw.

'Look here,' he said, 'are you really on the square?'

'Of course I am,' I answered, hurt.

'Because,' he said slowly, 'if anyone else gets hold of that letter it will be a bad look-out for her and me and perhaps for you, too.'

He couldn't have said anything more calculated to put me on my mettle.

'I shall defend it with my life,' I said.

At that he smiled, lifted his hand, and pushed the letter towards me.

'But you haven't addressed it!' I exclaimed.

'No,' he said, and added with a rush of confidence that excited me, 'and I haven't signed it either.'

'Will she be glad to get it?' I asked.

'I think so,' he said briefly.

I wanted to have it all cut and dried.

'And will there be an answer?'

'That depends,' he said. 'Don't ask too many questions. You don't want to know too much.'

With that I had to be content. Suddenly there was a lull in my mind, like the *détente*[9] after a retreating thunderstorm, and I realized it must be late. Looking at my watch, 'Golly!' I exclaimed, 'I must be off.'

'How are you feeling?' he asked solicitously. 'How's the knee, eh?'

'A.I.,' I said, bending it up and down. 'The blood hasn't come through the handkerchief,' I added, half regretfully.

'It will do, when you walk.' He gave me his hard, searching stare. 'You're looking a bit peaked,' he said. 'Sure you wouldn't like me to drive you some of the way? The trap's there and I can put the horse to in a jiffy.'

'Thank you,' I said, 'I'll walk.' I should have liked to drive, but suddenly felt the need of being alone. Being too young to know how to take my leave, I lingered awkwardly: besides, there was something I wanted to say.

'Here, you've forgotten the letter,' he said. 'Where shall you put it?'

'In my knickers pocket,' I said, suiting the action to the word. 'This suit has several pockets' — I indicated them — 'but a man who knew a policeman once told me that your trousers pocket is safest.'

He looked at me approvingly and I noticed for the first time that he was sweating: his shirt was sticking in dark patches to his chest.

'You're a good boy,' he said, shaking hands with me. 'Hop off, and be kind to yourself.'

I laughed at this, it seemed so funny to be told to be kind to yourself, and then I remembered what I wanted to say. 'May I come and slide down your straw-stack again?'

'I'll have it combed and brushed for you,' he said. 'And now you must scoot.'

He went with me to the stackyard gate and when I turned round a little later he was still standing there. I waved and he waved back.

*

They were all at tea when I arrived. I felt I had been away for months, so different was the atmosphere and so estranging the experience I had been through. At the sight of my knee they poured out sympathy and I told them how kind Ted Burgess had been.

'Ah, that's the fellow at Black Farm,' said Mr Maudsley. 'Good-looking chap, rides well, I'm told.'

'He's a man I want to see,' Lord Trimingham said. 'I expect he'll be playing in the match on Saturday. I'll have a word with him then.'

I wondered if Ted Burgess had been getting into trouble; and I looked at Marian, expecting her to make some comment, but she did not seem to have heard: her face had the hooded, hawk-like look it sometimes wore. I could hear the letter crackling in my pocket and wondered if it showed. Suddenly she got up and said:

'I think I'd better dress that knee for you, Leo. It's looking a bit messy.'

Glad to get away, I followed her. She went to the bathroom: it was the only one, I think, in the whole house. I had never seen it before; Marcus and I had a round bath in our room.

'Stay here,' she ordered, 'and I'll find you another bandage.'

It was a big room with, which seemed to me unnecessary, a wash-stand in it: for why should people want to have a bath and wash as well? The bath was encased in mahogany and had a mahogany lid. It looked like a tomb. When she came back she lifted the lid and made me sit on the edge of the bath while she took my shoe and stocking off, as if she didn't know that I was old enough to do it for myself. 'Now, put your knee under the tap,' she said.

The water trickled down my leg deliciously cool.

'My goodness,' she said, 'you did come a cropper,' but to my surprise she said nothing about Ted Burgess until almost the end, after she had put on the new bandage. The old one was lying on the edge of the bath, all creased and blood-stained, and she looked at it and said: 'Is that his handkerchief?'

'Yes,' I said. 'He said he wouldn't want it back, so shall I throw it away? I know where the rubbish-heap is'[10] – it wasn't officiousness, I wanted to save her the trouble. And I welcomed the chance to revisit the rubbish-heap, that grateful touch of squalor in all the magnificence.

'Oh, perhaps I'll wash it out,' she said, 'it seems to be quite a good handkerchief.'

Then I remembered the letter, which I had kept forgetting, for while I was with her I only thought about her. 'He asked me to give you this,' I said, pulling it out of my pocket. 'I'm afraid it's rather crumpled.'

She almost snatched it out of my hand and then looked round for somewhere to put it. 'Oh these dresses! Wait a moment.' She disappeared, taking the letter with her, and the handkerchief. A moment later she came back and said: 'Now, what about that bandage?'

'But you've put it on,' I said, showing her my knee.

'Good gracious, so I have. Now I'll put on your stocking.'

I protested; but no, she wanted to do it herself and I cannot say I minded. 'Was there an answer to the letter?' I asked, disappointed that she had taken it all so lightly. But she only shook her head.

'You mustn't tell anyone about this . . . letter,' she said, looking away from me; 'no one at all, not even Marcus.'

I was rather bored by all these injunctions to secrecy. Grown-ups didn't seem to realize that for me, as for most other schoolboys, it was easier to keep silent than to speak. I was a natural oyster. I assured Marian again that her secret was quite safe with me. I patiently explained that I couldn't anyhow tell Marcus, because he was in bed and I wasn't allowed to see him.

'Of course he is,' she said, 'I seem to forget everything. But you mustn't breathe a word, I should be terribly angry with you if you did.' Then, seeing me looking very hurt and on the point of tears, she melted and said: 'Oh no, I shouldn't, but you see it would get us all into the most frightful trouble.'

CHAPTER 8

One remembers things at different levels. I still have an impression, distinct but hard to analyse, of the change that came over the household with Lord Trimingham's arrival. Before, it had had an air of self-sufficiency, and, in spite of Mrs Maudsley's hand on the reins, a go-as-you-please gait: now everyone seemed to be strung up, on tip-toe to face some test, as we were in the last weeks at school, with the examinations coming on. What one said and did seemed to matter more, as if something hung on it, as if it was contributing to a coming event.

That this had nothing to do with me I realized: the quickly summoned smiles, the suppressed anxiety, were not for me; in the conversation, which was never allowed to die away, I took little part. Picnics or expeditions or visits were planned for almost every day: Mrs Maudsley would announce them after breakfast; to the rest of us it sounded like a command, yet her eye would flash an interrogation at Lord Trimingham as if he were a signal that must be consulted before the train went on.

'Suits me down to the ground,' he would say, or, 'Just what I was hoping we should do.'

I can remember sitting by some stream and watching the hampers being unpacked, the rugs spread out, and the footman bending down to change our plates. The grown-ups drank amber wine out of tall tapering bottles; I was given fizzy lemonade from a bottle with a glass marble for a stopper. I enjoyed the meal; it was the conversation afterwards, while the things were being packed away, that was the strain. I got as near to Marian as I dared, but she did not look at me; she seemed to have eyes only for Lord Trimingham who sat beside her. I could not hear what they were saying to each other, and I knew I shouldn't have understood it if I had. I should have understood the words, of course, but not what made them say them.

Presently Lord Trimingham looked up and said: 'Hullo, there's Mercury!'[1]

'Why do you call him Mercury?' asked Marian.

'Because he runs errands,' said Lord Trimingham. 'You know who Mercury was, don't you?' he asked me.

'Well, Mercury is the smallest of the planets,' I said, glad to know the answer but suspecting an allusion to my size.

'You're quite right, but before that he was the messenger of the gods. He went to and fro between them.'

The messenger of the gods! I thought of that, and even when the attention of the gods had been withdrawn from me, it seemed to enhance my status. I pictured myself threading my way through the Zodiac, calling on one star after another: a delicious waking dream, that soon became a real one, for in the midst of chewing a long succulent grass I dropped off to sleep. When I awoke I did not at once open my eyes; I had a feeling they would laugh at me for having slept and I wanted to put off the moment as long as possible; and I heard Marian say to her mother: 'I think he must be bored to tears, Mama, trailing round with us; he'd be much happier pottering about on his own.'

'Oh, do you think so?' Mrs Maudsley said. 'He's so devoted to you, Marian, he's your little lamb.'

'He's a darling,' Marian said, 'but you know what it's like when you're a child: a little of grown-up people's company goes a long way.'

'Well, I can ask him,' Mrs Maudsley said. 'Just now he makes us thirteen—I don't know if that matters. It's unfortunate about Marcus.'

'If Marcus has got measles,' said Marian carelessly, 'I suppose we shall have to put the ball off?'

'I see no reason for that,' said Mrs Maudsley with decision. 'We should disappoint so many people. And you wouldn't want to, Marian, would you?'

I didn't hear what Marian's reply was, but I was conscious of the clash of wills between them. After feigning sleep a little longer, I cautiously opened my eyes. Marian and her mother had moved away: most of the other guests were standing about, still talking; the two carriages were drawn up in the shade; the horses were tossing their heads and whisking their tails to keep the flies off. Upright on their boxes the coachmen towered above me; their cockaded silk hats almost touching the leafy branches and making deeper tones of dark against the shade. The play of shadows pleased me. As casually as I could I got up, hoping to escape notice; but Lord Trimingham saw me.

'Aha!' he said, 'Mercury's been off duty, taking a nap.'

I smiled back at him. I was aware of something stable in his nature. He gave me a feeling of security, as if nothing that I said or did would change his opinion of me. I never found his pleasantries irksome, partly, no doubt, because he was a Viscount, but partly, too, because I respected his self-discipline. He had very little to laugh about, I thought, and yet he laughed. His gaiety had a background of the hospital and the battlefield. I felt he had some inner reserve of strength which no reverse, however serious, would break down.

All the same, driving back on the one unoccupied box seat (the footman had the other), I was aware (though I did not admit it to myself) that I found the coachman's factual conversation more satisfying than the trifling, purposeless, unanchored talk that I had been listening to before I fell asleep. I liked giving and receiving information and he supplied it just as did the signposts and the milestones – to the appearance of which, as every few minutes they hove in sight, I eagerly looked forward. Sometimes he couldn't answer my questions. 'Why are there so many by-roads in Norfolk?' I asked. 'There aren't any where I live.' He didn't know, but generally he did, and with him I felt I was getting somewhere. With them there was nothing to catch hold of: gossamer threads that broke against my mind and tired it. The conversation of the gods! – I didn't resent or feel aggrieved because I couldn't understand it. I was the smallest of the planets, and if I carried messages between them and I couldn't always understand, that was in order, too: they were something in a foreign language – star-talk.

Under the multi-coloured roof of parasols below me – a Roman tortoise[2] against the sun – more than one man's boater was taking shelter. The buzz of talk reached me – how they kept it up! – but I was under no obligation of politeness to listen. At first I had been a little wounded by Marian's suggestion that I should be left out of future expeditions; but now I realized that she had made it for my benefit, and her 'he's a darling' kept coming back to me, like a sweet taste in my mouth. Of course I valued the prestige of being with them; I enjoyed our triumphal progress through the countryside, the passers-by staring at the carriages, the children running to open gates and scrabbling on the ground for the pennies which the coachman nonchalantly threw them. But I could imagine them in my mind, and bask in their radiance, just as well, and perhaps better, when I was away from them; for then I had the essence of the experience without its accidental drawbacks of arranging my face and trying to look interested when I wasn't. I thought of the outhouses, I thought of the bathing-place, I thought of the straw-stack down which I could now slide whenever I liked – I even thought of the rubbish heap. They were places which appealed to me in an intimate way and which I longed to revisit.

'Do you know Ted Burgess?' I asked the coachman.

'Oh yes,' he said, 'we all know him round here.'

Something in his tone made me say: 'Do you like him?'

'We're all neighbours,' the coachman answered. 'Mr Burgess is a bit of a lad.'

I noticed the Mister but the rest of the remark was disappointingly meaningless. Ted Burgess did not seem in the least like a lad to me.

At last we came to what I had been specially looking forward to – the hill, the one real hill of the drive, its one sensational feature. A warning notice loomed up and gradually came nearer:

> To Cyclists
> Ride with Caution.

I had made a joke to myself about this. 'Two cyclists ride with caution' meant that any other number could take what risks they liked. I tried to explain this to the coachman but he was busy with the brakes. Down we went, the horses' hindquarters, writhing and flecked with sweat, pressed up against the dashboard. Looking back I saw the carriage behind us similarly labouring. As the brakes grew hotter a pungent smell of burning rose, which for some perverse reason was incense to my nostrils. The sense of strain and crisis grew: all sensation was sharpened to a point.

At last we were at the bottom, and both carriages came to a stand. Now the reverse process faced us – less exciting, less fraught with dread, but scarcely less spectacular, for now the bearing-reins were slackened and the men of the party dismounted to make the ascent easier for the horses. A warm humanitarian feeling possessed me: I begged to be allowed to get down too.

'Why, you won't make any difference!' said the coachman, rather to my chagrin, but all the same he helped me down those springy skimpy footholds on which one might so easily slip. I aligned myself with the men and tried to fit my short stride to their long ones.

'My word, how cool you look!' Lord Trimingham said, touching his face with a silk handkerchief. He wore a white linen suit and, unlike the others, had a panama hat, which was attached to his coat by a button and a black cord: it looked extremely elegant, as did all his clothes: perhaps one noticed them the more because of the contrast with his face. 'This is the hottest day we've had so far.'

I took a few prancing steps to show how little I regarded it; but I remembered what he had said, and when we were all back in our places, and the horses were moving at their slow swinging trot, my obsession with the heat returned. Perhaps today would break a record. If only it would, I thought, if only it could! I was in love with the exceptional, and ready to sacrifice all normal happenings to it.

My first thought, on arriving, was to hurry to the game-larder; but in this I was thwarted. For one thing, tea was ready, and for another I had a letter from my mother, which had come by the afternoon post. 'Master Leo Colston, c/o Mrs Maudsley, Brandham Hall, near Norwich.' I looked at the address with pride: yes, that was where I was.

I liked to be specially alone when reading my mother's letters: even the game-larder was too exposed for that. Sometimes I took refuge in the lavatory but now that I had a room of my own I was assured of privacy. Thither I retired, like a dog with a bone, but for the first time I could not feel really interested in my mother's letter. The small concerns of home, instead of coming close to me and enveloping me as I read about them, remained small and far away; they were like magic lantern slides without a lantern to bring them to life. I did not belong there, I felt; my place was here; here I was a planet, albeit a small one, and carried messages for the other planets. And my mother's harping on the heat seemed irrelevant and almost irritating; she ought to know, I felt, that I was enjoying it, that I was invulnerable to it, invulnerable to everything . . .

She had given me for the visit a black leather writing case which had an inkpot embedded in its top right-hand corner. I tried to write to her; but I was out of touch. It was not like at school, when I carefully edited my letters until hardly anything remained except the fact that I was well and the hope that she was; I wanted to tell her about my promotion and the ampler ether, the diviner air that I now breathed. But even to me my efforts sounded feeble. Viscount Trimingham said I was like Mercury — I run errands — Marcus's sister Marian is still very nice to me, I think I like her the best of them all — it is a pitty she is going to be married only then will she be a Lady Viscount — what could it mean to her, what did it mean to me, that made me feel so self important? I did say something about all this and about Marcus being unwell (though of course I didn't mention measles); I told her of all the festivities, past and to come — the picnics, the cricket match, the birthday party, and the ball; I thanked her for saying I might bathe, and I promised not to bathe unless someone was with me; and I was her loving son. But even that sounded false, and a touch condescending, as if an immortal was acknowledging kinship with a mortal.

Poor effort as it was, the letter took me a long time to write, and it was past six when, hot-foot, I reached the game-larder. I expected something sensational and I was not disappointed. The mercury had declined to eighty-five; but the marker, nearly half an inch above it, recorded ninety-four. Ninety four! Perhaps it was a record, a record at any rate for England, where I believed the shade temperature had never reached a hundred. It was my ambition that it should. Only six degrees to go! A mere trifle, the sun could easily accomplish that; perhaps it would, tomorrow. As I stood musing I seemed to feel within me the world's tremendous meteorological effort to excel itself, to pass into a region of being which it had never attained before. I was myself the mercury[3] (had I not been called Mercury, I thought confusedly) soaring ever to new heights; and Brandham Hall with its still unexplored altitudes of feeling was the mountain on which my experience would be won. I felt intoxicated and light-headed, as though some miraculous boon had been granted to me, something that took me outside myself and the limitations of my normal

personality. Yet it was not a solitary experience, it was linked insepar-
ably with the expectation that I saw reflected in the faces round me.
They too were looking forward to a fulfilment, and I knew its stages
as distinctly as if they had been rungs in a ladder: the cricket match,
my birthday party, and the ball.

And then? Then there was to be a coming together, which my
mind, hesitating and half unwillingly, was learning to associate with
Marian and Lord Trimingham. Yet there were the stirrings of rapture
in that thought too; the shedding, the sacrifice of the part of me that
found its happiness in her.

'Enjoying yourself?' said a voice behind me.

It was Mr Maudsley, also bent on meteorological investigation.

Wriggling (I could not help wriggling when he spoke to me) I told
him that I was.

'Been pretty hot today,' he remarked.

'Is it a record?' I asked eagerly.

'I shouldn't be surprised,' he said. 'I shall have to look it up. Hot
weather suit you?'

I said it did. He took up the magnet. I did not want to see the
testimony to the day's heat obliterated but muttered something and
hurried off.

Confused by the encounter I forgot what my next move was to
be, and found myself straying near the lawn, where figures in white
were strolling about as aimlessly as I. It was far from my intention
to join them; I wanted to be alone with my sensations, and I made
for the ha-ha which separated the lawn from the park.[4] I knew from
experience that it was high enough to hide me. But it was too late;
I had been sighted.

'Hi!' called Lord Trimingham's voice. 'Come here! We want you!'

He came to the edge of the ha-ha and looked down at me.

'Trying to sneak past in dead ground,' he said.

I did not recognize the military allusion, but the general purport
of the accusation was quite clear to me.

'Now you're always running about,' he said, 'can you find Marian
and ask her to make a four at croquet? It's all we're any of us good
for. We've looked for her and we can't find her, but I believe you
have her in your pocket.'

Involuntarily my hands went to my pockets, and he laughed.

'Well,' he said, 'you must bring her in alive or dead.'

I trotted off. I had no idea where to look, and yet it never occurred to me that I should not find her. My footsteps took me round the house, away from its noble and imposing aspects, which meant so little to me, past the huddle of buildings at the back, which meant so much, and along the cinder track that led to the abandoned out-houses. And it was there that I met her, walking rather quickly and with her head held high.

She did not see me at first and when she did she eyed me stonily. 'What are you doing here?' she said.

I felt guilty as children do when asked their business by a grown-up person; but I had my answer ready, and I felt sure that it would please her.

'Hugh asked me to tell you –' I began.

'I asked you to tell me?'

'No, not you, Hugh.'

'Not you, you,' she repeated. 'I can't understand a word you say. Is it a game?'

'No,' I said wretchedly, for it seemed I was fated to mispronounce Hugh's name. 'Hugh, you know Hugh.'

'Yes, of course I know myself,' she said, apparently more mystified than ever. We were standing still, but I noticed that she was breathing rather quickly. 'Now let's talk about something else,' she said, as though she had humoured me long enough. For a moment it occurred to me that she didn't want to talk about Lord Trimingham and was deliberately putting me off; but I had to deliver my message.

'It's not you, it's Viscount Hugh,' I said; there could be no mis-understanding now, and I waited to see her face light up. But it didn't; her eyes moved quickly to and fro and she looked almost vexed.

'Oh, Hugh,' she said, almost like an owl hooting. 'How stupid of me. But you do pronounce his name in a funny way.'

It was the first unkind thing she had said to me and I suppose I looked dashed, for she noticed my embarrassment and said more kindly:

'But people have different ways of saying it. Well, what does he want?'

'He wants you to play croquet.'

'What time is it?' she asked.

'Nearly seven o'clock.'

'We don't dine until eight-thirty, do we? All right, I'll go.'

Friendship restored we walked along together.

'He said I was to bring you dead or alive,' I ventured to say.

'Oh, did he? Well, which am I?'

I thought this very funny. After we had joked a bit she said:

'We're going to luncheon with some neighbours tomorrow. They're all grown up, as old as the hills, quite mossy, and Mama thinks you might be bored. Should you mind staying here?'

'Of course not,' I replied. I remembered it was she, and not her mother, who thought I might be bored, but I didn't hold it against her; she was like the girl in the fairy story whose words turned to pearls as they fell from her lips. [5]

'What shall you do to amuse yourself?' she asked.

'Well,' I said, playing for time, 'I might do several things.' This sounded rather grand.

'What for instance?'

I was flattered by her interest; but pinned down I could only think of one thing.

'I might go for a walk.' Even to me this sounded a pedestrian thing to do.

'Where shall you walk to?'

I had an inkling that she was guiding the conversation, and half clairvoyantly I followed her lead.

'Well, I might slide down a straw-stack.'

'Whose?'

'Well, perhaps Farmer Burgess's.'

'Oh, his?' she said, and sounded so surprised. 'Leo, if you go that way, will you do something for me?'

'Of course. What is it?' But I knew before she spoke.

'Give him a letter.'

'I was hoping that you'd say that!' I exclaimed.

She looked at me, seemed to debate with herself, then said:

'Why? Because you like him?'

'Ye—es. Not so much as Hugh, of course.'

'Why do you like Hugh better? Because he's a Viscount?'

'Well, that's one reason,' I admitted, without any false shame. Respect for degree was in my blood and I didn't think of it as snobbery.

'And he's so gentle, too. I mean, he doesn't order me about. I thought a lord would be so proud.'

She considered this.

'And Mr Burgess,' I went on, 'he's only a farmer.' I remembered his reception of me before he knew where I came from. 'He's rather rough.'

'Is he?' she said, but not as if she regarded it as a fault. 'I don't know him very well, you see. We sometimes write each other notes . . . on business matters. And you say you like taking them.'

'Oh yes, I do,' I said, enthusiastically.

'Because you like T– Mr Burgess?'

I knew she wanted me to say I did, and I was ready to accommodate her, the more so that an overwhelming desire to testify came over me, and I saw my chance to voice it.

'Yes. But there's another reason.'

'What is it?'

I had no idea that when I came to them the words would be so difficult to say; but at last I brought them out.

'Because I like you.'

She gave me an enchanting smile, and said:

'That's very sweet of you.'

She stood still. We had reached a parting of the ways. One path, an ill-kept one, led to the back premises; the other, a broader one which I seldom took, led to the front of the house.

'Which way were you going?' she asked.

'Well, I was going with you – to the croquet lawn.'

A cloud came over her face. 'I don't think I shall go after all,' she said, almost snappily. 'I'm rather tired. Tell them I've got a headache. Or tell them that you couldn't find me.'

The bottom seemed to drop out of my world. 'Oh!' I exclaimed. 'But Hugh will be so disappointed!'

It wasn't only that: I should be disappointed at being deprived of my catch, and of the triumph of bringing her in alive or dead.

A gleam of humour returned to Marian's face. 'I get so mixed up with all these Hughs,' she said. 'Do you mean that I shall be disappointed, or that Hugh will be?'

'Hugh,' I said, trying to whistle it as she did, though I didn't quite like doing that, it sounded like mockery.

'Well, then, I suppose I must go,' she said. 'What a slave-driver you are! Only I think I'll go alone, if you don't mind.'

I did mind, terribly. 'But you'll tell them I sent you, won't you?' I begged.

She looked back at me teasingly. 'Perhaps I will,' she said.

CHAPTER 9

Between the next day, Tuesday, and the cricket match, which was on Saturday, I three times carried messages between Marian and Ted Burgess: three notes from her, one note and two verbal messages from him.

'Tell her it's all right,' he said the first time; then: 'Tell her it's no go.'

It wasn't difficult to find him, for he was usually working in the harvest fields on the far side of the river; from the sluice platform I could see where he was. The first time I went he was riding on the reaper, a new-fangled machine which cut the corn, but did not bind it; it was called the 'Spring-balance',[1] I remember. I walked beside it until the standing corn was between us and the three or four farm-labourers who were binding the sheaves, and then he stopped the horse and I handed him the letter.

Next day the area of uncut corn had dwindled; and he was standing with his gun watching for the rabbits and other creatures which clung to their shelter till the last moment before bolting out; this was so exciting that for a time I quite forgot the letter and he stood with narrowed eyes apparently having forgotten it too.[2]

My excitement mounted for I thought that this last stronghold would be stuffed with game; but I was wrong: the last stalks fell and nothing came out.

The man on the reaper drove it off towards the gate that led to the next field; turning their backs on us the labourers plodded to the hedgerow to retrieve their coats and rush-baskets. The farmer and I were left alone.

The field that had been cut looked very flat, and he was much the tallest thing in it. Standing there, the colour of the corn, between red and gold, I had the fancy that he was a sheaf the reaper had forgotten and that it would come back for him.[3]

I gave him the envelope which he at once tore open; and then I knew he must have killed something before I came, for, to my horror, a long smear of blood appeared on the envelope and again on the letter as he held it in his hands.

I cried out: 'Oh, don't do that!' but he did not answer me, he was so engrossed in reading.

The other time I went in search of him he was not in the field but in the farmyard and it was then he gave me the letter to take back.

'No blood on this one,' he said humorously, and I laughed, for there was a part of me that accepted the blood and even rejoiced in it as part of a man's life into which I should one day be initiated. I had a great time sliding down the straw-stack; indeed I did this on all three occasions when I took him letters; it was the climax of the expedition and when I got back to the party reassembled at tea, I was able to tell them with perfect truth that that was how I spent my afternoons.

They were golden afternoons in more than one sense, and I did not realize till Thursday came, and Mrs Maudsley told me, in her after breakfast orderly-room, as someone called it, that they were going out to lunch at a house where there were children, and I was to go with them, how right Marian had been to say I should be happier at home. There is a lot of ice to be broken between children, they do not make friends easily, their worlds are private, even their games are mysteries; and I could not readily learn the rules when I remembered the much more important business that I was leaving undone. Perhaps their kind of make-believe was a little insipid to me because it shed no blood.

For I took my duties as a Mercury very seriously, all the more because of the secrecy enjoined on me,[4] but most of all because I felt I was doing for Marian something that no one else could. She chattered to her grown-up companions to pass the time; she turned a smiling face to Lord Trimingham, sat next to him at meals, and walked with him on the terrace; but when she handed me the notes, young as I was, I detected an urgency in her manner which she did not show to others — no, not to Lord Trimingham himself. To be of service to her was infinitely sweet to me, nor did I look beyond it. I did, however, impose on my errands to and fro a meaning of my own —

several meanings indeed – for I could not find one that satisfied me. Even in the world of my imagination no hypothesis as to why Marian and Ted Burgess exchanged their messages quite worked. 'Business' they both said. 'Business' to me was a solemn, almost sacred, word; my mother spoke it with awe: it was connected with my father's office hours, with earning a living. Marian did not need to earn a living but Ted Burgess did; perhaps she was helping him; perhaps in some mysterious way these notes meant money in his pocket. Perhaps they even contained money: cheques or bank-notes, and that was why he said: 'Tell her it's all right' – meaning he had received it. I was thrilled to think I might be carrying money, like a bank-messenger, and be set upon and robbed; what confidence she must have in me, to entrust me with such precious missives!

And yet I only half believed in this, for no bank-note that I could see ever came out of the envelope. Perhaps she was telling him something, something that might be useful to him in farming: I could not imagine what, but then I knew nothing about farming. Or perhaps she was comparing notes with him, notes about the temperature, for instance, the daily readings of the thermometer which she had means of finding out that he had not. The last days' readings, though they did not reach Monday's height, had been satisfactory: eighty-three on Tuesday, eighty-five on Wednesday, nearly ninety-two on Thursday and on Friday. (I have since had the curiosity to check my figures by the official records, and found them not far out.) Or if it was not an interest in the temperature, it might be something that corresponded in the adult mind to such an interest, which I should understand if it was explained to me. Betting, perhaps: I knew how important betting was to grown-up people. Perhaps they were having bets on how soon this or that field would be finished.

Suppose he was in some kind of trouble and she was trying to help him out. Suppose he was wanted by the police and she was trying to save him. Suppose he had committed a murder (the smear of blood made it easier to think he had). Suppose only she knew about it, and was keeping him informed of the movements of the police?

This, being the most sensational, was also my preferred solution to the problem. But it did not really satisfy me, and when I was in her presence or in his, receiving the notes or delivering them, it struck me as inadequate as the others. Neither he nor she behaved, it seemed to me, as people would in any of the circumstances that I had imagined.

Behind my instinctive wish to find an imaginatively satisfying explanation there lurked a sneaking curiosity, of which I was half ashamed, to know the real one. But I did not act on it. I had no desire to play the spy; my privilege in being associated with the movement of the heavenly bodies had so inflamed my self-esteem that I did not require minor proofs of my own cleverness. Also I suspected that if I found out the real reason I should be disappointed. And so it proved: I was.

Two things happened on the Friday before the cricket match; and one in a way led to the other. The first was that Marcus, cleared of the imputation of measles, came downstairs. He was not allowed to go out, but it was understood that he would be well enough to watch the cricket match. I knew of course that he was better, but his coming down took me by surprise: his temperature had only been normal that morning for the first time, and my mother would have kept me in bed another day. I supposed all doctors had the same rules. Still, I was very pleased to see him when he appeared at luncheon, for though he was not a great friend, he gave me the sense of familiar companionship for which there is no substitute. I could say to him whatever was uppermost in my mind in a language that we shared; I did not have to translate what I said, or flounder in grown-up thoughts and ways of expression. Or so I thought. We sat together and chattered at a great pace, oblivious of the others; and then, half-way through the meal, the implication of his being again in circulation suddenly dawned on me.

I should not be able to carry any more messages. It was one thing to engage in this clandestine traffic while I was on my own. I was free to go and come as I pleased; I was asked only the most perfunctory questions as to what I did with myself, and to these sliding down the straw-stack provided a sufficient answer. But I could not so easily pull the wool over Marcus's eyes – those rather expressionless grey eyes that took in so much more than they seemed to. He was less interested in pretending than I was; he did not have as much imaginative life; he would play at being Lord Roberts or Kitchener or Kruger or de Wet with me,[5] but only for a limited time and only on condition that the English won: he was a strong patriot as well as being no supporter of lost causes. I could tell him many things but not my fantasy of myself as Robin Hood and his sister as Maid Marian.

He would slide down a straw-stack with me once or twice, but he would not want to make a daily habit of it – the way he took my references to it was proof. It was one thing to hoodwink a few farm-labourers, who anyhow were not interested in what I did; it was another to give Ted Burgess a letter, or take even a verbal message from him, with Marcus looking on. Besides – the difficulties began to crowd into my mind – he wouldn't want to talk to the farmer at all, except in the most distant way, and would oppose my doing so; in matters of degree he was a realist, though unlike me he did not carry his snobbery into the heavens. He certainly would not want to go into the kitchen and hang about while Ted laboriously composed a letter.

The more I thought about these expeditions in Marcus's company the more impracticable did they seem and the less I liked the prospect of them. Nor, though I was practised in deceit and an uncritical upholder of the no-sneaking tradition, did I relish the idea of deceiving Marcus – not on moral grounds, for any system of ethics, as distinct from the school code, I barely recognized – but because I felt it would spoil our relationship.

So for one part of me. Another part was still in love with the adventure and told me how dull the colours of my life would be without it. My counsels of prudence hadn't reckoned with that; they had not reckoned with the emotional impoverishment (an intimation of which, like the first pangs of a want, was beginning to steal over me) which I should suffer when I could no longer run to do Marian's bidding. I did not realize how much, in Marcus's absence, the focus of my life at Brandham Hall had changed. How could I tell her that I didn't mean to serve her any longer, and that Robin Hood was faithless to his trust?

My exchanges with Marcus, which had been as urgent as and much more expansive than those of Dr Livingstone and Stanley,[6] grew more desultory; half in hope, half in dread, I awaited the end of the meal. At last it came, and I was again visited by a feeling between hope and fear that I should be excused my afternoon commission. Before, Marian had given me the notes soon after breakfast – soon after, in fact, her mother had given us our orders for the day.

According to our wont I was scampering off with Marcus when I heard her calling me. Supposing he followed?

'Just half a tick, old dunderhead,' I said, 'the Lady Marian hath somewhat to communicate to me. I'll be with you anon.'

While he stood hesitating I hurried off and found her at a writing-table, in which room I can't remember, for the house was peppered with writing-tables, but I remember shutting the door after me.

'Marian,' I began, and I was just about to tell her what a difference to our routine Marcus's arrival on the scene would make, when I heard the latch click. Like lightning she thrust an envelope into my hand; like lightning I transferred it to my pocket. The door opened and Lord Trimingham stood on the threshold.

'Ah, a love-scene,' he remarked. 'I heard you call,' he said to Marian, 'and thought you were calling me, but it was this lucky fellow. But can I snatch you from him now?'

She rose with a quick smile and went to him, just giving me a backward look.

When they had gone I felt in my pockets to make sure the letter was safely there. My pockets were not very deep and the letters had a way of working up. Sometimes I took this precaution a dozen times during my journey. But today something felt different and in a moment I realized what it was. The letter was unsealed.

I found Marcus and told him where I was going.

'What! the old straw-stack again?' he said languidly. 'And on a day like this! There'll be nothing left of you, methinks, but one spot of train-oil, shiny on the top and thick and smelly underneath.'[7]

We bickered a little about this and then I asked him what he was going to do.

'Oh, I suppose I shall find some way of killing time,' he said. 'I may sit at yonder window and watch them spooning.'[8]

We both laughed a good deal about this, for it was the aspect of grown-up behaviour that we found the silliest. Then a thought shocked me into seriousness.

'I'm sure your sister Marian doesn't spoon,' I said, 'she's got too much sense.'

'Don't you be too sure,' said Marcus darkly. 'And come to

that, old turnip-top, Dame Rumour[9] hath it that she spoons with you.'

At this I hit him and we wrestled together until Marcus cried 'Pax! you've forgotten I'm an invalid.'

Elated by my victory I left him, and made tracks for the game-larder. It was three o'clock. The thermometer stood at ninety. It might still go up. Passionately I willed it to, and seemed to feel around me the unspoken response of Nature to my plea. From the distance came the sounds of croquet – the sharp smack of the mallet on the ball, the tap of the balls hitting each other, and exclamations of triumph and protest. No other sounds disturbed the stillness.

I was half-way through the belt of trees above the water-meadow when automatically my hand went to my pocket, encountering the sharp edge of the flap of the unsealed envelope. With no further intention in my mind I pulled it out and looked at it. There was no address (or direction, as Mrs Maudsley called it, why I could not imagine) on the envelope: there never was. But the open flap disclosed some writing which, at the moment, was the wrong side up.

Among the complexities of our school code was a very wholesome respect for the Eleventh Commandment.[10] But we also had a strong sense of justice, and if we were found out we did not expect to be let off. For most offences the appropriate penalties were known, and though we might grumble at them we did not think them unjust: certainly I did not. They were as inevitable as the law of cause and effect. If you put your hand into the fire it got burnt; if you were caught cribbing you were punished: there was nothing more to be said.

We had little sense of right and wrong in the abstract, but to be liable to punishment one must have broken some rule; and when a border-line case occurred, and a boy was punished for doing something 'wrong' that was not a contravention of any recognized rule, then we were indignant and considered him the victim of injustice.

The rules about reading other people's letters were fairly well defined. If you left your letters lying about and somebody read them, then it was your fault, and you were not justified in retaliation. If somebody rifled your desk or locker and read them then it was their fault, and you were justified in taking vengeance. Even if Jenkins and

Strode had not bullied me I should still have felt justified in calling down curses on them.

In class and out I had often passed round notes at school. If they were sealed I should not have dreamed of reading them; if they were open I often read them – indeed, it was usually the intention of the sender that one should, for they were meant to raise a laugh. Unsealed, one could read them, sealed one couldn't: it was as simple as that. The same rule applied to post-cards: one read a post-card that was addressed to someone else, but not a letter.

Marian's letter was unsealed and therefore I could read it. So why hesitate?

I hesitated because I wasn't sure she had meant me to read the letter. The others had been sealed. She had given me this one in a hurry; she might have meant to seal it.

But she hadn't.

In our code we attached great weight to facts and very little to intentions. Either you had done something or you hadn't: and what your motives might have been didn't matter. A slip counted against you just as much as something done deliberately. If Marian had made a slip, well, then, she must pay for it. That was only logical. But to my surprise I couldn't think of her in that way, as just an example in an argument. I wished her well, I wanted to be of use to her, my feelings were entangled with hers. I could not disregard her intentions.

For a time I struggled in the unfamiliar toils of moral casuistry. Why couldn't everything be plain sailing, as it had always been? Why did Marian's face and presence keep recurring to me, dividing my thoughts against themselves?

And how did I know that she hadn't *wanted* me to read the letter – that she hadn't left it open on purpose, so that I could find out something which would be useful to both of us? As a proof of her regard for me? There might even be something about me in the letter – something kind, something sweet, that would make me glow . . . gloat . . .

It was this hope, I think, that finally decided me, though I went over many other arguments to give me the excuse of meaning well. One was that this might be the last letter in the series: I had practically made up my mind to take no more. And another, illogically, was that to know the contents would help me to make up my mind: if they were sufficiently important, if they were matters of life and death (as I rather hoped), if Marian's safety was at stake, if she would get into the most frightful row —

Well, then, I might go on with the messages, Marcus or no Marcus.

But I would not take the letter out of the envelope: I would only read the words that were exposed, and three of them were the same, as I could see from upside down.

> 'Darling, darling, darling,
>> Same place, same time, this evening.
> But take care not to —'

The rest was hidden by the envelope.

CHAPTER 10

Not Adam and Eve, after eating the apple, could have been more upset than I was.[1]

I felt utterly deflated and let down: so deep did my disappointment and disillusion go that I lost all sense of where I was, and when I came to it was like waking from a dream.

They were in love! Marian and Ted Burgess were in love! Of all the possible explanations, it was the only one that had never crossed my mind. What a sell, what a frightful sell![2] And what a fool I had been!

Trying to regain my self-respect, I allowed myself a hollow chuckle. To think how I had been taken in! My world of high intense emotions collapsing around me, released not only the mental strain but the very high physical pressure under which I had been living; I felt I might explode. My only defence was, I could not have expected it of Marian. Marian who had done so much for me, Marian who knew how a boy felt, Marian the Virgin of the Zodiac[3] – how could she have sunk so low? To be what we all despised more than anything – soft, soppy – hardly, when the joke grew staler, a subject for furtive giggling. My mind flew this way and that: servants, silly servants who were in love and came down red-eyed to prayers – post-cards, picture post-cards, comic post-cards, vulgar post-cards, found in shops on the 'front': I had sent some of them myself before I knew better.

'We are having an interesting time in Southdown'[4] – a fat couple, amorously intertwined. 'Come to Southdown for a good spoon' – two spoons with human faces, one very thick, one very thin, leering at each other.

And always, or nearly always, the thin–fat motif; the man or the woman grossly out of proportion, under- or over-sized: the man or the woman, the man or the woman . . .

I laughed and laughed, half wishing Marcus had been with me to share the joke, and at the same time miserable about it, and obscurely aware that ridicule, however enjoyable, is no substitute for worship. That Marian of all people should have done this! No wonder she wanted it kept secret. Instinctively, to cover her shame,[5] I thrust the letter deep into the envelope and sealed it.

Yet, it must be delivered.

I climbed the stile into the water-meadow and at once the sun caught me in its fierce embrace. What strength it had! The boggy pools that fringed the causeway were almost dried up; the stalks that had been below the water-line showed a band of dirty yellow where the sun had scorched them. And standing on the sluice platform I saw almost with dismay how far the level of the river had sunk. On the blue side, the deep side, I could see stones at the bottom that had never been visible before; and on the other side, the gold and green side, the water was almost lost to view beneath the trailing weeds which, piled one on another, gave a distressing impression of disarray. And the water-lilies, instead of lying on the water, stuck up awkwardly above it.

All this the sun had done, and it had done something to me too, it had changed the colour of my thoughts. I no longer felt the bitter shame for Marian that I had felt in the shadow of the trees. Whether I realized the helplessness of Nature to contend with Nature I don't know; but my heart, which could not bear to feel unkindly towards her, softened the strictures that my mind was heaping on her, so that the act of spooning, when associated with her, no longer seemed the most damaging activity that a human being could engage in. But it did not help me to find a new attitude; I was too honest with myself to say 'Spooning is all right because she does it,' or, 'Other people mustn't spoon, but *she* can.' After all, she had to have someone to spoon with, and what was right for her –

Almost for the first time I thought of Ted Burgess as her spooning-partner. It was not a pleasant thought. Where was he? Not in the field the men were reaping; I could see that at a glance.

I went down to them. 'Mr Burgess is up to the farm,' they told me; 'he's got a job on there.' 'What is it?' I asked. They smiled but did not enlighten me.

It was the best part of a mile to the farm. My thoughts troubled me and I tried to concentrate them on the straw-stack, and the pleasure of sliding down it – the one known factor among all these doubtful ones. I still conceived the act of spooning visually, comic post-card fashion; an affront to the eye and through the eye to the mind. Silliness, silliness, a kind of clowning that made people absurd, soft, soppy . . . Pitiful at the best, but who wanted pity? It was a way of looking down on people and I wanted to look up.

As I opened the farmyard gate he was coming out of one of the stable doors. He saluted me, as he always did; a gesture half mocking, half playful, but with something of respect for me, or for the Hall, in it, which I enjoyed. I noticed that his arm had turned a darker shade of brown, and for this I envied him. It was difficult to connect him with silliness, or with spooning.

'How's the postman?' he asked. This was a name he had given me. It was the kind of liberty that grown-ups took with children. I liked it from Lord Trimingham, but I wasn't so sure I liked it from Ted Burgess.

'Very well, thank you,' I said rather distantly.

He gave his battered leather belt a hitch.

'Brought anything for me?' he asked. I handed him the letter. He turned away from me to read it, as he always did, then put it in the pocket of his corduroy trousers.

'Good boy,' he said. And when I looked surprised he added, 'You don't mind being called a good boy, do you?'

'Not at all,' I answered primly. And then it seemed the moment, and I heard myself saying:

'I'm afraid I shan't be able to bring you any more letters.'

His mouth fell open and his forehead wrinkled.

'Why not?' he asked.

I explained the difficulty about Marcus.

He listened moodily and the vitality seemed to ebb out of him. I could not help feeling half pleased to see him so discountenanced and chap-fallen.

'Have you told her this?' he asked.

'Who?' I parried, hoping to embarrass him still further.

'Miss Marian, of course.'

I admitted that I hadn't.

'What will she say? She counts a lot on getting these notes through.'

I moved about uneasily and he pressed his advantage.

'She won't know what to do, you see, no more shall I.'

I was silent, then I said:

'What did you do before I came?'

At that he laughed and said, 'You're an old-fashioned one, aren't you? Well, it wasn't so easy then.'

I was pleased by this.

'Look here,' he said suddenly. 'She likes you, doesn't she?'

'I . . . I think so.'

'And you want her to like you, don't you?'

I said I did.

'And you wouldn't like her to stop liking you?'

'No.'

'Now why?' he said, coming nearer to me. 'Why wouldn't you like it? What difference would it make to you if she stopped liking you? Where would you feel it?'

I was half hypnotized by him.

'Here,' I said, and almost instinctively my hand strayed towards my heart.

'So you have a heart,' he said. 'I thought perhaps you hadn't.'

I was silent.

'She won't like it, you know,' he said, 'if you don't take the letters. She won't be the same to you, you mark my words. You won't like that, will you?'

'No.'

'She counts on having 'em, same as I do. It's something that we both look forward to. They're not just ordinary letters. She'll miss them, same as I shall. She'll cry, perhaps. Do you want her to cry?'

'No,' I said.

'It isn't hard to make her cry,' he said. 'You might think she was stiff and proud, but she isn't really. She used to cry, before you came along.'

'Why?' I asked.

'Why? Well, you wouldn't believe me if I told you.'

'Did you make her cry?' I asked, almost too incredulous to be indignant.

'I did. I didn't do it on purpose, mind you. You think I'm just a rough chap, don't you? Well, so I am. But she cried when she couldn't see me.'

'How do you know?' I asked.

'Because she cried when she did see me. Doesn't it follow?'

To me it didn't seem to follow, but I had an inkling of what he meant. Anyhow, she had cried, and the thought brought tears to my own eyes.

I found myself trembling, troubled by his vehemence, by the unfamiliar sensations he had aroused in me, and the things he had made me say. He noticed this and said, 'You've had a hot walk. Come on in out of the sun.'

I would rather we had stayed outside; for in the badly lit, sparsely furnished kitchen, with its bare, hard, worn surfaces, its utter lack of the femininity that children of both sexes feel at home with, I instinctively felt that he was too much on his own ground. And though he had moved me strangely I still did not want to go on taking the letters.

'I thought I should find you in the field,' I said, hoping this would be a safe topic.

'So you would have,' he replied. 'I came back to take a look at Smiler.'

'Oh, is she ill?' I asked.

'She's in the family way.'

'What's that?' I asked. 'Do you mean she gets in your way?' Horses did get in the way, and I thought he might count himself as a family.

'No,' he said, shortly. 'She's going to have a foal.'[6]

'I see,' I said, but I didn't see. The facts of life were a mystery to me, though several of my schoolfellows claimed to have penetrated it, and would have been quite willing to enlighten me. But I was not so much interested in facts themselves as in the importance they had for my imagination. I was passionately interested in railways, and in the relative speed of the fastest express trains; but I did not understand the principle of the steam-engine and had no wish to learn. Yet now my curiosity was kindled.

'Why is she having one?' I asked.

'It's Nature, I suppose,' he said.

'But does she want to, if it makes her ill?'

'Well, she hasn't much choice.'

'Then what made her have one?'

The farmer laughed.

'Between you and me,' he said, 'she did a bit of spooning.'

Spooning! The word struck me like a blow. Then horses could spoon, and a foal was the result. It didn't make sense. I put my hand to my mouth, a nervous gesture that I believe dates from that day; I felt my ignorance shaming me like a physical defect.

'I didn't know horses could spoon,' I said.

'Oh yes, they can.'

'But spooning's so *silly*,' I said, and was glad to have said it. It was almost like getting a tooth out. I could not associate silliness with animals. They had their dignity: silly they were not.

'You won't think so when you're older,' he replied, with a quietness of manner he had not used to me before. 'Spooning isn't silly. It's just a word that spiteful people use for something . . .' He broke off.

'Yes?' I prompted him.

'Well, for something that they'd like to do themselves. They're envious, see. That makes them spiteful.'

'If you spoon with someone does it mean you are going to marry them?' I asked.

'Yes, generally.'

'Could you spoon with someone without marrying them?' I pursued.

'Do you mean me?' he said. 'Could I?'

'Well you, or anyone.' I felt I was being very crafty.

'Yes, I suppose so.'

I reflected upon this.

'Could you marry someone without spooning with them first?'

'You could, but . . .' He stopped.

'But what?' I demanded.

He shrugged his shoulders. 'It wouldn't be a very lover-like thing to do.'

I noticed that he used the word 'lover' not in a disparaging sense, as I was accustomed to hearing it used, rather the opposite. I wasn't going to let him impose his standards on me, but I wanted to know what he thought.

'Would it be worse to spoon with them without marrying them?' I asked.

'Some folks would say so. I shouldn't,' he said shortly.

'Could you be in love with someone without spooning with them?' I asked.

He shook his head.

'It wouldn't be natural.'

For him the word 'natural' seemed to be conclusive. I had never thought of it as justifying anything. Natural! So spooning was natural! I had never thought of that. I had thought of it as a kind of game that grown-ups played.

'Then if you spoon with someone, does it mean they will have a baby?'

This question startled him. His ruddy face went mottled, and his cheek-bones seemed to stand out under his skin. He drew a long breath, held it, and let it out in a noisy sigh.

'Of course it doesn't,' he said. 'What made you think such a thing?'

'You did. You said that Smiler had been spooning, and that was why she was going to have a foal.'

'You're sharp, aren't you?' he said, and I could see him casting about in his mind for an answer. 'Well, it isn't the same for horses.'

'Why isn't it?' I demanded.

Again he had to think hard.

'Well, Nature doesn't use 'em same as she does us.'

Nature again! I didn't find the answer satisfactory, and I didn't like the idea of being used by Nature. I felt that he was keeping something from me, and I took a fearful pleasure in baiting him.

'Now, isn't that enough questions for one day?' he said, persuasively.

'But you haven't answered them,' I protested. 'You've hardly told me *anything*.'

He got up from the wooden chair and prowled about the room, every now and then looking down at me with an expression of distaste.

'No, and I don't think that I will,' he answered almost pettishly. 'I don't want to go putting ideas into your head. You'll learn soon enough.'

'But if it's something so nice – ?'

'Yes, it is nice,' he conceded. 'But you don't want to come to it before you're ready.'

'I'm ready now,' I said.

He laughed at this, and his face altered.

'You're a big boy, aren't you? How old did you say you were?'

'I shall be thirteen on Friday the 27th.'

'Well,' he said. 'Let's make a bargain. I'll tell you all about spooning, but on one condition.'

I knew what he was going to say, but for form's sake I asked: 'What is it?'

'That you'll go on being our postman.'

I promised, and as I promised the difficulties in the way seemed to dissolve. Really he needn't have added that final bribe. I suppose he wanted to make assurance doubly sure,[7] but the softening-up process, as we should call it now, which he had put me through had been enough. He had made me realize something of what Marian and he meant to each other, and though I did not understand the force that drew them together, any more than I understood the force that drew the steel to the magnet,[8] I recognized its strength. And with its strength went a suggestion of beauty and mystery that took hold of my imagination in spite of all my prejudice against it.

But I can't pretend that Ted's promise of enlightenment didn't weigh with me, though I had no idea why I wanted so much to know what spooning was.

'You've forgotten something,' he said suddenly.

'What?'

'The straw-stack.'

He was right. I had forgotten it. It seemed to stand for something I had outgrown – physical exertion for its own sake: I felt much less keen about it now.

'You hop up the ladder,' he said, 'and I'll be writing something.'

CHAPTER II

Meteorologically Saturday was a disappointing day; the thermometer only rose to seventy-eight, clouds came up – the first clouds I had seen at Brandham since I came – and the sun shone fitfully. And that is how I remember the day – in snatches.

I remember a conversation at the breakfast table. Marcus was having the luxury of breakfast in bed.

'It all depends,' Denys was saying, 'on whether we can get Ted Burgess out before he's set.'

I pricked up my ears.

'I don't fancy he's their best bat,' Lord Trimingham said. 'In my opinion, —— and ——' (I have forgotten their names) 'are more likely to make runs than he is. He's just a hitter, and the pitch is a bit bumpy.'

I glanced across at Marian who was sitting next to Lord Trimingham, but she made no comment.

'But he'll flog the bowling,' Denys persisted, 'and then where shall we be?'

'We'll get him caught in the deep field,' Lord Trimingham said.

'But if he *breaks the back* of the bowling?'

'If he shows signs of doing that, I shall put myself on,' said Lord Trimingham, with a smile. He was our captain.

'I know you're a useful bowler, very useful, Hugh,' said Denys, 'no one knows that better than I do. But if he were to just *capture* the bowling –'

'I don't think you'll find he will,' said Mrs Maudsley unexpectedly. 'I don't know a great deal about cricket, but I seem to remember that you made the same prophecy last year, Denys, and this Mr Burgess got out for a duke or whatever they call it.'

'Duck, Mama.'

'Well, duck then.'

Denys subsided in the general laugh, which was more at his expense than Mrs Maudsley's. His unfinished features, handsome when you didn't look at them too closely, turned red, and I too felt uncomfortable. As schoolboys we snubbed each other unmercifully and it seemed the right thing to do: it was our code. But I knew it was a deviation from the code of grown-ups, and I was a stickler for codes.

Presently, however, Denys piped up again.

'And you know we haven't settled the side yet. Who *is* going to be the A. N. Other?'

At this there was a silence. One or two of the breakfasters glanced at me but I saw no significance in this. I was interested in the composition of our side, of course, and had speculated as to who would be playing; but in the Olympian deliberations of the selection committee I had taken no part.

'It's rather a delicate question, isn't it?' said Lord Trimingham, stroking his chin.

'Yes, it is a delicate question, I grant you, Hugh, but we shall have to decide it one way or another, shan't we? I mean, we've got to put eleven men in the field.'

That was undeniable, but no one offered an opinion.

'What do you think, Mr Maudsley?' asked Lord Trimingham. 'There are two candidates for the place, I believe.'

Lord Trimingham often appealed to his host in this way, and it always came as a surprise, for since his lordship's arrival it had seemed as though he, and not Mr Maudsley, was the master of the house. Mr Maudsley, though he spoke so seldom, was never at a loss for an answer.

'Perhaps we had better go into conclave,' he said, and the men of the party rose rather self-consciously and trooped out.

I hung about the smoking-room door (a room into which I had never penetrated) so as to lose no time in satisfying my curiosity and carrying the news to Marcus. They were so long deliberating that I thought they must have gone out another way, but at last the door opened, and one after another, with portentously grave faces, they emerged. I tried to look as though I was passing the door by accident. Lord Trimingham came last.

'Hullo, there's Mercury!' he said, and his face, which he had to pull about to register any special feeling, contracted into a grimace.

'Hard luck, old fellow,' he said, 'I'm afraid I have bad news for you.'

I stared at him.

'Yes. We couldn't get you into the team because Jim' (Jim was the pantry boy) 'played last year and the year before and he's a promising bowler and we daren't leave him out. Miss Marian will be furious with me but you can tell her it's not my fault. So you're to be twelfth man.'

His whole speech so surprised me that I had hardly time to feel disappointed before I was again raised to a pinnacle of happiness.

'Twelfth man!' I gasped. 'So I shall be in the team! . . . at least,' I added, 'I shall sit with them.'

'So you're pleased?' he said.

'Rather! You see I never expected *anything*! Shall I go down with you?'

'Yes.'

'Shall I get ready now?'

'You can, but we don't start till two o'clock.'

'Will you tell me when it's time to go?'

'The band will strike up.'

I was racing off to tell the news to Marcus when he called me back.

'Do you feel like taking a message?'

'Oh yes.'

'Ask her if she's going to sing "Home, Sweet Home"[1] at the concert.'

I darted off and found Marian, as I thought I should, arranging the flowers. Lord Trimingham's message at once went out of my head.

'Oh Marian, I'm playing!'

'Playing?' she said. 'Aren't you always playing?'

'No, I mean this afternoon, in the cricket match. At least I'm twelfth man, which is nearly as good. I shouldn't be able to bat, of course, even if one of our side was to die.'

'So it's no good hoping for that,' she said.

'No . . . But if one of the batsmen got very out of breath I could run for him, and I could field too, if somebody broke his leg or sprained his ankle.'

'Who would you like it to be?' she asked teasingly. 'Papa?'

'Oh *no*.'

'Denys?'

'No.' But I wasn't able to put quite so much conviction into this denial.

'I believe you want it to be Denys. Or do you want it to be Brunskill?' Brunskill was the butler. 'He's very stiff in the joints. He'd easily break.'

I laughed at this.

'Or Hugh?'

'Oh *no*, not him.'

'Why not?'

'Oh, because he's hurt himself already . . . and besides . . .'

'Besides what?'

'Besides he's our captain and I like him so much, and – oh Marian!'

'Yes?'

'He asked me to give you a message.' I recollected myself. 'Two really, but one doesn't matter.'

'Tell me about the one that doesn't matter. And why doesn't it matter?'

'Because it's about me. He said you weren't to be angry with him –'

'Why shouldn't I be angry with him?'

She pricked her finger on the thorn of a white rose. 'Blast!' she exclaimed. 'Why shouldn't I be angry with him?'

'Because I wasn't in the Eleven.'

'But I thought you were.'

'No, only twelfth man.'

'Of course, you told me. What a shame. I *shall* be angry with him.'

'Oh no, please not,' I exclaimed, for by the vindictive way she was thrusting the flowers into their vases I thought she really might be. 'It wasn't his fault, and anyhow captains have to – I mean, it would be awful if there was favouritism. So it wouldn't be fair if you were cross with him. Now,' I added hurriedly, dismissing the topic of her anger, 'would you like to hear the other message?'

'Not specially.'

I was very much taken aback at this reply, but again I put it down to the facetiousness that grown-ups practised on young people.

'Oh, but . . .' I began.

'Well, I suppose I had better hear it. You said it mattered more than the other. Why?'

'Because it's about you,' I said.

'Oh.' She took some dripping roses from the white enamelled bowl where they were lying, and held them up and examined them critically. 'Pretty poor specimens, aren't they?' she said, and it was true that compared with her they did look wilted. 'But I suppose you can't expect much of roses at the end of July, and in all this heat, too.'

'It isn't quite the end,' I reminded her, always calendar-conscious. 'It's only the twenty-first.'

'Is it?' she said. 'I lose count of the days. We live in such a whirl of gaiety, don't we? Parties all the time. Don't you get sick of it? Don't you want to go home?'

'Oh no,' I said, 'unless you want me to.'

'I certainly do not. You're the one ray of light. I couldn't do without you. How long are you staying, by the way?'

'Until the thirtieth.'

'But that's so near. You can't go then. Stay until the end of the holidays. I'll arrange it with Mama.'

'Oh, I couldn't. Mother would miss me. She does miss me, as it is.'

'I don't believe it. You're flattering yourself. Stay another week then. I'll arrange it with Mama.'

'I should have to write home –'

'Yes, of course. Well, now that's all settled. And the flowers are arranged, too. Can I trust you to carry one of these vases for me?'

'Yes, please,' I said. 'But Marian –'

'Yes?'

'You haven't heard Hugh's other message.'

Her face clouded. She put down the vases she was carrying and said almost irritably:

'Well, what is it?'

'He wants to know if you will sing "Home, Sweet Home" at the concert.'

'What concert?'

'The concert tonight after the cricket match.'

Marian's face took on its most sombre look; she thought a moment and then said:

'Tell him I'll sing it if he will sing – oh well – if he'll sing "She Wore a Wreath of Roses".'[2]

With my schoolboy's exaggerated sense of fairness I thought this a most satisfactory arrangement, and as soon as I had finished carrying the flowers for Marian, which perforce I had to do at a walking pace, I ran off to find Lord Trimingham.

'Well, what did she say?' he asked eagerly.

I told him the bargain Marian had proposed.

'But I don't sing,' he said.

His voice was much more expressive than his face. I knew at once that the answer had been a blow. He had said 'I don't sing' not 'I can't sing' but it was obvious that he couldn't and I wondered why I hadn't thought of it before. At school such rebuffs were all in the day's work, and I was surprised that he was so dejected; but I wanted to cheer him up, so I said, my mind working quicker than usual, 'Oh, it was only a joke.'

'A joke?' he repeated. 'But she knows I don't sing.'

'That was what made it a joke,' I patiently explained.

'Oh, do you think so?' he said, his voice brightening. 'I wish I could be sure.'

It might have been better if I had left him with his original impression.

Later in the morning I saw Marian again, and she asked me if I had taken Lord Trimingham her message. I told her I had.

'What did he say?' she asked.

'He laughed,' I said. 'He thought it was a very good joke, because, you see, he doesn't sing.'

'Did he really laugh?' She looked put out.

'Oh yes.' I was beginning to fancy myself as an editor as well as a messenger.

With Marcus's full approval I put on my school cricket-clothes but when I asked him if I could wear the school cap – a blue one made in segments converging on a crowning button, and having a white gryphon woven on the front[3] – he was doubtful. 'It would be all right,' he said, 'if it was an England cap, or even a county cap or a club cap. But being only a school cap, people might think you were putting on side.'[4]

'They wouldn't if it was to keep the rain off, you old heifer.'

'It won't rain, stomach-pump.'

We argued for some time about the propriety of wearing a cap, heaping ingenious insults on each other.

Sunshine and shadow outside, sunshine and shadow in my thoughts. Since Marcus's return I had become vaguely aware that I was leading a double life. In one way this exhilarated me; it gave me a sense of power and called out my latent capacities for intrigue. But also I was afraid, afraid of making some slip, and at the back of my mind I knew that the practical difficulty of keeping Marcus in the dark about the letters still existed, though I had been half persuaded to ignore it. I carried about with me something that made me dangerous, but what it was and why it made me dangerous, I had no idea; and soon my thought of it was banished by the imminence of the cricket match, which was making itself felt throughout the house. I caught glimpses of white-clad figures striding purposefully to and fro, heard men's voices calling each other in tones of authority and urgency, as if life had suddenly become more serious, as if a battle were in prospect.

We had a stand-up, buffet luncheon, all going to the sideboard and helping ourselves, and this seemed a tremendous innovation. It relieved the excitement and suspense to be always jumping up, and Marcus and I busied ourselves with waiting on the others. Waiting on, and waiting for them; for we had long ago finished our meal, and were kicking our heels, when Lord Trimingham caught Mr Maudsley's eye and said: 'Ought we to be moving now?'

I remember walking to the cricket ground with our team, sometimes trying to feel, and sometimes trying not to feel, that I was one of them; and the conviction I had, which comes so quickly to a boy, that nothing in the world mattered except that we should win. I remember how class distinctions melted away and how the butler, the footman, the coachman, the gardener, and the pantry-boy seemed completely on an equality with us, and I remember having a sixth sense which enabled me to foretell, with some accuracy, how each of them would shape.

All our side were in white flannels. The village team, most of whom were already assembled in the pavilion, distressed me by their nondescript appearance; some wore their working clothes, some had already taken their coats off, revealing that they wore braces. How can they have any chance against us? I asked myself, for though less conventional than Marcus I did not believe you could succeed at a game unless you were dressed properly for it. It was like trained soldiers fighting natives. And then it crossed my mind that perhaps the village team were like the Boers,[5] who did not have much in the way of equipment by our standards, but could give a good account of themselves, none the less; and I looked at them with a new respect.

Most of the members of the opposing sides knew one another already, those who did not were formally made acquainted by Lord Trimingham. The process of successively shaking hands with person after person I found confusing, as I still do; the first name or two held, then they began to trickle off my memory like raindrops off a mackintosh. Suddenly I heard: 'Burgess, this is our twelfth man, Leo Colston.' Automatically I stretched my hand out and then, seeing who it was, for some reason I blushed furiously. He, too, seemed embarrassed but recovered himself more quickly than I did, and said, 'Oh yes, my lord, we know each other, Master Colston and I, he comes to slide down my straw-stack.'

'Stupid of me,' said Lord Trimingham, 'of course, he told us. But you should make him run errands for you, Burgess, he's a nailer[6] at that.'

'I'm sure he's a useful young gentleman,' said the farmer, before I had time to speak. Lord Trimingham turned away, leaving us together.

'I didn't see you when I came,' I blurted out, eyeing the farmer's white flannels, which transformed him almost as much as if he had been wearing fancy dress.

'I was with the mare,' he said, 'but she's comfortable now, she's got her foal. You must come and see them.'

'Are you the captain?' I asked, for it was difficult to think of him in a subordinate position.

'Oh no,' said he, 'I'm not much of a cricketer. I just hit out at them. Bill Burdock, he's our skipper. That's him over there, talking to his lordship.' Of course I was used to hearing the servants call Lord Trimingham his lordship, but it seemed odd to me that Ted should, and involuntarily I glanced round to see if Marian was there;

but the ladies from the Hall had not appeared. 'Look, they're spinning the coin,' he said, with an eagerness that was almost boyish. 'But it won't signify; his lordship never wins the toss.'

This time he did, however, and we went in first.

The game was already under way when Mrs Maudsley and her train arrived. I could hardly contain my disapproval of their lateness. 'They simply wouldn't start,' Marcus confided to me. 'See you again, old man.' He went down with them to a row of chairs below the steps; I sat with the team in the pavilion.

I have never voluntarily watched a cricket match since, but I realize that conditions at Brandham were exceptional; the Triminghams had always been interested in the game and Mr Maudsley carried on the tradition; we had a scoreboard, scoring cards, white sheets, and a chalk line to mark the boundary. All these correct accessories gave the match the feeling of importance, of mattering intensely, which I required from life; had it been conducted in a slipshod manner I could not have taken the same interest in it. I liked existence to be simplified into terms of winning or losing, and I was a passionate partisan. I felt that the honour of the Hall was at stake and that we could never lift our heads up if we lost. Most of the spectators, I imagined, were against us, being members of the village, or neighbouring villages; the fact that they applauded a good shot did not give me a sense of unity with them; had we worn rosettes or colours to distinguish us I could hardly have looked the other party in the eye, while I would willingly have clasped the hand of the biggest blackguard on our side.

Above all I was anxious that Lord Trimingham should do well, partly because he was our captain, and the word captain had a halo for me, partly because I liked him and enjoyed the sense of consequence his condescension gave me, and partly because the glory of Brandham Hall – its highest potentialities for a rhapsody of greatness – centred in him.

The first wicket fell for fifteen runs and he went in. 'Trimingham's a pretty bat,' Denys had said on more than one occasion; 'I grant you he's not so strong on the leg side; but he has a forcing stroke past cover point that's worthy of a county player and I very much doubt if even R. E. Foster can rival his late cuts.[7] I very much doubt it.'

I watched him walk to the wicket with the unconscious elegance of bearing that made such a poignant contrast with his damaged face;

the ceremony of taking centre – actually he asked for middle and leg – a novelty in those days – had its awful ritual solemnity. And he did give us a taste of his quality. The beautiful stroke past cover point reached the boundary twice; the late cut, so fine it might have been a snick, skimmed past the wicket, and then came a bumping ball on the leg stump – looking dangerous as it left the bowler's hand – and he was out, having added only eleven to our score.

A round of applause, subdued and sympathetic and more for him than for his play, greeted his return. I joined in the muted clapping and, averting my eyes, muttered 'Bad luck, sir,' as he came by; so what was my surprise to see Marian applauding vigorously, as for the hero of a century;[8] and her eyes were sparkling as she lifted them to his. He answered with the twisted look that served him as a smile. Can she be mocking him? I wondered. Is it another joke? I didn't think so; it was just that, being a woman, she didn't know what cricket was.

Further disasters followed; five wickets were down for fifty-six. These Boers in their motley raiment, triumphantly throwing the ball into the air after each kill, how I disliked them! The spectators disposed along the boundary, standing, sitting, lying, or propped against trees, I imagined to be animated by a revolutionary spirit, and revelling in the downfall of their betters. Such was the position when Mr Maudsley went in. He walked stiffly and stopped more than once to fumble with his gloves. I suppose he was fifty but to me he seemed hopelessly old and utterly out of the picture: it was as though Father Time had come down with his scythe to take a turn at the wicket. He left behind a whiff of office hours and the faint trail of gold so alien to the cricket field. Gnome-like he faced the umpire and responded to his directions with quick, jerky movements of his bat.[9] His head flicked round on his thin lizard neck as he took in the position of the field. Seeing this, the fielders rubbed their hands and came in closer. Suddenly I felt sorry for him with the odds so heavily against him, playing a game he was too old for, trying to look younger than he was. It was as though an element of farce had come into the game and I waited resignedly for his wicket to fall.

But I waited in vain. The qualities that had enabled Mr Maudsley to get on in the world stood by him in the cricket field – especially the quality of judgement. He knew when to leave well alone. It cannot be said that he punished the loose balls – he never hit a boundary – but he scored off them. He had no style, it seemed to me; he dealt empirically with each ball that came along. His method was no method but it worked. He had an uncanny sense of where the fielders were, and generally managed to slip the ball between them. They were brought in closer, they were sent out further, they straddled their legs and adopted attitudes of extreme watchfulness; but to no purpose.

A bowler whose fastish swingers had claimed two wickets earlier in the innings now came on. One of his deliveries hit Mr Maudsley's pads and he appealed, but the appeal was disallowed, and after that his bowling became demoralized and he was taken off. In the next over a wicket fell and Denys joined his father. The score was now 103 of which Mr Maudsley had made 28. The ladies, as I could tell from their motionless hats, were now taking a proper interest in the game: mentally I could see the searchlight beam of Mrs Maudsley's eye fixed on the wicket.

Before he left the pavilion Denys had told us what he meant to do. 'The great thing is not to let him tire himself,' he said. 'I shall not let him run a single run more than I can help. I wanted him to have someone to run for him, but he wouldn't. When a ball comes to me I shall either hit a boundary or I shall leave it alone. I shall leave it absolutely alone.'

For a time these tactics were successful. Denys did hit a boundary – he hit two. He played with a great deal of gesture, walking about meditatively when his father had the bowling, and sometimes strolling out to pat the pitch. But his methods did not combine well with his father's opportunist policy. Mr Maudsley, always anxious to steal a run and knowing exactly when to, was frequently thwarted by Denys's raised arm, which shot up like a policeman's.

Once or twice when this happened the spectators tittered but Denys appeared to be as unconscious of their amusement as he was of his father's growing irritation, which also was visible to us. At last, when the signal was again raised against him, Mr Maudsley called out, 'Come on!' It was like the crack of a whip; all the authority that Mr Maudsley so carefully concealed in his daily life spoke in those two words. Denys started off like a rabbit but he was too late; he had hardly got half-way down the pitch before he was run out. Crestfallen and red-faced he returned to the pavilion.

There was now no doubt as to who dominated the field. But oddly enough though I did not grudge my host his success I could not quite reconcile it with the spirit of the game. It wasn't cricket; it wasn't cricket that an elderly gnome-like individual with a stringy neck and creaking joints should, by dint of head-work and superior cunning, reverse the proverb that youth will be served. It was an ascendancy of brain over brawn, of which, like a true Englishman, I felt suspicious.

Mr Maudsley did not find anyone to stay with him long, however. The last three wickets fell quickly, but they had raised our score to 142, a very respectable total. Tremendous applause greeted Mr Maudsley as he came back, undefeated, having just made his fifty. He walked alone – the footman, his last companion at the wicket, having joined the fieldsmen, with whom no doubt he felt more at home. We all rose to do him honour; he looked a little pale but much less heated than the village team, who were perspiring freely and mopping their faces. Lord Trimingham took the liberty of patting him on the back; gentle as the pat was, his frail frame shook under it.

During the tea-interval the game was replayed many times, but the hero of the hour seemed content to be left out; indeed it soon became as difficult to associate him with his innings as with the financial operations he directed in the City. At five o'clock our team took the field; the village had two hours in which to beat us.

CHAPTER 12

I still have the scoring cards but whereas I can remember our innings in detail, theirs, although the figures are before me, remains a blur, until the middle. Partly, no doubt, because our batsmen were all known to me personally, and theirs, with one exception, were not. Also because it looked such an easy win for us – as the scores, all in single figures, of the first five batsmen testify – that I withdrew some of my attention: one cannot concentrate on a walk-over. The excitement of our innings seemed far away and almost wasted – as if we had put out all our strength to lift a pin. I remember feeling rather sorry for the villagers, as one after another their men went back, looking so much smaller than when they had walked to the wicket. And as the game receded from my mind the landscape filled it. There were two bows: the arch of the trees beyond the cricket field, and the arch of the sky above them; and each repeated the other's curve. This delighted my sense of symmetry; what disturbed it was the spire of the church. The church itself was almost invisible among the trees, which grew over the mound it stood on in the shape of a protractor, an almost perfect semi-circle. But the spire, instead of dividing the protractor into two equal segments, raised its pencil-point to the left of the centre – about eight degrees, I calculated. Why could not the church conform to Nature's plan? There must be a place, I thought, where the spire would be seen as a continuation of the protractor's axis, producing the perpendicular indefinitely into the sky, with two majestic right angles at its base, like flying buttresses, holding it up. Perhaps some of the spectators enjoyed this view. I wished I could go in search of it, while our team was skittling out the village side.

But soon my eye, following the distressful spire into the heavens, rested on the enormous cloud that hung there, and tried to penetrate its depths. A creation of the heat, it was like no cloud I had ever seen. It was pure white on top, rounded and thick and lustrous as a snow-drift; below, the white was flushed with pink, and still further below, in the very heart of the cloud, the pink deepened to purple. Was there a menace in this purple tract, a hint of thunder? I did not think so. The cloud seemed absolutely motionless; scan it as I would, I could not detect the smallest alteration in its outline. And yet it *was* moving – moving towards the sun, and getting brighter and brighter as it approached it. A few more degrees, and then –

As I was visualizing the lines of the protractor printed on the sky I heard a rattle and a clatter. It was Ted Burgess going out to bat; he was whistling, no doubt to keep his spirits up.

He was carrying his bat under his arm, rather unorthodox. How did I feel about him? Did I want him, for instance, to come out first ball? Did I want to see him hit a six and then come out? I was puzzled, for until now my feelings had been quite clear: I wanted everyone on our side to make runs, and everyone on their side not to.

The first ball narrowly shaved his wicket and then I knew: I did not want him to get out. The knowledge made me feel guilty of disloyalty, but I consoled myself by thinking that it was sporting, and therefore meritorious, to want the enemy to put up a fight; besides, they were so far behind! And in this state of uneasy neutrality I remained for several overs while Ted, who got most of the bowling, made several mis-hits including one skier, which the pantry-boy might have caught had not the sun been in his eyes.

Then he hit one four, and then another; the ball whistled across the boundary, scattering the spectators. They laughed and applauded, though no one felt, I think, that it was a serious contribution to the match. More mis-hits followed and then a really glorious six which sailed over the pavilion and dropped among the trees at the back.

A scatter of small boys darted off to look for it and while they were hunting the fieldsmen lay down on the grass; only Ted and his partner and the two umpires remained standing, looking like victors on a stricken field. All the impulse seemed to go out of the game: it was a moment of complete relaxation. And even when the finder had triumphantly tossed the ball down into the field, and play began again, it still had a knock-about, light-hearted character. 'Good old Ted!' someone shouted when he hit his next boundary.

With the score-card in front of me I still can't remember at what point I began to wonder whether Ted's displayful innings might not influence the match. I think it was when he had made his fifty that I began to see the red light and my heart started pounding in my chest.

It was a very different half-century from Mr Maudsley's, a triumph of luck, not of cunning, for the will, and even the wish to win seemed absent from it. Dimly I felt that the contrast represented something more than the conflict between Hall and village. It was that, but it was also the struggle between order and lawlessness, between obedience to tradition and defiance of it, between social stability and revolution, between one attitude to life and another. I knew which side I was on; yet the traitor within my gates felt the issue differently, he backed the individual against the side, even my own side, and wanted to see Ted Burgess pull it off. But I could not voice such thoughts to the hosts of Midian prowling round me under the shade of the pavilion verandah.[1] Their looks had cleared marvellously and they were now taking bets about the outcome not without sly looks at me; so spying a vacant seat beside Marian I edged my way down to her and whispered:

'Isn't it exciting?' I felt this was not too much betrayal of our side.

When she did not answer I repeated the question. She turned to me and nodded, and I saw that the reason she didn't answer was because she couldn't trust herself to speak. Her eyes were bright, her cheeks were flushed, and her lips trembled. I was a child and lived in the society of children and I knew the signs. At the time I didn't ask myself what they meant, but the sight of a grown-up person so visibly affected greatly increased my emotional response to the game, and I could hardly sit still, for I always wriggled when excited. The conflict in my feelings deepened: I could not bear to face the fact, which was becoming more apparent to me every moment, that I wanted the other side to win.

Another wicket fell and then another; there were two more to go and the village needed twenty-one runs to pass our total. The spectators were absolutely silent as the new batsman walked out. I heard their captain say 'Let him have the bowling, Charlie,' but I doubted whether Ted would fall in with this; he had shown no sign of wishing to 'bag' the bowling. It was the last ball of the over; the new batsman survived it, and Ted, facing us, also faced the attack.

Lord Trimingham had two men in the deep field, and long on was standing somewhat to our right. Ted hit the first ball straight at us. I thought it was going to be a six but soon its trajectory flattened. As it came to earth it seemed to gather speed. The fieldsman ran and got his hand to it, but it cannoned off and hurtled threateningly towards us. Mrs Maudsley jumped up with a little cry; Marian put her hands in front of her face; I held my breath; there was a moment of confusion and anxious inquiry before it was discovered that neither of them had been touched. Both the ladies laughed at their narrow escape and tried to pass it off. The ball lay at Mrs Maudsley's feet looking strangely small and harmless. I threw it to long on, who, I now saw, was one of our gardeners. But he ignored it. His face twisted with pain he was nursing his left hand in his right and gingerly rubbing it.

Lord Trimingham and some of the other fielders came towards him and he went out to meet them; I saw him showing them his injured hand. They conferred; they seemed to come to a decision; then the group dispersed, the handful of players returned to the wicket, and Lord Trimingham and the gardener returned to the pavilion.

Confusion reigned in my mind: I thought all sorts of things at the same time: that the match was over, that the gardener would be maimed for life, that Ted would be sent to prison. Then I heard Lord Trimingham say: 'We've had a casualty. Pollin has sprained his thumb, and I'm afraid we shall have to call on our twelfth man.' Even then I did not know he meant me.

My knees quaking I walked back with him to the pitch. 'We've got to get him out,' he said. 'We've got to get him out. Let's hope this interruption will have unsettled him. Now, Leo, I'm going to put you at square leg. You won't have much to do because he makes most of his runs in front of the wicket. But sometimes he hooks one, and that's where you can help us.' Something like that: but I scarcely heard, my nervous system was so busy trying to adjust itself to my new role. From spectator to performer, what a change!

Miserably nervous, I followed the movements of the bowler's hand, signalling me to my place. At last I came to rest in a fairy ring, and this absurdly gave me confidence, I felt that it might be a magic circle and would protect me. Two balls were bowled from which no runs were scored. Gradually my nervousness wore off and a sense of elation took possession of me. I felt at one with my surroundings and upheld by the long tradition of cricket. Awareness such as I had never known sharpened my senses; and when Ted drove the next ball for four, and got another four from the last ball in the over, I had to restrain an impulse to join in the enemy's applause. Yet when I saw, out of the tail of my eye, a new figure going up on the scoreboard, I dare not look at it, for I knew it was the last whole ten we had in hand.

The next over was uneventful but increasingly tense; the new batsman stamped and blocked and managed to smother the straight ones; the lower half of his body was more active than the upper. But he got a single off the last ball and faced the bowling again.

It was not the same bowling, however, that had given Ted Burgess his boundaries in the preceding over. As I crossed the pitch I saw that a change was pending. Lord Trimingham had the ball, and was throwing it gently from one hand to the other; he made some alterations in the field, and for a moment I feared he was going to move me out of my magic circle; but he did not.

He took a long run with a skip in the middle but the ball was not very fast; it seemed to drop rather suddenly. The batsman hit out at it and it soared into the air. He ran, Ted ran, but before they reached their opposite creases it was safe in Lord Trimingham's hands. It was evidence of our captain's popularity that, even at this critical juncture, the catch was generously applauded. The clapping soon subsided, however, as the boy who kept the telegraph moved towards the scoreboard. The figures came with maddening slowness. But what was this? Total score 9, wickets 1, last man 135. Laughter broke out among the spectators. The board boy came back and peered at his handiwork. Then to the accompaniment of more laughter, he slowly changed the figures round.

But funny though it seemed, the mistake didn't really relieve the tension, it added to it by suggesting that even mathematics were subject to nervous upset. And only eight runs – two boundaries – stood between us and defeat.

As the outgoing met the incoming batsman and exchanged a word with him, at which each man nodded, I tried for the last time to sort my feelings out. But they gathered round me like a mist, whose shape can be seen as it advances but not when it is on you, and in the thick, whirling vapours my mind soon lost its way. Yet I kept my sense of the general drama of the match and it was sharpened by an awareness, which I couldn't explain to myself, of a particular drama between the bowler and the batsman. Tenant and landlord, commoner and peer, village and Hall — these were elements in it. But there was something else, something to do with Marian, sitting on the pavilion steps watching us.

It was a prideful and sustaining thought that whereas the spectators could throw themselves about and yell themselves hoarse, we, the players, could not, must not, show the slightest sign of emotion. Certainly the bowler, digging his heel into the ground, a trick he had before starting his run, and Ted facing him, his shirt clinging to his back, did not.

Lord Trimingham sent down his deceptively dipping ball but Ted did not wait for it to drop, he ran out and hit it past cover point to the boundary. It was a glorious drive and the elation of it ran through me like an electric current. The spectators yelled and cheered, and suddenly the balance of my feelings went right over: it was their victory that I wanted now, not ours. I did not think of it in terms of the three runs that were needed; I seemed to hear it coming like a wind.

I could not tell whether the next ball was on the wicket or not, but it was pitched much further up and suddenly I saw Ted's face and body swinging round, and the ball, travelling towards me on a rising straight line like a cable stretched between us. Ted started to run and then stopped and stood watching me, wonder in his eyes and a wild disbelief.

I threw my hand above my head and the ball stuck there, but the impact knocked me over. When I scrambled up, still clutching the ball to me, as though it was a pain that had started in my heart, I heard the sweet sound of applause and saw the field breaking up and Lord Trimingham coming towards me. I can't remember what he said — my emotions were too overwhelming — but I remember that his congratulations were the more precious because they were reserved and understated, they might, in fact, have been addressed to a *man*; and it was as a man, and not by any means the least of men, that I joined the group who were making their way back to the pavilion. We went together in a ragged cluster, the defeated and the surviving batsmen with us, all enmity laid aside, amid a more than generous measure of applause from the spectators. I could not tell how I felt; in my high mood of elation the usual landmarks by which I judged such things were lost to view. I was still in the air, though the scaffolding of events which had lifted me had crumbled. But I was still aware of one separate element that had not quite fused in the general concourse of passions; the pang of regret, sharp as a sword-thrust, that had accompanied the catch. Far from diminishing my exultation, it had somehow raised it to a higher power, like the drop of bitter in the fount of happiness; but I felt that I should be still happier – that it would add another cubit to my stature – if I told Ted of it. Something warned me that such an avowal would be unorthodox; the personal feelings of cricketers were concealed behind their stiff upper lips. But I was almost literally above myself; I knew that the fate of the match had turned on me, and I felt I could afford to defy convention. Yet how would he take it? What were his feelings? Was he still elated by his innings or was he bitterly disappointed by its untimely close? Did he still regard me as a friend, or as an enemy who had brought about his downfall? I did not greatly care; and seeing that he was walking alone (most of the players had exhausted their stock of conversation) I sidled up to him and said, 'I'm sorry, Ted. I didn't really mean to catch you out.' He stopped and smiled at me. 'Well, that's very handsome of you,' he said. 'It was a damned good catch, anyway. I never thought you'd hold it. To tell you the truth I'd forgotten all about you being at square leg, and then I looked round and there you were, by God. And then I thought, "It'll go right over his head," but you stretched up like a concertina. I'd thought of a dozen ways I might get out, but never thought I'd be caught out by our postman.' 'I didn't mean to,' I repeated, not to be cheated of my apology. At that moment the clapping grew louder and some enthusiasts coupled Ted's name with it. Though we were all heroes, he was evidently the crowd's favourite; and I dropped back so that he might walk in alone. His fellow-batsmen in the pavilion were making a great demonstration; even the ladies of our party, sitting in front, showed themselves mildly interested as Ted came by. All except one. Marian, I noticed, didn't look up.

As soon as we were back at the Hall I said to Marcus, 'Lend me your scoring card, old man.'

'Why, didn't you keep one, pudding-face?' he asked me.

'How could I, you dolt, when I was fielding?'

'Did you field, you measly microbe? Are you quite sure?'

When I had punished him for this, and extracted his score-card from him, I copied on to mine the items that were missing.

'E. Burgess c. sub. b. Ld Trimingham 81,' I read. 'Why, you might have put my name in, you filthy scoundrel.'

'"C. sub." is correct,' he said. 'Besides, I want to keep this card clean, and it wouldn't be if your name was on it.'

CHAPTER 13

The supper at the village hall was graced by various local notabilities, as well as by the two teams; it seemed to me far the most magnificent occasion I had ever been present at. The decorations, the colours, the heat, the almost overpowering sense of matiness (a quality I greatly valued) went to my head quite as much as the hock-cup which was poured into my glass. At times I lost all sense of myself as a separate entity; at times my spirit fluttered round the peaked ceiling of the hall, among the Union Jacks and paper streamers, a celestial body, companion of the stars. I felt that I had fulfilled my function in life, nothing more remained for me to do: I could live for ever on my capital of achievement. My next-door neighbours, both of them members of the village team (for we were dovetailed; at this democratic festival it was not thought proper for two members of the Hall party to sit together) must have found me poor company, for though I communed with them freely in the spirit, I had almost nothing to say to them in the flesh. Not that they minded; they were intent upon their food, and sometimes made remarks to each other across me as if I was not there. These I could seldom understand but they evoked hilarious laughter; a nod or a grunt passed for a sally, until to my besotted sense the whole world seemed one laugh.

After the supper Mr Maudsley made a speech. I expected it would be a very halting one, for I had never heard him say half a dozen words consecutively. But he was amazingly fluent. Sentence after sentence poured out, just as if he was reading it; and just as when he was reading prayers, his voice was uninflected and monotonous. Because of this, and the speed he went at, some of his jokes misfired; but those that took effect were all the more successful because of their dry delivery. With what seemed to me consummate skill he contrived to bring in almost every player by name and find something noteworthy in his performance. As a rule I turned a deaf ear to speeches, classing them with sermons as things intended for the grown-up mind; but this one I did listen to, for I hoped to hear my own name mentioned, nor was I disappointed. 'Last, but not least, except in stature, our young David, Leo Colston, who slew the Goliath of Black Farm if I may so describe him, not with a sling, with a catch.'[1] All eyes were turned on me, or so I thought; and Ted, who was sitting nearly opposite, gave me a tremendous wink. Wearing a lounge suit and a high starched collar he looked even less like himself than he did in flannels. The more clothes he put on, the less he looked himself. Whereas Lord Trimingham's clothes always seemed part of him, Ted's fine feathers made him look a yokel.

Speeches droned on – it was as if the flight of time had been made audible – and then songs were called for. On the dais at the end of the hall stood an upright piano, with a revolving plush-upholstered stool set invitingly in front of it. But now a murmuring began, the import of which at last reached me: where was the accompanist? He was called for but he did not appear. Explanations were forthcoming. He had sent a message that he was seedy, but inexplicably the message hadn't been delivered. A wave of disappointment swept the assembly. What was a cricket match, what was a supper, without songs? A chill settled on our wine-warmed spirits and there was no more wine to thaw it. It was early: the evening stretched ahead, an unending blank. Would no one volunteer to fill the gap? Lord Trimingham's ill-matched eyes, which always had the gleam of authority behind them, roved round the room and were avoided as sedulously as if they had been an auctioneer's; certainly I kept mine fixed on the table-cloth, for Marcus knew that I could play the piano a little. But suddenly, when everyone seemed to be rooted in their places, immovably, never to rise, never to look up, as long as an accompanist was being sought for, there was a movement, a flutter to the vertical, almost as if a standard was being raised; and before the relaxation of relief had had time to ease our stiffened bodies, Marian had walked swiftly down the hall, and was seated at the piano-stool. How lovely she looked in her Gainsborough-blue dress[2] between the candles! From there, as from a throne, she looked down at us. Amused and a little mocking, as though to say: I've done my part, now you do yours.

It was the custom, so I afterwards learned, that the first singers should be members of the two teams; all were called upon and some were badgered, but it was pretty well known, I fancy, who would oblige and who would not. The former, it appeared, had brought their music with them; this they produced apparently from nowhere, sometimes with a guilty and self-conscious, sometimes with a brazen, air; but one and all they seemed to be in awe of the accompanist, standing as far away from her as they could. Her playing fascinated me and I listened to it rather than to the songs. I could see her white, slender fingers (in spite of the perpetual sunshine, she had managed to keep them white) sliding over the keys, and what delicious sounds she coaxed out of that old tin-pot piano! I could tell how irregular its touch must be, but the runs came as smooth as water trickling. What fire there was in the loud passages, and what sweetness in the soft! And it was almost miraculous the way she was able to flick up the key that stuck and put it back in commission. A tactful as well as a skilled accompanist, she followed the singers and did not try to hurry or retard them; but her performance was in such a different class from theirs that the two did not quite match: it was as though a thoroughbred had been harnessed to a cart-horse. The audience appreciated this and their applause was respectful as well as rollicking.

When Ted Burgess was called upon he did not seem to hear and I thought he actually hadn't heard. But when his friends in various parts of the room began to repeat his name, adding facetious encouragements, 'Come on, Ted! Don't be bashful! We all know you can!' – he made no movement to rise, he sat on in his place looking stubborn and embarrassed. The company enjoyed this; their cries redoubled and became almost a chorus, whereat he was heard to mutter, rather ungraciously, that he didn't feel like singing. Lord Trimingham joined his voice to theirs. 'Now don't disappoint us, Ted,' he said (the 'Ted' surprised me: perhaps it was a concession to good fellowship). 'You didn't keep us waiting in the cricket field, you know.' In the laughter that followed Ted's resistance seemed to crumble; he got up clumsily, carrying a fat roll of music under his arm, and stumbled towards the dais. 'Careful now!' somebody called out, and there was more laughter.

Marian appeared to take no interest in all this. When Ted reached her she raised her eyes and said something and he reluctantly handed her his sheaf of songs. Quickly she looked through them and put one on the music rest: I noticed that she dog-eared the page, which she had never done before. 'Take a Pair of Sparkling Eyes,'[3] announced Ted, as if they were the last thing one could want to take, and someone whispered, 'Cheer up, it isn't a funeral!' At first the singer's voice was much less audible than his breathing, but gradually it gained strength and steadiness and colour and lent itself to the dancing lilt of the song, so in the end it was quite a creditable performance, which the audience seemed to appreciate all the more for its shaky start. An encore was called for, the first of the evening. Again Ted had to confer with Marian; their heads came close together; again he seemed to demur, and abruptly he left the piano, and made a bow in token of refusal. But the applause redoubled; they liked his modesty and were determined to overcome it.

The new song was a sentimental one by Balfe.[4] I don't suppose it's ever sung now, but I liked it, and liked Ted's rendering of it and the quaver which threaded his voice.

> *When other lips and other hearts*
> *Their tales of love shall tell*
> *In language whose excess imparts*
> *The power they feel so well.*

I remember the pensive look on the faces of the audience as they listened to this resigned and mellifluous presage of infidelities to come, unaware of its underlying bitterness; and I expect my face reflected it, for it seemed to me that I knew all about other lips and other hearts telling their tales of love, and knew how sad it was, and yet how beautiful; nor was I a stranger to the language whose excess imparts the power it feels so well. But what sort of experience, if any, I connected it with, I have no idea. To me it was a literary mood evoked by the sounds of words I liked, words from the grown-up world, which made poetry for me and which yet had reality too — the reality of their meaning for grown-ups, which I was content to take on trust. Songs were about such matters. It never occurred to me that there might be hard feelings when other lips and other hearts began to tell their tales of love, or that they told them in any other way than to the accompaniment of a piano in a concert-room. Least of all did I connect such manifestations with the phenomenon called spooning: I should have been horrified if I had. I sat in ecstasy as though listening to the music of the spheres,[5] and when the lover finally asked nothing more than that his sweetheart, in the midst of her dallyings with another, or others, should remember him, tears of happiness came into my eyes.

At the conclusion of the song there was a call for the accompanist, and Marian left her stool to share the applause with Ted. Half turning she made him a little bow. But he, instead of responding, twice jerked his head round towards her, and away again, like a comedian or a clown wise-cracking with his partner. The audience laughed and I heard Lord Trimingham say, 'Not very gallant, is he?' My companion was more emphatic. 'What's come over our Ted,' he whispered across me to my other neighbour, 'to be so shy with the ladies? It's because she comes from the Hall, that's why.' Meanwhile Ted had recovered himself sufficiently to make Marian a bow. 'That's better,' my companion commented. 'If it wasn't for the difference, what a handsome pair they'd make.'

As though alive to the difference Ted came down from the dais blushing furiously, and once back in his place he turned a frowning, sulky face to the congratulations and sly witticisms of his friends.

I minded his discomfiture and yet I enjoyed it too, for it made the party go, keeping it up, enriching it with the spice of malice. Ted the mountebank was just as popular as Ted the hero, perhaps more so, for prolonged hero-worship puts a strain upon one's vanity. Comic or romantic, the songs that followed were less eventful; mistakes were made which Marian negligently covered up but they were mistakes that did not catch the imagination of the audience, indeed being all on one side they slightly diminished the hilarity of the evening by giving it the air of a music lesson. This, too, had its piquancy for me, for it affirmed the superiority of the Hall, and I was beginning to bask in this and add it to my other sensations, when, in a pause that followed the last song, I heard Lord Trimingham say: 'What about our twelfth man? Can't he give us something? Latest from school and all that. Come on Leo.'

For the second time I was called upon to exchange the immunities of childhood for the responsibilities of the grown-up world. It was like a death but with a resurrection in prospect: the third time it happened, there was none. Even as I left my seat – for it never occurred to me that I could refuse — and felt my mouth going dry, I knew that I should get back to what I had been, just as certainly as, the third time, I knew that I should not. I had no music, but I had a song — Lord Trimingham was right about that. I had several songs. One I had sung at a school concert and it never dawned on me until I reached the platform that I couldn't sing it by myself.

'Well, Leo,' Marian said, 'what is it to be?' She spoke in her ordinary voice, as if there was no one else in the room, and it didn't matter if there was.

Envisaging the walk back to my place, the catastrophic absence of applause, the sense of failure stripping me naked, I said helplessly:

'But I haven't the music.'

She smiled, a starry smile which I still remember, and said:

'Perhaps I can play the accompaniment without. What is it?'

'The Minstrel Boy.'[6]

'My favourite song,' she said. 'How high does it go?'

'To A,' I said, proud of my top note, half afraid she would say she couldn't play it in that key.

She said nothing but took a ring off her finger and rather deliberately laid it on the piano-top. Then she settled herself with a swish of silk that seemed to radiate outwards like a perfume, and played the opening bars.

I suppose I had no reason to be grateful to her for this second deliverance from what I dreaded almost more than anything: looking a fool in public. For the first I had: she had taken a lot of trouble to see that I was properly turned out. For the second it was not her I had to thank, but her gift for music. Yet I think I valued the second intervention even more, for it was not her kindness that had rescued me, but one of her graces. I would not have gone to war for a kindness, perhaps, but for a grace I would, and did. For I had no doubt, as my voice floated upwards, who was going, or why. It was I, and for her. She was my Land of Song. Never did a soldier devote himself to death more wholeheartedly than I did; I looked forward to it intensely, I would not have missed it for the world. As for my harp, I could hardly wait for the moment when I should tear its chords asunder. It should never sound in slavery, I proclaimed: and I can honestly say, it never has.

I knew the song so well that I did not have to think about singing it; my thoughts were free to wander as they pleased; and although, unlike the other singers, who kept their eyes on the music, I turned and faced the audience, I could see Marian's fingers at work, catch the gleam of her white arms and whiter neck, and imagine not one, but a whole series of deaths which I should die for her. Each was quite painless, of course: a crown without a cross.

By the silence in the hall I could tell the song was going down well, but I wasn't prepared for the storm of clapping which, owing to the confined space, had far greater impact and head-turning quality than the applause which had greeted my catch. I didn't know, what I afterwards learned, that far from thinking me a fool for going on to the platform apparently unprovided with the means to sing, the company had taken it as a sporting gesture. Forgetting to bow I stood, while feet stamped and the demands for an encore grew louder. Marian didn't join me; she sat at the piano with her head a little bowed. Once more at a loss, I went to her side, and with some difficulty attracted her attention. I said, unnecessarily:

'They want me to sing again.'

'What else can you sing?' she asked, without looking up.

'Well,' I said, 'I can sing a song called "Angels ever bright and fair,"[7] but it's a sacred song.'

For a moment her sombre face relaxed into a smile; then she said, in her abrupt way, 'I'm afraid I'm no good to you. I don't know the accompaniment to that one.'

The bottom dropped out of my world for I was longing to repeat my triumph, and my emotional temperature was so high that I had no stamina left in me to meet disappointment. But while I was trying to look as if I didn't mind a voice from the audience said, in a strong local accent, 'I think I've got it 'ere,' and the next moment the speaker was on the platform with a tattered, paper-covered volume called, I still remember, 'The Star Folio of Popular Songs'.

'Shall we skip the first bit?' asked Marian, but I begged her to let me sing it.

> *'Oh worse than death, indeed! Lead me, ye guards,*
> *Lead me on to the rack, or to the flames;*
> *I'll thank your gracious mercy.'*

So ran the recitative, concluding with Handel's habitual pom . . . pom. I was proud of being able to sing it for it was in the most uncompromising minor and the intervals were very tricky; also I had enough music in me to know that without it the dulcet air that followed was much less effective. And I liked singing it because the idea of something worse than death had a powerful appeal to my imagination; the Minstrel Boy had gone to his death but the heroine of this song was threatened with something worse than death. What it was, I had no idea, but with my passion for extremes I contemplated it with ecstasy. Besides, it was a woman's song, and I could feel that I was undergoing these harsh experiences not only for Marian, but with her . . . Together we confronted the fate worse than death; together we soared to our apotheosis:

> *Angels! Ever bright and fair,*
> *Take, oh take me to your care.*
> *Speed to your own courts my flight*
> *Clad in robes of virgin white*
> *Clad in robes of virgin white.*

My being was incandescent with a vision of angels, robes, virginity, and whiteness, eternally prolonged; and with the sensation of soaring that the music's slow ascent so powerfully evoked. But none of this, I think, got into my voice, for I regarded singing as a discipline no less than cricket: nothing of what one felt must be betrayed.

Marian stayed at the piano and left me to take the applause alone. But as it grew more insistent she suddenly got up and took my hand and bowed to the audience; and then, disengaging her hand, she turned and dropped me a low curtsey.

I returned to my seat but not at once to my pre-song self: the readjustment was too sudden. I had a feeling that my success (for I couldn't doubt it had been one) had set me a little apart; no one said anything to me until someone asked if I meant to take up singing professionally. I was slightly dashed by this, for singing was an accomplishment not much esteemed at school and now that I had proved my prowess at it I was inclined to belittle it. 'I would rather be a professional cricketer,' I said. 'That's the spirit,' somebody observed; 'Ted had better look out.' Ted did not take this up. Regarding me speculatively he said, 'You took those high notes a treat. A real choirboy couldn't have done it better. You could have heard a pin drop. We might have been in church.'

That was just it; after my religious contribution no one seemed disposed to come forward with a secular song. It was getting late; reaction into the spectator's security made me sleepy. I must have dozed for the next thing I heard was Marian's voice singing 'Home, Sweet Home'.[8] After the musical hazards of the evening, the boss shots, the successes snatched from the jaws of failure, the anxiety for myself and others, it was bliss to listen to that lovely voice extolling the joys of home. I thought of my home, and how I should return to it after pleasures and palaces; and I thought of Marian's and how inappropriate to it the epithet humble was. She sang with so much feeling: did she really long for peace of mind in a thatched cottage? It didn't make sense to me. But I knew there were much grander places than Brandham Hall; perhaps that explained it. She was thinking of some of the bigger houses in the district, where they went visiting. It was only afterwards that I remembered she was singing the song by request.

Alone of those who were asked to, Marian would not give us an encore. The applause that normally brings singer and audience together in her case had the opposite effect; the harder we clapped, the further away from us she seemed. I did not resent this or even regret it; nor, I think, did anyone. She was not of our clay, she was a goddess, and we must not think that by worshipping her we could lower her to our level. If she had said, 'Keep your distance, worms!' I should have rejoiced, and so, I think, would most of us. The day, the evening, had been full to overflowing: nothing had been withheld and perhaps we were never more conscious of the sum of our good luck than when Marian denied this final boon.

'Frog-spawn,' said Marcus as we walked back together, 'you didn't do so badly after all.'

I thought it was decent of him to be pleased with my success, so I said, magnanimously,

'Lor lumme, toadstool, in my place you might have done as well, or better.'

He said reflectively:

'It is true that on certain occasions I should have tried not to look like a sick cow.'

'On what occasions?' I demanded rashly, adding, 'It's better than looking like a stuck pig, any day.'

Marcus ignored this.

'I was thinking of the time when somebody not a million miles from here was knocked down by a cricket ball, and lay on his back with his feet in the air, showing his posterior to all the gaping villagers of Brandham, Brandham-under-Brandham, Brandham-over-Brandham, and Brandham Regis.'

'I didn't, you po-faced, pot-bellied –'

'Yes, you did, and another time was when you were singing the "Minstrel Boy", which is a silly song anyhow, and you rolled your eyes just like a sick cow – you really *did*, Leo, – and you sounded like one, too – a cow that is just going to *be* sick. Oo – er – yar –' he gave a dramatic imitation of what I knew was a physically impossible feat. 'I was sitting with Mama pretending to be a villager – poor dear, she didn't want them on both sides of her – and she was convulsed, and so was I – I shouldn't like to tell you what I nearly did.'

'I can guess, you bed-wetter,' I said. This was an unkind thrust, but I was really put out. 'If you weren't such an infernal invalid, with knees like jelly and arms like sparrow's elbows, I should –'

'Yes, yes,' said Marcus, pacifically, 'you didn't really do so badly. I wasn't as ashamed of you as I expected to be. And you got rid of that brute Burgess, though it was the biggest fluke I ever saw. God, when I saw him at the piano with Marian it made me go all goosy.'

'Why?' I asked.

'Don't ask me, ask Mother. At least don't ask her; she feels like I do about the plebs. Anyhow, we've said good-bye to the village for a year. Did you notice the stink in that hall?'

'No.'

'You didn't?'

'Well, not particularly,' I said, not wanting to seem insensitive. 'I suppose it was a bit whiffy.'

'Phew! Three times I nearly had to cat: I had to hold myself with both hands. You must have a nose like a rhinoceros, and come to think of it, you *have*: the same shape, the same two bumps, and just as scaly. But I suppose you were too busy mooing and rolling your eyes and sucking up the applause. Golly, you did look pleased with yourself.'

I felt I could afford to disregard this.

'And you looked so *pi*, Leo, really dreadfully *pi*. So did everybody, while you were singing that church thing about the angels taking care of you. They all looked as if they were thinking about their dear dead ones, and Burgess looked as if he might be going to blub. Of course it's difficult to know how Trimingham feels because of his face, but he didn't half crack you up to Mama. He'll eat out of your hand now.'

Having allowed me this dewdrop Marcus paused. We were approaching the house – the S.W. prospect, I suppose, since the village lay that side; but I still can't remember what it looked like though I remember how bright the moonlight was. I could hear voices in front of us, but none behind; we had been the last of the party to leave, largely because I lingered to receive further congratulations on my performance, which was partly, no doubt, why Marcus was sore about it, or pretended to be. He peered dramatically into the bushes and waited till we were demonstrably out of earshot.

'Can you keep a secret?' he said, dropping our schoolboy language.

'You know I can,' I answered.

'Yes, but this is very important.'

I gave extreme pledges of secrecy; that I should fall down dead if I betrayed his confidence was one of the least binding.

'Very well, I'll tell you, though Mama made me promise not to tell anyone. But can't you guess?' Marcus was evidently afraid that his revelation might fall flat.

I couldn't.

'Marian's engaged to marry Trimingham – it'll be announced after the ball. Are you glad?'

'Yes,' I said, 'I am. I'm sure I am.'

CHAPTER 14

I remember Sunday morning as a whitish blur, soundless, featureless, and motionless. All my wishes had come true, and I had nothing left to live for. This is usually taken to mean a state of despair, with me it was bliss. Never, even after the downfall of Jenkins and Strode, had I had such a supreme sense of personal triumph. I realized that it was due to extraordinary luck; the ball might have been a few inches higher, no one might have been able to play my songs. But that didn't detract from my achievement; luck was in love with me, like everyone else. I stood so high in my own regard that I was beyond the need for self-assertion, for putting myself across. I was I. It was thanks to me that we had won the cricket match; thanks to me that the concert had been the success it was. These were facts which could not be gainsaid.

A more partial triumph might have made me cocky as Marcus thought I should be; but mine was too undeniable, too absolute. It moved me to awe and wonder, almost to worship. At last I was free from all my imperfections and limitations; I belonged to another world, the celestial world. I was one with my dream life. Of this I needed no confirmation from anyone; and when at breakfast I was again congratulated on my achievements, it had no more effect than more fuel under a kettle already boiling.

But it was not only for myself that I was triumphant. Marcus's disclosure had crowned my happiness anew. Of outside influences, Marian's favour had been the Jacob's ladder of my ascent;[1] had the balance of my feelings for her been disturbed by a harsh look, I should have fallen, like Icarus.[2] And now she was just where I wanted her: united to Lord Trimingham, my other idol. Though I was not worldly, I got some extra satisfaction from the suitability of the match.

These were high matters which appealed to my imagination. But they also affected my daily life, or would affect it. I took it for granted that my rôle of postman would now cease.

I was glad of this for several reasons. I still did not see how my secret missions could be combined with Marcus's return to normal life. They had excited me and become a habit with me and before the cricket match I hadn't really wanted to abandon them. The current of my endeavour flowed in them; I was most myself when I was carrying them out. I liked the secrecy and the conspiracy and the risk. And I liked Ted Burgess in a reluctant, half-admiring, half-hating way. When I was away from him I could think of him objectively as a working farmer whom no one at the Hall thought much of. But when I was with him his mere physical presence cast a spell on me, it established an ascendancy which I could not break. He was, I felt, what a man ought to be, what I should like to be when I grew up. At the same time I was jealous of him, jealous of his power over Marian, little as I understood its nature, jealous of whatever it was he had that I had not. He came between me and my image of her. In my thoughts I wanted to humiliate him, and sometimes did. But I also identified myself with him, so that I could not think of his discomfiture without pain, I could not hurt him without hurting myself. He fitted into my imaginative life, he was my companion of the greenwood, a rival, an ally, an enemy, a friend – I couldn't be sure which. And yet on Sunday morning he had ceased to be an unresolved discord and become part of the general harmony.

At the time I did not wonder why; I was content to accept the peace that my thoughts offered me. But now I do wonder and I think I know. I had disposed of him. Twice I had overcome him in fair fight. Of what use were the fours and sixes of this village Jessop[3] when I had caught him out and snatched victory from him? My catch would be remembered when his sparkling innings was forgotten. And in the same way I had eclipsed him at the concert. His songs of love had moved me and brought him plenty of applause; but it was applause mixed with laughter, for a personal not a musical success; they clapped him for his hesitations and mistakes, as well as for the rough charm of his singing, they clapped him as they might have clapped him on the back. And what a figure he had cut on the platform, with his red face, his board-stiff suit, and his strength turned to heaviness. Whereas I, with my songs of death, my high, pure, Church music, had captured the admiration as well as the emotions of the audience. From the human plane of badinage and teasing, of jollity and good fellowship, I had transported them to the region of the angels. I had given them real music, purged of human frailty, not a knock-about turn; and Marian had set her seal on this, she had left her throne and taken my hand and curtsied to me. If the Cricket Concert of 1900 was remembered, it would be remembered for my songs – my songs of death, not for his songs of love. I had killed him, he was dead, and that was why I no longer felt him as a discordant element in my orchestra.

I remember how on that enchanted morning, one of the servants, no longer a companion-in-arms but shrunk to his former status, came up to me and said, 'You saved the situation for us, Master Leo. We should have been done for if you hadn't caught him. Of course his Lordship took the wicket in a manner of speaking, but it was you really. And we didn't half enjoy your songs.'

Now the thought of the farmyard had lost its magic for me: it was as dead as a hobby that one has grown out of. I had never really relished its strong smells or the feeling that some dangerous animal might get loose and turn on me. As for the straw-stack, I had tasted to satiety every experience it had to offer, and I now thought, as Marcus did, that straw-stack sliding was a puerile occupation, unworthy of a fully-fledged private schoolboy. I was, in fact, a little ashamed of it. I was looking forward to taking up my old life with Marcus, to renewing our talks and jokes and to furbishing up our private language. I thought of some new juicy insults to try out on him.

So sure was I that Marian would have no more messages for me to carry that I did not dream of asking her. Indeed I thought it would be tactless to ask her, just as it was tactless to ask one's schoolfellows if they had been doing something that one knew they had given up. It would be a mistake to mention it to her. The whole thing was done with. Totally ignorant as I was of love affairs, and little as I knew about their conventions, I felt sure that when a girl was engaged to a man she did not write letters to another man calling him 'darling'. She might do it until the day of the engagement, but not after. It was automatic; it was a rule; like leaving the wicket at cricket when you were out; and it scarcely crossed my mind that to comply with it might be painful. I had plenty of experience of *force majeure*[4] and I only rebelled against it when it was manifestly unjust. Private injustice was the lot of schoolboys, as witness Jenkins and Strode, but grown-up people were exempt from it, for who was there to be unjust to them?

It no longer seemed to me that my life would be the poorer for the cessation of my secret traffic between the Hall and the farm. My feeling for Marian was possessive only when Ted entered into it, and Ted was now eliminated. I didn't seriously regard Lord Trimingham as a rival: he was on a higher plane, the plane of imagination. I sincerely wanted Marian's happiness, both for her sake and mine; my happiness would be crowned by hers. I thought of happiness as following naturally on the attainment of some aim, like winning a cricket match. You got what you wanted and were happy: it was quite simple. Who could not want to get Lord Trimingham? — and by getting him, so Marcus told me, Marian would also get his house. Married to her he could afford to live there. The trail of gold followed her, too.

All this was eminently satisfactory as a subject of contemplation, and I thought about it, almost with rapture, when I was not thinking about myself and my own achievements. I had an overwhelming desire to tell my mother about it, and in the space between breakfast and starting for church I wrote her a long letter, in which I represented Marian and myself as living on twin pinnacles of glory. I also told her that Marian had asked me to stay another week. Mrs Maudsley had confirmed the invitation in her after-breakfast orderly-room: she said a great many sweet things to me. Among them was a compliment that I specially treasured: she was glad that Marcus had found such a nice friend. I told my mother this, and added, 'Please let me stay if you're not too lonly without me, I have never been happier than I am now except with you.'

I posted the letter in the hall letterbox and was relieved to see some letters showing through the glass door. I had a morbid fear that they might have already been collected, though the post did not go until the afternoon.

Waiting for the other church-goers to assemble, I wondered how I should spend the afternoon, and my thoughts, as to some very distant object, flew to Ted. He had promised to tell me something, what was it? I remembered: he was going to tell me all about spooning, and at the time I had been very eager to hear. Now I was much less eager, hardly eager at all. But perhaps some time, not this afternoon, I would let him tell me; I had fifteen more days at Brandham and it would be only polite to go and say good-bye to him.

One thing more was added to me before I left for church. Though there were clouds about, the temperature, I knew, was rising: the weather hadn't broken after all.

Again I was lucky with the Psalms; the Sunday before there had been forty-four verses; this Sunday there were forty-three,[5] seven below the danger-line. Truly Providence was on my side. Also I knew we should not have the Litany, as we had had it last Sunday: this also was a great gain. Less than ever was I in a mood to repent of my sins or to feel that other people should repent of theirs. I could not find a flaw in the universe and was impatient with Christianity for bringing imperfection to my notice, so I closed my ears to its message and chose as a subject of meditation the annals of the Trimingham family emblazoned on the transept wall. I had a special interest in it now that Marian was to be admitted to its ranks; she would be a Viscountess, Marcus had told me; and for the first time I noticed that wives were included in the mural tablets: hitherto I had thought of the family as an entirely masculine phenomenon. It did not say, however, that they were Viscountesses: Caroline his wife . . . – Mabelle his wife . . . – what an affected way of spelling Mabel! The next moment it seemed pretty and aristocratic, such was the Trimingham spell. 'Marian his wife' – but I would not let myself think of that: to me they were both immortal. Immortal – the word had a lovely quality which gave new lustre to my reverie. Why should the race of Triminghams ever die out? My excitement mounting I thought of the ninety-ninth Viscount, then the hundredth, and tried to calculate in what century he would occur. The thought of their unbroken line, stretching down the ages, moved me deeply. And yet, I told myself, it *has* been broken; there is no memorial to the fifth Viscount. My mind disliked the lacuna and tried to by-pass it. At last, by dint of persuading myself that the missing memorial must be in another part of the building, I managed to regain my altitude.[6] The solemn atmosphere of church reinforced the sufficiency of earthly glory; in a mystical union of genealogy and mathematics, the time flashed by.

Again Lord Trimingham was the last to leave. I thought that Marian would wait for him, but she didn't, so I did. Most of my shyness with him had worn off, and I was disposed to think that everything I did or said became me. But I did not want to broach at once the subject that was uppermost in my mind.

'Hullo, Mercury,' he said.

'Can I take a message for you?' I asked, too tactful (and I was proud of this) to suggest the name of the recipient.

'No, thank you,' he replied, and I noticed the contentment in his tone. 'It's very good of you to offer to, but I don't think I shall have many more messages to send.'

It was on the tip of my tongue to ask why not, but I thought I knew and said instead, less tactfully,

'She hasn't left her prayer-book behind *this* time?'

'No; but did you ever know such a scatter-brained girl?' he said, as if to be scatter-brained was something to be intensely proud of, and as if I must know any number of girls who were.

I said I did not, and hoping to draw him out and at the same time, perhaps, to collect a compliment for myself I added:

'Doesn't she play the piano well?'

'Yes, and don't you sing well?' he answered, taking the bait at once.

Delighted with the success of my ruse I cut a few capers, after which it seemed quite easy to ask:

'Why is there no fifth Viscount?'

'No fifth Viscount?' he echoed. 'What do you mean? There are plenty of fifth Viscounts.'

'Oh, I expect there are,' I answered airily, not wishing to seem ignorant of the peerage. 'But I meant in the church. There isn't a fifth of your Viscounts, not a fifth Viscount Trimingham.'

'Oh, I see,' he said. 'I didn't know you meant him. I'd forgotten which number he was. But yes, there was one.' He was silent.

'But why isn't he there?' I insisted.

'Well, you see,' said Lord Trimingham, 'it was rather a sad story. He was killed.'

'Oh,' I exclaimed, agreeably titillated, for this was more than I had hoped for. 'In battle, I expect.' I remembered how many of the Viscounts had served in the forces.

'No,' he said, 'not in battle.'

'In an accident?' I promoted, 'climbing a mountain perhaps? or rescuing somebody?'

'No,' he answered, 'it wasn't really an accident.'

I could see he didn't want to tell me, and a week ago I should have stopped probing him. But now, on the crest of my wave, I felt I could afford to go on.

'What was it?'

'If you really want to know,' Lord Trimingham said, 'he was killed in a duel.'

'Oh, what *fun*!' I cried, astonished that he didn't want to discuss this ancestor, who now seemed to me the most interesting of the Triminghams. 'What had he done? Was it to avenge his honour?'

'Well yes, in a way,' Lord Trimingham admitted.

'Had someone insulted him? You know, called him a coward or a liar? – Of course, I know he wasn't,' I added hastily, fearful of seeming to associate myself with the insult.

'Well no, they hadn't,' Lord Trimingham said. 'He fought the duel about somebody else.'

'Who?'

'A lady. His wife, as a matter of fact.'

'Oh.' My disappointment was almost as bitter as when I realized what the messages I had been carrying between Ted and Marian were about. But Marcus had told me that only an outsider spoke of a woman as a lady. It was one of his shibboleths. Now I could tell him that Lord Trimingham did, which was something. Trying to sound interested I said:

'The Viscountess?'

'Yes.'

'I didn't know,' I said, my voice dull and heavy, 'that people fought duels about ladies.'

'Well, they did.'

'But what had she done?' I didn't much care, but it was only polite to ask.

'He thought she was too friendly with another man,' said Lord Trimingham, shortly.

I had an inspiration.

'He was jealous?'

'Yes. It happened in France. He challenged the man to a duel, and the man shot him.'

I was struck by the unfairness of this, and said so. 'It ought to have been the other way round.'

'Yes, he was unlucky,' Lord Trimingham said. 'So they buried him in France, away from his own people.'

'Did the Viscountess marry the other man?'

'No, but she lived abroad, and the children came to live in England, all except the youngest, who stayed with her in France.'

'Was he her favourite?' With the egotism of my sex, I assumed that the child was a boy.

'Yes, I suppose so.'

I was glad to have had the explanation, and unsatisfactory as it was to my sensation-loving mind, I was impressed by his unsensational way of telling it. Something of the sadness of human life came through to me, its indifference to our wishes, even to the wish that calamity should be more colourful than it is. The ideas of acceptance and resignation were hard for me to entertain: I thought that emotions should be more dramatic than the facts that caused them.

'If she hadn't been the Viscountess would he have minded so much?' I asked at length.

He laughed in a puzzled way.

'I don't imagine that the fact of her having a title made any difference. He gave it to her, he couldn't feel snobbish about it.'

'Oh, I didn't mean that,' I exclaimed, realizing that my delicacy in not wanting to describe a Viscountess as a mere wife had led to confusion. 'What I meant was, would he have minded so much her having another . . . friend, if he hadn't been married to her but just engaged?'

Lord Trimingham thought this over.

'Yes, quite as much, I should think.'

As I ruminated on his answer, it slid into my mind, for the first time, that there was a parallel between the fifth Viscount's situation and his own. I dismissed the idea at once, so sure was I that Marian had given up being too friendly with Ted. But it affected my imagination and I said, for anger always interested me:

'Was he angry with her too?'

'I don't think so,' Lord Trimingham answered. 'More upset.'

'She hadn't done anything wicked?'

'Well, she'd been a bit unwise.'

'But wasn't it her fault as well as the man's?'

'Nothing is ever a lady's fault; you'll learn that,' Lord Trimingham told me.

This remark, confirming something I already felt, made an immense impression on me.

'Was the man a very wicked man?' I asked. I didn't much believe in wickedness, but the word thrilled me.

'He was a good-looking blackguard, I believe,' Lord Trimingham said, 'and it wasn't the first time . . .' He broke off. 'He was a Frenchman,' he added.

'Oh, a Frenchman,' I said, as if that explained everything.

'Yes, and a good shot, by all accounts. I don't suppose he was a specially wicked man, judged by the standards of his time.'

'But now would he be?' I was determined to find wickedness somewhere.

'Yes, now it would be murder, at least in England.'

'But it wouldn't be murder if the fifth Viscount had shot him instead, would it?' I asked.

'It would be now,' Lord Trimingham said.

'That doesn't seem very fair,' I observed. I tried to picture the scene as I had read about it in books: the coffee and pistols for two in the early morning, the lonely place, the seconds measuring out the distance, the dropped handkerchief, the shots, the fall.

'Did he — the fifth Viscount — bleed very much?' I asked.

'History doesn't relate. I shouldn't think so. A bullet wound doesn't bleed very much, unless it hits an artery or a vein . . . Duelling's been abolished in England, and a good thing, too.'

'But men still shoot each other, don't they?' I asked hopefully.

'They shot me,' he answered, with what I took to be a smile.

'Yes, but that was in a war. Do they still shoot each other over ladies?' I imagined a carpet of prostrate women, over whom shots rang out.

'Sometimes.'

'And it's murder?'

'In England, yes.'

I felt that this was as it should be; and then, anxious to have his opinion on a question that had long exercised me, I said:

'The Boers break the rules of war, don't they?' My father had bequeathed his pacifism to me, but Lord Trimingham, the war-hero, had shaken it.

'The Boer's not a bad feller,' said Lord Trimingham tolerantly. 'I don't dislike him personally. It's a pity we have to shoot so many of them but there you are. Hullo,' he added, as if surprised at a sudden discovery. 'We've caught Marian up. Shall we go and talk to her?'

CHAPTER 15

All through luncheon fragments of my conversation with Lord Trimingham kept coming back to me. Two things stood out: one was that whatever happened it was never a lady's fault, and the other, that it might be necessary to kill someone although you didn't really dislike him. These were new ideas to me and their magnanimity appealed to me very much.

At the longed-for moment when our elders ceased eating their peaches and began to look about them instead of showing off to each other (grown-up conversation always seemed to me a form of showing off) I caught Marcus's eye and we did our usual bunk. Hardly were we out of earshot, however, when Marcus said:

'I'm afraid I can't come with you this afternoon.'

'Why ever not, you sewer-rat?' I demanded, acutely disappointed.

'Well, it's like this. Nannie Robson, our old Nannie, lives in the village and she isn't very well and Marian said would I go and spend the afternoon with her. What good I shall do her I don't know, and zounds, man, how her house smells! Enough to raise the roof. But I suppose I must go. Marian said she was going herself after tea. Cripes, partner, you can think yourself lucky not to have a sister.'

Still trying to control my disappointment I said:

'Shall you tell Nannie Robson about the engagement?'

'Good lord, no. It would be all round the village if I did. And don't you tell anyone, either. I shall chop you up into the teeniest weeniest little pieces if you do.'

I retorted suitably.

'Now what will you do?' asked Marcus languidly. 'How will you occupy your silly self? Towards what destination will you drag your evil-smelling carcase? Not to that bally old straw-stack?'

'Oh no,' I said. 'I've said good-bye to that. I might hang round the rubbish-heap awhile and then —'

'Well, don't get carted away by mistake,' Marcus said. I was angry with myself for giving such an easy score, and we had a slight tussle before parting.

After more than a week of neglect the rubbish-heap had suddenly regained its fascination for me. I liked pottering about on its malodorous confines, scanning its surfaces and probing its depths for the accidentally discarded treasures which, someone had assured me, many if not most dustmen came across during their rounds, enabling them to retire on fortunes. But first I bent my steps to the game-larder. Although I felt a little lonely, my exaltation of the morning had not worn off; it gave an upward impetus to all my thoughts, as the sun did to the gossamers; and as usual I cast about in my mind for a subject of contemplation which would raise them still higher. Some of these, I knew, would lose their power because I could only think of them in a limited number of ways; even my catch, even my song, had, I suspected, yielded me all the ecstasy they could. My memory and imagination would add nothing to them. But I was always finding new facets to Marian, and here was one ready for my use: her kindness to her old nurse. My mother used to read to me from a book called *Ministering Children*[1] in which two high-born young ladies – Anne Clifford and Lady Gertrude were their names, I think – did acts of charity and rescue-work among the needy villagers. To these my imagination added a third, Marian, and I began to fit her into the story, making her, I need hardly say, the most outstanding of the trio for beauty as well as for good works.

Eighty point nine, said the thermometer. This was an advance of nearly three degrees on yesterday, but I felt that the sun could do still better, give us a greater grilling, and it turned out I was right.

My thoughts swung back. To give Marian social precedence over Lady Gertrude I had cheated: I anticipated her marriage. 'Last but not least on a grey palfrey came the Viscountess Trimingham (ninth of her line), and she, too, dismounted at the door of the humble cottage, carrying a bowl of steaming soup' – I was going to say, but just as I was wondering how she could carry it on horseback, for my imaginings, which would swallow a camel, sometimes also strained at a gnat – I heard a voice behind me that made me jump.

'Hullo, Leo! Just the man I was looking for' – and there she was, in every other way so like my vision of her that it almost surprised me she was not carrying something – but she was: I saw it now, a letter.

'Will you do something for me?' she said.

'Oh yes. What shall I do?'

'Just take this letter.'

It shows how little thought I had of Ted in connexion with her that I said,

'Who to?'

'Who to? Why, to the farm, you silly,' she answered, half laughing, half impatient.

The scaffolding of my life seemed to collapse: I was dumbfounded.

Many thoughts besieged my mind but only one found lodging, and it was overwhelming: Marian was engaged to Lord Trimingham but she hadn't given up her relationship with Ted, she was still being friendly with another man. What that meant I had no idea but I knew what it might lead to: murder. The dread word shook me to my foundations, I had no defence against it; and almost without thinking I cried out:

'Oh, I can't.'

'You can't?' she echoed, mystified. 'Why not?'

I have been asked difficult questions in my life, but only one that has given me more trouble to answer. In a flash I saw the betrayals it would involve, if I were to give my reasons. The iron curtain of secrecy, which it was my deepest instinct to keep intact, would be riddled with holes. I should not have answered at all, I should have left her without answering, had not a stronger dread – the dread of something terrible happening – forced me to speak.

'It's because of Hugh.'

'Because of me?' she repeated. A smile softened her lips and she opened her blue eyes very wide.

I remembered closing mine, screwing them up. If I had had the quickness of mind to accept her interpretation of the name, this story might have ended differently, but my one concern, the one channel in which my will-power flowed, was to get his name out; and the trivial but maddening circumstance of her misunderstanding it confused me still further.

'No, not you,' I said. 'Hugh.' I tried to hoot it, whistle it as she did. Marian's brow darkened.

'Hugh?' she said. 'What has Hugh to do with it?'

I gave her a despairing look: I had a wild notion of running round to the other side of the game-larder, putting it between us. But I had to stand my ground: people didn't literally run away from questions. Remembering a word Lord Trimingham had used, I muttered:

'He might be upset.'

At that her eyes blazed. She came a step forward and stood over me, her nose hawk-like, her body curved to pounce.

'What has he got to do with it?' she repeated. 'I told you, this is a business matter between me and . . . and Mr Burgess. It has nothing to do with anyone else, no one else in the world. Do you understand, or are you too stupid?'

I stared at her in terror.

'You come into this house, our guest,' she stormed, 'we take you in, we know nothing about you, we make a great fuss of you – I suppose you wouldn't deny that? – I know I have – and then I ask you to do a simple thing which a child in the street that I'd never spoken to would do for the asking – and you have the infernal cheek to say you won't! We've spoilt you. I'll never ask you to do anything for me again, never! I won't speak to you again!'

I made some gesture with my hands to try to stop her – to push her away from me or to bring her closer – but she almost struck out at me in her fury: I thought – and it was a moment of relief – that she was actually going to hit me.

All at once her manner changed; she seemed to freeze.

'You want paying, that's what you want,' she said quietly, 'I know.' She produced her purse from somewhere and opened it. 'How much do you want, you little Shylock?'[2]

But I had had enough: I snatched the letter which she still held crumpled in her hand, and ran away from her as fast as I could.

For a time no thoughts would come to me, I was so blasted by her anger. Then I began to realize, beyond the immediate ache and smart, how much, in losing Marian's friendship, I had lost: it seemed to me that I had lost everything that I valued, and this cut even deeper than her cruel words.

I was not a hypersensitive child. I was used to people being angry with me and made it a point of honour not to mind. I had been called far worse names than Marian had called me, and by people who, I believed, liked me, without turning a hair. I was myself no mean master of invective. Of all the insults she had heaped on me the one that hurt me most was 'Shylock', because I didn't know what it meant and therefore couldn't deny it. I didn't know if it was personal, like the smell that schoolboys are, or were, so apt to attribute to each other, or moral. The suspicion that everybody was going about saying I was a Shylock and disliked and despised me for it added to my wretchedness.

But if in the realm of experience I was fairly tough, in the realm of the imagination I was not. Marian inhabited that realm, she was indeed its chiefest ornament, the Virgin of the Zodiac;[3] she was as real to my contemplation as she was to my experience – more real. Until I came to Brandham Hall the world of my imagination had been peopled by fictitious beings who behaved as I wanted them to behave; at Brandham Hall it was inhabited by real people who had the freedom of both worlds; in the flesh they could give my imagination what it needed and in my solitary musings I endowed them with certain magical qualities but did not otherwise idealize them. I did not need to. Marian was many things to me besides Maid Marian of the green-wood. She was a fairy princess who had taken a fancy to a little boy, clothed him, petted him, turned him from a laughing stock into an accepted member of her society, from an ugly duckling into a swan. With one wave of her wand she had transformed him, at the cricket concert, from the youngest and most insignificant person present to a spell-binder who had held them all in thrall. The transfigured Leo of the last twenty-four hours was her creation; and she had created him, I felt, because she loved him.

And now, again like an enchantress, she had taken it all away and I was back where I had started from – no, much lower. She had taken it away, not so much by her anger and harsh words – those, on the plane of experience, I knew how to make allowances for – as by the complete withdrawal of her favour. As the distance increased between us my alarm diminished but my heart grew heavier.

For I saw – it was relentlessly borne in upon me – that everything she had done for me had been done with an ulterior motive. She hadn't been fond of me at all. She had pretended to be fond of me so that she could inveigle me into taking messages between her and Ted Burgess. It was all a put-up job.

As this realization sank into me I stopped running and began to cry. I had not been so long at school that I had lost the power of crying; I cried a good deal and felt calmer for it. A sense of my whereabouts returned to me: I noticed for the first time where I was – on the causeway leading to the sluice.

On the platform of the sluice I paused, out of habit. No one was at work; I had forgotten it was Sunday. I should have to go on to the farm. At once I was seized with an almost invincible reluctance: I'll go no further, I thought, I'll creep back to the house and lock myself in my bedroom and perhaps they will leave some food outside the door and I shan't have to see anyone. I looked down at the water. It had sunk much lower. The surface of the pool was still blue, but many more boulders than before showed ghostly, corpse-like, at the bottom. And on the other side, the shallow side, the change was greater. Before, it had been untidy, now it was a scene of mad disorder: a tangled mass of water-weeds, all high and dry, and, sticking out from them, mounds of yellow gravel, like bald patches on a head. The clusters of round, thin, grey-green rushes, whose tufted tops had made me think of an army of spearmen with pennons, were now much taller than a man; and for a yard or more above the water-line they were coated with a grey deposit – mud. But many had fallen over, let down by their native element, back-broken under their own weight; they lay pointing this way and that, all discipline gone. The army of spearmen had been routed.[4] Their companions in arms, the grass-green reeds that tapered to a point like swords, had escaped the blight and kept their colour; but they too were bent and broken.

As I stood watching, trying to remember what the river looked like before this happened to it, and in my agitation lifting first one foot and then the other, like a restive horse, I heard the letter crackle and knew I must go on.

All the way across the fields instances of Marian's duplicity kept pricking me, each with its separate sting. In my black mood I persuaded myself that every kindness she had done me, including the present of the green suit, had had the same end in view. She had got me out of going on the family's afternoon expeditions on the pretext that they bored me, whereas she really wanted to have me free for the message business; she had invited me to stay an extra week for the same reason, and not because she wanted me or thought that Marcus did; for the same reason, this very afternoon, she had got rid of Marcus: it was not to do his old nurse a kindness. Everything, it seemed, fell into place. I even believed that but for Ted she would not have played my accompaniments at the concert, or taken my hand or curtsied to me.

My tears flowed afresh and yet I could not bring myself to hate her or even to think badly of her, for that would have increased my wretchedness. 'Nothing is ever a lady's fault,' Lord Trimingham had said, and to this comforting maxim I clung. But it must be somebody's fault: it must be Ted's.

The burden of my mission grew heavier, but when I reached the cart track that climbed the hillside to the farm I accidentally found a way to lighten it. My foot struck a stone; the stone rolled; and I began to kick it, running to and fro across the rutted surface. It became a kind of game, to kick the stone before it stopped, or fell into a rut, and to find it when it got lost in the grass verges – no easy task for they were as brown as it was. Doing this I got very hot, the stone hurt my toes and took the polish off my treasured shoes; but this was a relief to me, and I half hoped I should injure myself too much to go on. And I had a curious experience, almost an illusion, as though a part of me was stationed far away, behind me, perhaps in the belt of trees beyond the river; and from there I could see myself, a bent figure, no bigger than a beetle, weaving to and fro across the ribbon of road. Perhaps it was the part of me that would not take the letter. This dual vision remained with me, dividing me from myself, until I reached the farmyard gate.

I had let myself go on crying because it didn't matter when nobody could see me, and I thought I could stop whenever I liked. But I found that though I could check the tears, I couldn't control the sobbing, also I was out of breath from running, which made it worse. So I hung about by the gate, thinking that Ted might come out and see me. Then I would hand him the letter and run off without speaking to him.

But he didn't come, and I must try to find him. It didn't occur to me that I should go back without delivering the letter, my state of mind didn't affect that obligation. So I crossed the stackyard and knocked at the kitchen door. There was no answer and I went in.

He was sitting on a chair behind the table with a gun between his knees, so absorbed that he didn't hear me. The muzzle was just below his mouth, the barrel was pressed against his naked chest, and he was peering down it. He heard me and jumped up.

'Why,' he said, 'it's the postman!'

He stood the gun against the table and came across to me, with a swish of the brown corduroy trousers that he wore in the hottest weather. Seeing the hesitations and reservations in my face he said, 'I oughtn't to be like this when callers come, but I was that hot. Do you mind? Shall I put a shirt on? There are no ladies present.'

One of the ways he had of winning me was by deferring to me.

'N-no,' I began to say, but a hiccup interrupted the word.

He looked at me closely, much as he had looked down the barrel of his gun.

'Why, you've been crying!' he said. 'You oughtn't to be crying at your age.' I couldn't tell if he meant I was too old or too young to cry. 'Now what's the matter? Somebody's been upsetting you – a woman, I shouldn't wonder.'

At that I began to cry again, whereupon he whipped a handkerchief out of his pocket and before I could protest began to wipe my eyes. Oddly enough I didn't mind him doing this; I had an instinct that, unlike the people of my own class, he wouldn't think the worse of me for crying.

My tears had ceased to flow and I felt calmer. 'Now what can we do to cheer you up?' he said. 'Would you like to see Smiler and her foal?'

'N-no, thank you.'

'Would you like to slide down the stack? I've put some more straw under the drop.'

'No, thank you.'

He looked round the room, evidently trying to think of something else that might distract me. 'Would you like to take my gun outside and let it off?' he asked persuasively. 'I was just going to clean it, but I can do that afterwards.'

I shook my head. I wouldn't fall in with anything he proposed.

'Why not?' he said. 'You've got to start some time. It kicks but it wouldn't hurt you half as much as that catch you held. Ah, that was a beauty, that was. I haven't forgiven you yet.'

At the reference to my catch something gave in me and I felt more myself.

'Well, would you like to come out and see me shoot something?' he suggested, as if my salvation lay in shooting. 'There's some old rooks⁵ round here that could do with a peppering.'

I couldn't go on saying no, and followed him out into the stackyard. For some reason I imagined that shooting was a long business, a matter of patient waiting for some psychological moment, but no sooner were we outside the door than the gun went to his shoulder.

The bang took me completely by surprise. It frightened me out of my wits, which was perhaps the best thing that could have happened to me. Half dazed I watched the bird twirl slowly down to earth a few yards from us. 'Well, that's the end of him,' said Ted, and taking it by the claws, he so alive, the bird so dead, he threw it into a bed of nettles. Overhead sounded a flurried, indignant outcry. I looked up: the rooks were wheeling about the sky, growing more distant every moment. 'They won't come back in a hurry,' Ted remarked. 'They're artful, they are. I was lucky to get that one.'

'Do you ever miss?' I asked.

'Good Lord, yes, but I'm a pretty good shot, though I say it. Now, would you like to see me clean the gun?'

No one is quite the same after a loud bang as before it: I went back into the kitchen a different person. My grief had changed to sulkiness and self-pity, a sure sign of recovery. The deed of blood had somehow sealed a covenant between us, drawn us together by some ancient, sacrificial rite.

'Now you take this cleaning-rod,' he said, 'and this bit of four-by-two' – picking up a piece of frayed, white, oily rag – 'and you thread it through the eye of this cleaning-rod, same as you would a needle.' Screwing his eyes up, for the kitchen was not well lighted, he suited the action to the word. The slightest movement brought into play the muscles of his forearms; they moved in ridges and hollows from a knot above his elbow, like pistons working from a cylinder. 'And then you press it down the breech, like this, and you'll be surprised how dirty it comes out.' He pushed the wire rod up and down several times. 'There, didn't I say it would be dirty?' he exclaimed, triumphantly showing me the rag, which was filthy enough to satisfy one's extremest expectations. 'But the barrel'll be quite clean now, you look – and then look through the other which I haven't cleaned. That'll show you.' He spoke as if I had denied there would be a difference. Taking the gun to the window he made me look through it. He held it level with one hand; I could hardly hold it with two, resting the other under the barrel. But I got a strange thrill from the contact, from feeling the butt press against my shoulder and the steel cold against my palm.

'Put your head lower if you can,' he said, 'and get the sight between the barrels: then you can think you're taking a real shot.'

I did so, and the sense of power was intensified. I devoted to destruction several objects that I could see through the kitchen window, then slowly swung the muzzle round, picking out things I might blow to pieces in the room itself, until at last it pointed straight at Ted.

'Hi, you mustn't do that,' he said, 'that's against the rules. Never point a gun at anybody, even when it isn't loaded.'

Already feeling almost a murderer, I hastily handed the gun back to him.

'Now I'll just clean the other barrel,' he said, 'and then I'll make you a nice cup of tea.'

Should I accept his offer? Tea would be waiting for me at Brandham Hall . . . I saw his cricket bat standing in a corner, and to gain time I said:

'You ought to oil your bat, too.'

It was rather pleasant to give instructions after receiving so many.

'Thanks for reminding me. I shall want it again on Saturday.'

'May I oil it for you?' I asked.

'Of course you can. It's an old one, but it does drive. Yesterday was my top score. I don't suppose I'll ever make another fifty.'

'Why not?'

'Not if you're about.'

I laughed at this.

'Lord Trimingham gave me the ball to keep,' I said, wondering if he would turn pale at the name; but he only said, 'I'll put the kettle on in the scullery. It's too hot for a fire here. I'll get the linseed oil.'

I handled the bat as reverently as if it had been the bow of Ulysses,[6] and wondered which of the bruises on its much-scarred surface had been caused by the stroke I caught him off. The oil came in an alien container: 'Price's Cycle Axle Oil' was printed on the tin, and there was a picture of a lady and a gentleman bicycling gaily along a country road, looking at me and at the future with surprised but pleased and confident expressions.

I poured a little oil on to the middle of the bat and began to work it in gently with my fingers; the wood seemed to drink it thirstily and gratefully, as if it too was suffering from the drought. The rhythmic rubbing half soothed and half excited me; it seemed to have a ritual significance, as if I was rubbing out my own bruises, as if the new strength I was putting into the bat would pass into its owner. I was thinking more normally now: I belonged to the present, not to a ruined past and a menacing future. Or so I felt.

Suddenly he came in and said:

'Have you a letter for me, postman?'

I gave it to him. I had forgotten it.

'It looks as if you had been sleeping on it,' he said, and took it with him into the scullery. He came back with a tablecloth and some tea-things.

'I'm on my own today,' he said, 'my daily woman doesn't come on Sundays.'

'Oh, do you have a woman every day?' I asked politely, though not perhaps without an oblique reference to the many servants at Brandham Hall.

He shot me a quick look and said, 'No, I told you she doesn't come on Sundays, and only in the morning on Saturdays.'

I don't know what made me think of Marian, but I did. Suddenly I felt I could not stay to tea, I must get back to face the music, which I now felt more able to do.

'Have you any message for her?' I asked.

'Yes,' he replied, 'but do you want to take it?'

I was totally unprepared for this question, and felt the tears coming back.

'Not very much,' I said, 'but if I don't she'll be so angry.'

It was out. I hadn't meant to say it, but the surprise of having my wishes consulted weakened me.

'So it was her,' he said, and lit a cigarette, the first I'd ever seen him smoke. I don't know what he had meant to say but what he said was: ''Tisn't fair to ask you to do it for nothing. What can I do to make it worth your while?'

'Nothing,' I ought to have answered, and 'nothing' is what I should have answered, half an hour before. But since then many impressions had overlaid my mind, already tired and strained by too much emotion. Ted had once more imposed himself on me with his gun, his cricket bat, his self-sufficiency, his panoply of masculine endowments and accomplishments. The fact that he did not seem to be angry with me gave me nothing to resist. Like many uneducated people he was readier than the educated to talk to a child on equal terms; his age was a physical but not a conversational barrier.

With the wish to please him some of my old relish for my mission returned; the case against it seemed far away and much less cogent. Instead of saying 'nothing' I temporized; I did not reject his bribe as I had Marian's money. Besides, I remembered something.

'The last time I was here,' I said accusingly, 'you said you'd tell me something.'

'Did I?'

'Yes, you said you'd tell me all about spooning. That's partly why I came.' This was not true; I had come because Marian made me; but it served for an argument.

'So I did, so I did,' he said. 'I'm just going to get some tea-cups,' he added, and presently returned with them. I can see the tea-cups now. They were deep and cream-coloured, with a plain gold line round the outside and inside at the bottom, worn by much stirring, a gold flower. I thought them rather common-looking.

It was odd to see a man laying the table, though of course the footman did it at the Hall.

Ted cleared his throat and said:

'I did enjoy your singing at the concert.'

'I enjoyed yours too,' I said.

'Oh, mine was nothing. I've had no lessons, I just open my mouth and out it comes. I made a pretty good fool of myself, really. But you sang just like – well, like a lark.'

'Oh well,' I said lightly, 'I practised those songs at school. We've quite a good teacher. He's an LRAM.'[7]

'I never had much schooling,' Ted said, 'but when I was a nipper, hardly bigger than you' (his using me as a standard of smallness came as a shock to me) 'Mother took me one Christmas to hear the carol-singing in Norwich Cathedral, and there was a lad there with a voice just like yours. I've never forgotten it.'

Gratified as I was by the comparison, I sensed that he was putting me off: it was a trick all grown-ups had.

'Thank you very much,' I said, 'but you said you were going to tell me about spooning.'

'So I did, so I did,' he repeated, moving the plates about the tablecloth with clumsy fingers. 'But now I'm not sure that I shall.'

'Why not?' I demanded.

'It might spoil it for you.'

I thought about this and my tired mind suddenly turned angry.

'But you promised!' I exclaimed.

'I know I did,' he said, 'but it's a job for your dad, really. He's the one to tell you.'

'My father's dead,' I said, 'and' – contempt for the stupid pastime suddenly blazed up in me – 'I'm quite sure he never spooned!'

'You wouldn't be here if he hadn't,' Ted said grimly. 'And I believe that you know more about it than you let on.'

'I don't, I don't,' I cried passionately, 'and you did promise to tell me.'

He looked down at me irresolutely and said, 'Well, it means putting your arm round a girl, and kissing her. That's what it means.'

'I know that,' I exclaimed, wriggling and throwing myself about in my chair, outraged by his perfidy. 'That's on all the post-cards. But it's something else too. It makes you *feel* something.'

'Well,' he said heavily, 'it makes you feel on top of the world, if you know what that means.'

I did know: it was what I had felt last night and this morning. But I didn't think it was the same as the pleasure of spooning and I said so.

'What do you like doing best?' he asked me suddenly.

I had to think: it was a fair question and I was annoyed with myself for not being able to answer it.

'Well, something that happens in dreams, like flying, or floating, or –'

'Or what?' said he.

'Or waking up and knowing that somebody you dreamed had died was really alive.' I had dreamed this several times about my mother.

'I've never had that dream,' he said, 'but it'll do, it gives you the idea. Think of it, and add some, and then you'll know what spooning's like.'

'But —' I began. But my protest was drowned by a commotion in the scullery: rattling, bubbling, and hissing.

'The kettle's boiling over,' exclaimed Ted, jumping up. He came back with the tea-pot in one hand and in the other a plum cake on a plate. My mouth watered: I would stay, but only on condition —

'You haven't really told me,' I said, 'what spooning is.'

He carefully put down the tea-pot and the plate, and said patiently, 'Yes, I have, it's like flying, or floating, or waking up and finding someone you thought was dead is really there. It's what you like doing best, and then some more.'

I was too exasperated to notice how exasperated he was.

'Yes, but *what* more?' I cried. 'I know you know, and I won't take any more messages for you unless you tell me.'

Some primitive instinct told me that I had him in a corner; it also warned me that I had tried him too far. He towered above me, as hard and straight and dangerous as his gun. I saw the temper leap into his eyes it had when he caught me sliding down the straw-stack. Armoured by his nakedness he took a step towards me.

'Clear out of here quick,' he said, 'or you'll be sorry.'

CHAPTER 16

Brandham Hall
Near Norwich.
Norfolk.
England.
The World.
The Universe
etc.

DEAR MOTHER (I wrote),

'I am sorry to tell you I am not enjoying myself here. When I wrote to you this morning I was enjoying myself, but not now, because of the errands and the messages. They are very kind to me as I wrote to you this morning and I like being here, but please, dear mother, send a telegram to say you want me to come back at once. You could say that you want me to come home for my birthday because you would miss me too much and I would much rather spend it with you. My birthday is on Friday July the 27th. so there is still plenty of time. Or if this is too exspensive you could say please send Leo back – I will write exsplaining. I don't want to stay here any longer than I or you can help. It is not that I am not enjoying myself, but the messages.'

Here I paused. I knew I ought to be more explicit about the messages, but how, when my lips were sealed? And did I know myself what they were? I did not, except that they were to arrange meetings between Ted and Marian. I knew that they were very secret and aroused the strongest feelings – feelings which, until this afternoon, I had not known that grown-up people possessed, feelings which might lead – well, lead to murder. That was only a word to me, but it was a fearsome word, and though I didn't understand the logic of the emotions, Ted's violence, and his threats, and his gun, which I had come to think of as a symbol of himself, gave me an inkling of how the thing might happen in real life.

And Lord Trimingham would be the victim: I did not doubt that: the fate of the fifth Viscount made it all too plain.

I could not tell my mother any of this, but I could use other arguments, arguments she would appreciate, to make my aversion to the errands sound more plausible.

'It is nearly four miles there and back, and I have to cross the river by a narrow Plank and go along a ruff farm road which is very exausting in the Grate Heat' ('in the great heat' was a stock phrase of my mother's and, as I have said, she dreaded the reality for which it stood), 'and on both sides there are some wild animals or nearly so which frighten me. This I have to do nearly every day otherwise they would be angry, they depend so much on the messages.'

So much for the material and physical objections to the errands. Now I would deal with their moral aspect; this, I felt sure, would influence my mother. She had two phrases, Rather Wrong, and Very Wrong; the former she applied often, the latter sparingly, to any course of action that she didn't approve of. I did not believe in the idea of wrong myself, but I saw this was the moment to invoke it.

'I should not mind this so much,' I went on, 'only I feel that what they are making me do is Rather Wrong and perhaps Very Wrong' (I thought I would get them both in) 'and something you would not like me to do as well. So please send the telegram as soon as you get this letter.

I hope you are quite well, dear Mother, as I am and should be very happy if not for the Errands.

Your loving son
LEO
XXXXXXXXXXXXX

P.S. I am looking forward very much to coming home.

P.P.S. I have unfortunately missed the post today, but if this letter arrives by the first post on Tuesday July 24th. your telegram will arrive here about 11.15 on Tuesday morning and if it arrives by the second post the telegram will arrive by 5.30 P.M. on Tuesday at latest.

P.P.P.S. Perhaps you could send a telegram to Mrs Maudsley too.

P.P.P.P.S. The Heat is Grate and growing Grater.'

I was naturally a good speller, and if I hadn't been tired and excited I shouldn't have made so many mistakes.

Although I felt much better for writing the letter, the afternoon had put my mental age back and dealt my spirit a shrewd blow, or I could not have written it. I do not quite know where the wound went deepest. True my feelings had been hurt, but they had been hurt twice over and the second blow had in a way deadened the first. Ted's outburst had almost obliterated Marian's: it had finished off the demolition of my temporary emotional structure. For the second time that afternoon I had taken to my heels: I had run out of the house as fast as my legs could carry me. Looking back, I saw Ted standing at the farmyard gate, waving to me and shouting; but I thought he was meaning to give chase, and I ran the faster, like a street-urchin fleeing from a policeman, nor did I draw breath until my breath gave out. I did not cry, however, because he was a man, and his anger touched a hardier nerve in me than Marian's had. By the time I reached the sluice, the frontier between his land and ours, my fright had begun to wear off, for I was beyond the reach of his arm, or even of his gun, which I still dreaded.

To bleed from many wounds may be more serious than to bleed from one, but the pain, being less localized, is also easier for the mind to bear.

Perhaps more important to my well-being than my feelings was my *amour propre*.[1] This had suffered in various ways, but it had also been bolstered up by Ted's references to my prowess at cricket and singing, and in a way it dwelt in a part of me which was almost inaccessible to my feelings: I had excelled at cricket, I had excelled at singing: these were assets which hard words could not devalue. At the same time it depended to some extent on public recognition, and this is what I foresaw would be lacking when I returned to Brandham Hall.

I had got it into my head (the most unlikely thing that could happen) that Marian would have told everyone what she had told me, that I was a stupid little boy, a swollen-headed brat, etc., and worst of all a Shylock. I imagined that when I entered the drawing-room, rather late for tea, everyone would treat me as an outcast: and this, even after my other experiences, was a prospect that daunted me.

In fact, the opposite happened. I wasn't even late; I was greeted with acclaim; inquiries, both facetious and solicitous, were made as to how I had spent the afternoon, which I answered as best I could;

and I was drawn into the circle in a place of honour near the tea-kettle – the shining silver tea-kettle which had always been my admiration.

Marian was presiding over it. I had never seen her so animated. She did not put the finesse into pouring out the tea that her mother did, asking questions all round the table, making each cup seem like a present, for she seemed to know by instinct, or to remember from other times, just how everybody liked their tea. 'Yours is with lemon, isn't it?' she would say, and so on. We were a full house. Among the week-end guests were some older people whom I welcomed because they generally had more to say to me than the younger ones. I can't remember their faces but I can remember hers, and the challenge in her eye and the lift of raillery in her voice. Her eyes were always fiercer than her mouth; they glinted while it smiled. The guests seemed to enjoy being made fun of, for there was flattery in it too. Lord Trimingham was sitting beside her on a low chair, I could only see his head, and it struck me that this was how they would be when she came to reign at Brandham – she in full view and he half in shadow. There was a sparkle on everything she did. In her mother's absence she seemed to be reigning already: there was such decision in her face and in her gestures. I wondered where Mrs Maudsley was; she had never been away at tea before. This was another mastery than hers, less subtle but more brilliant.

When my turn came Marian looked into my eyes and said 'Three lumps or four, Leo?' and I said four because small boys are supposed to like a lot of sugar. It raised a laugh, as I had hoped it would.

Tea was made a feature of at Brandham. The cakes and sandwiches and jam we had! Half of it went back into the servants' hall. If I thought of Ted eating his lonely tea at his kitchen table scored with knife cuts, it was to wonder how I ever came to be there; it had left a lurid feeling in my mind, as if it had been the cage of a wild animal. The decorous sounds we all made eating and drinking, the light chatter, the unemphatic voices, the small safe sounds of things being moved about and passed from hand to hand, the glitter of the trail of gold – how captivating it all was, and yet I shouldn't have relished it so much if I hadn't known the other.

When I took my cup to Marian to be refilled (I claimed this privilege as a guest of older standing) her eyes held a message which I did not miss. 'Stay behind,' they said, 'or come and see me afterwards.'

But in spite of that and in spite of having enjoyed it all so much, I didn't. I went back to my room and locked the door and wrote the letter.

It seemed to me that if I went away, and only if I went away, the relationship between Ted and Marian would cease. I didn't ask myself how it had been kept up before I came. I reasoned: there is no one else to take the notes but me; they have to be taken and brought back on the same day, because only after breakfast does Marian know what her mother's plans will be; if I'm not there to do it they can't meet, and Lord Trimingham will never know that his bride-to-be is too friendly with another man. If I stay I shall have to do as she tells me: the only thing is to go. I saw no flaw in the logic of this.

I didn't ask myself why these missions, which had once been my delight, were now my bugbear. It was I who had changed, not they. For the first time in my life I had a strong sense of obligation in a matter that didn't really concern me — a sense of ought and ought not. Hitherto my maxim had been to mind my own business, as it was the maxim of most of my schoolfellows. If anyone attacked me I tried to defend myself. If I had broken a rule I tried to escape the consequences. Where no rules were, and when I was not being attacked, I had no sense at all of two independent elements, unrelated to my concerns, called right and wrong, to which my actions could be referred for approval or disapproval. But now for some such scruple I felt constrained to take preventive action — and at a sacrifice to myself, for I didn't want to leave Brandham.

Of course I had had plenty of provocation from Marian and Ted, but I had the fairness to see that I had attacked them first. They were defending themselves against me. I thought I knew what was best for myself, best for them, best for Lord Trimingham, best for everybody: so I was leaving. I did not feel I was running away. But I was. I was shaken and frightened and did not trust myself or anyone.

The hall box had been cleared and my letter would have to wait till morning. The other had got a start of it by more than half a day. But I did not doubt that it would bring the telegram of recall.

Crossing the hall I ran into Lord Trimingham. 'Just the man!' he said, as Marian had said before him. 'Do you want to earn my good opinion?'

The others had offered me heavier bribes but I saw no risk in taking this.

'Oh, yes!'

'Well, find Marian for me, there's a good feller.'

My heart sank. She was the last person I wanted to see.

'But I thought you weren't going to send her any more messages!' I protested.

For the first time in our acquaintanceship, if I read the signs aright, he looked put out, and I thought he was going to turn on me as the others had. He said, rather sharply:

'Oh, don't worry if you're busy. It's just that I wanted to say something to her. She's going to London tomorrow and I may not get another chance.'

'She's going to London?'

'Yes, till Wednesday.' He spoke of her possessively, I thought.

'She never told me,' I said, in the offended tone of a servant who has not been apprised of a coming visitor.

'She has a lot to think about just now, or I'm sure she would have. Now be a saint and find her, unless you can produce her out of your hat.'

Suddenly, with intense relief, I remembered a valid objection. 'Marcus told me she was going down to see Nannie Robson after tea.'

'Confound Nannie Robson. Marian's always going there, and she says the old girl's losing her memory and forgets whether she's been or not. Robson by name, Robson by nature, Mrs Maudsley used to say. She ought to be called Robdaughter now.'

I thought this an excellent joke, and was just running off when he called me back. 'Don't overdo it,' he said, with a return to his old genial manner. 'You're looking a bit pale. We mustn't have two invalids in the house.'

'Oh, who's the other one?'

'Our hostess, but she doesn't want it talked about.'

'Is she *very* ill?' I asked.

'Oh no, it's nothing much.' I could see he wished he hadn't told me.

CHAPTER 17

On my way to pay my deferred visit to the rubbish-heap I met Marcus.

'Bon soir,[1] thou dusky varlet, whither away?' he said.

I told him my destination.

'Oh, don't let's go there. Je le trouve trop ennuyeux,'[2] he said. 'Let's think of somewhere else.'

I sighed. It was to be a French conversation. French was one of the few school subjects which Marcus was better at than I was. He had had a French governess who had given him a good accent; he had also, unlike me, been abroad and there picked up words and phrases his governess would not have taught him. And he had an annoying habit, when one mispronounced a word, of repeating it with the right pronunciation. But he was not a prig, and had allowed his real French to be overlaid by a smattering of the pidgin French we all sometimes talked. I was his guest, with a guest's obligation to comply. I had to admit that he had been decent in not insisting before on a form of conversation at which he shone and I didn't. I don't think he would have insisted on it then had he not still felt sore about my Saturday's success. He thought I still needed taking down a peg, not knowing that this had been amply done already; and I was half aware of his intention and resented it. Often when we talked there was a spirit of verbal rivalry between us; we trod a knife-edge between affection and falling out; but this time our latent animosity was nearer to the surface.

'Je suggère que nous visitons les outhouses,'[3] I proposed laboriously.

'Mais oui! Quelle bonne idée! Ce sont des places délicieuses.'[4]

'I thought a place meant a square,' I remarked.

'Bon! Vous venez sur!' he said deflatingly, but lapsing, I was relieved to hear, into a kind of French that was less lesson-like. 'Et que trouvons-nous là?'[5]

'Le deadly nightshade, for one thing,' I replied, hoping to edge him into English.

'Vous voudriez dire la belladonne, n'est-ce pas?'[6]

'Oui, atropa belladonna,' I replied, trumping his French with Latin.

'Eh bien, je jamais!' he rejoined, but I knew that I had scored, for the 'Eh bien, je jamais', though ironical, was a current admission of being impressed, and we returned for a while to our mother tongue, or rather to medieval and facetious versions of it.

Nearly every term it happened that certain words and phrases ran like wild-fire through the school and acquired a sort of fetishistic value. Everyone used them, but no one ever knew who started them. Conversely other words, which seemed intrinsically harmless, were made taboo, and their use excited the utmost derision. We had to guard our tongues against them. I could still hear my tormentors hissing 'vanquished' at me. In a few weeks the vogue would pass and the words regain their normal value. 'Vous venez sur' (you're coming on) and 'Eh bien, je jamais' (well, I never) were two of the latest.

The outhouses were about ten minutes' walk away. They were adjuncts of an old kitchen garden which had been made, as such gardens sometimes were, at a considerable distance from the house. The path, a track of earth mixed with cinders, led through a long shrubbery of rhododendrons and I imagine that when they were in flower it was much frequented; but now it was gloomy and forbidding and rather frightening, which was partly the secret of its attraction for me. Several times I had started out to revisit the deadly nightshade, and had turned back before I reached it, overcome by an irrational dread; but only once, when I met Marian coming along it, had I ever seen anyone on the path. But with Marcus at my side my alarm was reduced to an agreeable pioneering thrill.

'Je vois l'empreinte d'un pied!'[7] he cried, reverting to French.

We stopped and bent down. The path was very dry, the grass withered, the earth powdery; but it did look like a footmark, a small one. Marcus gave a whoop intended for a Red Indian war-cry.

'Eh bien, je jamais! Je dirai à Maman que nous avons vu le spoor de Man Friday.'[8]

'Ou Mademoiselle Friday,' I suggested wittily.

'Vous venez sur! Certes, c'est la patte d'une dame. Mystère! Que dira Maman? Elle a un grand peur des voleurs!'[9]

'I should have thought your mother was very brave,' I said, rebelling. 'Braver even than mine,' I added, not wanting the talk to stray too far from my affairs.

'Mais non! Elle est très nerveuse! C'est un type un peu hystérique,' he said, with all the detachment of a doctor. 'En ce moment elle est au lit avec une forte migraine, le résultat de tous ces jours de strain.'[10]

I was glad that Marcus had broken down at the last word, but sorry to hear about his mother.

'But why is it a strain?' I asked. 'She seems to have so many people to help her.' Like a housewife of today, I thought of strain in terms of housekeeping.

He shook his head mysteriously and raised his finger.

'Ce n'est pas seulement ça. C'est Marianne.'[11]

'Marian?' said I, anglicizing it.

'Mais oui, c'est Marianne.' He lowered his voice. 'Il s'agit des fiançailles, vous savez. Ma mère n'est pas sûre que Marianne – '[12] he rolled his eyes and put his finger to his lips.

I didn't understand.

'Will stick to her engagement, if you must be told in English.'

I was thunderstruck, not only at the news but at Marcus's indiscretion. And I am almost sure that if he had not been carried away by his own French, and by trying to act the Frenchman, and by showing off to me, he would have been more careful. How much did he suspect? How much did his mother suspect? He was her favourite, that I knew; she didn't care about Denys, she rarely spoke to Mr Maudsley, at any rate in my hearing. Perhaps she confided in Marcus, as my mother sometimes confided in me – things that surprised me. Perhaps all women were liable, at moments, to *let on*. But how much did she *know*?

A thought struck me.

'Vous avez vu votre soeur chez Mademoiselle Robson?'[13] I brought out, after much consideration.

'Robsón,' repeated Marcus, with a heavy accent on the second syllable. 'Mais non! Quand je suis parti, la Marianne n'était pas encore arrivée. Et la pauvre Robson était bien fâcheuse,[14] because she says that Marian hardly ever comes to see her,' said Marcus rapidly. 'I say this in English for your benefit, you insular owl.'

'Lord Trimingham told me,' said I impressively, and ignoring the insult, 'that Marian says that Nannie Robson has well – has perdu sa mémoire,'[15] I wound up with a slight flourish.

'Perdu sa fiddlesticks!' retorted Marcus, again breaking down. 'Sa mémoire est aussi bonne que la mienne, et cent fois meilleure que la vôtre, sale type de woolgatherer!'[16]

I clouted him for this, but the news disquieted me.

'Lord Trimingham also said that Marian is going to London to-morrow,' I said. 'Pourquoi?'[17]

'Pourquoi?' said Marcus, much more Frenchly than I had. 'En part, parce que, comme toutes les femmes, elle a besoin des habits neufs pour le bal; mais en grand part, à cause de vous, vous –'[18] the epithet failed him, and he puffed out his cheeks instead.

'A cause de moi?' I said. 'Because of me?'

'Vous venez sur!' came the swift retort. 'Yes, because of you! She has gone to get what perhaps you will understand if I say it is a cadeau.'

'A present!' I said, and for a moment compunction seized me. 'But she has given me so many presents.'

'This is a very special one for your birthday,' said Marcus, speaking deliberately and loudly, as to a deaf person or a half-wit. 'Entendez-vous, coquin? Comprenez-vous, nigaud?[19] But you'll never guess what it is.'

In my excitement I forgot my dread of Marian's presents and their Danaan implication.[20]

'Do you know what it is?' I exclaimed.

'Yes, but I don't tell les petits garçons.'

I shook him till he cried 'Pax'.

'Well, swear that you won't tell anyone I told you,' I had shaken some of the French out of him too.

'I swear.'

'Swear in French, si vous le pouvez.'[21]

'Je jure.'

'And swear that you'll look surprised when Marian gives it to you – though you can't help looking surprised, mooncalf, you were born that way.' And he mimicked my face.

'Je jure,' I intoned, ignoring his grimaces.

'Will you try to understand if I say it in French?'

I didn't answer.

'C'est une bicyclette.'

To a child of today this might have seemed an anti-climax, to me it opened the gates of heaven. A bicycle was the thing I wanted most in the world, and had least hope of getting, for it was, I knew by inquiry, beyond my mother's purse. I plied Marcus with questions about it – its make, its size, its tyres, its lamp, its brakes. 'C'est une bicyclette Oombaire,'[22] said Marcus, so Frenchly that at first I didn't recognize the famous name; but to my other questions he would only answer 'Je ne sais pas' in a maddening up and down sing-song.

'Je ne l'ai pas vue,' he said at last. 'C'est un type qui se trouve seulement à Londres that is only found in London, espèce de block-head.[23] But I can tell you one thing that you haven't asked me.'

'What?'

'Sa couleur, or as you would say, its colour.'

'What colour is it?'

'Vert – un vert vif.'

It was very slow of me but I took the word to be verre, and I stared at him, no doubt moon-faced and owlish, wondering how a bicycle could be the colour of a lively glass.

At last he enlightened me.

'Green, green, mon pauvre imbécile, bright green,' and just as this vision was beginning to dawn on me in all its splendour, he added, 'Et savez-vous pourquoi?'[24]

I could not guess.

'Parce que vous êtes vert vous-même – you are green yourself, as the poor old English say,' he translated, to leave me in no doubt. 'It is your true colour, Marian said so.' And he began to dance round me, chanting 'Green, green, green.'

I cannot describe how painful this disclosure was to me. Momentarily it took away all my pleasure in the thought of the bicycle. Most of Marcus's gibes had run off me like water, but to be called green, that went home. And like other revelations of the day it cast a black shadow[25] on the past which I had thought so secure. The green suit, that happy-making present, Lincoln green, the green of the greenwood, Robin Hood's green – it too had been a subtle insult, meant to make me look a fool.

'Did she really say that?' I asked.

'Mais oui! Vraiment!'[26] and he went back to his chanting and his dance.

Perhaps schoolboys no longer dance round each other, but they did once, and it was a most unnerving and exasperating experience for the victim. For a moment I hated Marcus, and I hated Marian: I saw how green I must look to her and realized how she had taken advantage of it. I would strike back, and in French.

'Savez-vous où est Marian en ce moment-ci?'[27] I asked carefully.

Marcus stopped dead and stared at me. 'No,' he said, and his voice sounded strangely English. 'Do *you* know where she is?'

'Oui,' I replied, thrilled to have turned his French against him. 'Je sais bien.'

This was quite untrue; I had no idea where she was, though I guessed she was with Ted.

'Where, where?' he said.

'Pas cent lieues d'ici,'[28] I answered, not knowing the French for miles and giving the impression, I suppose, that Marian was near at hand.

'But where, where?' he repeated.

'Je ne dis pas ça aux petits garçons,' I retorted, and began to dance round him in my turn, chanting 'petit garçon, petit garçon, ne voudriez-vous pas savoir?'[29]

'Pax,' cried Marcus at last, and I stopped gyrating.

'But do you really know where she is, honest Injun?' Marcus asked.

'Mais oui, mais oui, mais oui,' was all I would vouchsafe.

If I had remembered what a tell-tale Marcus was I should never have proclaimed my supposed knowledge of Marian's whereabouts; though the fact that I really did not know paradoxically made it seem less of a betrayal. Nor should I have done so had we been talking in English: I should have kept a guard on my tongue. But my French *persona* ran away with me. Trying to compete in French with Marcus, I felt a different being – as no doubt he did. In a foreign language one has to say something, or look silly, even if the something were better left unsaid. But what weighed most with me was the feeling I was doing Marian a bad turn. By saying I knew where she was I got rid of some of my spleen against her; by not knowing, I salved my conscience.

We were walking in silence, every now and then taking a few skips to release the tension and let the bad blood out, when suddenly I saw something which turned me cold.

We were in sight of the outhouse where the deadly nightshade grew, and the deadly nightshade was coming out of the door.

For a second I actually thought it had been endowed with movement and was coming towards us. Then the phenomenon explained itself: the bush had grown so much since my last visit that the hut no longer held it.

On the threshold which it guarded we paused and peered in. Marcus was for pushing past it into the shed: 'Oh, don't,' I whispered, and he smiled and drew back: it was our moment of reconciliation. The shrub had spread amazingly; it topped the roofless walls, it pressed into their crannies, groping for an outlet, urged by a secret explosive force that I felt would burst them. It had battened on the heat which had parched everything else. Its beauty, of which I was well aware, was too bold for me, too uncompromising in every particular. The sullen heavy purple bells wanted something of me that I could not give, the bold black burnished berries offered me something that I did not want. All other plants, I thought, bloom for the eye; they are perfected for our view: the mysterious principle of growth is manifest in them, mysterious yet simple. But this plant seemed to be up to something, to be carrying on a questionable traffic with itself. There was no harmony, no proportion in its parts. It exhibited all the stages of its development at once. It was young, middle-aged, and old at the same time. Not only did it bear its fruit and flowers together but there was a strange discrepancy between the size of its leaves: some were no longer than my little finger, others much longer than my hand. It invited and yet repelled inspection, as if it was harbouring some shady secret which it yet wanted you to know. Outside the shed, twilight was darkening the air, but inside it was already night, night which the plant had gathered to itself.

Torn between fascination and recoil I turned away, and it was then we heard the voices.

Actually there was only one voice, or only one voice audible. I recognized it at once, though Marcus didn't; it was the voice of 'When Other Lips',[30] speaking, no doubt, the language whose excess imparts the power it feels so well. But what I heard was a low insistent murmur, with pauses for reply in which no reply was made. It had an hypnotic quality which I had never heard in any voice: a blend of urgency, cajolery, and extreme tenderness, and with below it the deep vibrato of a held-in laugh that might break out at any moment. It was the voice of someone wanting something very much and confident of getting it, but at the same time willing, no, constrained, to plead for it with all the force of his being.

'A loony talking to himself,' whispered Marcus: 'shall we go and see?'

At that moment a second voice became audible, toneless, unrecognizable but distinct. Marcus's eyes lit up.

'Eh bien, je jamais! c'est un couple,' he whispered, 'un couple qui fait le cuiller.'

'Fait le cuiller?' I echoed, stupidly.

'Spooning, you idiot. Let's go and rout them out.'

Terrified equally at the thought of discovering or being discovered I suddenly had an inspiration.

'Mais non!' I whispered, 'Ça serait trop ennuyeux. Laissons-les faire!'[31]

I started resolutely on the homeward path and Marcus, after more than one backward glance, with a bad grace followed me. Through the mad pounding of my heart, and my general gratitude for deliverance, I found time to congratulate myself. It was the word 'ennuyeux' that had done the trick: Marcus had used it to discredit the rubbish-heap; in all his large vocabulary it carried the greatest weight of disparagement. Precociously sophisticated, he knew that to be boring was the unforgivable sin.

'Confounded cheek, I call it!' Marcus fumed when we were out of earshot. 'Why should they come here to spoon? I wonder what Mama would say.'

'Oh, I shouldn't tell her, Marcus,' I said quickly. 'Don't tell her. Promise you won't. Jurez, jurez, je vous en prie.'[32]

But he wouldn't oblige me, even in French.

Our amity restored we walked along, sometimes sedately, with open, guileless faces, sometimes barging into each other with sudden charges. I thought of many things.

'How long do engagements last?' I asked. Marcus would be sure to know.

'Cela dépend,'[33] he announced oracularly. 'Perhaps you would rather I answered in English?' he said suddenly. 'It is a language more suited to your feeble intelligence.'

I let this pass.

'In the case of grooms, gardeners, skivvies, and such-like scum,' said Marcus, 'it may go on for ever. With people like ourselves it generally doesn't go on very long.'

'How long?'

'Oh, a month or so. Deux mois, trois mois.'[34]

I thought about this.

'Engagements are sometimes broken off, aren't they?'

'That's what is worrying Mama. But Marian would never be so *folle*[35] – fou for you, Colston, in the masculine it describes you exactly – write it out a hundred times, please – so *folle* as to leave Trimingham *planté là*.[36] What did I say, Colston?'

'Planté là,' I repeated humbly.

'Please construe it.'

'Planted there.'

'Planted there, indeed! Sit down. Next, next, next, next, next. Can no boy give a proper rendering of "planté là"?'

'Well what does it mean?' I asked.

'"Planté là" means . . . it means . . . well, almost anything you like except "planted there".'

I took this from him, too: my thoughts had veered again, and were now swarming like flies round a honey-pot. The green bicycle! Even if it was an insult – and I had no doubt of that – I could swallow the insult. Could I bring myself *not* to swallow it, that was the question. The bicycle was already dearer to me than anything I possessed. I was sure that if I went away before my birthday I should not get it. They would be offended with me and return it to the shop, or perhaps give it to Marcus, though he had one already. I pictured myself riding it through our village street, which had become much nearer and clearer to me during the last few hours – jumping off and standing it against one of the posts that held the hanging chains that guarded our road frontage. How everyone would admire it! I couldn't ride a bicycle but I should soon learn. Mother would put a steadying hand on the saddle, so would the gardener . . . up and down the hills I should go, soaring, floating . . .

And yet I wasn't comfortable about it. There was a trap somewhere, I felt sure; and though I didn't know the term hush-money, its meaning flittered, bat-like, about my mind.

I was too tired to hold any one thought for long, even the image of the bicycle. I had been so pleased with my handling of the situation at the outhouses: now I found myself wondering whether instead of whispering to Marcus, it wouldn't have been better to have given a shout that would have warned them.

'Vous êtes très silencieux,' said Marcus. 'Je n'aime pas votre voix, which is ugly, oily, and only fit to be heard at a village sing-song. Et quant à vos sales pensées, crapaud, je m'en fiche d'elles, je crache upon them. Mais pourquoi avez-vous perdu la langue?[37] Your long, thin, slimy, spotted serpent's tongue?'

At his bedroom door we parted. There was plenty of time before dinner, and I stole down into the hall to look at the post-box. My letter was still there, leaning against the pane, with other letters behind it. I fingered the door and to my intense surprise it opened. I had the letter in my hand; tear it up and I had the bicycle too. A moment of excruciating self-division followed. Then I slipped the letter back, and tip-toed upstairs with a thudding heart.

CHAPTER 18

When I came down to breakfast the next morning the letter was gone. Oh, the peace of that moment! There were two absentees from the breakfast table, Marian and her mother. Marian, I learned, had caught the early train to London; Mrs Maudsley was still in bed. I speculated on the nature of her complaint. Un type hystérique, Marcus had said. What were her symptoms? Did she have fits? All I knew about hysteria was that sometimes servants had it; I didn't know what form it took, but I couldn't connect it with Mrs Maudsley who, besides being a lady, was always so calm. That tense still look of hers that caught you in its searchlight beam! She had been invariably kind to me; kinder in some ways, perhaps kinder in all ways, than Marian had been. Yet because of her very stillness, I found her presence repressive: I shouldn't have dared to love her, if she had been my mother. Marcus did, but perhaps she showed another side of herself to him. She brought out all the clumsiness in Denys; when he saw her eye on him he always looked as if he was going to drop something – or had dropped it. Yes, with Mrs Maudsley away one breathed more freely.

Did Marian love her? That I could not tell: I had seen them watching each other like two cats; and then, as cats do, turn away again, indifferently, as if whatever was at stake between them had somehow faded out. It wasn't my idea of love; my idea of love was more demonstrative.

I had loved Marian, or so I should have said, if anyone in my confidence had asked me (but there was no one: I certainly should not have told my mother). How did I feel to her? I asked myself the question as we knelt at prayers, when my thoughts should have been turned towards forgiveness: but I couldn't answer it. I was still half expecting to see her mocking face across the table, and when I didn't see it and realized I shouldn't till Wednesday, relief surged up in me.

By Wednesday, by Tuesday indeed, I should have got my marching orders: I should have finished with Brandham: already I felt in it but not of it.

Even when she was everything I most admired, even when to hear her voice speaking my name with its ironic, intimate inflexion had brought me as much happiness as a human relationship could give me, I had always been a little frightened of her, and fearful of falling below her standard. What that consisted in I don't quite know, for it was not only her beauty. I don't think I ever heard her say a clever thing, though I shouldn't have recognized it if I had. No, it was her air of good-humoured impatience with things and people – her getting to a point before they did, and leaving it while they were still fumbling with it, her disturbing faculty of guessing what they were going to say before they said it, that made her seem superior to them. She arrived, while they plodded; her short cuts made them seem heavy-footed and prosy. She wasn't superior in the sense of being patronizing; she took a great interest in people, and never spoke to any of us as if he or she was someone else. But she had her own angle on us, and it was generally a slightly disconcerting one: she saw us not as we saw ourselves or as other people saw us. To me her vision of me as the Green Huntsman had always been intoxicating, a mirror in which I never tired of seeing myself: it was like a rebirth. And only she could perform the miracle: it was no good my saying to myself: 'This is how Marian sees me.' The portrait wouldn't come to life unless she held the mirror.

And now the mirror was cracked. Only I knew how much calculation underlay her apparent inconsequence, and all my thoughts of her were steeped in green and poisoned; I could hardly bear to look at my green suit. No use to tell myself, now, that she had given it me before I took to letter-carrying, because she had always thought of me as green; Marcus had told me so, and it didn't occur to me he might have lied.

So I was relieved at her absence; relieved from the strain of having to keep up with her, of being what I thought she wanted me to be at every minute, a psychological exercise that had lost its magic; and relieved from the threat of an emotional show-down, involving perhaps further recriminations and unkind words, the desire for which I had read in her eyes, I thought, the day before.

It is I, the elder, the old Leo, who am making this post-mortem; at the time I didn't analyse my feelings much: I was content to feel the pressure of circumstances relax, and myself slipping into my humdrum, pre-Brandham state of mind, with nobody's standards to live up to except my own.

Four of the week-end visitors had taken the early train with Marian, so we were a small party, only seven: Mr Maudsley, Lord Trimingham, Denys, Marcus, and myself, and an elderly Mr and Mrs Laurent, of whom I remember nothing except that they were quite unformidable. Even the table had shrunk, and was now hardly longer than our dining-table at home, which I should see so soon. The cats were away; a wonderful feeling of *détente*[1] prevailed. Denys took advantage of it to give us a long harangue on the best way of combating poachers. 'But you forget, Papa,' he said more than once, 'that this park is an *exposed* park. Anyone can get into it, anyone, anywhere, and we be none the wiser.' He rambled on, working himself up, arguing with himself when no opposition offered. He would not have dared to, with his mother there; but Mr Maudsley never snubbed him in my hearing, except that once, on the cricket field.

Presently our host rose, and we rose with him. 'Have a cigar?' he abruptly inquired, his sunken eyes scanning face after face, including mine. He often asked this question at times of day which even I knew to be inappropriate: it was when he suddenly remembered his duties as host that he proffered this pistol-shot hospitality. We all smiled and shook our heads, and left the dining-room to the servants. No orderly room, no plans for the day, no messages to take, no problems. We were free!

As I was going out Marcus said, 'Come with me, I want to tell you something.' Agreeably titillated, and wondering what it could be, I followed him into Mrs Maudsley's sitting-room — the blue boudoir, it was called. I should never have dared to venture into it, but Marcus was a privileged person where she was concerned.

· He shut the door and said, rather self-consciously:

'Have you heard this one?'

'No,' I said, instinctively, without waiting to hear.

'It's very funny and rather rude.'

I was all ears.

Marcus composed his face into solemn lines and said:

'The awe-inspirers have gone away.'

I rolled my eyes in agonized conjecture, hoping that somewhere on the confines of sight I might see this as very funny and rather rude, but I couldn't, and finally had to say so.

Marcus frowned and put his finger to his cheek. Then he shook himself in exasperation and said:

'Oh, I've got it wrong. I remember now. Be sure to laugh: it's frightfully funny.'

I composed myself to guffaw.

'It's: "The awe-*mongers* have gone away."'

I tittered slightly from nervous reaction, not from having seen the joke. Marcus realizing this, was vexed.

'You needn't laugh if you don't want to,' he said loftily, 'but it *is* very funny.'

'I'm sure it is,' I said, for I knew how ill-advised, as well as ill-mannered it is, not to appreciate a joke when it is told one. Worse still, it laid one open to the charge of being a thickhead.

'A man who is a prefect at a public school told a friend of mine, and he *rocked* with laughter,' Marcus said. 'It was after some ushers[2] had been sacked for spooning or something like that. They had been frightfully strict in form, cursing everybody and giving them impots,[3] which made it all the funnier. Can't you see it now?'

'Not quite,' I confessed.

'Well, *monger* – you can have an ironmonger, or a fishmonger, or a cheesemonger or a costermonger, but have you ever heard of an awe-monger before?'

'I can't say I have.'

'Well, *isn't* it funny?'

'Yes, I suppose it is,' I said doubtfully. Then, as I realized the ingenious use of the words, I began to laugh quite heartily. 'But why is it rude?'

'Because "awe" is a rude word, you dolt.'

'Is it?' I said, feeling as small as only someone can who has been caught out in ignorance of salacious matters. 'Why is it rude?'

For answer Marcus laughed and laughed. He shut his eyes, wagged his round head from side to side, and shook all over. At last he said:

'You're the best joke of all.'

I joined in the laugh, for fear of not seeming sporting, and then when he had laughed his fill I asked a second time, though it cost a great sacrifice of pride to say it:

'But why is "awe" a rude word? Please tell me.'

But he wouldn't enlighten me and it's my belief he couldn't.

That day and the next were two of the happiest I spent at Brandham Hall. They did not compare with Saturday and Sunday morning; I did not feel, to use Ted's phrase, 'on top of the world'. Those were days of buoyant emotional health, of positive well-being such as I had never known. These were days of convalescence: I felt as if I was slowly picking up after a long illness; or as if in the middle of a tournament I had suddenly been whisked out of the field and put down among the spectators.

No one paid us a visit, nor did we pay any; for the first time at Brandham Hall it was like family life, not like a party. The strain of entertaining and being entertained was over: there was no obligation to talk or listen, we could be as uncommunicative as we liked. Denys took the opportunity to talk a great deal, but the rest of us put in a word when we felt like it. Many things in and about the house (though never its south-west prospect) became visible to me which hadn't been visible before, so busy were we keeping the ball of sociability rolling. The weather grew more settled as well as hotter; on Monday the temperature was 82.9, on Tuesday it was 88.2: the climax in the 100s that I hoped for seemed to be again approaching.

'Marian will be boiled in London,' Lord Trimingham said; 'there's nothing so hot as shopping.' I saw her in a crowded bicycle shop, oil melting in all directions. 'Oh dear, it's got on to my skirt, what shall I do? – and this is a new one I've just bought for my engagement.' But she wouldn't have said that; she would have laughed and said something to make the salesman laugh; I remembered how it had been at Norwich. Out she comes, her oily dress sweeping the pavement, gathering up the dust; and behind her, in my mind's eye, is a small green bicycle, a boy's bicycle, complete with all the latest devices, including a brake front and rear, made like a horse-shoe, not one of those outmoded models working on the tyre of the front wheel such as Marcus had, which wore thin and wouldn't hold you. Whenever she came into my thoughts, the bicycle followed her like a familiar, going by itself, keeping very close to her, dogging her footsteps.

A green bicycle! How difficult it is to keep out of one's mind a painful thought that attaches itself, leech-like, to a thought one welcomes! If Marcus had not given me that unkind explanation of the bicycle's colour, I might not have posted my letter to mother.

Upon the certainty of her swift response my happiness reposed. I hoped she would not think it too extravagant to send a second telegram: I rather dreaded having to show Mrs Maudsley mine: it might give her a fit, or something.

On Tuesday morning I found a letter by my plate. The handwriting was unknown to me, the postmark was Brandham Rising, a nearby village. I couldn't think whom it could be from, for only two people wrote letters to me, my mother and my aunt. I was so consumed with curiosity that I could hardly listen to what anybody said, but I couldn't satisfy it because I hated to read my letters in public. As soon as the signal for departure — now so casual and informal — was given, I ran up to my room. To my intense annoyance the housemaids were occupying it, as they so often were when I wanted it to myself; and I had to curb my impatience till they were gone.

Black Farm.
Sunday

DEAR MASTER COLSTON,

'I am writing straight off to say how sorry I am I sent you off like that. It has quite upset me that I sent you off like that. I didn't mean to, it wasn't on purpose, but at the last minute I jibed at telling you something. Perhaps when you are older you will understand how it was and forgive me. It was quite natural you should want to know being a boy of your age but the fact is I didn't feel like telling you at the moment. But I oughtn't to have taken on so specially after telling me your Dad was dead — only I got my rag out as I do sometimes, that's how it was.

I ran after you and called to you to come back but I expect you thought I was chasing you.

I don't expect you'll want to come again in a hurry but if you would like to come next Sunday at the same time I will try and tell you what you asked, and have some shooting and stay to tea. It was a shame you missed your tea, I hope they kept some for you at the Hall.

Please believe I am sincerly sorry if I was rather rough, and don't have hard feelings about me.

> Yours faithfully
>> (this was crossed out)
> Your faithfull friend
>> TED.

P.S. You oiled my bat a treat.'

I read the letter over several times and was nearly convinced of its sincerity. But a part of me still suspected that it was a ruse to make me take more notes. I had been taken in so often, I had been so green! And I thought, perhaps with justice, that it was all very well for Ted to be ashamed of telling me something which he hadn't been ashamed of using as a bait. I didn't guess — what I now think may have been the case — that he was apologizing for the one as for the other.

In any case the letter made no difference. If the prospect of a pleasant Sunday afternoon with Ted learning the facts of life had its attractions, I put it away from me, knowing I should be the other side of England.

My mother believed in the logic of the emotions; she did not think they should be tested, still less regulated, by the lessons of experience. If I had been nice to her ten times running and nasty to her the eleventh it would upset her just as much as if the ten times hadn't existed; and if (for the sake of argument: I hope I never was) I had been nasty to her ten times running and nice the eleventh, she would have in the same way discounted the other ten. She relied on the feeling of the moment, and would have thought it 'rather wrong' to do otherwise. Unconsciously I had taken after her and accepted her example as a law of life. But now I couldn't: my emotions had become circumspect and self-protective.

An older person would have seen that the letter needed an answer. It didn't occur to me to answer it — I was too prone to regard a letter as a present. But there was a phrase in it that puzzled me, so I thought I would seek out Lord Trimingham and ask for enlightenment (to my mind he was still Viscount though my tongue had learned to call him Lord).

*

At this hour he generally repaired to the smoking-room to read the newspaper and discuss 'deep affairs of state' (as mother used to say when my father was closeted with his friends). Thinking he might be thus engaged I softly pushed the door ajar and peeped in, ready to take flight, but seeing him alone, went in.

'Hullo,' he said, 'have you taken to smoking?'

I wriggled and tried to find a suitable answer. Not finding one, I circled about in front of his chair.

'Don't do that,' Lord Trimingham said. 'You make me giddy.'

I laughed, and blurted out:

'Do you know anything about Ted Burgess?'

Now that I had neutralized him it was safe to mention him.

'Yes,' he said, surprised. 'Why?'

'I only wondered,' said I, feebly.

'Oh, you're thinking of that catch, I expect,' said Lord Trimingham, kindly supplying me with a reason. 'Well, he's quite a decent feller' – I remembered he had said this about the Boers – 'but he's a bit wild.'

'Wild?' I repeated, thinking at once of lions and tigers. 'Do you mean he's dangerous, Hugh?'

'Not to you or me. He's a bit of a lady-killer, but there's no great harm in that.'

Lady-killer: what did that mean? I didn't like to ask too many questions. I did not think, however, Ted would kill Marian: man-killer, that was what I had been afraid of. Now the fear had passed away, lost its reality with the rest of my life at Brandham Hall. I could scarcely believe that I had once felt I ought to warn Lord Trimingham of his peril. The ninth Viscount would never know that I had saved him from the fate of the fifth. By removing myself I had removed the danger: it was my master-stroke. I should not have cared to see it as an act of self-sacrifice even if it had been one; for there is nothing clever in self-sacrifice, nothing to pride oneself on. Considering the scenes that Marian and Ted had made me, it was excusable that I should regard myself as the lynch-pin of the whole business.

Ever since I had arranged with mother for my recall, I seemed to be living a posthumous life at Brandham, but I still took a retrospective interest in the situation, in what might have happened if I would have let it.

'Anything else I can tell you about him?' Lord Trimingham asked. 'He's a bit hot-tempered, a word and a blow, you know, flies off the handle.'

I reflected on this, and then asked the question I had come to ask, not realizing how apt it was.

'What does it mean, getting your rag out? Has it something to do with cleaning a gun?'

Lord Trimingham laughed. 'No, it hasn't,' he said. 'But it's funny you should ask: it means what I just said – flying into a temper.'

At that moment Mr Maudsley came in. Lord Trimingham rose, and I, after a moment's hesitation, followed suit.

'Sit down, Hugh, please sit down,' Mr Maudsley said, in his dry, level voice. 'You've got a new recruit to the smoking-room, I see. Have you been telling him some smoking-room stories?'

Lord Trimingham laughed.

'Or showing him the pictures?'

He indicated a row of small dark canvases, set deep in heavy frames. I looked at the one nearest to me, and saw men wearing broad-brimmed hats, smoking long pipes, sitting on tubs with tankards in their hands, or playing cards. Drinking with the men or serving them were women. They wore no hats; their hair was pulled back from high bare foreheads and kept in place by plain white handkerchiefs. One woman was leaning on the back of a man's chair, watching the card players with avid eyes: the chair-back pressed against her breasts, which bulged over its rim and were of a dirty colour between pink and grey. This made me feel uncomfortable. I didn't like the look of the picture or its feeling; pictures, I thought, should be of something pretty, should record a moment chosen for its beauty. These people hadn't even troubled to look their best; they were ugly and quite content to be so. They got something out of being their naked selves, their faces told me that; but this self-glory, depending on nobody's approval but their own, struck me as rather shocking – more shocking than their occupations, unseemly as those were. They had forgotten themselves, that was it; and you should never forget yourself.

No wonder the pictures were not shown to the public, for who could want to look at them? And they couldn't be very valuable, being so small.

'He doesn't like them,' said Mr Maudsley, flatly.

I wriggled.

'I thought they might be above his head,' Lord Trimingham said. 'Teniers is an acquired taste, in my opinion.'[4] He seemed anxious to change the subject, and said, without changing it very much:

'We were talking about Ted Burgess when you came in, and I told Leo he was a lady-killer.'

'He has that reputation, I believe,' Mr Maudsley said.

'Yes, but it's no business of mine, is it, what he does with his week-ends?' Lord Trimingham seemed to shoot a glance at me – one never knew which way he was looking – and added quickly, 'I've been talking to him about joining up. I approached him tactfully, of course – easy does it. A likely man, single – no ties – he'd make a first-rate NCO. Of course it's different with a rifle, but he's a good shot too, by all accounts.'

'He has that reputation, I believe,' said Mr Maudsley for the second time. 'When did you see him, Sunday? I only ask because somebody noticed him in the park.'

'Yesterday, as a matter of fact,' Lord Trimingham said, 'and I went up to the farm. But I'd tackled him about it once before. I'm not much of an advertisement for Army life, I'm afraid.'

He sometimes alluded to his disfigurement, to accustom himself to the idea of it, I now think, and to make those with him feel he didn't mind. It didn't always work that way, however. After an uneasy pause Mr Maudsley asked:

'What did he say?'

'The first time he said he didn't want to, he was quite happy as he was, and let others do the fighting. But yesterday he seemed to have changed his mind – he thought he'd like to have a crack at them. I said he might never get out there. The situation's changed since Roberts went into Pretoria, though De Wet's still likely to give trouble in the Transvaal.'[5]

'So you think he'll go?' said Mr Maudsley.

'I think he may, and for myself I'm sorry; he's a good chap and I shan't easily find another tenant like him. But there you are, war's war.'

'He won't be altogether a loss to the district,' Mr Maudsley said.

'Why?' asked Lord Trimingham.

'Oh, what you were saying just now,' Mr Maudsley answered

vaguely. There was a silence. I had not quite followed the drift of the conversation, but something in my heart was troubled by it.

'Is Ted really going to the war?' I asked.

'So you're on "Ted" terms!' said Lord Trimingham. 'Well, it's on the cards he will.'

If only grown-ups would be more explicit! I tried to think that 'on the cards' meant some very remote contingency. As I was shutting the door I heard Mr Maudsley say to Lord Trimingham:

'They say he's got a woman up this way.'

I didn't know what he meant, but thought he was perhaps referring to Ted's daily woman.

CHAPTER 19

I had told my mother, and myself, that the telegram might arrive by eleven-fifteen. Eleven-fifteen came, but not my marching-orders. I was not cast down, indeed I was relieved. My belief that the telegram would come was unshakeable and now I had an extra respite in hand: a respite from the respite, so to speak; for I didn't relish the prospect of breaking to Mrs Maudsley the news of my abrupt departure (which I had fixed in my mind for Thursday at latest), nor did I know how I should get it to her, since she was in bed. In bed my imagination could not reach her: she might as well have been abroad.

The explanation was, of course, that my letter had been delayed. It would come by the second post.

I spent most of the day with Marcus. We were on excellent terms. Marcus had quite got over the irritation – or at any rate the signs of it – that he may have felt with me on the score of my late success: that wonder had not lasted the traditional nine days, and was now but sparingly referred to. We wandered rather aimlessly about the park, speculating what the next term would bring, testing each other's vocabularies, bandying insults, and offering each other physical violence, and sometimes walking arm in arm. He told me many secrets, for he was shamelessly given to gossiping, a thing I disapproved of but privately enjoyed. Contrary to the proverb, I thought that tales out of school didn't matter so much.[1] He told me about the coming ball, enlarging on its splendours; he coached me in the part I should have to play. He told me that Marian would bring me some white gloves from London – I didn't mind missing them, but ah the bicycle, the green familiar trailing after her: that rankled! He took a programme from his pocket and showed it me: Valse, Valse, Lancers, Boston, Barn Dance ('that's for old fogies like you' Marcus obligingly explained; 'it's out of fashion now'), Valse, Valse, Polka. Then supper, and again Valse, Valse, etc., down to Sir Roger de Coverley and Galop. 'But oughtn't Galop to have two l's?' I asked. 'Not in French, crétin,' Marcus told me crushingly: 'What a lot you have to learn. But I'm not sure we shall have Sir Roger *and* a Galop: il est un peu provincial, vous savez,[2] to have both. We shall decide at the last moment. Papa will probably give it out.' 'And when will the news of the engagement be given out?' I asked. 'We may not give it out,' said Marcus: 'we rather think that we may let it *spread*. It won't take long to spread, I can tell you. But you and I will have been sent to bed by then. They won't let us stay up after twelve, out of respect for your tender years, mon enfant. Oh, you are so yo—o—oung!' he carolled languishingly. 'And do you know what you are as well?'

'No,' I said, unsuspectingly.

'Well, don't get angry, but you're just a teeny, weeny bit green, *vert*, vous savez.'

I hit him and we fought for a bit.

It was all most agreeable and most unreal, hearing of these happenings in which I should take no part. Ever since I came the ball had loomed up as an obstacle to be got over somehow. I was only just learning to dance, I couldn't reverse properly, and was sure I should acquit myself badly. But to imagine the ball without being there was another matter.

I didn't feel that I was deceiving Marcus; such dissimulation as I practised was necessary to my plan – my plan that was to be for everybody's good. Inconceivable as it seems to me now, I was a man of action in those days, and in action I was a realist for whom the end justified the means. My end, at any rate, was irreproachable. It wasn't like taking the messages, which could only, I was convinced, end badly, and therefore Marian and Ted were wrong to try to deceive me. Rather Wrong, Very Wrong? Wrong was not a word I had much use for; the idea of Right and Wrong as two gigantic eavesdroppers spying on my movements was most distasteful to me. But surely something which might end in murder must be wrong.

So I listened unconcerned while Marcus talked about the ball but when, proceeding from the greater to the lesser, he began to tell me of the preparations for my birthday (they were a deadly secret, he informed me) I did have twinges of conscience. And not only of conscience, but of regret. For everyone, it appeared, had something for me; the green suit and its accompaniments did not count – they had been strictly unbirthday presents. 'Another thing that's worrying Mama,' said Marcus, 'is the cake. Not the cake itself, vous savez, mais les chandelles.[3] Mama is what do you call it, superstitious; she doesn't like the number thirteen – though of course everyone has to be thirteen some time, especially you, you saignant baker's dozen!'

I thought this really witty and looked at Marcus with a new respect.

'But we've thought of a way out, only it's too secret to tell you, you'd blab to everyone. But the great moment, the clou[4] of the evening, if you can understand that, dunderhead, will be when Marian gives you the bicycle. At the tolling of six o'clock the doors will be thrown open and she'll come in riding it, and wearing tights, she says, if Mama will let her, which I doubt. She may have to wear bloomers.'

I closed my eyes against the enchanting vision and for a moment my old feeling for Marian came back. Too late: the die was cast. It was six o'clock on Tuesday not on Friday, and at any moment now the telegram would come.

'Are bloomers safer than tights?' I asked.

'Safer, good heavens no, but they're not so fast.'[5]

'But shouldn't they be fast, for bicycling, I mean?'

'Its not that kind of fast,' said Marcus, with unexpected patience, 'it's the other kind, the kind that women are who are not quite-quite. Men can be fast, I think, but then it's different. Bloomers were fast too, until a woman we knew took to wearing them for bicycling in Battersea Park.'

'I still don't see why tights are faster,' I confessed.

'Eh bien, je jamais! Ask yourself!'

I did, but got no answer.

'And she wants to wear black tights, too.'

'Are they worse?'

'Of course they are, you owl! Much worse, Mama says. Pas comme il faut – entièrement défendu.'

The shadows lengthened, the light changed, taking on its golden tint. The weather now obeyed the rules; at all times of the day it was exactly what it should be. No caprices, no cloudings over or threat of sudden storms. It was as good as its word, one could rely on it. I have never known again – even abroad, even in Italy – the meaning of Set Fair. It was as though the majestic claims of science to absolute certainty had miraculously been realized in the skies. This guaranteed serenity, as of a landscape by Claude,[6] had a curious effect upon one's spirits. One could ask for nothing more, and the stirrings of discontent, instead of finding an outlet in the weather, instead of finding their image in the weather, were silently rebuked by it.

We were turning into the drive, with an idea of going down into the village, when we saw a telegraph boy complete with red-piped uniform, pill-box hat, and scarlet bicycle, pedalling vigorously towards us. My mind was so full of bicycles that his seemed like a materialization, and its colour somehow a mistake.

'A telegram!' we both exclaimed, and Marcus signalled to the boy to stop. I was so sure the telegram was for me that I held my hand out for it.

'Maudsley?' queried the boy cheekily.

'*Mr* Maudsley,' Marcus corrected him. I withdrew my hand, and fixed my eyes on Marcus's face, wondering how he would take the news; for I was still sure the telegram was from Mother.

Marcus opened it. 'It's only Marian,' he said, as if a telegram from her hardly counted, 'to say she's coming by the late train tomorrow. Mama told her she hadn't given herself time for all her shopping. I expect she's staying on to buy your bicycle. Now let's go and déranger the villagers – sales types!'[7]

How short-sighted I had been, I thought, to expect my mother to wire! Of course she wouldn't. A telegram cost sixpence and we had to count our sixpences. A letter summoning me would come tomorrow, if not by the first post, by the second. Another reprieve, another carefree day, in body at Brandham Hall, in heart at home.

Wednesday morning brought *Punch*. I had to bide my time listening to the chuckles of my elders, which seemed more unrestrained now that Mrs Maudsley was not there; but at last I got possession of it. I opened it with caution for (as Marcus had discovered) I could not always see a joke, and sometimes had to have it explained to me by an older person, like a sum. So that when I did see one on my own it was a double triumph. To my delight, the paper was full of references to the heat: they made my single experience seem a universal one. Here was the sun, 'The Real Scorcher'[8] (there were, gratifyingly, several jokes about bicycles), bending low over the handlebars, curly rays coming out of his head, a sultry smile on his face; and in the background Mr Punch under an umbrella, mopping his brow, while Dog Toby, with his tongue hanging out, wilted behind him.

I laughed loudly and ostentatiously, meaning to be heard, for it is something to have seen a joke. But what was this, under the heading 'A Great Thought for Every Day in the Year'?[9]

'De Wet, having been frequently routed by Lord Methuen, has succeeded in cutting the railway at three points' – and there was more in the same strain, sneers at our conduct of the war. Was this funny? I didn't think so – I thought it unpatriotic, as perhaps it would be thought today. I always had a side, sometimes several sides, and now my side was England.

I was horrified, and, when opportunity offered, with due disgust I showed the offending passage to Lord Trimingham.

To my chagrin and surprise he laughed and laughed. I did not presume to criticize him, but surely this was too much? He, a veteran of the war, to think it funny to be made fun of! To laugh, when the side he had represented so gallantly and at such cost to himself, was ridiculed! I couldn't make it out.

But Wednesday morning did not bring a letter from my mother. I was not dismayed, however. On the contrary, I felt as if all the certitude that had been spread over the last twenty-four hours was gathering into a bomb that would explode at tea-time. Meanwhile, how should I spend the day? It was already very hot; my meteorological awareness, sharpened by practice into a sixth sense, foretold a record. Several times that morning I had to stop myself from going down to the game-larder and nibbling at the unripe fruit of knowledge.

This would be my last day at Brandham, unless they wanted me to stay till Friday, as a compromise, in which case, I told myself, I might get the presents after all, though in a hole and corner fashion and without the glory of a cake. I rather hoped they would, for the thought of the bicycle still sometimes pierced the perfect armour of my made-up mind.

'Have you forgotten anything?' This was a question my mother always asked when I was going to school, or going anywhere, though I went about so little. 'Is there anyone you ought to *thank*?' was another of her questions.

The people I ought to thank could all be thanked tomorrow or whichever day I left – Marian, Marcus, my host and hostess, and the servants. In imagination I saw myself thanking them, thanking them for having me. I might have to thank them for the presents, too. Thanks were something you kept till the last moment; they were the very essence of farewell and thinking of them brought departure nearer. Good-bye, Brandham! Was there anyone else?

Then I remembered Ted. I didn't think I had much to thank him for, but he had written me a letter, and it was on the cards that he was going to enlist. The thought of this still troubled me. I ought to say good-bye to him.

It wouldn't take long but how could I dispose of Marcus? I couldn't say good-bye to Ted with Marcus there. I had an idea.

Mother had consented to my bathing, but I had never bathed because, soon after her permission came, the river above the sluice had sunk so low it was too shallow even for a non-swimmer. The men of the party still sometimes went down to the pool below the sluice; but shrunken though it was, it was too deep for me.

'Marcus,' I said, 'il est très ennuyeux, mais . . .' French failed me.

'Spit it out in English, if it's easier,' said Marcus kindly. 'It's very boring, but . . .'

'Ted Burgess told me he'd give me a swimming lesson,' I said rapidly. This wasn't true but I had heard so many lies and lying is infectious; besides he had said he would do anything to make 'it' worth my while. I explained why I should need grown-up assistance.

'It will only take un petit quart d'heure,'[10] I wound up, pleased with this.

'Would you desert me?' said Marcus, tragically.

'But you deserted me,' I argued, 'when you went to Nannie Robson's.'

'Yes, but that's *different*. She's my old nurse and he . . .' I didn't know the epithet but it sounded unprintable. 'Well, don't let him drown you.'

'Oh no,' I answered, poised for flight.

'I shan't mind if you drown him,' Marcus said. He had a habit of speaking badly of people, especially those of a lower social status. It was a façon de parler,[11] as he might have said, and didn't mean much.

From the footman who in a dour, discouraging way was always

ready to oblige me, I obtained a length of rope; and armed with this, my bath-towel and my bathing-suit, I started for the river. My bathing-suit had only once before got wet: when Marian spread her dripping hair on it.

Mounting the sluice I saw Ted in the field, driving the reaper. It was the last field left with standing corn; in all the others the corn was gathered into stooks. Usually I went to him, but this was a last, a privileged occasion, and he should come to me. I signalled to him but he didn't see me; swaying and bumping on the seat of the 'spring-balance' he kept looking down to make sure that the blades were engaging with the wheat, and then up at the horse's head. At last one of the men saw me and told him. He stopped the horse and slowly dismounted, and the man got up in his place.

I went across to the second, smaller sluice to meet him but before we reached each other he stopped, which was most unlike him. I stopped too.

'I didn't think you'd come again,' he said.

'I came to say good-bye,' I told him. 'I'm going away tomorrow, or Friday at latest.' We seemed to be talking across a small but noticeable gulf.

'Well, good-bye, Master Colston, and good luck,' he said. 'I hope you'll enjoy yourself, I'm sure.'

I stared at him. I was not very observant but I saw that the strangeness in his manner was borne out by his appearance. Once he had reminded me of a cornfield ripe for reaping; now he was like corn that had been cut and left in the sun. I suppose he wasn't more than twenty-five. He had never looked young to me; young men in those days didn't try to look young, they aped the appearance of maturity. But now I could see in his face the features of a much older person. Sweating though he was, he looked dried up, the husk of the man he had been. He had taken in his belt another notch, I noticed. I might have said to him, as he had said to me, 'Who's been upsetting you?' but what I said was:

'Is it true you are going to the war?'

'Why,' said he, 'who told you?'

'Lord Trimingham,' I answered.

He said nothing to that.

'Did you know Marian was engaged to him?' I asked.

He nodded.

'Is that why you're going?'

He shuffled his feet as horses do, and for a moment I thought he was going to flare out at me.

'I don't know that I *am* going,' he said with a touch of his old spirit. 'That's for her to say. It isn't what I want, but what she wants.'

I thought this a cowardly speech, and still do.

'Look here, Master Colston,' he said suddenly, 'you haven't told anyone about this, have you? It's only a business matter between me and Miss Marian, but –'

'I haven't told anyone,' I said.

He still looked anxious.

'She said you wouldn't, but I said, "He's only a youngster, he might talk."'

'I haven't told anyone,' I repeated.

'Because we don't want to get ourselves into trouble, do we?'

'I haven't told anyone,' I said again.

'I'm sure we're both very much obliged to you, Master Colston, for doing what you have,' he said, almost as if he was proposing a vote of thanks. 'It isn't every young gentleman would want to give up his afternoons to carrying messages like an errand boy.'

He seemed to have become acutely conscious of the social gap between us. He was keeping his distance in more ways than one. At first I had been flattered by his calling me 'Master Colston', but suddenly I wished he wouldn't, and I said:

'Please call me postman, as you used to.'

He gave me a rueful smile.

'I'm still sorry I shouted at you same as I did on Sunday,' he said 'It's natural for a boy of your age to want to know those things and us older ones ought not to stand in your way. And it was a promise, as you said. But I dunno, I didn't feel like it – not after hearing you sing. I'll tell you now, if you like, and keep my promise. But I don't mind telling you I'd rather not.'

'I wouldn't dream of troubling you,' I said, loftily and as I thought a grown-up person might say it. 'I know someone who'll tell me. As a matter of fact, I know several people who will.'

'So long as they don't tell you wrong,' he said, half anxiously.

'How could they? It's common knowledge, isn't it?'

I was rather pleased with the phrase.

'Yes, but I should be sorry . . . You got my letter, didn't you? I wrote right off but it didn't go till Monday.'

I told him I had got it.

'Then that's all right,' he said, and seemed relieved. 'I don't write letters much, except on business, but it did seem mean, well, after what you'd done for us, giving up your own time, which is precious to a boy.'

A lump came into my throat, but all I could think to say was:

'That's quite all right.'

He looked towards the belt of trees behind which lay the Hall, his glance avoiding mine.

'So you're off tomorrow?'

'Yes, or Friday.'

'Oh well, we may be seeing each other, some time.' At last he crossed the gap and hesitatingly held his hand out. I think he still thought I might not take it. 'So long then, postman.'

'Good-bye, Ted.'

As I was turning away, grieved to be parting from him,[12] a thought started up in me and I turned back.

'Shall I take one more message for you?'

'That's very good of you,' he said, 'but do you want to?'

'Yes, just this once.' It could do no harm, I thought; and I should be far away when the message took effect, and I wanted to say something to show that we were friends.

'Well,' he said, once more across the gap, 'say tomorrow's no good, I'm going to Norwich, but Friday at half-past six, same as usual.'

I promised I would tell her. On the top of the sluice I stopped and looked back. Ted, too, was looking back. He took off his old soft hat and waved it, shading his eyes and waving vigorously. I tried to take off mine, and wondered why I couldn't. Then I saw why. In one hand I was carrying my bathing-suit, in the other my towel; the rope was draped like a halter round my neck. Suddenly I felt exceedingly uncomfortable; my movements were cramped and my neck was sweating. I hadn't noticed my encumbrances till now, nor apparently had Ted. I had forgotten what I came for and remembered something that I hadn't come for. Swinging my dry bathing-suit, which now was warm to the touch, and with the halter chafing my neck, I walked back across the blistering causeway. What a fool I should look, I thought, if Marcus saw me.

———

CHAPTER 20

On the tea-table lay my mother's letter. The order of release had come.

I realized then how much I had been counting on it, and my relief was a measure of the insecurity that I had felt since Sunday. Since Sunday I had enjoyed a great many things, and with all my being, so it seemed, but, underneath, the foundations were still crumbling. At the sight of the letter, various physical processes that unbeknown to me had been disorganized by the strain began to function normally; I talked a lot and ate voraciously. If I did not make an excuse to dart away and read the letter, it was partly to postpone the sense of flatness that I knew from experience would follow certitude, and partly because breaking the news to Mrs Maudsley was the one task left to me at Brandham that I dreaded. I had seen many guests leave Brandham unlamented, and it might have occurred to me that Mrs Maudsley would take my departure philosophically too, had I not been so much the centre of my own world and, as I thought, of hers.

But I reached my bedroom at last and this is what I read:

My Darling Boy,

'I hope you won't be disappointed at not getting a telegram and I hope you won't be disappointed by this letter.

Your letters both came by the same post, wasn't it strange? It took me a minute or two to discover which had been written first. In the first you begged me to let you stay on an extra week because you were so happy – and I can't tell you how I enjoyed hearing about the cricket and the songs, and how proud of you it made me. Then in the second letter you said you weren't at all happy, and would I send you a telegram asking Mrs Maudsley to send you back. Well, my darling, I couldn't bear to think you were unhappy, and I needn't tell you how much I miss you, at all times when you are away, and not only at your birthday, though especially then. So before I began my morning jobs I started off to the post office to send the telegram. But on the way it seemed to me that perhaps we were both acting in haste, which is seldom wise, is it? I remembered that only a few hours before you wrote the second letter you said you were happier than you had ever been in your life, and this hurt me a little, I confess, because I hope you have been happy here too. And I wondered what could have happened in a few hours to make you feel so different and wondered if you hadn't exaggerated something a little – we all do that at times, don't we? – it's what's called making a mountain out of a molehill. You said it was because you had to run errands and take messages, and you didn't like doing that. But, I seem to remember you once enjoyed taking them and besides, my darling, we can't always do what we like. I think it would be ungrateful to Mrs Maudsley after all her kindness to you if you were to grudge her this small service. (My mother quite understandably assumed that the "they" of my letter referred to Mrs Maudsley.) It's very hot here too, and I have often felt anxious for you, but you have always told me you enjoyed the heat, especially since Miss Maudsley gave you the thin suit (I'm longing to see it, and you in it, my darling, you do believe that, don't you? though I'm not sure that green is *quite* the right colour for a boy). You have often walked more than four miles at home (once you walked all the way to Fordingbridge and back, do you remember?) and I am sure that if you took things *very quietly* and didn't *run*, as you sometimes do, making yourself unnecessarily *hot*, you wouldn't find the walks too much for you.

You said that what you were doing might be wrong, but, my darling, how could it be? You told me Mrs Maudsley never misses going to church and all the family and the visitors go too, and that you have family prayers every day which isn't the case in *all* large houses, I feel quite sure (or even in small ones!) so I *can't* think she would want you to do anything *wrong* – besides, what *can* be wrong in taking a message? But I do think it would be rather wrong, though of course not *very* wrong (you *are* a funny old thing!) if you even *showed* her that you didn't want to go. She wouldn't be angry, I feel sure, but she'd be *puzzled* and wonder what sort of a home life you had had.

But of course, I do know that the heat knocks one up (it isn't "grate", my darling, it's "great" – I never knew you spell that wrong before – "grate" heat would be something quite different) and I am sure that if you went to

Mrs Maudsley and explained things to her, and asked her *very nicely* if someone else could take the messages, she would say yes. You told me more than once that there are twelve servants in the house: surely she could spare one of them to go? But I expect she has no idea that you don't like going – indeed, I rather hope she hasn't.

My darling, I do hope that you won't feel disappointed and hurt with me, but I do think it would be a *mistake* for you to leave so suddenly. They wouldn't understand, and might think me a spoilt and unreasonable mother! – which I am, my darling, but don't want to be in this instance. From what you have told me about them they would be very nice friends for you in after life. I hope this doesn't sound worldly, but we have to be worldly sometimes; your father didn't care about social life but I think he made a mistake, and since he died I haven't been able to do much in the way of making friends for you. I should like to ask Marcus here – but I don't know how we should entertain him – he must be used to *such* grand ways!

The ten days will soon pass, and so, my darling, I think we ought to be *patient*. I say this to myself as much as to you, for I long to see you and the sweetest part of your dear letter was where you said you were looking forward to coming home. But we can't expect to be happy *all* the time, can we? We both know that. Perhaps it wouldn't be good for us to be. And you are like your mother, sometimes up and sometimes down. I remember only a little while ago you were rather unhappy because some bigger boys teased you for using a long word, but you soon forgot about it and were as happy as ever. I feel sure that by the time this reaches you, you will be feeling so much happier that you will wonder how you ever came to write the letter.

Goodbye, my darling, darling boy. I shall write again for your birthday and send you a little present: my real present I am keeping until you come back: I wonder if you can guess what it is?

With all my love, my precious Leo,

Your loving

Mother

xxxx

P.S. What a long letter! But I thought you would like to know *exactly* how I felt. I do think it would be a mistake if you left now. All this will be an *experience* for you, my darling.'

Children are more used than adults to having their requests met by a flat refusal, and also less capable of taking the refusal philosophically. In spite of the reasonableness of its tone, my mother's letter amounted to a flat refusal, and as such it not only blocked my mental view, it utterly disorientated me. I literally did not know what to do next, in the smallest particular: I did not know whether to stay in my bedroom or go out of it. I should have liked to talk to somebody about my plight but instinctively dismissed this desire before it was formulated; I could talk to no one: to be a non-conductor was my function: I was a Tower of Silence on which lay whitening the bones of a dead secret[1] – no, not dead in that sense, but very much alive and death-dealing and fatal.

Or so I thought. For with my mother's letter cutting off escape, the perilous aspect of the situation again rose before me, for it was, in fact, the only aspect I could see.

Soon from pure restlessness I left my room. Half hoping, half dreading I should meet someone, I wandered about among the premises at the back, the wash-house, the dairy, the various outbuildings whose purpose I hardly knew but whose placid, normal functioning somehow reassured me; I even paid a half-hearted visit to the rubbish-heap. I tried to accustom myself to the feel of my new position, bring myself into harmony with it, as one does when wearing a new suit; but I couldn't. Some servants passed me and smiled. I wondered how they were able to go about their jobs so tranquilly, as if everything was just as it had been and should be, and no calamity was pending. From there I made my way towards the front of the house, furtively, keeping behind trees and bushes, until at last I heard the sounds of croquet on the lawn, and voices, too far away from me to distinguish the speakers. I wondered if Marian had come back.

As far as I had a purpose, it was to avoid being alone with her. She, I dimly realized, was the rock on which I had split. Ted had frightened me more, perhaps, but she had hurt me more; with men, as with boys, I knew more or less where I was: I did not expect them to be nice to me. Schoolboys have a much clearer perception of each other's characters than grown-ups have, for their characters are not obscured by a veil of good manners: they deal in hard words, they have no long-term policy, as men have, for asserting themselves, they prefer short profits and quick returns. Ted was like a schoolboy, angry one moment, good-humoured the next; I did not feel, until the end, that he had any greater regard for me than one thrusting male has for another, and I was prepared to take him on those terms, and though I idealized him, and myself in him, I had sunk no great capital of confidence in him.

But in Marian I had. Against her I had no such defences. She was my fairy-godmother. She combined the rôles of both fairy and mother: the magical benevolence of the one, the natural benevolence of the other. I had no more imagined that she could turn against me than that the good fairy of a fairy story could turn against the hero she protected. But she had, and so had my real mother: that was a betrayal, too. The difference was that mother did not know what she was doing and Marian did.

So my policy was to keep clear of her. I knew that it was shortsighted and that I should have to see her some time, if only to give her Ted's message. And as to that I was gradually coming to a conclusion that needed more resolution than anything I had yet done at Brandham Hall. I did not know if I should be able to bring myself to do it when the moment came: but it was the logical outcome of seeing myself as the pivot of the situation: I and only I could make the machinery break down, and if the machinery broke down so would the situation. On one thing I was determined, that I would take no more messages.

Our first meeting was uneventful. Marian was at dinner but she had brought two guests down with her; the table had lengthened again, the talk was general; she smiled at me as she used to and teased me a little across the table; then Marcus and I went off to bed.

Next morning, Thursday morning, Mrs Maudsley appeared at breakfast. She greeted me warmly – no, not warmly, for warmth was not in her nature – but with a full and flattering sense of what was due to a guest who had been unavoidably but most regrettably neglected. I studied her, looking for symptoms of hysteria, but could detect none. She was paler, I thought, than she had been, but she was always pale; her glance still had its special quality of not travelling but arriving, and her movements were as deliberate as ever. Yet tension had returned to the breakfast table; again I was afraid of making an awkward gesture, of spilling something, of drawing unfavourable attention to myself. And after breakfast, instead of the relaxation of the past three days, the feeling of beginning the day on bottom gear, there came her voice at which other conversation died, and the ominous 'Now, *today* . . .'

As Marcus and I were going out he whispered to me wickedly 'The awe-mongers have come back,' and I tittered, but at the disloyalty, not at the joke. I was going to reply when a voice behind us said, 'Marcus, I want to borrow Leo from you for a moment,' and I found myself following Marian.

I can't remember where the interview took place but I know that it was indoors and that the usual feeling one has that someone might come in was absent.

She asked me how I had been getting on without her and I said 'Very well, thank you,' which I thought safe and non-committal, but it didn't please her, for she said, 'That's the first unkind speech I've heard you make.' I hadn't meant it unkindly and a man would not have thought it was unkind, yet immediately I felt contrite and began to wonder how I could propitiate her. She was wearing a new dress; I had got to know the others and noticed the difference. 'Did you enjoy yourself?' I asked. 'No,' she replied. 'Someone asked me out to dinner but I felt more like dying than dining. I missed Brandham every minute. Did you miss me?'

I was thinking what I should answer, for I didn't want to be caught out a second time, when she said, 'Don't bother to say "yes" if you didn't.' She said this with a smile and I said untruthfully 'Of course I did,' and as I said it I half thought I had, at any rate I wished I had. She sighed and said, 'I expect you think me a ghastly old governess, don't you, slanging you and calling you names. But I'm not really — really I'm a good-natured girl.'

I didn't know what to make of this, was she saying she was sorry, as Ted had? Only once before had I known her apologize, except for something entirely accidental, like treading on somebody's toes. And this was her sole reference to the episode: she seemed to regard it as closed. 'I suppose you went about with Marcus?' she asked. 'Did you get into any mischief?'

'Oh no,' I answered righteously. 'We talked French.'

'French!' she said. 'I didn't know that French was one of your accomplishments. What a lot you can do — singing, cricket, French!' Her beautiful eyes searched me for a weak spot and found it. But I was wary, I only said:

'Marcus is much better at French than I am. He knows the irregular verbs.'

'Very irregular, I dare say,' Marian said. 'But anyhow you enjoyed yourself?'

'Oh yes,' I said politely. 'I'm sorry you didn't.'

'No, you're not,' she said surprisingly, 'you're not sorry in the least. You couldn't care if I dropped dead in front of you. You're a hard-hearted little boy, but then all boys are.'

Although she made it sound a compliment, and I would rather have been called hard-hearted than soft-hearted, I didn't altogether relish this. But I couldn't tell if Marian was serious.

'Are men hard-hearted too?' I asked to change the subject. 'I'm sure Hugh isn't.'

'Why?' she said. 'What makes you think he isn't? You're all alike, millstones, blocks of granite – or the beds at Brandham, if you want something *really* hard.'

I laughed. 'My bed isn't hard,' I said.

'You're lucky. Mine is, harder than the ground.'

'I've never slept on the ground,' I said, interested by her comparison, 'but I know a boy who has. He said it made his hip sore. Did you find that?'

'What makes you think I've slept on the ground?' she countered.

'Because you said your bed was harder.'

'Well, so it is,' she said, 'a great deal harder.'

I guessed then that she didn't mean a real bed.

'But Brandham is such a nice place,' I said, groping towards something.

'Who said it wasn't?'

'Well, you said the beds –'

'Were hard? Well, so they are.'

She was silent and I felt for the first time that she was unhappy. This was a revelation to me. I knew that grown-up people were unhappy – when a relation died, for instance, or went bankrupt. At such times they were sure to be unhappy: they had no option: it was the rule, like mourning after a death, like a black margin round the writing paper. (My mother still used it for my father.) They were unhappy to order. But that they should be unhappy in the way that I was sometimes, because something in my private life, to which perhaps I couldn't give a name, had gone wrong – that hadn't occurred to me. And in any case I should never have associated unhappiness with Marian. She seemed to have happiness at her beck and call, like her other moods, and to be above the need for it. I thought I knew why she was unhappy, but I wanted to make sure.

'Do soldiers have to sleep on the ground?' I asked.

She looked at me surprised; her mind was far away.

'Yes, I suppose so. Yes, of course they do.'

'Did Hugh have to?'

'Did I – no – no, yes, no, yes – I never slept on the ground.'

I had never seen her confused before.

'Not you,' I stammered, aghast anew at this stupid pitfall of pronunciation. 'Hugh, Hugh, Hugh,' I hooted.

'Oh Hugh,' she said expressionlessly. 'Yes, I've no doubt he had to.'

I said, a little shocked by her callousness about Lord Trimingham, 'And will Ted have to?'

'Ted?'

Her astonishment should have warned me, but my mind's antennae were blunted and I went on:

'Yes, when he goes to the war.'

She stared at me stupefied and her mouth fell open.

'Ted going to the war? What do you mean?' she said.

It had never crossed my mind that she didn't know. In a flash I remembered that Lord Trimingham had seen him on Monday, after Marian had left. But it was too late to draw back.

'Yes,' I said. 'Hugh told me. Hugh asked him to join up and he said he might. Hugh said it . . . it was on the cards he would go.' I wanted to make it perfectly clear to Marian, and incidentally to myself, what Ted's position was. I knew that I had put too many 'Hughs' into it (this was not quite accidental: I was sheltering myself behind him) but I was utterly unprepared for the outburst that followed.

'Hugh!' Marian exploded. 'Hugh! Do you mean that Hugh has persuaded Ted to enlist? Do you really mean that, Leo?'

I was frightened, but realizing that I was not the main object of her anger, I mumbled:

'He said he'd tackled him.'

'*Tackled*?'

I thought she didn't know what 'tackled' meant. 'It's a word they use in football,' I explained, 'for . . . bringing a man down.'

'Oh!' cried Marian, and it was as if something had pierced her. 'You mean Hugh *made* Ted say he'd go?'

Her face had gone white and her eyes were like dark holes in a sheet of ice.

'No,' I said. 'I don't think he *made* him, how could he? Ted's as strong as he is – stronger, I should think.' This seemed a conclusive argument to me. But not to Marian.

'That's where you're wrong,' she said. 'Ted is as weak as water. Hugh's far stronger.'

I could not understand this at all. It seemed, like many things that grown-ups said to each other, the opposite of the truth. But now a new look came into Marian's face, fear contending with anger.

'He might have, he might have,' she repeated, more to herself than to me. 'Did he say *why* he wanted Ted to go?'

The ice-holes yawned as if they would draw me under.

'Yes,' I said, and if I had been vindictive I should have enjoyed seeing Marian shrink away. 'He said he was a single man with no ties and would make a first-rate NCO. That's a kind of officer who isn't a real officer,' I explained. People were always explaining things to me and I rather enjoyed explaining back. 'Hugh also said that Ted was a good shot, but it was different with a rifle. He meant it's easier to miss with a rifle.'

Marian's face changed again. Something peered out of it from behind her eyes. 'He *is* a good shot,' she said, 'he *is* a good shot. My *God*, if Hugh *dares*! But I'll not let him,' she went on wildly: I could not tell whom she meant, Ted or Hugh. 'I'll soon put a stop to it! I'll make Ted put a stop to it! I tell you, Ted's a dangerous man when his blood's up.'

I shivered, and my mood, which had to some extent pursued its own course, independent of her ravings, began to take its colour from hers.

'No, he won't go to the war,' she said more quietly. 'I'll see to that. Blackmail's a game two can play at.'

I didn't know what blackmail meant, and with all my thirst for knowledge, was too frightened to ask.

'I'll tell Hugh –' she broke off. 'A word would do it.'

'What word? what will you tell him?' I demanded.

She stared at and through me.

'I'll tell him I won't marry him if Ted goes.'

'Oh, but you mustn't!' I cried, seeing at once how fatal such a course would be, seeing too the fifth Viscount stretched before me, dead from a tight-lipped bullet wound that didn't bleed. 'You see, Hugh doesn't *know*.'

'Doesn't know?'

'He doesn't know about the messages.'

She screwed her eyes up tight as if she was trying to work a sum out in her head. 'Doesn't *know*?' she repeated. 'Then why does he want Ted to go to the war?'

'Oh,' I exclaimed, thankful to be on firm ground at last. 'I told you. It's because he's patriotic — what my father called a "Jingo"[2] — and he wants to raise men for the Army. I *know* it's that — he almost said so when he said he wasn't an advertisement for Army life himself.'

She looked at me as if I was another person and she wasn't sure who. 'You may be right,' she said doubtfully, but with the lift of hope in her voice. 'You may be right. In that case,' she said inconsequently, 'it's just silly of Ted and I shall tell him so.'

'Why is it silly?' I asked. For us children 'silly' was a word of very strong, though generalized, disapproval. I wanted to defend Ted from it. 'Why is it silly?' I repeated, when she didn't answer.

'Oh, because it is. Why should he go, because Hugh asks him to?'

Afterwards I guessed why she said Ted was silly. She thought he was making a scruple of her being engaged to Hugh, and was going to the war to salve his conscience. But that didn't occur to me then, and I said, with unconscious cruelty, still trying to defend him from the charge of silliness:

'But perhaps he *wants* to go!'

Her eyes grew round with terror.

'Oh, but he couldn't!' she cried.

I saw the look but misconstrued it, thinking her terror was for Ted, not for herself. All at once a thought long kept at bay, from loyalty to Lord Trimingham, from a confused recognition of its hopeless unsuitability, rose to my lips:

'Marian, why don't you marry Ted?'

It was only for a moment, but in that moment her face reflected all the misery she had been going through; it was a heart's history in a look. 'I couldn't, I couldn't!' she wailed. 'Can't you see why?'

I thought I did, and since so many barriers between us were being overturned, I added – it seemed only logical:

'But why are you going to marry Hugh if you don't want to?'

'Because I must marry him,' she said. 'You wouldn't understand. I *must*. I've *got* to!' Her lips trembled and she burst into tears.

I had seen grown-up people with red eyes, but I had never seen a grown-up person cry before, except my mother. My mother when she cried became unrecognizable. Marian didn't: she was just Marian in tears. But there was a change – in me. For when she cried she was not Marian the deceiver, Marian who for her own purposes had taken me in and then called me green, but the Marian of the first days, Marian who had taken pity on me, who had rescued me from being laughed at, Marian who had curtsied to me at the concert, Marian of the Zodiac, Marian whom I loved.

The sight of her tears loosened mine and I cried too. How long we cried I do not know, but suddenly she looked up and said – her voice altered by her tears but not sobbing, and as though it had nothing to do with our previous conversation:

'Did you go down to the farm while I was away?'

'No,' I said, 'but I saw Ted.'

'Did he have a message for me?' she asked.

'He said today was no good as he was going to Norwich. But Friday at six o'clock, same as usual.'

'Are you sure he said six o'clock?' she asked, puzzled.

'Quite sure.'

'Not half-past six?'

'No.'

For answer she rose and kissed me; she had never kissed me before.

'And you won't mind taking our notes as usual?'

'No,' I breathed.

'Bless you,' she said. 'You're a friend in a thousand.'

I was still savouring these words and remembering the kiss, when I looked up and saw I was alone.

I had remembered my plan, but I had forgotten, and Marian had apparently forgotten, that my birthday was to be kept on Friday at tea-time. I thought I should be spending it at home when I asked Ted if I should take a message. I didn't think I should be present when the message took effect.

CHAPTER 21

My conversation with Marian left behind a glow which at first I was only too content to bask in. At some level of consciousness, not perhaps the deepest, we were reconciled. That was a great thing; once it would have been the great thing – but there was still a reservation in me somewhere, not about her but about what she was doing. Dimly I felt that the two must be kept separate – just as her unhappiness and her tears had to be kept separate from my conception of her as a divinity: they were mortal, she was not.

That was one reason for my improved morale: I could think of her almost as I used to. And I could think of the green bicycle coasting after her without wishing it had been another colour; green had nearly lost its horrors for me. There was another reason, too, why I felt the springs of being starting up again. The air had been cleared: so many things had been said: I myself had said quite daring things, things that had carried weight with an older person.

Yes, I was on much better terms with myself and with the world. But I had learned one thing during the last days: it didn't follow, because I was happier, that things were inevitably going better. It didn't follow, because certain secrets had been dragged into the daylight, that they were no longer dangerous.

If Lord Trimingham really suspected Marian of being too friendly with Ted, what would happen when she persuaded him not to join the Army, as she certainly would? 'It's not what *I* want, it's what *she* wants,' Ted had said: 'she has the say-so.' Marian had said that Ted was dangerous, I didn't think he was, because he had been so mild when I last saw him, but I knew how hot-tempered he could be, and egged on by Marian he might –

This was the point of greatest danger, the point where the paths of the ninth Viscount and the fifth converged.

As a theory it appealed more to my fears than to my mind. Although

I had an exaggerated idea of the rights of landlords I didn't think Lord Trimingham could legally compel Ted to join up, nor did I think he would call him out, as his ancestor had done in the same circumstances.

The more I studied the problem and the unknown factors in it the more abstract did it become; the persons of the drama began to lose their dimensions and be elongated into the familiar lines, AB, BC, CA.[1]

But Ted less than the others. I knew exactly what Lord Trimingham wanted. He was a constant: he wanted to marry Marian. I knew what Marian wanted, or what she intended, which was not the same thing: to marry Lord Trimingham and keep Ted by her. And what did Ted want? What she wanted, he had said, but I doubted it. He was much the most impulsive of the three, as I had cause to know. Sometimes he felt like it, to use his own phrase; sometimes he didn't. Whereas they always felt like it. It now occurred to me that when he heard that Marian and Lord Trimingham were engaged he didn't feel like it, and tentatively revised his previous answer to his landlord about joining up.

I feared for Lord Trimingham, I wept with Marian, but for Ted I grieved. Only he, it seemed to me, had a real life outside the problem, a life unconnected with it to which he was always reaching. Into that other life he admitted me as a real person, not only as an errand boy who must be petted or scolded to make him function. Perhaps this was unfair to Marian and Lord Trimingham, who had both treated me with signal kindness. But to them, I knew, I was a go-between, they thought of me in terms of another person. When Lord Trimingham wanted Marian, when Marian wanted Ted, they turned to me. The confidences that Marian had made me had been forced out of her. With Ted it was different. He felt he owed me something — me, Leo: the tribute of one nature to another.

I did not like to think of him giving up the things he cared for and sleeping on the ground. I could not believe that it was softer than the beds at Brandham; besides, he might be killed. There was a lot of him to be killed, and what there was he carried about with him, it was not spread out over houses and parklands.

Who had started it all, I wondered, whose fault was it? This was not an inquiry I found sympathetic: it might bring sin in, and I wanted to keep sin out: sin was undiscriminating and reduced to a uniform shade of grey many fine actions which might otherwise have been called Golden Deeds.

Still, whose fault was it? 'Nothing is ever a lady's fault,' Lord Trimingham had said, thereby ruling Marian out, and I was glad, for now I had no wish to inculpate her. He had not said, 'Nothing is ever a lord's fault,' but no one could hold him to blame: he had done nothing that he shouldn't: I was clear about that. Nor had he said, 'Nothing is ever a farmer's fault,' and lacking the benefit of this saving clause the fault, if fault there were, must lie with Ted. Ted had enticed Marian into his parlour, his kitchen, and bewitched her. He had cast a spell on her. That spell I would now break – as much for his sake as for hers.

But how?

I had taken a first step by falsifying the time of his appointment. Marian would not find him in the outhouse at six o'clock; and would she wait a whole half-hour for him? I doubted it; I relied on the impatience which was one of her most obvious characteristics. She could not wait. She could not wait to hear an explanation; she could not wait for one to finish a sentence; the boredom of waiting upset her physically. Two minutes' grace, I was sure, would be the utmost she would give to Ted: and in the exasperation of waiting her feelings for him might alter. To keep a grown-up person waiting was a serious offence, even among themselves. She might be angry with him, for she could be angry as well as he. 'I'll never come again! I'll never come again!' And Ted: 'Well, if you waited for me, so have I waited for you, and a lot longer too, and I'm a busy man, and it's harvest-time.' 'Pooh! You're only a farmer, it doesn't matter keeping farmers waiting.' 'Oh, I'm only a farmer, am I, well, we'll see,' etc., etc.

I pictured quite a pretty quarrel between them, reproaches, recriminations, and finally rupture, all growing out of the seed of distrust I'd sown. And then the situation would subside, like a pricked gathering on one's finger.

How much happier we should have been, I reflected, if the situation had never arisen! Not Lord Trimingham, he was happy, but only because he was kept in ignorance. But Marian, Ted, and myself, Leo Colston; what had we got out of it to compensate us for what we had lost? We had reached, all three of us, a point when everything that happened, however distantly related, however apparently unconnected, only mattered in so far as it helped, or hindered, Marian's meetings with Ted. These meetings had come to dominate our lives: nothing else really counted. Why did Marian loathe London, or say she did? Why did Ted feel obliged to give up farming which he loved, for soldiering in South Africa, which he hated? Why had I been reduced to trying to get myself recalled from Brandham Hall, where I had been so happy? In each case the answer was the same: the Marian—Ted relationship.

How everything else had been diminished by it and drained of quality! — for it was a standard of comparison that dwarfed other things. Its colours were brighter, its voice was louder, its power of attraction infinitely greater. It was a parasite of the emotions. Nothing else could live with it or have an independent existence while it was there. It created a desert, it wouldn't share with anyone or anything, it wanted all the attention for itself. And being a secret it contributed nothing to our daily life; it could no more be discussed than could some shameful illness.

I did not know it by the name of passion. I did not understand the nature of the bond that drew the two together; but I understood its workings very well. I knew what they would give for it and give up for it; I knew how far they would go — I knew there were no lengths they would not go to. I realized they got something out of it I could not get: I did not realize that I was jealous of it, jealous of whatever it was they gave each other, and did not give me. But though experience could not tell me what it was, my instincts were beginning to have a clue.

What an Eden Brandham Hall had been before this serpent entered it![2] I fell to reconstructing my visit as it might have been if I had never slid down Ted Burgess's straw-stack. Some facts I suppressed, others I distorted, others I magnified. There would have been no ridicule, no making fun of me: every day would have been a high-light, like the shopping expedition to Norwich, like my catch at the cricket match, like my song at the concert. I should have been infinitely valued and esteemed, but at the same time I should have been perfectly free to go my own way; the affection showered on me would have imposed no obligations. I could not conceal from myself the fact that this sun of the twentieth century, of which I had such high hopes, had shone on me: even today, which seemed a chilly, disappointing day after yesterday, the thermometer had climbed to nearly eighty-one degrees. But I should have enjoyed it, so I told myself, in a different spirit, in a mood of continuous, conscious lyricism. In the windless stillness in which I wandered and wondered, everything I saw would have ministered to my happiness; everything would have had its proper quality and spoken to me of itself. The flowers, the trees, the house, the distant views, would have had the same value to my physical eye as they had to the eye of contemplation; the separateness, the distance between them, the air of existing only for themselves and me, which I demanded for the realization of my Golden Age, would have been my private, undisturbed possession. And so with the figures of the landscape. From Mrs Maudsley downwards (for I put her first) I should have come to know and love them in the unique splendour of their separate entities, stars of varying magnitudes, but each with its appointed place in the heavens, and each worshipful.

Instead, my orbit had contracted in proportion as my rate of progress had increased; until I was now dizzily whirling round a tiny flaming nucleus like a naphtha flare in a street-market, impenetrable darkness round me, my sole prospect my own imminent destruction.

Il faut en finir,[3] as Marcus might have said, il faut en finir.

But what spell could I employ to break the spell that Ted had cast on Marian?

I had no knowledge of Black Magic and relied on the inspiration of the moment. If while concocting the spell I could excite myself and frighten myself, I felt it had a better chance of success. If also I had the sense of something giving way, inside me and outside, that was still better. The spell that had brought about the downfall of Jenkins and Strode had fulfilled all these conditions.

But those were spells whose operation was confined to the world of my experience, the schoolboy world. I had never launched a spell against a grown-up person. My present victims were not only grown-ups, they belonged to the world from which my spells derived their power; I should be trying to turn their own weapons against them.

But I must not think of them as victims. This I told myself over and over again, and I still do. They would not suffer at all. The other spell, Ted's spell, would be destroyed but they would not be harmed. Afterwards, as in *A Midsummer Night's Dream*, they might not even be able to recognize each other.[4] 'Who is that man over there?' Marian might ask me. 'I seem to know him and yet I don't . . . Oh he's a *farmer*? Then I don't think I want to know him.' So ran one dialogue, and another ran: 'Who is that lady, Master Colston? I thought I knew her, and yet I don't. She's pretty, isn't she?' 'Oh don't you know? That's Miss Maudsley, Miss Marian Maudsley.' 'Oh is it, indeed, then she's not for the likes of me.'

Or perhaps they would be invisible to each other: that would be still more thrilling. In any case, order would have been restored: social order, universal order: and Puck or whoever he is who has produced this miracle will vanish gracefully from the scene.[5]

The spell must be something that would tax me to the utmost, involve me in doing something that I dreaded; and it must have a symbolical appropriateness, too.

The idea came to me while I was talking to Marcus, and I don't think he noticed any change in my expression.

I put on my bedroom slippers, and my brown Jaeger dressing-gown over my nightshirt, and crept down the staircase – careful to take the left-hand flight, whose turn it was, for in an enterprise of this sort every formality must be observed. Through the closed door of the drawing-room came sounds of singing. Often there was singing after dinner, I knew: but we were not allowed to sit up for it. Marian was at the piano, I recognized her touch, and the singer must be the man who had come down from London with her. He had a good tenor voice, much more even than Ted's, but not altogether unlike it. I knew the song: it was called 'The Thorn'.[6]

> 'From the white-blossomed sloe
> My dear Chloe requested
> A sprig her fair breast to adorn; . . .
> No, by Heaven, I exclaimed,
>   May I perish
> If ever I plant in that bosom a thorn.'

I had never quite understood what the song meant, but it appealed to some of my strongest feelings. Why was the lady (or woman, as

Marcus had warned me to call her, but I was always forgetting that) afraid that some jealous rival might laugh her to scorn? I did not know, but I sympathized with her, for I knew how unpleasant it was to be laughed at in that way. And I sympathized – how deeply I sympathized – with the lover's resolve to devote himself to death rather than expose her to such an insult.

After the song came a little desultory clapping, muffled and faint compared with the applause that had greeted my songs in the village hall; then silence.

The front door stood open to the night; it had been left open every night since I arrived, except the first, to keep the house cool. But it wasn't cool; under my Jaeger dressing-gown I was sweating.

I stared at the tall oblong of darkness in front of me. Behind me the hall, lit here and there by oil lamps, ended in darkness too. But under the drawing-room door a sliver of quite bright light glowed, and lay wedge-shaped upon the floor. What would happen, what would they say, if I pushed the door open and went in and said to Mrs Maudsley, 'I'm still awake – can I listen to the music?'

I dared not do it, yet I nearly did it, so strong was my shrinking from what lay before me. I tried to leave my moorings, I set my face towards the darkness outside and got as far as the threshold, but I couldn't cross it. The future was like a wall in front of me, impenetrable to thought.

I turned back to the hall. The presences the other side of the drawing-room door were a comfort to me; they did not know that I was there, but they were like spectators at the quayside who wave to the ship as it goes out, and cheer the lonely passenger, even if their farewells are not for him.

I found that by moving close to the drawing-room door, touching it, I could hear something of what was being said inside. They were discussing what the next song should be, 'In the Gloaming', or 'Kathleen Mavourneen'.[7] Someone said, 'Let's have both,' and perhaps I should have stayed to listen to them, for they were favourite songs of mine, and then crept back to bed. But my wretched habit of wriggling overcame me: I made a noise and someone within was asked to go and investigate – Denys, I think. I heard footsteps coming across the floor, and fled.

It was dark as I expected it would be, but much less difficult to find my way. That I might lose myself had been one of my chief fears – my chief practical fears. Another still haunted me and grew with every step I took – that they would have shut and locked the front door before I got back. Then I should have to stay outside till morning, and try to sleep on the ground.

The night was not only a strange world to me, it was a forbidden world. Little boys had no business to be about at night: the night was for grown-ups, and bad grown-ups too: thieves, murderers and such.

But what I was going to do had to be done at night, or it would lose its virtue. I had persuaded myself of that: the very fear it inspired in me convinced me.

I sped along between the rhododendrons, keeping my thoughts at bay, and passing one by one the landmarks at which (I had promised myself) I would turn back if my terrors became unbearable: I had bribed them in this fashion before I left my bedroom.

As I went along I rehearsed what I meant to do, for I knew how easy it is, in the excitement of doing something for the first time, to forget the proper way to do it, the separate stages and which follows which. More than once I had known perfectly, in theory, how to do a chemistry experiment, but when confronted by the bunsen burner and the tube and all the rest of it, so different in reality from what they had been in thought, I had lost my head and made a mess of it.

This, too, was to be a chemistry experiment, and one of the conditions had already been complied with: it was to be done at night: preferably by moonlight, preferably during an eclipse, but anyhow at night. First, the ingredients must be gathered. A single berry would be sufficient for my purpose, but as every part of the plant was poisonous it would be more effective if every part of the plant was used: leaf, stem, flower, berry, and root. To obtain a specimen of the last named might not be easy, as the root might be some distance underground, so it was advised to provide oneself with a pocket-knife fitted with a stout blade, for the purpose of paring off a portion of the root. No trowel or spade being available this must be done by the fingers, digging out the earth at the plant's base, the head of course coming into contact with the lower branches (this was a contact that I specially dreaded). The desired length of root having been cut off would then be placed in the dressing-gown pocket or other convenient receptacle, care being taken to touch none of the ingredients with the lips as every part of the plant is poisonous (NB If this can be done while holding the breath it will be more effective). The whole to be carried at a fast trot and without stopping to the magician's bed-chamber where other utensils must be held in readiness, viz.

> Four candles (for combustion)
> One mettle container (silver)
> I perferated utensil
> Four books (small) for supporting the last named
> Four boxes of matches
> Water for boiling
> Watch for timing
> Wet sponge in case of fire

The metal container was a cup my mother had given me: it was one of a series, graduated in size, which fitted into each other and so took up only a small space. They were of silver, gilt-washed inside, and had been given to mother as a wedding present. They were meant for picnics and she hoped I should use mine for this purpose, on my visit, though actually I never did, for there were always plenty of glasses. She also believed, I suspect, that the cup would be a mark of gentility, showing that I came from a good home. As an alembic it was almost perfect, being egg-shell thin.

The perforated utensil on which, more than on anything else, the success of my spell depended was the drainer from the soapdish on my washstand, a white enamelled makeshift that did not match the set. It had a large hole in the middle and other holes all round through which, I thought, the candle flames would find their way: supported by the books it would make a kind of tripod.

Then having arrived and having reduced the ingredients in the cup to a mash or pulp to add water but not too much as this will require longer to boil. Boiling takes place when bubbling begins (212 Fahr.). This should be at midnight, and at the same time chant the spell (words of spell to be supplied later) thirteen times backwards, thirteen times forwards, saying, 'And I am thirteen too,' not so loud as to be heard in the passage but loud enough for someone listening in the room to hear, and if the magician sweats to add some drops of his own sweat for this is most effective.

Afterwards on no account to touch the liquid with the lips but pour it down the WC, leaving all utensils clean and workmanlike, remembering that others have to use them after you.

How much of these instructions I was able to repeat I cannot tell; I had written them down on a blank page of my diary, which I meant to tear out, for safety's sake, as soon as I had ceased to be proud of them. But I forgot to do that, as I forgot many other things, the following day.

Though my eyes got gradually accustomed to the darkness I was almost on top of the outhouses before I saw the thick blur of the deadly nightshade. It was like a lady standing in her doorway looking out for someone. I was prepared to dread it, but not prepared for the tumult of emotions it aroused in me. In some way it wanted me, I felt, just as I wanted it; and the fancy took me that it wanted me as an ingredient, and would have me. The spell was not waiting to be born in my bedroom, as I meant it should be, but here in this roofless shed, and I was not preparing it for the deadly nightshade, but the deadly nightshade was preparing it for me. 'Come in,' it seemed to say; and at last after an unfathomable time I stretched my hand out into the thick darkness where it grew and felt the shoots and leaves close softly on it. I withdrew my hand and peered. There was no room for me inside, but if I went inside, into the unhallowed darkness where it lurked, that springing mass of vegetable force, I should learn its secret and it would learn mine. And in I went. It was stifling, yet delicious, the leaves, the shoots, even the twigs, so yielding; and this must be a flower that brushed my eyelids, and this must be a berry that pressed against my lips . . .

At that I panicked and tried to force my way out but could not find the way out: there seemed to be a wall on every side, and I barked my knuckles. At first I was afraid of hurting the plant, then in my terror I began to tear at it, and heard its branches ripping and crackling. Soon I cleared a space round my head, but that was not enough, it must all be clear. The plant was much less strong than I supposed: I fought with it: I got hold of its main stem and snapped it off. There was a swish; a soft, sighing fall of leaf on leaf; a swirl, a débris of upturned leaves, knee-deep all round me: and standing up among them, the torn stem. I seized it and pulled it with all my might, and as I pulled the words of the missing spell floated into my mind out of some history lesson – 'delenda est belladonna![8] delenda est belladonna!' I heard the roots creaking and cracking, felt their last strength arrayed against me, the vital principle of the plant defending itself in its death-agony. 'Delenda est belladonna!' I chanted, not loudly, but loud enough for anyone listening to hear, and braced myself for a last pull. And then it gave, came away in my hands, throwing up with a soft sigh a little shower of earth which rustled on the leaves like rain; and I was lying on my back in the open, still clutching the stump, staring up at its mop-like coronal of roots, from which grains of earth kept dropping on my face.

CHAPTER 22

I slept deeply that night and for the first time since I came to Brandham Hall was still asleep when the footman called me. I felt very strange and could not collect myself. The feeling of strangeness did not wear off when he had drawn the curtains. It was something inside me, I knew, but it was also something outside. I just remembered to say, 'Good morning, Henry!' otherwise he would have gone out without speaking: he never spoke to me unless I spoke to him first – and not always then.

'Good morning, Master Leo, many happy returns!'

'Why, it's my birthday! I had quite forgotten.'

'You may have, Master Leo,' said the footman, 'but there's others haven't. Time's running on! You're thirteen now, you'll soon be fourteen: fifteen, sixteen, seventeen, eighteen, and every year bringing new troubles.'

I didn't quite like this speech, though I knew it was kindly meant, and only reflected the ingrained pessimism of Henry's outlook. But I still felt strange: what could it be? I looked at the window and one explanation dawned on me.

'Good gracious, it's raining!'

'It's not raining *yet*,' said Henry grudgingly. 'But it will before the day's out, mark my words. Not that we don't need it. All this hot weather isn't natural.'

'Oh, but it's summer!' I exclaimed.

'Summer or not, it isn't natural,' Henry repeated. 'Why, every-thing's burnt up and they do say' – here he looked down at me ominously – 'that quite a lot of people have gone mad.'

'Oh,' I exclaimed, for mental derangement, like most forms of calamity, had a special interest for me.

'The Dog Days, you know,'[1] he said, confidentially, shaking his head.

225

Still interested in the effects of the weather I asked:

'Do you know of any dog that's gone mad, personally, I mean?'

Again he shook his head. 'It isn't only dogs go mad,' he remarked with gloomy relish: 'it's human beings.'

'Oh, not anybody here?' I asked, all ears.

'I'm not saying it is,' said Henry oracularly, 'and I'm not saying it isn't. But what I do say is, A miss is as good as a mile, any day.'

I could make nothing of this, and if his manner had not been so chilling I should have asked him to explain it. He was bending over the washstand, ritually removing the water jug from the basin and replacing it with a brass hot-water can, over which he draped a face-towel. Suddenly he said accusingly:

'There's a piece of the soap-dish missing.'

'It's over there,' I answered guiltily, pointing to the writing table which, for reasons of space, had been put at the end of the bed. Henry came across and stared at my handiwork.

It looked like a little heathen altar, or a study for Stonehenge. The four books formed the temenos,[2] within stood the four candles, close together; above them, resting on the books, lay the drainer from the soap-dish, and on the drainer, ready to receive the ingredients, my silver cup. The water-bottle, the damp sponge, the four boxes of matches, were set at ritual intervals. Only my watch was absent from the roll-call. Flimsy and childish-looking as the structure was, it did somehow bear witness to occult intention, as if it was ready to do what harm it could, and I felt exceedingly embarrassed at having to confess myself its architect.

Henry shook his head slowly; I knew what he meant: Here is someone else whose brains have been turned by the heat. But all he said was:

'It looks as if you've been having a field day.'

This was a compendious comment he often used to indicate Olympian tolerance for actions which, though harmless, were below the comprehension line.

'But,' he added grimly, 'it's not my job to clear them up.'

As soon as Henry had gone I got out of bed and gingerly dismantled my spell-mechanism. Once the various objects were separated and back in their proper place they seemed to lose their collective power for evil. They had only acquired it while I slept, for last night, after my struggle with the deadly nightshade, they had seemed the whitest magic, hardly magic at all. I had been so strung up by the encounter that my journey back, with its prospect of being locked out, had had no terrors for me. I walked in at the open door as if it had been eleven in the morning, not eleven at night.

And now the skies were grey: that was one reason why I felt strange. We had had cloudy days before, but not dull days, threatening rain. I was so used to being greeted by the sun that its absence was as disconcerting as a frown on a face that has always smiled. It told me summer was over and a sterner season lay ahead.

My experience of the night before had somehow prepared me for this. Not in vain had I allied myself with the weather; my summer was ended, too. I had emptied myself out over the deadly nightshade, purged myself of the accretions of fantasy that had been accumulating since I came to Brandham Hall. No one had ever told me to beware of them, but now I told myself. Good-bye to make-believe! I tried, with tolerable success, to think of my struggle in the outhouse as a mere gardening operation, the destruction of a poisonous weed of whose existence I ought long ago to have warned my hostess.

Now that I was thirteen I was under an obligation to look reality in the face. At school I should be one of the older boys to whom the others looked up. When I thought of last night's performance at the outhouse, of my efforts to impose my puny self upon events, when I thought of my career as a magician, the mumbo-jumbo which I had practised and which I had taught to others, I grew hot. And my letter to my mother – that pitiful petition for recall – how I despised myself for writing it. Looking back on my actions since I came to Brandham, I condemned them all: they seemed the actions of another person.

I condemned them unheard. I did not stop to ask myself how, if they were to do again, I should improve on them. I saw them all as instances of a gross piece of quackery, that had begun the moment I arrived at Brandham – had indeed begun before, when Jenkins and Strode had fallen off the roof. Ever since then I had been playing a part, which seemed to have taken in everybody, and most of all myself. It would not have taken in my old nurse, who had been very quick to spot in me, or any child, a tendency to ape an alien personality. She had no objection to one's being any kind of animal, or any kind of human being, high or low, young or old, dead or alive, provided it was a pretence, provided you could say *who* you were, when challenged. But if the assumed personality was a distortion of one's own ego, the 'I' decked out in borrowed plumes meant to impress, somebody one would like to be thought to be, then she was down on one. 'Who are you being now?' she would ask me. 'Oh, nobody special. Just Leo.' 'Well, you're not my Leo. You're another little boy and I don't like him.'

All the time at Brandham I had been another little boy and the grown-ups had aided and abetted me in this: it was a great deal their fault. They like to think of a little boy as a little boy, corresponding to their idea of what a little boy should be – as a representative of little boyhood – not a Leo or a Marcus. They even had a special language designed for little boys – at least some of them had, some of the visitors: not the family: the family, and Lord Trimingham too who was soon to be one of them, respected one's dignity. But there are other ways, far more seductive to oneself than the title 'my little man', to make one feel unreal. No little boy likes to be called a little man, but any little boy likes to be treated as a little man, and this is what Marian had done for me: at times, and when she had wanted to, she had endowed me with the importance of a grown-up; she had made me feel that she depended on me. She, more than anyone, had puffed me up.

No doubt, as Henry said, the heat had something to do with it. The heat had knocked out Mrs Maudsley – the heat and Marian. Perhaps Marian *was* the heat? It had also knocked out Marcus, and he had taken it more sensibly than anyone: he had come out in spots and retired to bed. He had no wish to be thought other than he was: he could have told me he had measles, but he didn't. He was never taken in by himself: even his pretences were not for themselves but had an ulterior object. Once or twice his French personality had run away with him but its main object was to score off me. He was interested in what really went on around him, not in what his imagination could make of it. That was why he was fond of gossip: he wanted to know about people, not to imagine about them. It would not have pleased him in the least to imagine himself a romantic outlaw, defending a deadly secret to the death: he would much rather tell the secret and see what happened. I had never admired Marcus so much as I did on the morning of my thirteenth birthday.

This is what I think now, but it is also what I felt then, and my feelings were of a substance thicker than thought and pressed more heavily on my tired, bewildered mind.

In my attack upon the deadly nightshade I had gone a step too far, even for myself. Supposing someone had seen me 'savaging it'! Supposing someone – the imaginary listener I had evoked – had heard me chanting 'delenda est belladonna' to the night! He might well have thought me mad. It was bad enough to have been seen by myself.

The grey, liquid light that lay like rain-water on roofs and trees flowed softly into my small, tall room. Henry had taken away the Eton suit I wore for dinner (sometimes he took away my braces too, and I had to ring for them), and put out my green suit on the chair, with my underclothes, stockings, and garters neatly piled above. Having by forced marches reached the final stage, I was just about to put the suit on, when suddenly I thought I wouldn't. Not because of its colour or because it reminded me of Marian's duplicity – no, it was a suit like any other; but it was also my motley, the vesture of my make-believe. I was prepared to be called a green boy, which I was, but I didn't want to be taken for Robin Hood, which I was not. So I got out my Norfolk suit, which already had the appearance of having been put away for a long time, and the stockings that went with it, and my boots. Very odd I felt when I put them on, with all the pressures coming in new places and very odd I felt when I saw myself in the glass. But at any rate it was myself I saw, not a sea-green, corruptible parody.[3]

During prayers I was anonymous, a worshipper, exempt from mortal notice, but when we rose from our knees I was a birthday boy in a Norfolk jacket; and when I had been congratulated on being the one, the other, my costume, came in for comment: there was a return, a gentle, innocuous echo, of the teasing of earlier days. I wondered why I had ever minded it; but Lord Trimingham, who clearly thought I might mind, said, 'But he's quite right, and he's the only one of us who is. A Norfolk jacket in Norfolk, and besides, it's going to rain. We shall all have to change, but he won't.' Except for me, everyone at the table was dressed for a fine day. 'Yes,' said Marian, whose eyes had a mischievous gleam, 'but he looks as if he was going away, that's what I don't like. That suit is labelled Liverpool Street.'[4]

Beside my plate were two long envelopes, one in my mother's handwriting, one in my aunt's. Ordinarily I should have waited until the end of the meal to read them in private, but today this withdrawal had an air of furtiveness; I wanted all my movements to be public; so making the excuse that grown-ups made, I opened my mother's missive. At what was wrapped in tissue paper I did not look, but I took out the letter. It was full of loving messages and apologies. 'I have been so vexed with myself for not sending the telegram,' she said. 'At the time it seemed more *sensible* not to: but now I wonder if you weren't quite well, and didn't like to say so. You would tell me, my darling, wouldn't you? I didn't know I should miss you so much, but I do, I miss you dreadfully and ten days seems such a long time to wait. Still, they will pass. I hope you are quite happy again, I wish I could feel sure you were: if you are still taking the messages, and find it tiring, do take my advice and ask Mrs Maudsley to let someone else go. I'm sure she *gladly* would. And I was afraid, my darling, you would think I wasn't nice about your new suit, because I said it wasn't the right colour for a boy. But of course it is, why, soldiers wear it now, poor things – khaki's a sort of green, and so I'm giving you a tie to go with it. I hope it will go with it, greens are a little apt to clash, but you wouldn't know that.'

Here I peeped into the envelope, not meaning to take the tie out, but when I saw a corner of the stuff I couldn't help it: out it came, a long green serpent. 'Oh, what a lovely tie!' exclaimed several voices: 'And what a lucky little boy you are,' said one of the new visitors, whom I immediately disliked.

'But it won't go with that Norfolk suit, you know,' said Marian.

Blushing, I dived back into my letter, which was now only a shallow water, gently a-ripple with my mother's farewell.

The other letter was longer, for my aunt had much to tell about herself, much to surmise about me. She was an imaginative guesser and knew what one was likely to be doing, but did not always get it quite right. 'Norfolk is famous for its dumplings,'[5] she said, 'I expect you are having plenty of them.' As a matter of fact, I don't think we ever had one. 'I knew some Maudsleys once,' she hazarded, 'and they lived close to where you are; at Hanging Brandham or Steeple Brandham, I forget which. I expect you will have met them.' But alas, I hadn't. On another matter she was better informed. 'Your mother tells me you have a new suit, a green one, rather an unusual colour for a boy, perhaps, but *I think men's clothes are far too dingy, don't you?* They say a woman can never choose a tie for a man, but I think that's all rubbish, so *here goes!*'

Again I had to break off and peep into the envelope, and again a peep was not enough. A glance warned me that whatever shade of green was right for a boy, this shade was not, it was too mustardy. But as against that, it was already made up into a lovely bow, such as no human hand could tie, while a neat loop at the back made it, even for a hasty dresser, almost foolproof.

But this tie did not have the success of the other. Approval tarried, doubt spread through the room. A cloud was gathering on Marcus's brow, when suddenly Lord Trimingham said, stretching his hand across the table:

'Can I have a look at it?'

I pushed the tie across to him.

'I think it's charming,' he said, 'so gay. Wait a moment and I'll show you what it looks like on.'

He pulled off his blue and white spotted tie and after a little fumbling ('I can't quite get the hang of it') looped mine to his collar-stud. On him it didn't look the common thing that Marcus's deepening frown told me it was; it looked outré but elegant; and he sketched a little flourish with his hands and gave a smile meant to suggest some carefree occasion – Goodwood, perhaps? Even to me it was pathetic, how little his face would answer to his thoughts; but he seemed unconscious of that. 'What do you say?' he appealed to Mr Maudsley; 'What do you say, Marian?'

I kept the tie for years.

'And now,' said Mrs Maudsley, pushing back her chair, '*today*' – she paused, '*today* is Leo's day.' She smiled at me, and the smile broke against my face like a cool wave. 'How would you like to spend it, Leo?'

I was completely tongue-tied: I could not think of any way of spending it. Mrs Maudsley tried to help me out. 'What do you say to a picnic?'

'That would be very nice.'

'Unless it rains,' said Mrs Maudsley, scanning the heavens. 'Or a

drive to Beeston Castle, after luncheon?[6] You haven't seen it, have
you?'

'That would be very nice,' I repeated, miserably.

'Well, shall we do that, if it doesn't rain? I expect you'd like the
morning free to play with Marcus.'

'Yes, please.'

'And at five o'clock you'll cut your birthday cake . . . Yes, Denys?'

'I was only going to say, Mama, that we still don't know what *Leo*
wants.'

'I think we do,' said Mrs Maudsley, mildly. 'That suits you, doesn't
it, Leo?'

'Oh *yes*,' I said.

Mrs Maudsley turned to her elder son.

'Are you satisfied now, Denys?'

'I only meant, Mama, that on his birthday he ought to choose for
himself.'

'But hasn't he chosen?'

'Well, no, Mama, you've chosen for him.'

His mother's face expressed a prayer for patience.

'He did not offer an alternative, so –'

'I know, Mama, but on his *birthday* –'

'Can you suggest anything yourself, Denys?'

'No, Mama, because it's not *my* birthday.'

I saw Mrs Maudsley's fingers clench.

'I think you'll find the arrangements are satisfactory,' she said,
evenly. 'Now, for us *grown-ups* –'

As soon as Marcus and I were out of the room he said:

'No, Leo, you can't.'

'Can't what?'

'Wear that tie.'

'Why not?'

'Because,' explained Marcus, speaking slowly and spacing out the
words, 'it is a made-up tie.'

After we had scuffled a little, Marcus said, 'It's all right for Trimingham, of course – he can wear anything, but you, you have to be
careful.'

'Careful, what of?'

'Not to look like a cad. But I won't say any more about it because it's your birthday.'

I had plenty of time during the morning to savour my sensations. My new true personality tasted rather flat. For one thing it had no birthday spirit; it would not admit that this was a day different from other days, with special privileges of feeling and behaving. It was always warning me not to get above myself. When I had made a fool of myself in the eyes of other people, I fought against their judgement even while I smarted; but I could not so easily fight against my own judgement. My new mentor would not allow me to inspect the place where the crime had been committed, which, in common with other murderers, I hankered to do; it would not even let me visit the rubbish-heap to see if the corpse of the plant had found its way there. When the sun came out, as soon it did, shining between heavy piled-up clouds, I would not let my spirits rise to greet it. When we saw Marian and Lord Trimingham strolling together, heads bent towards each other, I strove to repress the uprush of delight I felt. All my relationships, both with people and things, seemed to have lost their edge. Even with Marcus, whose place in my regard had always been ambiguous, one thing at school and another at his home, I did not feel at ease; our friendship was the product of many fine adjustments, of many feelings nicely balanced, and I saw a round-headed boy a little shorter than myself, being specially nice to me, refraining from talking French because it was my birthday.

My birthday! It all came back to that. But I didn't feel it was my birthday: I felt I was an indifferent spectator at someone else's: someone in a Norfolk jacket buttoned across his chest, belted across his tummy, wearing thick stockings and laced boots whose serrated hooks grinning upwards were like mouthfuls of serpent's teeth swallowing his legs.

I did not realize that this attempt to discard my dual or multiple vision and achieve a single self was the greatest pretence that I had yet embarked on. It was indeed a self-denying ordinance to cut out of my consciousness the half I most enjoyed. To see things as they really were – what an impoverishment! Chafed in my flesh, chafed in my spirit, I wandered aimlessly about with Marcus, half wishing that he would barge into me, or call me names, or practise his superior

French on me, instead of wrapping me in the cotton-wool of his society manner.

Just before luncheon I stole up to my room and changed into my green suit, after which I felt more normal.

CHAPTER 23

Luncheon was seldom over before three o'clock and our drive was timed to start at a quarter past. But the clouds had gathered again. This time they had an ominous look, white upon grey, grey upon black, and the still air presaged thunder. One after another we went outside, stared at the sky, and came back with our verdicts.

It was the first time we had had to wait upon the weather, and the first time I had seen Mrs Maudsley undecided. It did not show in her face which, as always, bore the generalized expression of a portrait; but her movements were uneasy. At last she proposed we should wait a quarter of an hour to see what happened.

We were standing about the hall in the uncertainty that a provisional plan brings, when Marian said:

'Come with me, Leo, and tell me what the weather means to do.'

I followed her outside and conscientiously turned my eyes up to the lowering sky.

'I think – ' I began.

'Don't trouble to,' she said. 'What about a walk, if we don't drive?'

I don't suppose that anyone nowadays would dare to look as innocent as she did.

'Oh yes,' I said eagerly. 'Will you come with me?'

'I wish I could,' she answered, 'but it's not that sort of walk, it's this.' And as she spoke her hand touched mine which opened on a letter.

'Oh no!' I cried.

'But I say yes.'

She wasn't angry this time, she was laughing, and I began by resisting her half-heartedly. I was handicapped by having to hold the letter. Between us we must have made a great deal of noise, for I laughed too, louder than she did, louder than good manners permitted, as loud as any spooning holiday-maker on the sea-front; and I didn't want to stop, I wanted to go on to a conclusion. Daring each other with our eyes we lunged and dodged and feinted. I suppose she was trying to make me say I would take the letter; I had forgotten how the scuffle started and hardly knew whether I was defending myself or attacking her.

'Marian! Leo!'

At the sound of Mrs Maudsley's voice we broke away, Marian still laughing, I panting and ashamed.

Mrs Maudsley walked slowly down the steps.

'What were you fighting about?' she asked.

'Oh,' said Marian, 'I was teaching him a lesson –' She got no further, for at that moment, as Denys might have done, I dropped the letter. Crumpled, untouchable, it lay on the ground between us.

'Was that the bone of contention?' Mrs Maudsley asked.

Marian picked up the letter and stuffed it in my pocket.

'Well, yes, Mama,' she said. 'I wanted him to take this note to Nannie Robson, to tell her, poor old dear, that I would go and see her some time this afternoon. And would you believe it, Leo didn't want to! He pretended he had something on with Marcus. Yes, you did!' she insisted, smiling when I began to protest that I would take it.

'I shouldn't let it worry you, Marian,' Mrs Maudsley said, giving us each in turn her straightest look. 'You say she often doesn't remember whether you've been or not; and I thought that Leo and I would take a walk in the garden. It's too threatening to go to Beeston now. Come along, Leo; I don't believe you've seen the garden properly; Marcus isn't interested in flowers yet – that will come later.'

It was true that I hadn't seen the garden properly. Frankly, I preferred the rubbish-heap, for there I had a sense of adventure which was absent from the garden. But my mother had told me something about flowers, and botany was a subject I respected. In the abstract flowers delighted me; my fantasies were incomplete without banks of them in the distance. I liked to think about them and know that they were there. I liked to read about them, especially the more sensational kinds, the carnivores: the sundew, the pitcher-plant, and the teasel which could turn insects into soup. But pure flower-gazing was a habit I had not acquired, and in Mrs Maudsley's company I rather dreaded it. Still breathless from the struggle, and obscurely feeling I needed some protection from her I said:

'Would you like Marcus to come with us?'

'Oh no, he has had you all the morning, he must spare you for an hour. He's very fond of you, you know, Leo, and so is Marian. We all are.'

I could not fail to be delighted at this speech, but how to answer it? Experience at school gave me no clue; such things were not said there. I invoked my mother's image and tried to use her tongue.

'You have all been so kind to me,' I ventured.

'Have we? I was afraid we had neglected you, Marcus being in bed and so on. And I was laid up, too. I hope that they looked after you all right?'

'Oh yes,' I said.

We walked on past the cedar tree to where the flower-beds began.

'Well, now,' said Mrs Maudsley, 'here's the garden. It looks a bit lop-sided, doesn't it? with that L-shaped wall? I'm not sure I should have made it like that, but they keep the east wind and the north wind off, and then such lovely roses grow on them. But are you really interested in flowers?'

I said I was, especially in poisonous ones.

She smiled.

'I don't think you'll find many of those here.'

To demonstrate my knowledge I began to tell her about the deadly nightshade, and then stopped. I found I did not want to speak about it. But she was only half listening.

'In one of the outhouses you say? You mean where the old garden used to be?'

'Yes, somewhere there . . . but . . . will you tell me what this rose is called?'

'Mermaid:[1] isn't it a beauty? Do you often go to the outhouses, as you call them? I should have thought it was rather a dank place.'

'Yes, but there might be poachers.'

'Do you mean real poachers?'

'Oh no, just pretence ones.'

We stopped by a magnolia with a pink blush on it, and Mrs Maudsley said:

'This always reminds me of Marian. How sweet of you to say you'd take her note to Nannie Robson. Does she often send you with messages?'

I thought as quickly as I could.

'Oh no, just once or twice.'

'It rather worries me,' said Mrs Maudsley, 'that I stopped you going just now. Perhaps you would like to go? You know the way, of course?'

Here was an opportunity of escape: the door stood open. But how was I to answer her question?

'Well, not quite, but I can ask.'

'You don't know the way? But I thought you had taken messages there before?'

'Yes, well, yes, I have.'

'But you still don't know the way?'

I didn't answer.

'Listen,' said Mrs Maudsley, 'I think perhaps the note should be delivered. You have it in your pocket, haven't you? I'll call one of the gardeners and ask him to take it.'

An icy chill went through me.

'Oh no, Mrs Maudsley,' I said, 'it's not a bit important, please don't bother.'

'It is important in a way, you see,' said Mrs Maudsley, 'because Nannie Robson will want to get ready for her – old people don't like being taken unawares. Stanton,' she called, 'could you come here a minute?'

The nearest gardener put down his tools and came towards us with a gardener's gait, swaying and slow. I began to see his face: it was like an executioner's. Instinctively I put my hands in my pockets.

The gardener touched his cap.

'Stanton,' said Mrs Maudsley, 'we have a note here for Miss Robson, rather urgent. Would you mind taking it?'

'Yes'm,' said Stanton, holding out his hand.

I dug my fingers into my pockets. Trying not to let the paper crackle, and wriggling helplessly, 'I haven't got it!' I exclaimed, 'I am very sorry, but it must have fallen out of my pocket.'

'Feel again,' said Mrs Maudsley. 'Feel again.'

I did, without avail.

'Oh, very well, Stanton,' Mrs Maudsley said, 'just tell Miss Robson that Miss Marian will be going there some time this afternoon.'

The man saluted and went off. I had an impulse to follow him, simply to get away, and had actually taken a few steps when I realized how hopeless such a move was, and came back.

'Had you changed your mind about the note?' asked Mrs Maudsley.

Hating sarcasm, as most children do, I made no answer, but gazed sullenly at a point half-way up my hostess's ample lilac skirt.

'Take your hands out of your pockets, please,' said Mrs Maudsley. 'Has no one ever told you not to stand with your hands in your pockets?'

Silently I obeyed.

'I could ask you to turn your pockets out,' she said, and at once my hands flew to cover them. 'But I won't do that,' she went on. 'I'll just ask you one question. You say you have taken messages for Marian before?'

'Well, I —'

'I think you said so. If you don't take them to Nannie Robson, to whom do you take them?'

I could not answer, but an answer came. There was a sound as if the sky was painfully clearing its throat, then all round the thunder muttered.[2]

Rain followed instantly. I can't remember how our interview broke up, or whether either of us said anything more, nor do I remember how we reached the house. But I remember running up to my room to take refuge there, and my dismay when I found it already occupied by another person. Not by the person himself but by his belongings: his glass, silver, leather, ebony and ivory, his hair brushes and sponge and shaving-tackle. I tiptoed out, not knowing where to go; so I shut myself in the lavatory, and was rather relieved than alarmed when impatient fingers rattled the door-knob.

All of us, except Marian and Mrs Maudsley, assembled at the tea-table. There were several faces strange to me: house guests for the ball. It was so dark outside that the lamps were lit; I couldn't rid myself of the idea that it was dinner-time, not tea-time. Lacking our hostess we stood about, watching the lightning flashes through the windows, and talking desultorily. Nobody said much to me; I was like a hero or a victim kept apart until the ceremonies should begin. My thoughts were in a tumult yet everything around me appeared normal; in the middle of the table was my cake, a white iced cake, surrounded by pink candles and with my pink name scrawled across it. At last, by a concerted movement in the room, I knew that Mrs Maudsley had come in. The others began to cluster around the tea-table, but I hung back.

'Sit here, please, Leo dear,' said Mrs Maudsley, and unwillingly I crept into the place beside her. But her manner was all affability: I needn't have been frightened.

'I've had to move you from your room,' she said, 'to Marcus's. I'm very sorry, but we had to have yours for another, older bachelor. Marcus is so pleased to have you back. I hope you don't mind?'

'Not at all,' I said.

'Do you see what's in front of you?' she asked.

Quite a lot was in front of me; crackers, flowers strewn on the table-cloth and – suddenly I saw it – another cake, a facsimile of the one in the centre, but tiny, topped by a single candle, and with my name written on it.

'Is it for me?' I asked stupidly.

'Yes, everything's for you. But you see, I don't like the number thirteen – isn't it silly of me? I think it's unlucky. So we've put twelve candles round the big cake, and then, when they're blown out, you shall light this one.'

'When will that be?' I asked.

'When Marian comes. She wants to be the first to give you a present. Don't try to guess what it is. The others are on the sideboard waiting for you.'

I peered across at the sideboard and saw several parcels, gaily done up in coloured paper. I tried to make out, from the shapes, what might be in them.

'Can you wait?' said Mrs Maudsley, gently teasing.

'How soon will it be?' I asked again.

'About six o'clock, we think. When Marian comes back from Nannie Robson's. She won't be long now, we were so late starting. My fault, I'm afraid, I wasn't ready.'

She smiled, but I noticed that her hands were shaking.

'Did you get wet?' I asked. I felt an irresistible impulse to make some reference to our talk. I couldn't believe she had forgotten it.

'Only a few spots,' Mrs Maudsley said. 'You didn't wait for me, you unchivalrous fellow.'

'Leo unchivalrous?' asked Lord Trimingham, who was sitting on Mrs Maudsley's other side. 'I don't believe it. He's a regular lady's man. Didn't you know he was Marian's cavalier?'

Mrs Maudsley didn't answer. Instead she said:

'Isn't it time that Leo cut the cake?'

I couldn't reach it in the middle of the table, so the cake was brought to me. I didn't make a very good job of cutting it.

'Leave a piece for Marian,' someone said.

'She ought to be here now,' said Lord Trimingham, looking at his watch.

'It's still raining,' Mr Maudsley said. 'We'd better send the brougham[3] down to fetch her. Why didn't we think of it before?'

He rang the bell, and gave the order.

'Was it raining when she started?' somebody asked; but no one could answer, no one had seen her go.

The cake was eaten, all but one thick wedge which lay on its side in the middle of the plate, with the candles burning round it.

We heard the carriage drive past the windows.

'She'll be with us in ten minutes now,' Lord Trimingham said.

'And then she has to change, hasn't she?' said Marcus.

'Sh,' said Denys. 'That's a secret, a most important secret.'

'What's a secret?' Mrs Maudsley asked. 'What's a secret, Denys?'

'That Marian's going to change.'

'If it's a secret, why tell it?'

Denys subsided, but it was Marcus who had given the show away, not he.

'She may not have waited for the carriage,' someone said, 'and be walking up in the rain. She'll have to change then, poor darling she'll be soaked.'

'What a kind-hearted daughter you have, Mrs Maudsley,' said another guest. 'It isn't every girl who would be so good to her old nannie.'

'Marian was always very fond of her,' Mrs Maudsley said.

'Now Leo, blow those candles out before they set fire to anything, and then light yours. And have you still room for a bit of your own special cake?'

I rose to do her bidding, and the room was soon filled with the sound of puffing. Slender as they were, the candles did not take extinction easily, and I was rather breathless before I began to blow. But stronger and fresher lungs lent me their aid.

'Oh, pinch them, pinch them! Lick your fingers first!'

At last the smouldering wicks were extinguished. I lit my one candle and cut myself a piece of my little cake; but I couldn't swallow it.

'He'd rather have his cake than eat it,' someone said.

There was a pause; during the last few minutes, I noticed, every action and almost every remark had been followed by a pause.

'She should be here any minute now,' Lord Trimingham said. No one questioned this.

'Let's have a round of crackers,' suggested Mr Maudsley. 'Here, Leo, come and pull one with me.'

Everyone found a partner; some their next door neighbours, some their opposite numbers. Several of the ladies screwed their faces up and held their heads back; one or two brave spirits seized the cardboard strip.

'Now all together!'

The detonations were splendid and prolonged. They joined with the thunder outside to produce a terrific salvo; and I think only my ears caught the sound of carriage wheels as they rolled past the windows.

Caps were put on, dunces' caps, forage caps, Roman helmets, crowns; tin whistles shrilled, languishing voices chanted sentimental rhymes. 'Another round, another round!' Everyone began to search among the débris for unused crackers; soon we were all rearmed, and confronting each other with flushed, challenging faces. This time my cracker-partner was Mrs Maudsley. She bent her head and compressed her lips.

'Leave one for Marian!' someone cried.

Again the detonations, the tearing paper, the smoke, the acrid fumes. When sounds and smells had died away and laughter was beginning, I saw the butler standing at Mrs Maudsley's elbow.

'Excuse me, madam,' he said, 'the carriage has come back but not Miss Marian. She wasn't at Miss Robson's, and Miss Robson said she hadn't been all day.'

This piece of news dismayed me just as much as if I had not been expecting it. Perhaps I was not expecting it: perhaps I had persuaded myself that Marian would be there. My insides began to revolt anew against my birthday tea. Across the table, under the caps which always made grown-ups seem still older than they were, the shining eyes, the faces, dark-red in the lamplight, had a wild, hobgoblin look. They reminded me of the pictures in the smoking-room – they had forgotten themselves.

'Where *can* she be?' asked someone, but not as if it mattered.

'Yes, where can she be?'

'She's *got* to change. She may be changing now. She may be upstairs, changing,' Denys said.

'Well, all we can do is to wait for her,' said Mr Maudsley equably.

Cap nodded at cap sagely, whistles began to blow, and a man was starting to read a riddle, shouting to make himself heard, when all at once Mrs Maudsley pushed her chair back and stood up. Her elbows were sticking out, her body was bent and trembling, and her face unrecognizable.

'No,' she said. 'We won't wait. I'm going to look for her. Leo, you know where she is; you shall show me the way.'

Before I knew what was happening she had swept me from the room, as much by the authority of her voice and manner as by her hand which, I think, touched my shoulder. 'Madeleine!' her husband's voice called after her; it was the only time I ever heard him call her by name.

As we passed through the hall my eyes caught sight of the green bicycle, and in an instant it was photographed on my mind. It was propped against the newel-post of the staircase, and somehow reminded me of a little mountain sheep with curly horns, its head lowered in apology or defence. The handlebars, turned towards me, were dwarfed by the great height of the saddle which, pulled out to its fullest extent for Marian to ride, disclosed a shining tube of steel six inches long.

The vision remained with me, imparting a distressing sense of something misshapen and misused, as I ran through the rain at Mrs Maudsley's side. I did not know that she could run at all; but I could hardly keep up with her, she ran so fast. Her lilac paper bonnet was soon soaked through; it flapped dismally as she ran, then clung to her head, dark and transparent, while the water dripped off the strings. I felt the rain oozing through my dunce's cap, cooling my head and coursing down my back.

Actually the rain was less heavy than it had been, the thunder was more distant and the lightning, instead of darting ice-blue from black clouds, wriggled slowly, an orange trickle, down a primrose-coloured sky. I was too frightened to mind the storm, though it increased my wretchedness; what I was most aware of – outside my misery – was the indescribable smell of rain filling the air.[4]

Mrs Maudsley said nothing but ran with wide, awkward steps, her skirt with its three rows of braid dragging at the gravel and swishing through the puddles, and soon I realized that it was she who was guiding me; she knew where we were going. When we came to the cinder path between the rhododendrons I tried to turn her back: I cried, 'Not this way, Mrs Maudsley.' But she paid no heed to me and plunged blindly on, until we came to the outhouse where the deadly nightshade had been. The tousle-headed stump was still lying on the path, limp and bedraggled. She stopped and peered inside at the leaves, wet but already withering. 'Not here,' she said, 'but here, perhaps, or here. You said there were poachers.' Not a sound came from the forlorn row of huts; only the rain pattering on their battered roofs. I could not bear to aid her in her search, and shrank back, crying. 'No, you *shall* come,' she said, and seized my hand, and it was then that we saw them, together on the ground, the Virgin and the Water-Carrier, two bodies moving like one. I think I was more mystified than horrified; it was Mrs Maudsley's repeated screams that frightened me, and a shadow on the wall that opened and closed like an umbrella.

I remember very little more, but somehow it got through to me, while I was still at Brandham Hall, that Ted Burgess had gone home and shot himself.

EPILOGUE

When I put down my pen I meant to put away my memories with it. They had had days, weeks, months to settle, but in the end they didn't, and that is how I came to write this epilogue.

During my breakdown[1] I was like a train going through a series of tunnels; sometimes in the daylight; sometimes in the dark, sometimes knowing who and where I was, sometimes not knowing. Little by little the periods of daylight grew more continuous and at last I was running in the open; by the middle of September I was considered fit to go back to school.

I didn't recover my memory of what happened at Brandham however, after the revelation in the outhouse. That, like my coming home, remained a blank. I didn't remember it and I didn't want to. The doctor said it would be good for me to unburden myself, and my mother tried to make me, but I wouldn't have told her if I could. When she volunteered to tell me what she knew I shouted at her to stop; and I have never known how much she did know. 'But you have nothing to be ashamed of,' she would say; 'nothing at all, my darling. Besides, it's all over now.'

But I didn't believe her, and the capacity for disbelief, so difficult to acquire, is equally difficult to eradicate. I didn't believe it was all over and I didn't believe that I had nothing to be ashamed of. On the contrary, it seemed to me that I had everything to be ashamed of. I had betrayed them all – Lord Trimingham, Ted, Marian, the whole Maudsley family who had welcomed me into their midst. Just what the consequences had been I neither knew nor wished to know; I judged their seriousness by Mrs Maudsley's screams, which were the last sounds heard by my conscious ear – for the tidings of Ted's suicide came to me voicelessly, like a communication in a dream.

His fate I did know, and it was for him I grieved. He haunted me.

Not only in the most dreadful way, by his blood and brains stuck to the kitchen walls,[2] but by a persistent picture of him cleaning his gun. The idea that he had cleaned it to shoot himself with was a special torment to me; of all the thoughts he might have had while cleaning it, the thought that he was going to use it against himself must have been the one furthest from his mind. The irony of this was like an arrow in my spirit.

It did not occur to me that they had treated me badly. I did not know how to draw up an indictment against a grown-up person. A certain set of circumstances had arisen and it was for me to deal with them, just as at school I had had to deal with the persecution of Jenkins and Strode. Then I had succeeded; I had turned their taunt of 'vanquished' against them. This time I had failed: it was I who was vanquished, and for ever.

At school a spell had saved me; and at Brandham, too, I had resorted to a spell. The spell had worked: I couldn't deny that. It had broken off the relationship between Ted and Marian, from whose continuance I had foreseen such direful consequences. It had uprooted the belladonna, and blasted it in Ted's very arms. But it had recoiled on me. In destroying the belladonna I had also destroyed Ted, and perhaps destroyed myself. Was it really a moment of triumph when I lay prostrate on the ground, and the uplifted root rained down earth on me?

I saw myself entering Ted's life, an unknown small boy, a visitant from afar, sliding down his straw-stack; and it seemed to me that from that moment he was doomed. And so was I – our fates were linked together. I could not injure him without injuring myself.

Yes, the supernatural powers I had invoked had punished my presumption. And why had they, when at school they had so clearly been on my side? The reason was, I told myself, that at Brandham Hall I had invoked these powers against each other, had tried to set the Zodiac against itself. In my eyes the actors in my drama had been immortals, inheritors of the summer and of the coming glory of the twentieth century.

So whichever way I looked, towards the world of experience or the world of the imagination, my gaze returned to me empty. I could make no contact with either, and lacking the nourishment that these umbilical cords convey I shrank into myself.

*

When Marcus and I met again at school we met almost as strangers. We were polite and distant with each other; we never went for walks together and never alluded to the past. No one commented on this; at school friendships were always being made and broken. I found new friends to go about with, but into these friendships I put little of myself – indeed, there was little left to put. But my daily glimpses of Marcus, reminding me of the need for secrecy, were like hammer-taps nailing me up.[3] Gradually my active dread of hearing anything about Brandham passed into indifference, a progressive atrophy of curiosity about people that extended in many directions, in fact in nearly all. But another world came to my aid – the world of facts. I accumulated facts: facts which existed independently of me, facts which my private wishes could not add to or subtract from. Soon I came to regard these facts as truths, and the only truths I cared to recognize. Pascal would have condemned them as being truth without charity;[4] they contributed little to experience or imagination, but gradually took the place of both. Indeed, the life of facts proved no bad substitute for the facts of life. It did not let me down; on the contrary it upheld me and probably saved my life; for when the First War came my skill in marshalling facts was held to be more important than any service I was likely to perform on the field. So I missed that experience, along with many others, spooning among them. Ted hadn't told me what it was, but he had shown me, he had paid with his life for showing me, and after that I never felt like it.

Many records came to light besides those hidden in the collar-box. My mother and I were both inveterate hoarders; I had kept all her letters, she all mine; it was only a matter of time before I found our Brandham correspondence. Among the letters was an envelope, sealed down but unaddressed. What was it? Then in a flash I guessed: it was the letter Marian had given me for Ted on the afternoon of my birthday. In equal measure I wanted to open it and not to open it. Eventually I compromised by keeping it beside me, a prize to be opened only when I had finished.

My acquired respect for facts bore fruit, enabling me to lay some unction to my soul[5] which at the time I had denied myself. Thus it became clear to me – chronology proved it – that Marian had been quite fond of me before there was any question of my acting as go-between. Afterwards she had redoubled her favours, making up to me and stuffing me with lies; but the episode of the green suit came first. I saw now, what I did not take in then, that her chief object in going to Norwich was to meet Ted Burgess: his must have been the raised hat on the other side of the Square. But it would be unduly cynical to say I was only a pretext for her journey. It would have been such an expensive pretext, for one thing – not that she minded about money. I felt pretty sure that she was genuinely concerned about my permanently over-heated state, and wanted to do me a good turn. Inexplicable as it seemed to me now, the conviction that she had never really cared for me had been the bitterest of the pills I had to swallow. Similarly Lord Trimingham's affability and condescension, on which I had set so much store, did not altogether proceed from the wish that I should be a convenient link between him and Marian. Ted's behaviour had been more suspect. What a change there had been in his demeanour when I told him I was a visitor at the Hall! And how he had alternately cajoled and threatened me when I began to jib at taking the messages! And yet he had been really sorry about it; he had even said he was sorry, as a good child should. Perhaps among all of us – and that went for me, too – he was the only one who had had a true impulse of contrition.

I was able to winnow out other facts which had been hidden from me at the time. Marcus it must have been who told his mother that I knew something of Marian's whereabouts when she gave out that she was with her old Nannie; he had goaded me, by his superior knowledge of French, into making that silly and disastrous boast. I had assumed that all schoolboys obeyed the 'no sneaking' rule as implicitly as I did – as Marcus himself did, as long as he was at school. It hadn't occurred to me that just as we changed our language and vocabulary when we went into polite society, so we changed our natures – or at least our expression of them.

And I, I was not so guilty as I believed myself to be in the long months that followed my visit, or so blameless as, in the years that followed them, I had come to think I was. I had come to blame the visit for everything, even for my vice of taking myself too seriously. I ought not to have read Marian's note; I ought not to have falsified the hour of Marian's rendezvous with Ted. The first had been regrettable though venial; and the second, if well meant, had been fatal in its consequences. But if I should not have done it now, in my middle sixties, it was because I had long ceased to have the wish to meddle, for good or ill, in other people's business. 'Once a go-between never a go-between' had become my maxim.

As to the spell, I shook my head, I could not take it seriously. It did not fit into the world of facts. The search for facts, which meant the search for truth, had such a tranquillizing and reconciling effect on me that by the end the episode at Brandham Hall, that Bluebeard's chamber in my mind,[6] had lost its terrors. It was no more horrific than a long and intricate bibliographical quest. It might have been something that had happened to another person. With the opening of the door, and the installation of electric light in the cupboard, the skeletons had crumbled into dust.

The facts that I had brought to light had been sufficient for my purpose. They were incomplete, of course. If I wanted to know more precisely how I stood *vis-à-vis* life — success and failure, happiness and unhappiness, integration and disintegration, etc. — I should have to examine other facts, facts beyond the reach of memory and gleaned from outside, from living sources. I should have to know what happened to the other persons in the story, and how the experience had affected them. The others! I did not take kindly to the fact of others: I did not mind their names in print, providing evidence, but I did not want them in the flesh: that way they were most troublesome.

As to these 'others' of Brandham Hall, somehow I could not think of them as going on after I had stopped. They were like figures in a picture, the frame enclosed them, the two-fold frame of time and place, and they could not step outside it, they were imprisoned in Brandham Hall and the summer of 1900. There let them stay, fixed in their two dimensions: I did not want to free them.

So with a quiet mind I was able to approach the last piece of evidence, the unopened letter.

Darling, it read — only one darling this time —

'Our trusty messenger must have made a bloomer. You *can't* have said six o'clock. Why, you'll be all covered with hay-seed, you'll have straw in your hair, you won't be fit to be seen! So I'm writing to say, Come at six-thirty if you can, because it's our dear postman's birthday and I have to be there to give him a little present, just the thing for a postman — he won't have to walk any more, poor pet, when he takes our messages! I'm giving him this. Mama is making other plans for him and he may not be able to outwit her, cunning as he is, and if he doesn't get through with it I shall be there at six, and wait till seven or eight or nine or Doomsday – darling, darling.'

The tears came into my eyes – tears which I had never shed, I think, since I left Brandham Hall. So that was why she had given me the green bicycle – to facilitate my journeys between the Hall and the farm. Eh bien je jamais! She was a cool one. I didn't mind; my only wish was that I had kept it, instead of letting mother give it away because I wouldn't use it.

The figures in the picture started moving; curiosity stirred in me again. I would go back to Brandham and find out what had happened after I left.

Defying augury I took a room at the Maid's Head,[7] and the next day I recklessly hired a car and drove to my objective.

My memories of the village were very hazy, but even so I shouldn't have recognized it. The angle of vision makes a difference: I was a foot taller than when I had seen it last, and it seemed many feet lower. A passing motor-car cut off half the height of the houses; I saw a woman standing at an upper window, and her head and shoulders were invisible, the window was so low. The place had changed with all the changes of fifty years – the most changeful half a century in history. I did not even feel a revenant; I felt a stranger.[8] What will have changed least? I wondered. The church. To the church I bent my steps, and having reached it I went straight to the transept. There were two new mural tablets.

Hugh Francis Winlove, ninth Viscount Trimingham, I read. Born Nov. 15th 1874, died July 6th 1910.

So soon! Poor Hugh! His could never have been a good life, I reflected, not in the doctor's sense. Suddenly I thought of him as a man much younger than I, he who had seemed so much older: a young man of thirty-six, but looking any age: his face too damaged by the hand of man to respond to the kinder surgery of the hand of God. It had never struck me that besides the damage one could see there might be other damage that one couldn't.

Requiescat.[9]

Had he ever married? I wondered. The tablet did not record a Viscountess. There seemed to be no way of telling. But yes, there was, for here was another tablet, stuck away in the corner.

Hugh Maudsley Winlove, tenth Viscount Trimingham. Born Feb. 12th 1901, killed in action in France June 15th 1944; also of Alethea, his wife, killed in an air-raid Jan. 16th 1941.[10]

If these were facts they were very odd facts. Little as I remembered of the circumstances of my departure, I was quite sure that Lord Trimingham was not married when I left: indeed his engagement to Marian had not yet been made public. How had he contrived to get married and have a son in less than seven months?

That the explanation didn't dawn on me shows what a deep impression the scene in the outhouse had left on my mind. I could not conceive of Marian going on after it: it was not only worse than death it was death too: she was rubbed out.

Shaking my head, still puzzled and a little irritated — for I, who had got the better of so many facts, did not like it when facts got the better of me — I sat down in what I thought was the pew I had occupied fifty years before, and found myself, like myself of an earlier date, looking for a memorial to the eleventh Viscount.

But there was none. Had the line died out? Then it occurred to me that the eleventh Viscount might be still alive.

Thinking back to my past, lost self, I remembered how impatient I had always been with the Litany and with Christianity's general insistence on sin. I did not want to think about it! Since then I had thought about it a great deal, though not in a religious spirit, and not as sin. I was resigned to my lot and sometimes congratulated myself on it; but when I rebelled against its drabness I knew where the blame lay, and my resentment against Brandham Hall and all its works had hardened into a general grudge against mankind. I did not call them sinners — sin was not among my terms of reference — but I did not like or trust them.

But what of the sense of praise and thankfulness that I had then? What of the song I used to sing with so much gusto (singing was one of the studies I had given up), 'My song shall be alway Thy mercy praising'?[11] I would not have sung it now, even if I could have reached the notes. There seemed so little room for praise or thanksgiving in the modern world, and the mercy of God, on which people were all too prone to throw themselves, had been left behind with the Psalms.

In the porch as I came in I saw a notice which said that the church was kept open to visitors partly for the purpose of private prayer; and would the visitor pray for the parish priest, for the congregation committed to his charge, and for the souls of the faithful who had passed away in the hope of a joyful resurrection.[12]

Though my church-going days were over, it seemed ungracious not to comply; and when I came to the souls of the faithful[13] I did not fail to say a prayer for Hugh, nor for his son and daughter-in-law; and then I remembered Ted, and though I could not be sure that he had been buried in consecrated ground and was eligible for the benefits of prayer, I said a prayer for him too. But still I was not satisfied. I remembered all the persons of our drama, and prayed for them, and in the end I even prayed for myself.

I went out of the church uncertain what my next step should be. I had come to Brandham without a definite plan of campaign, but with some vague idea of searching out the oldest inhabitant and asking him or her for information. The pub was the most likely place to find such a person, but it was early still and the pubs would not be open for an hour. Anyhow I do not like pubs and had rarely been inside one.

I stood in the churchyard and looked down on the cricket field. It was mid-May, and they had been mowing it and rolling and generally putting it in order for the season. Evidently cricket still flourished in Brandham. The pavilion was still there, facing me, and I tried to make out where I had been standing when I made my historic catch, wondering what it felt like to be a cricketer, for cricket was another thing I had been excused when I went back to school.

I turned and made my way down to the village, and as I entered the street I saw a man whose face seemed less unfamiliar to me than the others. He was a young man in the middle twenties, not the sort of person I was looking for; probably he was also a stranger to the place. Certainly he was a stranger to me, and I did not care about talking to strangers. But there was one question he might be able to answer.

He was wearing a sports coat and an old pair of corduroy trousers; his face was closed in thought.

'Excuse me,' I said, 'but is there still a Lord Trimingham living at Brandham Hall?'

He looked at me as though he shared my prejudice against strangers, and as though he wanted to be left alone, and yet didn't want to be left alone.

'There is,' he said, rather shortly, 'and as a matter of fact I am Lord Trimingham.'

Very much taken aback, I stared at him. I remembered his colouring; it was like a cornfield; a ripe cornfield in the month of May.

'You seem surprised,' he said, and his tone suggested that my surprise was uncalled for. 'But I live only in a corner of the house – the rest is let to a girls' school.'

I recovered myself a little.

'Oh,' I said, 'I didn't mean that, though I'm glad to know you live there. You see I stayed there many years ago.'

At that his manner changed completely and he said, almost eagerly:

'You stayed there? Then you know the house?'

'I remember parts of it,' I said.

'You stayed there?' he repeated. 'When would that be?'

'In your grandfather's time,' I said.

'My grandfather?' he said, and I saw that he was on his guard again. 'You knew my grandfather?'

'Yes,' I said, 'your grandfather, the ninth Viscount.' Out of some unsealed chamber of memory the pompous phrase slipped past my tongue. 'He was your grandfather, wasn't he?'

'Of course,' Lord Trimingham said, 'of course. I never knew him, I'm afraid: he died before I was born. But I believe he was a charming man, if I may say so of my own relation.'

'You may,' I smiled. 'He was a charming man.'

Lord Trimingham had lost a little of his aplomb: it was as though the breath of the May morning had gone out of him. He hesitated and then said:

'And did you also know my grandmother?'

This time it was for me to echo him.

'Your grandmother?'

'Yes, she was a Miss Maudsley.'

I took a long breath. 'Oh yes,' I said. 'I knew her very well. Is she still alive?'

'She is,' he said, without too much enthusiasm.

'And living where?'

'Here in the village, in a little house that used to belong to an old retainer of the family, called, I think, Nannie Robson. Perhaps you knew her, too?'

'No,' I said, 'I never saw her, though I heard about her ... Is your grandmother well?'

'Quite well, except that she's got rather forgetful lately, like old people do.' He smiled, a tolerant, youthful smile that seemed to relegate her without regret to the category of the old. 'Why don't you call and see her?' he went on. 'She'd like to see you, I'm sure. She's rather lonely. She doesn't have many visitors.'

The inhibitions of fifty years rose up in me, and took control of my face and voice.

'I think I'd better not,' I said, 'I'm not sure she would want to see me.'

He looked at me a moment, good manners struggling with curiosity in his face.

'Well,' he said, 'it's for you to say.'

Suddenly I remembered that Trimingham or no Trimingham he was much younger than I was and I could claim an older person's freedom of speech. At the same time I was aware of an Ancient Mariner in me who might be trying his patience.[14]

'Would you,' I asked, 'do me a great kindness?'

'Of course,' he said, with a fleeting glance at his wrist-watch. 'What is it?'

'Would you tell Lady Trimingham that Leo Colston is here and would like to see her?'

'Leo Colston?'

'Yes, that is my name.'

He hesitated. 'As a rule I don't drop in on her,' he said. 'I sometimes telephone ... What a boon it is. Was there a telephone here in your day?'

'No,' I replied. 'It might have made a great difference if there had been.'

'Yes, indeed,' said he. 'My grandmother is a great talker you know; old people sometimes are. But I'll go if you like ... I –' he stopped.

'It would be a great kindness,' I repeated, firmly. 'Like you I shouldn't want to . . . to take her unawares.' I thought of the last time I had done so.

'Very well,' said he, overcoming an obvious reluctance. 'Mr Leo Colston, was it? You think that she'll remember the name? She's rather forgetful.'

'I'm sure she will,' I said. 'I'll wait here for you.'

While he was gone I strolled about the street, searching for some object that would put me visually in line with the past. But nothing clicked. I saw the village hall, a sombre structure of smooth, dark red brick, that looked incongruous among the glittering, grey flint houses. I ought to have remembered it, for it was the scene of my last public triumph, but I didn't.

I saw my envoy coming towards me and went to meet him. His face was clouded: and the resemblance between him and Ted was stronger than ever.

'She didn't remember you at first,' he said, 'and then she remembered you very well. She said she would be very pleased to see you. She also asked me if I would give you luncheon, as she can't: would you like that?'

'Yes,' I replied, 'if you would.'

'I should be most happy to,' said he, not looking at all happy, 'if you don't mind taking pot-luck. But she wasn't sure you'd want to come.'

'Oh, why?' I asked.

'Because of something that had happened long ago. You were only a little boy, she said. She said it wasn't her fault.'

'Your grandfather used to say,' I said, 'that nothing is ever a lady's fault.'

He gave me a hard look.

'Yes,' I said, 'I knew your grandfather extremely well, and you are very like him.'

He changed colour, and I noticed he was standing away from me, as his grandfather had at our last meeting.

'I'm very sorry,' he said, reddening, 'if we didn't treat you well.'

I was touched by the 'we' and remembering his grandfather's fatal capacity for contrition I said hastily:

'Oh, you had nothing to do with it. Please don't give it another thought. Your grandmother —'

'Yes?' he said sombrely.

'Do you often see her?'

'Not very often.'

'Not many people go to see her, you said?'

'Not very many.'

'Did many people go to see her when she was at the Hall?'

He shook his head.

'I fancy not very many.'

'Then why does she go on living here?'

'Frankly I can't imagine.'

'She was so beautiful,' I said.

'I have often been told so,' he replied. 'I don't quite see it myself
. . . You know your way to the house?'

I answered, conscious of having said it once before:

'No, but I can ask.'

I noticed he didn't offer to go with me, but he told me how to
find the house. 'Luncheon about one?' he added, and I promised to
be there. I heard the rustle of his corduroy trousers as he walked
away. And after a second or two I heard it again. He was coming
back.

When he drew level with me he stopped and said, obviously making
an effort, but without looking at me.

'Were you the little boy who – ?'

'Yes,' I said.

Marian received me in a small, heavily curtained room looking on the
street, and below street-level – one went down a step to reach it.
She was sitting with her back to the light.

'Mr Colston,' the maid said.

She rose and held her hand out uncertainly.

'But is this really – ?' she began.

'I should have known you,' I said, 'but I couldn't expect you would
know me.'

Actually I shouldn't have known her. Her hair was bluish, her face
had lost its roundness, her nose had grown more prominent and
hawk-like. She was very much made up and had developed a great
deal of manner. Only her eyes, faded as they were, had kept their
quality, their frosty fire. We talked a little of my journey and of what

I had done in life: both subjects that were easily disposed of. For conversational purpose, an ounce of incident is worth a pound of routine progress, and my life had little incident to record. My temporary loss of memory at Brandham Hall had been the last dramatic thing that had happened to me. She went back to that.

'You lost your memory at the beginning,' she said, 'I'm losing mine at the end – not really losing it, you know, but not quite remembering what happened yesterday, like poor old Nannie Robson used to. My memory for the past is still quite clear.'

I pounced on this, and asked a question or two.

'One at a time,' she said. 'One at a time. Marcus, yes, he was killed in the first war, and Denys, too. I forget which went first: Denys, I think. Marcus was your friend, wasn't he? Yes, of course he was. A round-faced boy: he was Mama's favourite, and mine too. We were a very devoted family but Denys was never quite at home in it, if you know what I mean.'

'And your mother?' I prompted her.

She sighed. 'Poor Mama! it was a shame, those nervous people! I got over it, I got over it very well. We didn't have the ball, you know; it had to be cancelled. Your mother came down – I remember her very well, a sweet woman – grey eyes like yours, and brown hair, and a quick way of moving and talking. We had to put her up at the inn. The house was chock-full for the ball, everyone tumbling over each other, you not speaking, Mama screaming out all sorts of Biblical words. It was a nightmare! And then Papa took charge and restored order. By the next day everyone was gone who could go: you stayed until the Monday, I remember, and how you heard about Ted we never knew: perhaps Henry the footman told you: he was a friend of yours.'

'How did you know I knew?'

'Because one of the few things you said was "Why did Ted shoot himself? Wasn't he a good shot?" You see at first you thought he shot himself by accident, and a good shot wouldn't have: you don't have to be a good shot to shoot yourself. Ted had a weak streak in him like Edward has.'[15]

'Edward?'

'My grandson. He should have waited till it all blew over, as I did. I knew it would blow over, once I was Lady Trimingham.'

'And Hugh?'

'And me?' she queried puzzled.

'No,' I said, 'Hugh' — I hooted it.

'Oh *Hugh*,' she said. 'He married me; he didn't mind what they said. Hugh was as true as steel. He wouldn't hear a word against me. We held our heads very high. If anyone didn't want to know us we just ignored them, but everybody did. I was Lady Trimingham, you see. I still am. There isn't another.'

'What was your daughter-in-law like?' I asked.

'Poor Alethea? Oh, such a dull girl. She had such dreary, stupid parties — I hardly ever went to them. I was living at the Dower House and people came to me, of course, interesting people, artists and writers, not stuffy country neighbours. There are stuffy people, even in Norfolk. My son wasn't a sporting man, you know, he took after my father — he was the very image of him. But he hadn't Papa's drive. Papa was a wonderful man, and Mama was wonderful too — it is something to have had such very exceptional parents.'

'You haven't told me what happened to your mother,' I reminded her.

'Oh, poor Mama! she couldn't stay with us, you know, she had to go away, but we often went to see her, and she remembered all about us and was so glad I had married Hugh — she always wanted that, you know. I didn't really, but I was glad I had, or people might not have been as nice to me as they were.'

'And your father?'

'Oh Papa lived to be very old, nearly ninety, but he lost interest in the business after Mama left us, and when Marcus and Denys were killed he gave it up. But he often came to see us at the Hall, and when I was living at the Dower House he paid me many visits. We were always a very devoted family, you see.'

How happy, I thought, has my life been compared with hers. I couldn't bear to hear much more, and yet I wanted to have the picture fitted in completely.

'Isn't it rather dull for you, Marian,' I said, 'to be living here alone? Wouldn't you be happier in London?'

'Alone?' she said. 'Alone, what do you mean? But people come in shoals. I almost have to turn them from the door, I'm quite a place of pilgrimage, I can tell you! Everybody knows about me, you see, they know what I've been through, and naturally they want to see me – just as you did.'

'I'm very glad I have,' I said, 'and I'm glad to have met your nice young grandson, Edward.'

'Sh,' she said. 'You mustn't call him that, he likes to be called Hugh, though Edward is a family name, of course.'

I remembered the two Edwards in the transept.

'Well,' I said, 'it must be a comfort to you to have him near you.'

At that her face fell, and the mask she had been wearing since I came showed signs of cracking.

'He is,' then she corrected herself – 'he would be. But do you know, though we are the only two members of the family left, he doesn't come to see me very much?'

'Oh, surely –' I protested.

'No, he doesn't. Masses of people come but he does not – I mean not regularly – not regularly like I used to see old Nannie Robson, when she was old. Does he remind you of anyone?' she asked me suddenly.

'Well yes, he does,' I said, surprised at being asked. 'His grand-father.'

'That's it, that's it, he does. And of course he knows – he knows what he's been told, what his parents told him, for he's never spoken of it to me. And what other people may have told him – a village is a hive of gossip. And I think he has a grudge against me – you know why. The only person in the world who has! His own grandmother! And they tell me – he has never told me – that he wants to marry a girl – a nice girl, a Winlove cousin, a distant cousin, but still a Winlove – but he won't ask her because . . . because this is still weighing on him. He feels – or so they tell me – that he's under some sort of spell or curse, and that he'd hand it on. He's just plain *silly*! But no doubt he's heard some rumour, totally false of course, that worries him. Now this is where you come in.'

'I?'

'Yes, Leo, you. You know the facts, you know what *really* happened. And besides me, only you know. You know that Ted and I were lovers: well, we were. But we weren't ordinary lovers, not lovers in the vulgar sense, not in the way people make love today. Our love was a beautiful thing, wasn't it? I mean, we gave up everything for each other. We didn't have a thought except for each other. All those house-parties – people being paired off like animals at stud – it wasn't like that with us. We were made for each other. Do you remember what that summer was like? – how much more beautiful than any since? Well, what was the most beautiful thing in it? Wasn't it us, and our feeling for each other? Didn't you realize it, when you took our letters for us? Didn't you feel that all the rest – the house, the people coming and going – just didn't count? And wouldn't you feel proud to be descended from our union? the child of so much happiness and beauty?'

What could I say but yes?

'I'm glad you see it so,' she said, 'for you were our instrument – we couldn't have carried on without you. "Carried on" – that sounds a funny phrase – but you know what I mean. You came out of the blue to make us happy. And we made you happy, didn't we? You were only a little boy, and yet we trusted you with our great treasure. You might never have known what it was, have gone through life without knowing. And yet Edward –' she stopped.

'But you can tell him, Leo, tell him everything, just as it was. Tell him that it was nothing to be ashamed of, and that I'm nothing to be ashamed of, his old grandmother whom people come miles to see! There was nothing mean or sordid in it, was there? and nothing that could possibly hurt anyone. We did have sorrows, bitter sorrows, Hugh dying, Marcus and Denys killed, my son Hugh killed, and his wife – though she was no great loss. But they weren't our fault – they were the fault of this hideous century we live in, which has denatured humanity and planted death and hate where love and living were. Tell him this, Leo, make him see it and feel it, it will be the best day's work you ever did. Remember how you loved taking our messages, bringing us together and making us happy – well, this is another errand of love, and the last time I shall ever ask you to be our postman. Why does he think I stay on here, except to be near him? And yet he has this grudge against me, he won't come near me if he can help it, though shoals of people come that I don't want to see. Sometimes I think he would rather I didn't live here, but I won't believe it. And make him get out of his head this ridiculous idea that he can't marry: it's that that wounds me most. I don't want him to marry, Heaven knows, and bring some frightful woman to Brandham

Hall – though the Winlove girl is quite nice, I believe. But every man should get married – you ought to have got married, Leo, you're all dried up inside, I can tell that. It isn't too late; you might marry still; why don't you? Don't you feel any need of love? But Edward (only don't call him that), he must; he's young – he's young – he's the same age Ted was when you came to Brandham. He has all his life before him. Tell him he must get rid of these silly scruples – his grandfather would have had them, if I'd let him. Poor Ted, if he'd had more brains he wouldn't have blown them out. You owe it to us, Leo, you owe it to us; and it'll be good for you, too. Tell him there's no spell or curse except an unloving heart. You know that, don't you? Tell him to think kindly of his old grandmother, who only lives to love him.'

She ceased, greatly to my relief, for I had made several ineffectual attempts to stop her, having seen how she was tiring herself. We talked a little about indifferent subjects; the changes at Brandham, the changes in the world; and then I took my leave, promising to come again.

'Bless you,' she said, 'bless you! You're a friend in a thousand. Kiss me, Leo!'

Her face was wet with tears.

A foreigner in the world of the emotions, ignorant of their language but compelled to listen to it, I turned into the street. With every step I marvelled more at the extent of Marian's self-deception. Why then was I moved by what she had said? Why did I half wish that I could see it all as she did? And why should I go on this preposterous errand? I hadn't promised to and I wasn't a child, to be ordered about. My car was standing by the public call-box; nothing easier than to ring up Ted's grandson and make my excuses . . .

But I didn't, and hardly had I turned in at the lodge gates, wondering how I should say what I had come to say, when the south-west prospect of the Hall, long hidden from my memory, sprang into view.

NOTE ON THE TEXT

The present text follows, with the exceptions noted below, that of the first edition (Hamish Hamilton, 1953) which is, to all appearances, definitive, as Hartley made no alterations in subsequent reprints (Hamish Hamilton, 1954, 1966; Knopf, New York, 1954; Penguin, 1958, 1970, 1971; Heinemann, 1963; Stein and Day, New York, 1967) or to the many translations that appeared in his lifetime.

In preparing this edition I have also consulted the surviving holograph of *The Go-Between*, which exists in nine foolscap notebooks in the L. P. Hartley Archive at the John Rylands University Library, Deansgate, Manchester. It contains a blend of what is clearly first-draft material with second and third thoughts written over or around; many cancelled passages; and many passages uncancelled but not present in the printed editions. But by far the greater part is in final form with occasional marginal notes to the typist, Ursula Carrington, revealing only minor deviations from the printed text. Given the unusual speed with which Hartley wrote *The Go-Between* (see Introduction, section I, letter of 17 June 1952 to Sir Roderick Meiklejohn), and the heat of inspiration that such speed suggests, I would conclude that the holograph represents, with the exception of some preliminary drafting now apparently lost, *The Go-Between* as Hartley wrote and revised it virtually in one go, apart from changes subsequently incorporated into the typescript. As such it has considerable authority, and I have used it to correct what I believe are several errors in the first edition which, unnoticed by Hartley either when checking the typescript or marking proofs (and possibly even the result of interference by the publisher's house editor at the stage when s/he checked the author's corrected proofs), have since been perpetuated. They are few and small, but nevertheless worth incorporating in order that the text should reflect Hartley's intention as closely as possible. (Note: the Hartley Archive now includes, through the generosity of Mr John Assheton, further valuable material relating to the novel, including a typescript of Pinter's screenplay for the film and a notebook containing a variant text, in holograph, of the cricket match.)

With the kind permission of the late Miss Norah Hartley, therefore, the following changes have been made on the authority of the holograph (1953 = first edition):

Prologue (p. 9, l. 13) *interresting*: this is the holograph reading (1953 reads *interesting*). As this announces the theme of Leo's misspellings, I take the printed text to be an oversight or editorial sophistication.

Chapter 2 (p. 28, l. 22) *disapeared* (1953: *disappeared*). Another unintended sophistication.

Chapter 6 (p. 61, l. 9) *Psalms for the Day*. 1953 has the technically incorrect *Psalms for the day*, which the bibliographer in Leo would not perpetrate.

Chapter 6 (p. 66, l. 9) *spifflicating . . . A.1. . . . I don't know what to call her*. 1953 omits the holograph's ellipses which suggest better the sense of searching for terms.

Chapter 7 (p. 80, l. 6) *He's a man I want to see*. 1953 has *He's the man . . .*, which is less in keeping with Trimingham's class and manner.

Chapter 8 (p. 87, l. 12) *it is a pitty* (1953: *pity*).

Chapter 13 (p. 138, l. 31) The holograph has a double space between the end of the previous paragraph and Marcus's 'Frog-spawn' to indicate a narrative break. Omitted in 1953 and subsequent editions, it is restored here.

Chapter 14 (p. 144, l. 29) *lonly*. Another misspelling corrected in 1953, the holograph's *lonly* is in fact written twice, very carefully, so that the typist should make no mistake.

Chapter 16 (p. 166, l. 27). 1953 and subsequent editions print eight kisses after the signature; the holograph has thirteen, a total restored in the present edition as it was evidently designed to reflect Leo's obsession with the number.

Chapter 17 (p. 176, l. 35). Space restored between paragraphs to indicate a narrative break.

Chapter 18 (pp. 186–7, Ted's letter). The repetitions do not suggest a literate man, yet his spelling is perfect in 1953. The present edition restores the holograph's misspellings: *jibed* (not *jibbed*); *sincerly* (not *sincerely*); *faithfull* (not *faithful*).

For further holograph readings, see Textual Appendix.

TEXTUAL APPENDIX

Although this is not a full textual edition, the following selection of passages, either cancelled in the holograph or left uncancelled, is printed as being of particular critical interest. Any phrase following a slash (/) is to be understood to have been written above the preceding alternative.

Chapter 2 (p. 30, l. 33) After *but not her beauty* the holograph has the following cancelled passage:
I suppose it was my first evening, the honoured guest, I sat next to her at dinner, and what was my astonishment (I never quite got over it) when at the end of the meal she produced a cigarette and lit it. Open-mouthed I stared at her; and she laughed and said, 'Haven't you ever seen a lady smoke before?' I remember feeling shamefully inexperienced – and no doubt she thought so too, and that was one reason why she was so angry with me – she never guessed that such a suckling had it in him.

Chapter 4 (p. 49, l. 35). The holograph has the following cancelled alternative to the sentence beginning *The river dominated it* and the following paragraph:
The river dominated it – the two rivers I might say. To the left of the sluice, by which we stood, where it ran under the belt of trees, almost choked by weeds and rushes, it was green and bronze and golden: the water flashed and glinted under innumerable shadows. On the other side it was open to the sky and as blue as the sky: not a weed marred the surface. Also it was much broader; for as they told me later the current had hollowed out a pool: the land retreated round it from two bays. The pool was a mirror of the clearest blue [sentence deleted]. Only one thing broke the surface, and it was so far away [phrase deleted] and I was so ravished by the scene that at first I did not notice the dark spot: it was a man's head, the stranger's head.

Chapter 4 (p. 51, l. 18). The holograph has the following cancelled passage following on from *daring each other to go in first*:
and then I heard a wail, 'Oh, my hair's come down!' and saw that Marian's

hair, a long coil of it, had slipped out of her bathing cap and was floating. It was the first time I had seen her at a disadvantage and I felt so sorry for her. 'Oh dear, oh dear,' she cried, while a soft wind sprang up and waved/sported with the tendrils. 'Oh, I'll soon put that right,' Eulalie said. She caught hold of the escaping tresses and bundled them back [last word deleted], almost cruelly it seemed to me, back into their prison. 'Lucky for you you weren't in the water when it happened,' she said. I hated seeing her hair pushed back/disappear; I should [deleted] like to have seen it/had a vision of it floating round her as she swam, mingling with the river weed, almost as if she had drowned [last six words deleted].

Chapter 4 (p. 52, l. 23). The holograph has the following two similes (both uncancelled) from which the printed text derives:
on him had the effect of a feather on an elephant/it was like the smile on the face of the tiger — it pointed/made a contrast

Chapter 7 (p. 80, ll. 34–6). The holograph has the following uncancelled alternative passage:
And as a matter of fact the rubbish heap had a fascination for me: I used to visit it in secret and stare at it, the one touch of squalor in all their magnificence.

Chapter 7 (p. 81, l. 19). The holograph contains the following cancelled passage after *safe with me*:
I had every reason to be satisfied with my part of the business: I had done what I promised to do. Yet I was dissatisfied with the outcome. Why had the letter not been hailed with cries of joy — celestial like the morning stars singing together?

Chapter 9 (p. 93, l. 19). The holograph contains this cancelled passage after *apparently having forgotten it too*:
Bang! Bang-bang! Two rabbits fell; one lay still; the other feebly kicked. He did not go to it at once, however, but waited until the plot of corn, no larger now than a good-sized room, should be/was finished off. My excitement mounted for I thought that this last stronghold would be stiff/stuffed with game; but I was wrong: the last stalks fell and nothing came out. Then he took the dying rabbit by the/its feet and knocked its head against his boot. At this my excitement turned to nausea; my stomach heaved and I looked away. [But added] The utter indifference of the labourers steadied me; why, I felt, should I be more squeamish than they were?

Chapter 10 (p. 107, ll. 8–10). Opposite the paragraph *'But spooning's so silly . . . silly they were not* the holograph contains the following uncancelled passage:

It would put him in his place. Always I had to struggle against a sense of inferiority with him, and I resented it, for he was lower in the social scale than I was. Now I had turned the tables. Though he was unaware of it, I had convicted him of spooning, and immunity from spooning was the one department of life/incontrovertible claim we children had to be superior to grown-ups.

'Spooning's silly,' I repeated almost viciously. 'It's soppy.'

Chapter 14 (p. 141, l. 29). After *suitability of the match* the holograph has this uncancelled passage:

and the feeling Trimingham Hall would now belong to them [deleted] both of them, and the disparity between the owner and tenant, guest and host relationship, between money and birth, which had always [deleted] seemed an anomaly ever since Lord Trimingham arrived, would be wiped out.

These were high matters which appealed to/This was how the incidents of the day affected my imagination.

Chapter 16 (p. 168, l. 3). Opposite *Marian was presiding over it* the holograph has this uncancelled version:

I dared not meet her eye, I dare [deleted]/tried not even to look at her. My eyes were still smarting from the flame of her glance/As if the sun had scorched them [both of these alternatives deleted], The memory of her face bright/burning with anger still made my eyes smart, and the security I felt from others' smiles was no protection. I still felt her glance would burn me. And it was almost with the physical sensation of getting used to something hot that I stole my first glimpses of her.

Chapter 19 (p. 200, l. 19). After *'Good-bye Ted'* I promised I would tell her the holograph has the following fine uncancelled passage:

As I was turning away, grieved to be parting from him, almost in tears, he suddenly said:

'Were you going for a dip?'

I had entirely forgotten the object, or at least the pretext, of my visit. All at once I felt the rope halter chafing my neck, half strangling [deleted] choking me, it seemed, and the towel above it making me sweat, and saw the bathing suit dangling from my hand.

'Well yes', I said. 'I was wondering whether you could spare the time to give me a swimming lesson. I can't swim, you know.'

He looked at me irresolutely, then back at the field, then back [deleted] at me again. The trouble deepened in his face. 'I oughtn't to,' he muttered.

'I oughtn't to.' Then something seemed to give way in him, his face cleared, and he cried

'Oh hang/damn it all, let's bathe.' He began to pull his shirt off.

'But you haven't a bathing suit', I said/warned him.

'Oh I can/shall manage.'

'Yes I have,' he said, producing the slip garment from his pocket; 'only I didn't feel like bathing until you came along'.

[the following passage is inserted opposite:

I retired into the reeds behind the bank; he changed on the bank itself, as was his custom. I could hardly wait to get my clothes off. The impulse towards nudity which had assailed me ever since I came to Trimingham, the longing, half physical, half spiritual, to get everything off, to feel the sun on my skin, to have nothing between me and the elements, to be at one with the summer, now had the compulsion of a passion. All that I felt burdensome was coming/peeling away, even the greenness of my suit, and my own greenness. The galloping approach of fulfilment drummed in my ears; I tingled with expectancy.]

The swimming lesson was a huge success. Standing on the brick bastion that held the sluice   At first Ted plunged me like a fish, with the rope knotted round me. The feel of the water, warm beyond belief/my wildest dreams [last three words deleted], was utterly delicious. To be in it and out of it that hot/scorching day, at last at one with the blue, touching it, cleaving it/floating in it, was a miraculous like the [these two words deleted] fulfilment like a dream. Following Ted's directions/instructions, imitating/copying the wide sweep of his arms above me I felt that I was swimming, and he said/swore I was; to me my frog-like sprawlings/movements/gropings seemed the very poetry of motion. And I could see in Ted's foreshortened face, from which the creases of care seemed to have been ironed out, a truer reflexion of my own happiness.

Could I keep afloat a moment while he dived in? he asked. Yes, I said, confident I could keep afloat forever. His body floated over me in an arc of speed, black lightning blotting out/slitting through the sunlight. The spray of ripples of the splash broke over my face; my legs sank under me; I gave myself up for lost. So this is/was drowning! But his hand was already under my back; my feet were coming up; my hair floated backwards from my face and I could see again. Skilfully he unleashed me from my halter and threw it to the bank. – So, the last encumbrance gone, I enjoyed at least [sic] the freedom of the water, as I had enjoyed the freedom of the air: a freedom which the touch of his hand, guiding me this way and that, keeping the soft pull of gravity at bay, did nothing to diminish.

'But you must have a proper swim!' I said suddenly conscience-stricken, and realizing that my freedom was his servitude. He protested/did not want to; but I persuaded him to put me on the shelving/wooden ledge, under the guillotine [these three words deleted]/above the pool between the two brick bastions and under the guillotine, where the gently running water hardly reached my ankles/in shallow water hardly up to my ankles; and here I sat, with the water gliding past me, while he, below me, like an energy released, churned up the pool and shattered the reflexions.

It was only a petit quart d'heure, as I had promised Marcus, but when I was drying myself among the rushes, and Ted was sunning himself on the bank, having refused the offer of my towel, I felt it had put a lifetime between me and my former self. [The following is written opposite: He rubbed the grass stalk along his arm, and seemed as pleased to be himself/smiling with happiness at being himself as he had been the first time I met him.]

Our second leavetaking was much happier than the first, indeed it was almost cheerful. 'Now hold on to what you've learnt,' Ted said, 'and the next time you come you won't need me to help you.'

'Oh, but I shall,' I said, 'it wouldn't be the same –.' I stopped, for there/on was the shadow of a cloud on his face,/was the shadow of a cloud that did not come from the cloudless sky. I wanted to sum up a feeling in a word, but could not find the word/the word would not come; but a thought rushed up in me, and before I knew I had given it utterance.

'Shall I take one more message for you?'

'That's very good of you,' he said, 'but do [deleted] are you sure you want to?'

'Oh yes, I do, this once.' Even then I safeguarded myself.

He thought a moment. 'Well,' he said, 'tell her tomorrow's no good, I'm going to Norwich; but Friday at half-past six at the same place.'

I promised and held my hand out. 'No, no,' he laughed, 'it's unlucky to say goodbye twice,' but all the same he took it, and the pressure lingered with me like a pledge of faithfulness.

We were standing on the platform of the sluice. His eye turned to the fields and mine followed it. [Written opposite: The reaper was revolving in a tiny circle, scarcely its own length. Suddenly it stopped.] 'Good Lord,' he said, 'look what they've done, while I've been slacking! The whole field's reaped!'

It was quite true: [Written opposite: I had given him back to himself, which is perhaps the most one can ask of anyone] in all the fields as far as the eye could see, not an ear of corn was standing. He hurried off; [written opposite: He strode off with a springy skip, carrying with him the wonder of another person's life, a grown-up life whose mysteries I should never penetrate, though for a moment I had had a glimpse of them.] I lingered/ waited on the sluice, trying to store in memory [last three words deleted] commit to memory all its prospects: the two aspects of the river, the belt of trees behind me, screening the house; and in front the cornfields, reaped for harvest.

Suddenly [deleted] Ted was already far away. Suddenly he stopped, took off his old soft linen hat and waved it vigorously [deleted] shading his eyes and waving vigorously. I took my hat off and waved back.

Chapter 22 (p. 227, l. 15). The holograph reads as follows after *No one had ever told me*:
they were wrong but now, without being told, I suspected they must be. I did not realize that they were defences which my imagination automatically put up against experiences which, like Atlantic rollers to an untried swimmer, were much too strong. Nor did I realize that my unpractised imaginative faculty was [too hard deleted] exhausted but not paralysed [whole of this sentence deleted]. I only knew that when I thought of my struggle in the outhouse, I thought of it as an attempt [deleted from beginning of sentence to here] I tried to think of my struggle in the outhouse as a mere gardening operation, the uprooting of a poisonous weed of whose existence I had long ago meant to warn my hostess.

At thirteen . . .

Epilogue (p. 247, l. 24). The holograph contains this uncancelled redraft of a cancelled passage following *after that I never felt like it*:
It was only when I had finished writing the story of my visit to Trimingham [this is the holograph's name for Brandham] that I allowed myself to wonder what had happened afterwards. I reminded myself that I was over sixty: for all these years I had kept myself in ignorance, – why? Because I thought that the facts, if I came to know them, would spoil my life. My nature was too tender to bear them; they would print a permanent blight on my spirits, perhaps worse. Had the policy been a sound one? I did not think so. Why should I be suspicious of these facts, when I had given hospitality to thousands of others? At any rate my life was nearly over and I could take the risk of spoiling what was left.

NOTES

Epigraph

But, child . . . have trod: Emily Brontë, 'I saw thee child one summer's day', stanza 3: *Complete Poems*, ed. J. Gazari (Harmondsworth, 1992), pp. 40–42. See Introduction, section II. Hartley often invokes Emily Brontë (e.g., the epigraphs to *The Shrimp and the Anemone* (1944) and *The Sixth Heaven* (1946)); here the quotation introduces *The Go-Between*'s (*GB*) main themes of the loss of childhood innocence and death.

Prologue

1. *The past . . . foreign country*: in contrast, in Philip Larkin's *A Girl in Winter* (1947), part 2, chapter 1, England is a foreign country to suggest the alien nature of its post-war self.

2. *red . . . collar-box*: cf. chapter 6, n. 11.

3. *Eton collars*: broad starched collar worn over the coat collar; but snobbery (another of *GB*'s themes) also operates: Hartley, an Harrovian, lamented that he hadn't been sent to Eton: E. T. Jones, *L. P. Hartley* (Boston, 1978), p. 16.

4. *two . . . sea-urchins*: 'dry' to suggest the adult Leo's emotional sterility (cf. Marian's words at the end of the Epilogue), the urchins recall the rock-pool that opens *The Shrimp and the Anemone*. They initiate a list of *twos* that will eventually focus on the coupling of Marian and Ted.

5. *magnets*: symbolize (sexual) attraction, and especially, via the magnet in the thermometer (opening of chapter 3), that between Marian and Ted.

6. *negatives*: symbolizing memories that have been refused exposure to the light of common sense (cf. chapter 3, n. 3).

7. *as I handled them*: touch as a stimulant to memory recalls the childhood

memory released by taste in Proust's *Remembrance of Things Past*, tr. C. K. Scott Moncrieff and Terence Kilmartin (Harmondsworth, 1983), 1: 48–50.

8. *the secret . . . flashed upon me*: cf. Proust, *ibid.*, p. 50: 'And suddenly the memory revealed itself'.

9. *rainbow-hued*: the rainbow is an ancient symbol of the link between heaven and earth, paradise and the world of lost innocence; here it is a reminder of the Golden Age (n. 16): see also chapter 4, n. 2, and Richard Heinberg, *Memories and Visions of Paradise* (Los Angeles, 1989), pp. 75–6.

10. *past . . . future*: anticipating the Janus symbol: nn. 17, 18 below and chapter 5, n. 3.

11. *century*: the idea is exploited throughout *GB*: both sides exceed a century in the cricket match, but the thermometer never quite reaches 100 and the twentieth century fails to live up to Leo's expectations.

12. *the signs . . . in glory*: *GB*'s main symbol of aspiration – social, imaginative/mystical and moral – the zodiac will become associated with the upper-middle class and aristocratic inhabitants of the Hall (e.g., pp. 47, 246) until disillusion sets in.

13. *The Fishes . . . only in legend*: this zodiac begins with the sea creatures because the sea signifies the reservoir of the unconscious, and to recall *The Shrimp and the Anemone*, which associates the sea with childhood (see n. 4).

14. *the Lion . . . the Virgin*: Leo (24 July–23 August) is Leo's emblem (p. 8), the adjacent sign Virgo, the Virgin (24 August–23 September), Marian's (chapter 4, n. 19). Just as Leo attains merely the physical characteristics of adulthood rather than 'imperious manhood', Marian too falls short of the virginal ideal astrologically predicted for her. The lion is an emblem of the handsome and sexually fulfilled male in *The Will and the Way* (1973), p. 51.

15. *I had been ill . . . death*: most of Hartley's heroes reflect his own childhood illness: cf. Eustace in *The Shrimp and the Anemone*, Richard in *The Brickfield* (1964) and *The Betrayal* (1966).

16. *a Golden Age*: for its importance in relation to Virgo and the novel's war theme, see Introduction, section III.

17. *My birthday fell in late July*: originally 1 January in the holograph, hence allying him with Janus: see n. 10 above.

18. *the Archer and the Water-carrier*: Sagittarius (23 November–21 December, a centaur – half man, half horse – bearing a bow and arrow) and Aquarius (21 January–19 February, depicted as a man or boy pouring water from a jar). As *GB* unfolds, Sagittarius the warrior will be Trimingham's emblem, and Aquarius ('a farm-labourer'), Ted's (but as role-models for Leo they are aspects of 'the same man': Janus with his two faces again; and see chapter 15, n. 6).

19. *Hercules*: because of his twelve labours an emblem of heroic strength and identified with the sun as lord of the twelve signs of the zodiac: J. E. Cirlot, *A Dictionary of Symbols*, tr. Jack Sage (London, 1962), p. 138. Like Leo, the mythological Hercules also succumbed to the charms of a woman and suffered for it (he died when his wife gave him the poisoned coat of Nessus to wear in the belief that it would make him faithful to her).

20. *war*: the holograph names the Boer War here: see chapter 4, nn. 12, 13, and chapter 9, n. 5.

21. *portfolio*: function or office; but as a receptacle for documents, the word glances ironically at the diary.

22. *Thomas A'Beckett's blood*: Thomas à Becket, Archbishop of Canterbury, was born in London c. 1118, and assassinated in Canterbury Cathedral on 29 December 1170, with the apparent complicity of King Henry II.

23. *Kingsgate Castle*: on the north east tip of the Isle of Thanet, Kent, about a mile and a half from Hartley's own school in Cliftonville; see n. 24.

24. *the Lambton House saga*: originally Dumpton House in the holograph. Hartley located the school precisely for his mother in the letter of 21 November 1909 (see Introduction, section I).

25. *Eton . . . Harrow*: see n. 3 above.

26. *Vanquished! . . . made to suffer*: announces a theme that climaxes in the obliteration of Leo's memory by Mrs Maudsley's screams in chapter 23 and includes Leo's victory over Ted in the cricket match and the uprooting of the belladonna: see chapter 21, n. 8.

27. *an 'I could if I would' air*: *Hamlet*, 1.5.184 ('We could and if we would') as, after the appearance of the ghost, Hamlet swears his companions to secrecy and requires them not to imply that they know why he has assumed his 'antic [bizarre; clownish] disposition': interesting in view of the spectre in the epigraph poem and Leo's reference to his green suit as his (jester's) 'motley, the vesture of my make-believe' (chapter 22).

28. *'animal . . . mineral'*: game in which a team has to discover the identity of an object that is defined for them by the chairman in terms of these attributes; he can answer their questions only with a 'yes' or 'no'.

29. *mob*: *circle* – cancelled in the holograph – suggests that this is a demonic parody of the zodiac.

30. *Peau de Chagrin*: Honoré de Balzac's novel of 1831; English title *The Wild Ass's Skin*. As a philosophical fiction about politics, magic, the will, love and suicide, it is of general importance to *GB* (see Introduction, section IV). For the symbols Leo remembers, see the Penguin Classics edition, tr. H. J. Hunt (Harmondsworth, 1977), pp. 50–1. In view of Leo's vexation, it should be noted that French *chagrin* = (1) shagreen; (2) vexation.

31. *shot my bolt*: from archery (*bolt* = arrow): see n. 18 above.

32. *consume . . . smoke*: proverbial.

33. *a master of language*: anticipates his role as go-between, since Mercury, the god who carried Jupiter's messages between heaven and earth, was god of language and, in his Egyptian form, Hermes (Mercurius) Trismegistus, of magic. He also guided the souls of the dead (see n. 36).

34. *Southdown Hill School*: Hartley's own prep school was Northdown Hill School at Cliftonville; n. 23.

35. *'Brandham Hall'*: originally Trimingham (named after the village in north-east Norfolk) and also Framlingham (named after the small town north-west of Aldeburgh). Based on Bradenham Hall: Introduction, section I.

36. *embalmed . . . scattering of earth*: on the burial imagery, continued in next paragraph, see Introduction, section II.

37. *adaptability to life*: hinting at the Darwinian notion of survival by adaptation; Darwinism was topical again during and after the Second World War because of what it had revealed about the beast in man and the erosion and adaptation of certain human 'species' (e.g., the old, landed aristocracy: note Hugh's precarious role in *GB*): cf. Osbert Sitwell, *Left Hand, Right Hand!* (1944), Introduction.

38. *in 1952*: the holograph originally read 'now'; replaced by 'in 1950' then 'in 1952'.

39. *You flew . . . scorched*: Icarus, son of the magician Daedalus, escaped from the Cretan labyrinth, in which he and his father had been imprisoned by King Minos, on a pair of artificial wings held together by wax. Ignoring his father's advice he flew too high, his wings melted with the heat of the sun, and he was drowned (see also chapter 4, n. 7, and chapter 14, n. 2).

40. *angels*: in *Facial Justice* (1960) the Inspectors, who exist on a plane far above that of the egalitarian masses, are named after the archangels.

41. *the cliffs of Thanet*: see n. 23 above; the name suggests 'death' (Greek *thanatos*).

42. LEO: originally 'Tom'.

Chapter 1

1. *I should not . . . school*: because of illness and his father's wishes, Hartley himself was late going to boarding school: see L. P. Hartley, 'Three Wars', in G. A. Panichas (ed.), *Promise of Greatness: The War of 1914–18* (New York, 1968), p. 250.

2. *landau*: four-wheeled carriage, the roof of which was designed so that it could be completely closed, or half- or completely open.

3. *the San*: sanatorium, or school sick-room.

4. *a most searching smell*: later, smell will be an index of Leo's increasing sensual/sexual awareness: e.g., chapter 7, nn. 7, 10.

5. *South-Eastern . . . Railway*: i.e., the South Eastern and Chatham Railway, which served Kent.

6. *Marcus*: a part-anagram of Mercury (Mercurius in Latin; see chapter 8, n. 1), so that he is, in a sense, Leo's double, the wish-fulfilment image of what he could become given Marcus's social background.

Chapter 2

1. *the 9th . . . the fateful Friday*: Hartley's chronology is exact: there was a heat-wave in 1900 which lasted from 10 July until dispersed in thunder-storms on Friday 27 July. *Fateful* here has its literal sense of death-dealing: for the Fate Atropos in *GB*, see below n. 14.

2. *Pepys's*: Samuel Pepys (1633–1703), naval administrator who kept a 1.25-million-word diary in shorthand.

3. *a directory of Norfolk*: the holograph reads 'Kelly's Directory'.

4. *Winlove family*: originally 'Trimingham'.

5. *Gainsborough . . . Teniers the Younger*: Thomas Gainsborough (1727–88), the portrait and landscape painter; Sir Joshua Reynolds (1723–92), famous as a portrait painter and first president of the Royal Academy; Aelbert Jacobsz Cuyp (1620–91), Dutch landscape painter noted for idyllic rural scenes full of light; the spelling 'Ruysdael' suggests that Salomon van Ruysdael (c.1600–1670), the prolific Dutch landscape painter specializing in monochromatic river scenes, is intended; Meindert Hobbema (1638–1709) was another Dutch landscape painter specializing in idyllic water scenes and a favourite with English collectors. David Teniers the Younger (1610–90) was a Flemish painter specializing in genre paintings of peasant life (see chapter 18). The Dutch landscapes reflect Leo's obsession with the Golden Age, the Teniers series the social and sexual aspects of Ted's world.

6. *a double staircase*: in his Introduction (1963) to *GB*, p. 4, Hartley relates this (as well as other details such as the cricket match, deadly nightshade, and a letter asking to be allowed home: see Introduction, p. xiv, section I) to a visit to a schoolfriend's home.

7. *Threadneedle Street*: home of the Bank of England, thus identifying Mr

Maudsley with the profession of Leo's dead father (chapter 1), albeit at a considerably higher level.

8. *a magnet*: see Prologue, n. 5.

9. *a portrait by Ingres or Goya*: Jean-Auguste-Dominique Ingres (1780–1867), distinguished French Neo-classical painter of historical and religious subjects as well as portraits; Francisco de Goya (1746–1828), the Spanish painter and engraver, who produced over two hundred portraits.

10. *Denys . . . conceit*: in *The Brickfield* and *The Betrayal*, the name of the author-hero's blond and eventually weak and blackmailing companion-secretary.

11. *gnome-like . . . trail of gold*: traditionally gnomes were earth-dwellers and guardians of treasure. Contrast the inhabitants of Leo's zodiac. See also chapter 4, n. 9.

12. *string . . . eye*: recalls the image of the eye-beam as found in Petrarch and the Elizabethan sonneteers and taken to hyperbolic extremes in Donne's 'The Extasie' (in *Songs and Sonets*), ll. 7–8: 'Our eye-beames twisted, and did thred/Our eyes, upon one double string'.

13. *Marian*: in Hartley's short story 'The Cotillon' (originally published in 1932), Marion Lane finds herself dancing at a masked ball with the ghost of the lover she has betrayed (*Complete Short Stories* (1973), pp. 154–62).

14. *Atropa Belladonna*: this, the botanical name of the deadly nightshade, is corrected from 'Belladonna Atropos' in the holograph. Hartley records that the plant is based on an actual memory (see n. 6 above), but it is also symbolic. *Belladonna* is Italian for 'beautiful lady'; *Atropos* (as in the holograph's uncorrected version) is the Fate who, in Graeco-Roman mythology, marked one's death by cutting the thread of life (after the climactic visit to the outhouse in chapter 23, Leo's memory and personality stop and Ted kills himself). Note that in *The Brickfield* Richard, in fact out looking for his girlfriend Lucy, is thought to be searching for the Death's Head Hawk Moth, but denies it, saying: '*acherontia atropos* is so rare' (p. 139). Both *atropa* and *belladonna* suggest the plant's link with Marian, then, as does its literary source in Nathaniel Hawthorne's short story 'Rappaccini's Daughter', in which a luscious but poisonous purple-flowered shrub is identified with a beautiful *femme fatale* who, by kissing her young lover, poisons him: see Giorgio Melchiori, 'The English Novelist and the American Tradition', *Sewanee Review*, 68 (1960), 502–15. The plant also recalls the fleshy-berried ivy that possesses the wartime house to which Gavin Doddington returns for the first time since childhood in Elizabeth Bowen's 'Ivy Gripped the Steps' (1946): in *The Collected Stories of Elizabeth Bowen* (New York, 1981), pp. 686–711.

Chapter 3

1. *The thermometer . . . eighty-three*: i.e., degrees Fahrenheit (28 degrees centigrade).

2. *low shoes*: boots or high-sided shoes were the fashionable norm.

3. *photographed together*: the photograph can be described now that memories are unleashed and the rolled 'negatives' (Prologue, n. 6) exposed.

4. *a Norfolk jacket*: informal loosely fitting jacket with waistband, usually worn for cycling, fishing, etc.

5. *adaptability*: see Prologue, n. 37.

6. *cads*: the opposite of gentlemen in manners and behaviour.

7. *What causes . . . losing face*: war has caused Trimingham literally to lose his: chapter 4, n. 11.

8. *au fond*: at bottom.

9. *for the first time . . . social inferiority*: as Pip feels a misfit once introduced to Satis House and Estella: *Great Expectations*, chapter 8.

10. *fifteen shillings and eightpence halfpenny*: approximately 78.5p in today's coinage (but in 1900 worth considerably more than it is now).

11. *Hugh*: the Hugh/who joke, by which Marian attempts to raise doubts about Trimingham's very existence, is added later in the holograph, which originally read 'Trimingham'.

12. *going to Goodwood*: the racecourse in Sussex celebrated for the Goodwood Cup, one of the important social events in the summer horse-racing calendar.

13. *steel threads crossing each other*: modifies the metaphors at chapter 2, nn. 12, 14.

14. *muslin bag*: the bag used to strain the butter solids from the buttermilk after churning.

15. *Bags I the bags*: I claim the trousers: mid-nineteenth-century slang.

Chapter 4

1. *the Maid's Head in Wensum Street*: hotel in the oldest part of the city; a cancelled passage in the holograph names it as the Golden Lion, a fact which Leo says 'ministered to my self-esteem' (there were three Golden Lion inns – named after the city arms – in Norwich in the late nineteenth century).

2. *iridescence*: in connection with Marian, recalls the lost rainbow of the

Prologue (n. 9) and suggests the rainbow-goddess Iris, the messenger of Juno, queen of heaven, as Mercury is messenger of Jupiter. Cf. chapter 7, n. 2.

3. *the Cathedral . . . ecstasy continued*: the cathedral was begun in 1096; at 313 feet its spire is second only to that of Salisbury in height. Ecstasy and Ely Cathedral are linked strikingly in *Facial Justice*, pp. 61–3.

4. *Tombland*: Tombland Alley, opposite the Maid's Head.

5. *O altitudo!*: Sir Thomas Browne, *Religio Medici* [Religion of a Doctor] (1642), l. 9: 'I love to lose myself in a mystery to pursue my reason to an *o altitudo* [height; Latin]'. Browne (1605–82), essayist and physician, who spent much of his life in Norwich and was buried in the church of St Peter Mancroft, is often quoted by Hartley. The *statue* was not there in 1900, as Hartley notes in his Introduction (1963), p. 3; it was erected in October 1905.

6. *Lincoln Green*: introduces the Robin Hood legend (he and his 'merry men' were traditionally dressed in that colour) and the county of Hartley's maternal grandparents, whose farm at Crowland, Lincolnshire, he often visited as a child. But, as Leo learns, green is also the colour of immaturity and naïvety as well as of youth and growth. As an outlaw defiant of the Norman settlers, Robin Hood offers a broad parallel to Leo, socially marginal to and, through the messages, subversive of, the upper-class world of the Hall.

7. *hotter . . . attain to*: a cancelled phrase follows in the holograph: 'and be lost, calcined, cremated', which hints at the legend of Phaethon, who took command of the chariot of his father, the sun god, lost control, and nearly burned the earth to cinders, while he himself was displaced by one of Jupiter's thunderbolts and fell in flames to earth: Ovid, *Metamorphoses*, 2. 1–328. Like the Icarus myth (Prologue, n. 39), it connects height (and heat) with ambition and pride that ends in disaster.

8. *nudist*: the word belongs to the older Leo, since the *OED* dates it from the 1930s. Cf. the similar nudist longing in the cancelled swimming lesson passage at the end of chapter 19 (Textual Appendix, pp. 269–72).

9. *golden*: in *GB*'s symbolic structure, the Hall is associated with the gold of money, Ted with the gold of harvested corn (ch. 9). Marian belongs to the Hall but, as Virgo, is goddess of the harvest (n. 19 below).

10. *trousseau*: in the French sense of 'outfit, kit', without the bridal associations.

11. *wounded . . . got right*: with Trimingham's war-disfigured face, cf. chapter 3, n. 7.

12. *My father . . . pro-Boer*: similarly, in *The Brickfield*, Richard's father (also a bank manager) had been 'a pro-Boer, or nearly' (p. 18). The English pro-Boers were a considerable group whose voice was heard increasingly through 1900: see Stephen Koss, *The Pro-Boers* (Chicago and London, 1973).

13. *'The Soldiers . . . Ladysmith*: the first song was a particular favourite of the crowds who assembled to cheer the Boer War volunteers as they departed *en masse* in January 1900: see, e.g., the *Blackburn Weekly Telegraph*, 29 December 1900, cited in Koss, *The Pro-Boers*, p. 180. Thematically, the songs anticipate the debate between love and duty raised at the end of chapter 20. The *relief of Ladysmith* occurred in February 1900. See also chapter 9, n. 5.

14. *There was . . . gallows*: Ted rises up almost immediately, so that the passage recalls the gibbet set in a marsh landscape associated with the appearance of Magwitch in *Great Expectations*, end of chapter 1. (In *The Brickfield*, p. 23, a sluice is described as being 'evil-looking, like a guillotine'.)

15. *Burgess*: the surname denotes Ted's status as a free man (*OED burgess*, sense 3): note Denys's change of manner. Because his mother's parents were farmers, Hartley is often sensitive to their standing: e.g., *The Brickfield*, pp. 21−3.

16. *They lingered . . . in first*: see Textual Appendix (pp. 267−8) for cancelled passage at this point.

17. *a feather on a tiger*: for the origin of this slightly strange simile see Textual Appendix (p. 268).

18. *corduroy trousers*: in the late nineteenth century 'worn chiefly by labourers' (*OED*).

19. *the Virgin of the Zodiac*: see Prologue, n. 14. Note that the sigil for Virgo looks like the letter 'm' (for Marian): ♍. Virgo is traditionally portrayed holding an ear of corn from her role as goddess of the harvest: chapter 9, n. 3.

Chapter 5

1. *'fast'*: immoral; ignoring the proprieties.

2. *the Collect*: short prayer designed to 'collect' the congregation's thoughts together on a particular topic.

3. *two-sided, like Janus*: Janus was depicted with two faces, one looking forward and one back. He was the god of the new year (hence 'January': see Prologue, nn. 10, 17) and also the Roman god of war and peace, his temple being open during the former, shut during the latter: wounded, two-faced Trimingham, one of the Boer War's victims, thus stands as an emblem of the Golden Age advantages of peace and the terrible price of war.

4. *Together ... the Beast*: Leo's adverse comparison actually works to Trimingham's advantage since the Beast eventually changes into a handsome prince and marries Beauty. The theme of ugliness and enchantment is picked up later (see chapter 21, n. 4). Compare also the comments on Thaddeus and Ted in the Introduction, section III.

5. *de rigueur*: compulsory.

6. *It helps ... quiet*: the first sounding of the theme of social unrest which links the villagers with the Boers: see chapter 11, n. 5.

7. *les convenances*: propriety.

Chapter 6

1. *transept*: side arm of a cruciform church, therefore at right angles to the nave or body of the church.

2. *forty-four verses all told*: Psalm 105, 'O give thanks unto the Lord, and call upon his Name' (appointed in the Anglican Prayer Book for morning prayer). The holograph originally read 'forty-six', which suggests that Hartley initially thought of Psalm 106 ('O give thanks unto the Lord, for he is gracious') but, on checking, discovered that it was appointed for evening prayer (both are about the Israelites captive in Egypt).

3. *Edward*: originally 'George and Peter' (but *Edward* anticipates the family's link with *Ted* Burgess: see Epilogue, n. 15).

4. *not buried ... came to life*: the family and its forebears live again, as do the older Leo's memories, released from their burial chamber: Introduction, section II.

5. *'My song ... praising'*: Novello's English edition of Mendelssohn's popular *Lobgesang* (*Hymn of Praise*), Opus 52, the ninth movement of which – a duet for soprano (treble) and tenor – is a setting of the opening of Psalm 89 in this particular translation.

6. *'O God ... Heaven'*: the beginning of the Litany, which is appointed to be said occasionally after morning prayer.

7. *'miserable sinners'*: the phrase sounds right at the beginning with the invocation, in turn, of Father, Son and Holy Ghost to 'have mercy on us miserable sinners' to which the congregation triply responds.

8. *life ... laws*: Leo's argument is now with the Psalm he has stood through (n. 2), which ends: '[God] gave them [the Israelites] the lands of the heathen

and they took the labours of the people in possession; That they might keep his statutes and observe his laws'.

9. *How . . . profit a man*: recalling Matthew 16:26: 'what is a man profited, if he shall gain the whole world, and lose his own soul?'

10. *dog-cart*: small two-wheeled driving vehicle with two seats placed back-to-back.

11. *red collar-box*: its first mention since the opening of the Prologue. Here it marks the beginning of the 'new personality', which will end in trauma and amnesia until it is rediscovered and opened.

Chapter 7

1. *earthbound*: the holograph reads *terre à terre*.

2. *rainbow bridge . . . dream*: traditional pathway to paradise or the Golden Age: cf. Prologue, n. 9, and chapter 4, n. 2.

3. *some . . . drowning, I suppose*: an image made explicit in a cancelled passage: see chapter 4, n. 16.

4. *the mirror . . . dive*: an image taken over from another cancelled passage in chapter 4 (see Textual Appendix, p. 267). It is 'darker' because associated with Ted's formidable and mysterious masculinity. There may be a half echo of Milton's *Paradise Lost*, 4. 453–91, where Eve gazes at her reflection in a mirror-like lake 'that to [her] seemed another sky', then is led away from this moment of introspection to encounter a virile and frightening Adam.

5. *my sense of being abroad*: the 'foreign country' of *GB*'s opening sentence, which is also the fenland landscape of Hartley's own boyhood and family roots: see Introduction, section I.

6. *these old boys*: *old* in the Norfolk dialect sense indicating general – and disparaging – familiarity.

7. *All the heat . . . stimulated me*: cf. n. 10, and chapter 1, n. 4, and chapter 13, n. 9.

8. *a proper inkstand*: a luxury of the middle and upper classes, inkstands consisted of an ornamental base incorporating a pen-rest and a recess for the metal-mounted cut-glass ink bottles.

9. *détente*: relaxation.

10. *I know . . . rubbish-heap is*: the heap is allied to smells as a stimulant of nascent sexual excitement. Cf. *The Brickfield*, pp. 100, 112, where Richard is attracted by various smells including the stink of the outside privies.

Chapter 8

1. *'Hullo, there's Mercury!'*: see Prologue, n. 33, and chapter 4, n. 2.
2. *a Roman tortoise*: protection formed by a body of Roman soldiers locking together their shields over their heads.
3. *I was myself the mercury*: mercury here perhaps includes the mercurial quicksilver of the alchemists which is essential to, and symbolizes most of the processes of, the alchemical work that culminates in the philosophers' stone and its power to make gold, emblem of the Golden Age. It was often personified as a boy: C. G. Jung, *Psychology and Alchemy*, tr. R. F. C. Hull, 2nd edition (London, 1968), pp. 65–7.
4. *the ha-ha . . . park*: a ha-ha is a deep trench, often stone-lined, which functions as a boundary between the formal and less formal parts of an estate.
5. *fairy story . . . lips*: in 'The Fairy' (or 'Diamonds and Toads') the younger of a widow's two daughters is courteous to an old lady who is, in fact, a disguised fairy. She is rewarded by having every word she utters turned into roses, diamonds, or pearls. When her evil sister tries for the same reward, she speaks snakes and toads. As a result the younger sister is thrown out by her angry mother and meets a prince who marries her. The tale is ironically suggestive in relation to Marian, who is compelled to take Trimingham for her prince.

Chapter 9

1. *the 'Spring-balance'*: a development of the McCormick reaper originally patented in the US in 1834 and still sold in large numbers at the end of the nineteenth century. See also chapter 19.
2. *he was standing . . . forgotten it too*: in a cancelled passage in the holograph Ted shoots two rabbits, introducing the blood motif developed below, with its hints of warfare and blood-brotherhood. See Textual Appendix, p. 268.
3. *Standing there . . . for him*: as a sheaf, Ted is the rightful complement of Virgo-Marian: chapter 4, nn. 9, 19.
4. *Mercury . . . secrecy enjoined on me*: identifying another Mercurian role, that of guardian of silence: Edgar Wind, *Pagan Mysteries in the Renaissance*, revised edition (Harmondsworth, 1967), figure 23. When, a few lines later, Leo ponders over 'business' as the subject of the messages, we should recall that Mercury was also patron of merchants and trade.

5. *Lord Roberts . . . de Wet with me*: Leo lists the main leaders in the Boer War: Frederick Sleigh Roberts, Lord Roberts (1832–1914), was Commander-in-Chief of the British forces in South Africa, 1899–1900; Horatio Herbert Kitchener, Lord Kitchener of Khartoum (1850–1916), was Chief of Staff of Forces, 1899–1900, and Commander-in-Chief, 1900–1902; Paul Kruger (1825–1904) was president of the Boer republic of the Transvaal (he went into exile in Europe after the British invasion of the Transvaal in 1900); Christiaan de Wet (1854–1922) was a leading, and ingenious, Boer general.

6. *Dr Livingstone and Stanley*: David Livingstone (1813–73), missionary and explorer, had apparently disappeared after setting out to discover the source of the Nile in 1866. The journalist–explorer Henry Morton Stanley (1841–1904) tracked him down in 1871, finding him desperate for food and medical supplies. He greeted him with the celebrated 'Dr Livingstone, I presume?'

7. *train-oil . . . underneath*: Marcus refers to the oil obtained by boiling whale blubber.

8. *spooning*: (1) making love in a silly, sentimental way; (2) courting someone. *OED* dates (1) from 1831, (2) from 1877; probably derived from *spoon* = a simpleton.

9. *Dame Rumour*: often accuses people of 'spooning' but, in view of the Carthage reference at chapter 21, n. 8, there is an irony at the expense of Marian and Ted: Virgil's *Aeneid*, 4. 173–97 contains a celebrated passage in which Rumour flies through Africa spreading the tale of the illicit union of Dido, Queen of Carthage, with Aeneas: see Introduction, section III.

10. *the Eleventh Commandment*: do not be found out.

Chapter 10

1. *Not Adam . . . I was*: the Fall myth (Genesis 3 via Milton's account in *Paradise Lost*, Books 9 and 10, where the Fall is seen in terms of sexual shame) is frequent in Hartley's fiction: see chapter 21, n. 2, and *The Brickfield*, p. 140 (where the field of the title is 'like the Garden of Eden, in a way. You might find the Tree of Knowledge'; but Richard's lover, Lucy, dies there), and *The Betrayal*, p. 3 (where sexual knowledge is the 'serpent in the garden').

2. *What . . . sell!*: *sell* = deception, hoax, dates from the mid nineteenth century.

3. *Marian the Virgin of the Zodiac*: see chapter 4, n. 19.

4. *Southdown*: cf. the name of Leo's school (Prologue, n. 34). The holograph originally had 'Margate' (cancelled).

5. *to cover her shame*: Genesis 3:7, when Adam and Eve have fallen after eating the apple and, eyes opened, realizing their nakedness, make themselves coverings of fig leaves (until this point in the biblical paradisal tale, as in *GB*, nakedness is innocent).

6. *'She's going to have a foal'*: preceded in the holograph by 'She isn't well'. The sentence is uncancelled, and makes sense of Leo's assumption a few lines later, despite Ted's denial, that the mare is 'ill'.

7. *to make assurance doubly sure*: proverbial; but the context of spooning and birth recalls its origin in *Macbeth*, 4.1.83, Macbeth confronting the bloody babe.

8. *the force . . . magnet*: in the thermometer (opening of chapter 3).

Chapter 11

1. *'Home, Sweet Home'*: see chapter 13, n. 8.

2. *'She Wore a Wreath of Roses'*: parlour song by Joseph Payne Knight (1812–87), clergyman and song writer, involving the traditional 'woman as rose' symbol.

3. *gryphon . . . front*: replaces the holograph's 'wyvern', presumably because griffins incorporate Leo's lion.

4. *putting on side*: showing off.

5. *trained soldiers . . . the Boers*: the Boer forces, largely made up of Dutch farmers, were not a formal, uniformed army.

6. *nailer*: marvellous fellow.

7. *R. E. Foster . . . late cuts*: Reginald Erskine Foster, one of seven cricketing brothers who all played for Worcestershire. The year 1900 saw him score three centuries in succession as captain of Oxford University, which he followed in his first Gentlemen v. Players match with a first-innings score of 102 not out, and a second-innings score of 136. He captained England against South Africa in 1907.

8. *as for . . . century*: the innings, like the thermometer and the twentieth century, can't live up to expectation.

9. *Father Time . . . trail of gold . . . his bat*: cf. chapter 2, n. 11. The 'gold' suggests ripe corn and thus links up with Father Time's scythe to evoke Ted's harvesting (chapter 9, n. 3) and eventual death via the biblical association of flesh cut down like grass (e.g., Isaiah 40:6–8).

Chapter 12

1. *hosts of Midian . . . verandah*: Leo, again in ecclesiastical mode, recalls the hymn: 'Christian, dost thou see them/On the holy ground,/How the troops of Midian/Prowl and prowl around?/Christian, up and smite them . . .' The opening of stanza 2 may suggest the extent to which Leo senses Ted's responsibility for what is happening to Marian: 'Christian, dost thou feel them,/How they work within,/Striving, tempting, luring,/Goading into sin?' The Midianites were an enemy of the Jews: e.g., Numbers 31, Judges 6.

Chapter 13

1. *David . . . catch*: the biblical story of the boy who killed the enemy giant with a stone from his sling appears in 1 Samuel 17.

2. *Gainsborough-blue dress*: mid-blue favoured by the portrait painter: see chapter 2, n. 5.

3. *'Take a Pair of Sparkling Eyes'*: from Act 2 of Gilbert and Sullivan's *The Gondoliers* (1889). Like the other songs, it relates to the Marian–Ted–Trimingham triangle in that it encourages the lover to move from gazing to kissing to hand-holding, then (cf. 'Home, Sweet Home', n. 8 below) celebrates the virtues of living together in a cottage.

4. *song . . . by Balfe*: Michael William Balfe (1808–70), Irish composer and singer, who achieved considerable popular success with his opera *The Bohemian Girl* (1843). Ted's song, one of its hits, was often anthologized: it is sung by Thaddeus (note: Ted: Thad) in Act 3. See Introduction, section III. As Leo narrates, the song tells of infidelities to come while at the same time asking that this singing lover be remembered. The stanza continues: 'There may, perhaps, in such a scene/Some recollection be,/Of days that have as happy been,/And you'll remember me'.

5. *the music of the spheres*: in ancient and Renaissance thought, the harmony supposedly produced by the planetary spheres, each of which was believed to revolve at a particular pitch.

6. *'The Minstrel Boy'*: words by Thomas Moore, Irish composer and poet (1779–1852), set to a traditional melody. Leo sings it in the high key of A to show off his voice. The next paragraph paraphrases the song; the dying minstrel's destruction of his harp so that it 'shall never sound in slavery' relates to *GB*'s pro-Boer and love themes.

7. *'Angels . . . fair'*: from Handel's oratorio *Theodora* (1750), Act 1. The Christian virgin martyr of the title invokes heaven to aid her in withstanding Septimius's demand that she worship the Roman gods to celebrate Diocletian's birthday. She refuses and is taken to a brothel, but is saved by Didymus, who disguises himself as a soldier in order to effect the rescue. She dies and Didymus is executed. The angels and the virgin both represent Leo's idealizing view of Marian, and Didymus suggests Trimingham's role in redeeming Marian after she has given herself to Ted. The song, quoted complete here, was perhaps best known from its inclusion in *Beecham's Portfolio of Popular Songs*, 5 vols, 1887 (vol. 1 contains 'When Other Lips' and 'Home, Sweet Home', vol. 2, 'Angels! Ever Bright and Fair'). The popular 'Star Folios' (of songs, violin and piano pieces, etc.) were published by Paxtons of Oxford Street.

8. *'Home, Sweet Home'*: marks the end of the supper; but, like Ted's opening song (n. 3), it celebrates life in a 'lowly thatched cottage', rejecting 'palaces' and their 'splendour'.

9. *the stink . . . hall?*: Marcus has developed the nose of the upper classes; Leo, in not noticing the odour, is again an outsider; and cf. chapter 7, nn. 7, 10.

Chapter 14

1. *Jacob's ladder of my ascent*: Genesis 28:12, Jacob's dream of a ladder stretching from earth to heaven with angels going up and down it (the image recalls the angelic Marian of the Handel aria).

2. *Icarus*: see Prologue, n. 39. Note the juxtaposition of biblical and pagan in this sentence in the light of Theodora's choice (chapter 13, n. 7).

3. *village Jessop*: Gilbert Laird ('The Croucher') Jessop (1874–1955) was renowned for his record of eleven centuries scored within an hour or less between 1897 and 1913. Shortly after Leo's match (Saturday 21 July), playing for Gloucestershire against Yorkshire, Jessop scored pre-lunch centuries in both innings at Bradford on 24 and 25 July 1900.

4. *force majeure*: superior force.

5. *the Psalms . . . forty-three*: Psalm 107.

6. *I managed . . . my altitude*: cf. chapter 4, nn. 3, 5.

Chapter 15

1. *Ministering Children*: exemplary tale by Maria Louisa Charlesworth (1819–80); published 1854; sequel, 1862. Mentioned also in *The Shrimp and the Anemone*, chapter 5.
2. *Shylock*: proverbial for meanness, named after the usurer Jew of Shakespeare's *Merchant of Venice*. A nasty gibe given the anti-Semitism of the English upper classes of the time.
3. *Virgin of the Zodiac*: see chapter 10, n. 3.
4. *The surface of the pool . . . routed*: the pool which was associated with Ted's appearance in *GB* (see chapter 4, n. 14, chapter 7, n. 4) now suggests a battlefield and, symbolically, Ted's death.
5. *old rooks*: see chapter 7, n. 6.
6. *bow of Ulysses*: Homer, *Odyssey*, Book 21. Ulysses (or Odysseus) fought on the Greek side in the Trojan War and the epic poem traces his journey home to Ithaca. In Book 21, in disguise, he joins in an archery contest, with which his wife, Penelope, despairing of his return, challenges her many suitors: she will marry the one who can string and shoot her husband's bow. Seeing them unable to handle it, Ulysses demands the bow and turns it on the suitors. In connecting Ted with archery the simile allies him with Trimingham (Prologue, n. 18), suggesting his fitness as a suitor to Marian.
7. *LRAM*: Licentiate of the Royal Academy of Music (London).

Chapter 16

1. *amour propre*: self-respect.

Chapter 17

1. *Bon soir*: good evening.
2. *Je . . . ennuyeux*: I find it too boring.
3. *Je suggère . . . visitons les outhouses*: I suggest that we visit the outhouses.
4. *Mais oui . . . délicieuses*: But what a good idea! Such a delightful spot.
5. *Bon . . . trouvons-nous là?*: Good! You're coming on . . . And what shall we find there?
6. *Vous . . . n'est-ce pas?*: you intended to say the belladonna, didn't you?
7. *Je vois . . . pied!*: I see a footprint.

8. *Je dirai . . . Friday*: I'll tell Mother that we've seen Man Friday's track. (The reference is, of course, to the footprint spotted by Crusoe on his island in Defoe's *Robinson Crusoe*.)

9. *Certes . . . voleurs!*: It certainly is a woman's foot. Strange! What will Mother say? She's very scared of burglars!

10. *Mais non . . . strain*: Indeed not! She's very nervous – a rather hysterical type. At this moment she's in bed with a bad migraine, the result of all these days of strain.

11. *Ce n'est pas . . . Marianne*: It isn't only that. It's Marian.

12. *Mais oui . . . Marianne –*: Yes indeed, it's Marian. It's a question of the engagement, you know. My mother isn't certain that Marian –.

13. *Vous avez . . . Robson?*: You did see your sister at Miss Robson's?

14. *Mais non . . . fâcheuse*: Indeed not. When I left, Marian hadn't yet arrived. And poor Robson was rather offended.

15. *perdu sa mémoire*: lost her memory.

16. *Sa mémoire . . . woolgatherer*: Her memory is as good as mine and a hundred times better than yours, you foul woolgatherer.

17. *Pourquoi?*: Why?

18. *En part . . . de vous, vous –*: In part because, like all women, she needs new clothes for the ball; but mainly because of you, you –.

19. *Entendez . . . nigaud?* : Are you listening, you dog? Do you understand, you blockhead?

20. *presents . . . Danaan implication*: Virgil, *Aeneid*, 2. 49: *timeo Danaos et dona ferentes* (I fear Greeks even when they are bearing gifts): Aeneas is telling Dido the story of the deception perpetrated by the Greeks when they left the wooden horse outside the city, and quotes Laocoon's warning.

21. *si vous le pouvez*: if you can.

22. *Oombaire*: Humber. Richard receives a Humber bicycle for his seventeenth birthday in *The Brickfield*, p. 78.

23. *Je ne sais pas . . . blockhead*: I don't know. I haven't seen it. It's a kind found only in London . . . you utter blockhead.

24. *Et . . . pourquoi?*: And do you know why?

25. *black shadow*: cf. the 'shadow on the wall', end of chapter 23.

26. *Mais oui! Vraiment!*: Yes indeed! Truly!

27. *Savez-vous . . . ce moment-ci?*: Do you know where Marian is at this very moment?

28. *Pas . . . d'ici*: Not a hundred leagues from here.

29. *Je . . . savoir?*: I don't tell that to little boys . . . little boy, little boy, wouldn't you like to know?

30. 'When Other Lips': see chapter 13, n. 4.

31. *Ça serait . . . faire!*: That would be too boring. Let them get on with it!
32. *Jurez . . . prie*: Swear, swear, I beg you.
33. *Cela dépend*: That depends.
34. *Deux . . . mois*: Two months, three months.
35. *folle*: stupid.
36. *planté là*: in the lurch.
37. *Vous êtes . . . la langue?*: You're very quiet . . . I don't like your voice . . . And as for your disgusting thoughts, toad, I don't give a fig for them, I spit upon them. But why have you lost your tongue?

Chapter 18

1. *détente*: see chapter 7, n. 9.
2. *ushers*: an usher was an assistant-master (the pun is, of course, on *whore*).
3. *impots*: impositions, detentions.
4. *Teniers . . . my opinion*: see chapter 2, n. 5.
5. *Roberts . . . Transvaal*: see chapter 9, n. 5.

Chapter 19

1. *Contrary . . . so much*: a particular opprobrium attaches to such tale-telling: see F. P. Wilson (ed.), *The Oxford Dictionary of Proverbs*, 3rd edition (Oxford and London, 1970), *under* 'Tales out of school, Tell no'.
2. *il est . . . savez*: it is rather provincial, you know.
3. *vous savez . . . chandelles*: you know, but the candles. (*Saignant* a few lines later = bloody.)
4. *clou*: chief attraction.
5. *fast*: see chapter 5, n. 1.
6. *Claude*: the leading French ideal-landscape painter Claude Lorrain (1600–1682).
7. *déranger . . . types!*: aggravate . . . beastly fellows!
8. *'The Real Scorcher'*: *Punch*, 25 July 1900, p. 69.
9. *'A Great Thought . . . Year'*: the 'Great Thought' column, p. 68, has the following entry under 3–5 July: 'DE WET – after having been frequently routed by Lord METHUEN, who carried the Boer positions at the point of the bayonet, the enemy on each occasion anticipating by flight the impact of our infantry – has succeeded in cutting the railway at three points . . .'

Hartley's notes for these details indicate that he checked them in the Athenaeum copy.

10. *un petit quart d'heure*: a few minutes.

11. *façon de parler*: way of speaking.

12. *As I was . . . parting from him*: the holograph has the swimming lesson at this point: see Textual Appendix, p. 269.

Chapter 20

1. *Tower . . . dead secret*: Leo refers to the sacred towers, circular in structure, on the top of which the Parsees expose their dead to the sun and the vultures; they are found in the northern part of the Indian sub-continent.

2. *a 'Jingo'*: the sense 'patriot who advocates a warlike foreign policy' dates from 1878.

Chapter 21

1. *familiar lines . . . CA*: the letters denoting the shape of a triangle in geometry.

2. *What an Eden . . . entered it!*: see chapter 10, n. 1.

3. *Il faut en finir*: An end must be put to it.

4. *Afterwards . . . each other*: Leo explains sexual attraction between social unequals in terms of the magic juice that causes Titania, the fairy queen, to fall in love with Bottom, the weaver, with his ass-head in Act 3 Scene 1 of Shakespeare's play.

5. *Puck . . . the scene*: Puck is the mercurial, mischievous go-between spirit, servant to Oberon, the fairy king, in *A Midsummer Night's Dream*.

6. *'The Thorn'*: song by the theatre composer William Shield (1748–1829) to words by J. Rannie; in vol. 2 of *Beecham's Portfolio* (see chapter 13, n. 7).

7. *'In the Gloaming', or 'Kathleen Mavourneen'*: the first was composed by Annie Harrison (1851–1944) to words by Meta Orred and is sung by a lover about to leave his beloved; the second, a popular song on the same theme, was composed by Frederick William Crouch (1808–96) to words by a Mrs Crawford.

8. *delenda est belladonna!*: the belladonna must be destroyed. Echoing the words of Cato the Elder (*delenda est Carthago*) on the need to vanquish Carthage as it was a constant threat to Rome: William Smith, *Dictionary*

of Greek and Roman Biography and Mythology, 3 vols (London, 1862–4), 1.642.

Chapter 22

1. *The Dog Days, you know*: Henry refers to the period of extreme summer heat believed by the ancients to be caused by the heliacal rising of the Dog-star, Sirius; they lasted from 3 July to 11 August, and it was traditionally thought that dogs went mad at this time.

2. *temenos*: sacred enclosure.

3. *sea-green, corruptible parody*: recalling Thomas Carlyle's description of Robespierre in *The French Revolution*, 2.4.4: ' "A Republic?" said the Seagreen . . . "What is that?" O seagreen Incorruptible, thou shalt see!'

4. *Liverpool Street*: the London terminus for the Great Eastern line that served East Anglia.

5. *Norfolk . . . dumplings*: proverbially so; but the phrase also means 'inhabitants of Norfolk'.

6. *Beeston Castle, after luncheon*: Beeston is some 4.5 miles north of Bradenham.

Chapter 23

1. *Mermaid*: a vigorous climber with large, single, pale-yellow flowers; one of the anachronisms pointed out by Hartley in his Introduction (1963), p. 3. As an emblem for Marian it harks back to chapter 11, n. 2.

2. *the thunder muttered*: the heat-wave did, in fact, end in a thunderstorm on 27 July 1900.

3. *brougham*: one-horse closed carriage for up to four people.

4. *Actually the rain . . . filling the air*: parallels the union of Dido and Aeneas during a thunderstorm: see Introduction, section III, and chapter 9, n. 9 above.

Epilogue

1. *my breakdown*: explained more specifically in the holograph: 'Nervous prostration and loss of memory following shock was the diagnosis of my illness.' It recalls the young Osbert Sitwell's meeting in 1914 with his idol

Debussy which left him with no recollection of the encounter: 'The intensity of the emotion killed memory' (*Left Hand, Right Hand!*, Introduction).

2. *He haunted me . . . kitchen walls*: the betrayed lover in 'The Cotillon' (chapter 2, n. 13) kills himself by blowing his brains out.

3. *hammer-taps . . . me up*: a cancelled passage in the holograph specifies coffin nails: cf. Prologue, n. 36.

4. *Pascal . . . charity*: Blaise Pascal (1623–62), French scientist and theologian. Leo is probably thinking of something like: *la vérité hors de la charité n'est pas Dieu, et est son image et une idole . . .*' ('truth without charity is not God, it is his semblance and an idol'): *Pensées*, ed. Louis Lafuma (Paris, 1951), 1. 492.

5. *to lay . . . my soul*: *Hamlet*, 3.4.146–51. Hamlet has accused his mother of betraying her former husband, Old Hamlet, whose ghost reappears; but she, unable to see it, says it is Hamlet's fantasy. He replies: 'Mother . . . / Lay not that flattering unction to your soul, / That not your trespass, but my madness speaks. / It will but skin and film the ulcerous place, / Whilst rank corruption, mining all within, / Infects unseen.' (*Unction* = ointment.) Note the degree of woman-blame implicit in Leo's quotation, and cf. Prologue, n. 27.

6. *Bluebeard's chamber in my mind*: Bluebeard was the fabled character who murdered his wives and hung their bodies in a tower-room. Leo appears to echo the phrase from Thomas Carlyle (cited by *OED* from E. C. Brewer's *Dictionary of Phrase and Fable* (1870)): 'The Bluebeard chamber of his mind, into which no eye but his own must look'.

7. *the Maid's Head*: see chapter 4, n. 1.

8. *revenant . . . stranger*: despite the distinction between the two made here, the terms are virtually synonymous in Hartley's fiction: cf. the ghostly, avenging 'stranger' in 'A Visitor from Down Under' (*Complete Short Stories*, pp. 71–3).

9. *Requiescat*: may he rest (usually followed by *in pace*: in peace). From the Catholic 'Recommendation of a Soul Departing'.

10. *Hugh Maudsley Winlove . . . 1941*: after the mention of the First War (p. 247), this concludes *GB*'s tally of twentieth-century wars.

11. '*My song . . . praising*': see chapter 6, n. 5.

12. *and for the souls . . . resurrection*: echoing the priest's words in the Anglican Burial Service: (1) 'in sure and certain hope of the Resurrection to eternal life'; (2) 'Almighty God, with whom do live the spirits of them that depart hence in the Lord, and with whom the souls of the faithful . . . are in joy and felicity'.

13. *and when . . . faithful*: there is no Anglican equivalent to Leo's prayer:

he seems to say the Catholic Litany for the Dead, with its responses mentioning 'the souls of the faithful departed'.

14. *Ancient Mariner . . . patience*: Leo refers to the long-winded and aged sailor-narrator of Coleridge's ballad *The Rime of the Ancient Mariner*; the fact that by telling his tale he stops a guest from attending a wedding (which proceeds without him) is suggestively relevant to *GB*.

15. *like Edward has*: see chapter 6, n. 3.

PENGUIN MODERN CLASSICS

BRIDESHEAD REVISITED
EVELYN WAUGH

'Lush and evocative ... the one Waugh which best expresses at once the profundity of change and the indomitable endurance of the human spirit'
The Times

The most nostalgic and reflective of Evelyn Waugh's novels, *Brideshead Revisited* looks back to the golden age before the Second World War. It tells the story of Charles Ryder's infatuation with the Marchmains and the rapidly disappearing world of privilege they inhabit. Enchanted first by Sebastian at Oxford, then by his doomed Catholic family, in particular his remote sister, Julia, Charles comes finally to recognize his spiritual and social distance from them.

PENGUIN MODERN CLASSICS

LARK RISE TO CANDLEFORD
FLORA THOMPSON

LARK RISE/ OVER TO CANDLEFORD/ CANDLEFORD GREEN

'Our literature has had no finer remembrance in this century, no observer so genuinely enduring' John Fowles, *New Statesman*

The story of the three closely related Oxfordshire communities – a hamlet, the nearby village and a small market town – this immortal trilogy is based on Flora Thompson's experiences during childhood and youth. It chronicles May Day celebrations and forgotten children's games, the daily lives of farmworkers and craftsmen, friends and relations – all painted with the gaiety and freshness of observation that make this a precious and endearing portrayal of country life at the end of the last century.

With an Introduction by H. J. Massingham

Penguin Modern Classics

THE POORHOUSE FAIR
JOHN UPDIKE

'A work of art' *The New York Times*

Published just four years after John Updike graduated from Harvard, *The Poorhouse Fair* is a brilliant allegory about charity. The setting is a poorhouse – repository of the old, the infirm, and the impoverished – on the day of the annual summer fair. The people are the vividly realized, unforgettable characters that only Updike can create. Short and succinct, *The Poorhouse Fair* speaks to those fears all of us have of growing not old, but dependent.

'A first novel of rare precision and real merit ... A rich poorhouse indeed'
Newsweek

With a new afterword by John Updike

Contemporary ... Provocative ... Outrageous ...
Prophetic ... Groundbreaking ... Funny ... Disturbing ...
Different ... Moving ... Revolutionary ... Inspiring ...
Subversive ... Life-changing ...

What makes a modern classic?

At Penguin Classics our mission has always been to make the best
books ever written available to everyone. And that also means
constantly redefining and refreshing exactly what makes a 'classic'.
That's where Modern Classics come in. Since 1961 they have been an
organic, ever-growing and ever-evolving list of books from the last
hundred (or so) years that we believe will continue to be read over and
over again.

They could be books that have inspired political dissent, such as
Animal Farm. Some, like *Lolita* or *A Clockwork Orange*, may have
caused shock and outrage. Many have led to great films, from *In Cold
Blood* to *One Flew Over the Cuckoo's Nest*. They have broken down
barriers – whether social, sexual, or, in the case of *Ulysses*, the
boundaries of language itself. And they might – like *Goldfinger* or
Scoop – just be pure classic escapism. Whatever the reason, Penguin
Modern Classics continue to inspire, entertain and enlighten millions
of readers everywhere.

'No publisher has had more influence on reading habits than Penguin'
Independent

'Penguins provided a crash course in world literature'
Guardian

The best books ever written

PENGUIN CLASSICS

SINCE 1946

Find out more at www.penguinclassics.com